Froets
Froetschel, Susan
Fear of beauty : a novel /

34028082101966
NC $15.95 ocn793581790
01/29/13

3 4028 08210 1966
HARRIS COUNTY PUBLIC LIBRARY

W9-DDM-506

FEAR
OF BEAUTY

A Novel

FEAR
OF BEAUTY

SUSAN FROETSCHEL

SEVENTH
STREET
BOOKS™

59 John Glenn Drive
Amherst, New York 14228–2119

Published 2013 by Seventh Street Books™, an imprint of Prometheus Books

Fear of Beauty. Copyright © 2013 by Susan Froetschel. All rights reserved. No part of this publication may be reproduced, stored in a retrieval system, or transmitted in any form or by any means, digital, electronic, mechanical, photocopying, recording, or otherwise, or conveyed via the Internet or a website without prior written permission of the publisher, except in the case of brief quotations embodied in critical articles and reviews.

Cover image © 2013 Nabi Lukic/iStockphoto
Cover design by Grace M. Conti-Zilsberger

Inquiries should be addressed to
Seventh Street Books
59 John Glenn Drive
Amherst, New York 14228–2119
VOICE: 716-691-0133 • FAX: 716-691-0137
WWW.PROMETHEUSBOOKS.COM

17 16 15 14 13 • 5 4 3 2 1

Library of Congress Cataloging-in-Publication Data

Froetschel, Susan.
    Fear of beauty / by Susan Froetschel.
        p. cm.
    ISBN 978-1-61614-702-0 (pbk.) • ISBN 978-1-61614-703-7 (ebook)
    1. Women—Afghanistan—Fiction. 2. Sons—Death—Fiction.
3. Americans—Afghanistan—Fiction. I. Title.

PS3556.R59353F43 2012
813'.54—dc23

                                                                        2012031724

Printed in the United States of America

For my brother Mark and his love of agriculture

PROLOGUE

*And withhold yourself with those who call on their
Lord morning and evening, desiring His goodwill, and
let not your eyes pass from them, desiring the beauties
of this world's life. . . .*

—Koran 18:28

Those who claim to know the will of Allah can scold us—and change how we dress, talk, or behave. But they cannot control our senses or prevent us from detecting truth as we try to live the one true way.

The women of our village endured seasons when the crops withered in the fields for want of rain. We come from villages where families sell their daughters for survival. We have seen younger brothers sent to the cities to plead for work or beg for food. We take turns holding the infants in our arms, exhausted from wailing and disease.

Our village is a lifelong home for men. The women arrive as strangers. But hard work and children, the arrival of new wives, obscure this betrayal. Strangers can be like the fierce winds that batter our crops or gentle rains that make them green.

Years ago, leaders of Afghanistan decided to forgo railroads and highways to prevent invasions of our land. Yet for three decades, combat was never far. Intruders have a way of finding us, asking us to change and bend to their will. There is no end to worrying about the brothers and fathers, husband and sons, who return from battle dazed, humiliated, and bitter. The men blame women and sins for problems that never go away.

We cannot tell others what we want. Revealing our preferences only ensures that the opposite will occur. We work to control our-selves, and disguise efforts to impose our control over others. In the end, attempts to control others are futile.

We live in a land where extremes reign. I may join my sisters in their plan, destroying those who squeeze every joy out of us until everyday life stings like the desert sand whipped by unrelenting wind.

PART 1

1.1. The most essential element of combat power is competent and confident leadership. Leadership provides purpose, direction, and motivation in combat. . . . A good leader will . . . motivate his men by setting the example and always maintaining a positive can-do attitude.

—*Ranger Handbook*

Every soul shall taste of death . . . and the life of this world is nothing but a provision of vanities.

—Koran 3:185

PART II

CHAPTER 1

I remember the last day with my son, his smile bright and happy as he tugged my hand, urging me to join him on the mountainside. There was something I needed to see.

Our work in the fields never ended, especially during harvests, and we had much to do before dinner. The boy gently tugged on a pomegranate, showing how it stubbornly clung to the stem. *The fruit is not yet ready to pick.*

Laughing, I tried to put him off, explaining I wanted to make a special meal that evening, his favorite, a spicy lamb pie. But Ali had a stubborn charm. *I'd rather spend the day with you, even if we must eat raw turnips and potatoes tonight.* Mischievous, he insisted that I'd want to see what he had to show me.

Ali, my oldest, was small for his age, but wiry and tough of mind. It was why we were sending him to school early, to a maktab farther than the one attended by most boys in our village. Other villagers raised their eyebrows and whispered about us. Parsaa, my husband, calmly repeated a simple explanation. His son would attend the school that Parsaa had attended.

Only because the boy was leaving the next day, I accompanied him for the climb that day.

And so I headed out early for the field, but worked doubly hard, taking no breaks and giving the boy time to gather the goats and move them along the path to higher pastures. As the sun reached its highest point in the sky, I slipped into a stand of pines not far from the edge of our field to hide my tools and follow my son.

My husband's tribe descended from nomads who wandered along

the border between Afghanistan and Iran. Constant fighting pushed our leaders west to a remote area, and more fighting prompted another move to an isolated location where another language was spoken.

The upland valley was far from roads and other people, cornered by intimidating, rugged mountains. The entrance to the village, once a dirt road, was reduced to a treacherous footpath after villagers deliberately triggered an avalanche. Passage was impossible for motor vehicles.

Our nearby hills offered decent slopes for grazing goats and sheep. The tallest and nearest mountain, with views of the path leading to our village, was most frequented by the village men and boys for herding or scouting. Our family fields were at the base of a shorter mountain with the steepest slopes. Slightly to the west, this lopsided mountain exposed not the footpath but the village and river valley stretching beyond. Any climb required careful checks of foot and handholds.

Men posed more danger for me than any path, and the most desolate mountain was the only one that I as a woman could safely manage alone. I couldn't wander away often, or other villagers would suspect my intentions.

Our family kept secrets along one slope—a deep fold, strewn with huge boulders that were barriers against the wind or prying eyes. Old leaves, twigs, and grass caught among the crevices turned into rich soil over time, and dark reedy strands had gradually spread into these pockets. To avoid jealousies and questions, we climbed this part of the mountain only when others in our village were busy.

Ali was the only one of our children who knew.

Before that day and since, I often pondered my special feelings for Ali. Of course, he was the oldest, but his character most resembled mine, and the sense that I was running out of time with this child had nagged at me. That afternoon, I thought about how I'd miss our routines and conversations while he attended school, but didn't share these feelings aloud.

Mothers must teach their children to keep secrets, and we practice by spending time alone with them, showing our trust.

Without glancing at the mountain's biggest secret, my hidden garden, I followed Ali, trudging uphill. My shoes were too large, the soles brittle with age, but two pairs of thick knitted socks also protected my feet. Rather than use a path that wiggled around the mountain, we headed straight uphill through luxurious waves of grass in gray, gold, lavender, and green. The long strands pulled against my tombaan, and rather than push through, we stepped high, toes pointed, to move more quickly.

It didn't take long before I spotted the peaceful scene of our goats ambling along the slope, selecting sprigs here and there. Before heading upward, I scanned the path between the village and our fields below and saw no sign of followers. In case we met other villagers, I carried bread, yogurt, and fruit in my pack and would explain that Ali had forgotten his meal. Some would still scold me for making the boy soft, but it was an easy excuse for abandoning work and climbing the sharp hillside overlooking Laashekoh.

I glanced up to see Ali happily waving for me to hurry. That memory of his fearless joy is always with me.

Running, I took long strides, barely keeping up, but there was no rest as Ali turned, aiming higher uphill. Once past the grassy area and goats, we had to scramble over crumbling gray rocks to reach the mountaintop. Hurrying, without words, we moved deliberately, guarding against falling with hundreds of crumbling rocks. As we closed in for the top, each breath felt sharp. My feet were sore from curling and gripping around rocks and dirt, trying to keep balance, and I was grateful to step on cushions of lichen.

The boy darted without any signs of weariness, and I smiled at the serious tilt of his mouth and curls that could not be tamed by a pakool. I felt so close to him because he was curious, observant, quick at laughing off problems. Not because he was my firstborn. Others weren't shy about favoring firstborn children, but it had never felt right for me.

But I kept these thoughts to myself. I couldn't explain, not even to Parsaa, how clever Ali was, more like a friend than a son. He was thoughtful, maybe because he spent so much time in the hills alone with only the goats. Unlike other village children, he did not complain about working alone to herd the animals. He found adventure in every day.

Others would have found our relationship odd, so Ali and I had to plan and snatch time together. *You can't leave the goats for long, and I can't leave the pomegranates. Others will ask questions.*

You're a woman. You did not feel well. He responded in a matter-of-fact way. *Tell them they don't want to know the details.*

The boy was the oldest of five brothers and adept at getting his way. No matter what happened, his face was calm and sweet. He could cast his gaze at others, staring into their eyes, intently studying the shape of their thoughts. His gray eyes could smile without a twitch of the mouth. A mother should not boast about her children, but he was too observant and intelligent, that one, often disconcerting men twice his age or more.

Not far from the top, Ali paused and slowly crouched to the ground, gesturing for me to wait. He slowly inched forward along the ground toward the crest of the hill. Once there, he leaned against a huge boulder.

Waiting for his signal, I lifted my head to take in deep breaths and enjoy the clouds hovering so close. My body was good for steady work, walking, bending with a hoe, and stooping to select vegetables, but not for such an intense climb. Leaning my head against the nearest rock, I studied the world below. Surrounding the village compound, home for almost twenty families, were gleaming fields of gold and green in the late-morning light. As families grew, new blocks and passageways were added to homes, and walls of clay, smoothed to creamy perfection, twisted like a maze to provide privacy and protection.

Ali tried to tuck his hair under the pakool once again, before slowly lowering his head and crawling out from behind the boulder. No shouts or shots responded.

In the stillness, I suddenly detected a soft rumbling sound from afar.

Ali backed away. *Move slowly*, he cautioned in a whisper. *We don't know who might wait on the other side.*

I hurried to look, but he grabbed my arm and removed his gray pakool, handing it over. *It blends with the boulder*, he whispered. Letting my headscarf fall to my neck, I placed the pakool on my head and tucked my unruly hair inside. Crouching low, following Ali's example, I moved toward the crest to check out the source of the rumbling.

Beyond the river, as far as the eye could see, a series of unfolding beige hills shoved our river this way and that, the rocky crests softening in the distance. All the snowmelt and streams wound their way down the mountains and eventually met with that river.

Most days, the only interruption in the scene of these dusty hills was the glistening river or a lonely bird gliding with the wind. Sometimes bedraggled groups of refugees passed through, fleeing the fighting and invariably stopping by the river to drink or camp for the night. Most passersby did not realize a village was nestled amidst the craggy mountains and that they were under watch. The few parties who knew about our village sent scouts ahead, met with our men, and sometimes bought food. I expected to watch another caravan moving like tiny insects, taking all day to crawl along the river until they were no longer in our view.

But the group was not refugees. Powerful motorized vehicles, the color of the sand and rocks, moved back and forth along the river's desert side. The huge, ugly trucks towed equipment that I had never seen before, kicking up clouds of dust around a set of structures that had suddenly emerged not far from our river. I squinted to focus in the bright sun. Two flying machines, blades whirling in a circle, moved over the site, like growling birds courting in the sky. One slowly dropped to the ground as another lifted, glinting in the sunlight and quickly moving out of sight over the nearby mountains. In the distance, another approached, and I pointed.

Ali pulled my arm down and leaned to whisper in my ear. *They're called helicopters. The foreign soldiers are here. The Americans.* Hatred seared through me, but he showed no hint of worry or fear. I remember thinking at the time how children were better at sensing immediate rather than distant danger.

I simply repeated the strange word, *Americans*, the ones who attacked after the drought in 2001, when our region was at its weakest. Since then, increasing numbers of foreign soldiers brought new troubles, new divisions among our tribes.

Many families found it easier to relocate than work with foreign troops. The same had happened when I was young, after heavy bombing and fighting with another group of foreigners, the Russians. Entire villages had walked away from productive fields and moved south. Our parents didn't mind starting over if we were far from the fighting and the cities. We learned to do with less water, less food, less contact with the outside world, less of everything. The fighting didn't stop, but at least parents removed their families far away from the angry clashes over territory. Then the Americans invaded, and villages had to decide whether to relocate again.

Some criticize our leaders for not standing ground and confronting the intruders. But there were many demands and factions, and too many men fight for reasons that carried little meaning in the years that followed.

We had a saying that peace and poverty were better than fighting. But now the enemy was near. I had worked hard in the fields of our village, and anger ripped through me at the thought that we might abandon a place that had given us so much.

For now, the men were far away, mere dots. But moving quickly and changing the landscape with their machines, they were different from others who had passed through. The camp was too dusty and far to see weapons or faces, but the activity suggested a long stay. I tried to convince myself the encampment was an annoyance, like ants, not an invasion that would force us to flee our village.

My son was keen to incite a reaction. I didn't oblige, though I'm sure Ali could not miss the hard look in my eyes. *How many days have they been here?*

Ali explained how he had climbed the hill four days earlier and had not seen any sign of them. He was excited, more curious than afraid, and that bothered me.

I refused to speak about my hate. Some parents want their children to share their feelings and talk too much about the targets of their hate. I prefer that my children practice forming their own conclusions. Yesterday's enemy can be tomorrow's ally, and a neutral stance is the best approach. Fighting does not keep change at bay.

Uncle goes down there at night to meet with those who guide the refugees. Ali shook his head. *He won't be happy.*

The comment took me by surprise, and I was annoyed that my child knew more about the business of our village than I did. But males of any age can move about as they please. Only when no one is paying attention, during chores, can women snatch time alone. Women gather to make soap, wash clothes, or work in the fields, but such occasions rarely make us privy to village business or politics.

I wish I had been more curious that day. But even with our sons, women don't let on how much we know or don't know, and I could expect questioning glances if I stayed away from my work too long.

We should return, I whispered.

So you can make our dinner, Ali said. *And I will help.*

Sitting up, I laughed, and we backed away from the precipice, hurrying downward and ducking behind boulders scattered about in odd piles, as if strewn by some giant's hand. My son was swift and sure, again taking the lead, dodging back and forth off the trail, scampering along the rocks. Leaping and stretching his arms out, in his father's old payraan, Ali resembled a giant bird

Nearing the meadow, he leaped onto a huge boulder and called out to me.

We must hurry—others will ask questions, I scolded. Instead of following me downhill, he swayed back and forth along the ledge, teasing me.

Ali! I gasped. *Stop!*

Then climb up! He called out, taking another jump.

Hurrying away from the path to join him, I searched for handholds and climbed toward the circle of rocks overlooking our village in miniature and the winding river valley below. My throat was tight.

I wanted to shake him for recklessly ignoring the sheer cliff below, but the scene was beautiful, and I said as much. Ali didn't answer. Frowning, he bent close to the ground, near a large rock, flat and smooth, with the curves of an expensive sofa seen only in the wealthiest homes of Afghanistan.

Mixed with scrabble on the one side of the rock was the dusty stub of a cigarette. I poked at the stray with a stick and saw tiny marks etched on its side. I could not guess the source. Few men in our village wanted or could afford foreign tobacco.

I didn't like the idea of a stranger loitering on the hillside so close to my secrets. With my shoe, I tucked the dirty thing back into its hiding spot, before circling the clearing. The sudden drop-off made me dizzy, and I backed away to sit next to Ali on the sofa-rock. He pointed toward two large rocks—a frame to the scene of thirty-odd structures that made up our village.

Someone is watching us, Ali commented. I just nodded, but he pressed, *Should we tell the others?*

Not yet, I whispered. *It could be someone from our village.* I held his stare and didn't have to explain that prying on fellow villagers could be more dangerous than observing foreign soldiers. *This shelter looks temporary*, I tried to reassure him.

Placing my hand on his shoulder, I suggested that he walk ahead and whistle if he spotted any disturbance. Waiting for the sound of his footsteps to fade away, I returned to the rocky ledge—and knelt, reaching for an opening that I had detected while climbing. A rock partially covered the opening, and I pushed it aside before feeling cool metal.

Looking about, I checked that Ali was well on his way before extracting the small flat box. Inside was a pile of documents, all similar, with lines and characters that I could not read. There was also a stack of strange money, with images of a stern man, no hair on the top of his head. It wasn't Afghan currency, and again, I couldn't read the few notations.

Such documents and foreign currency were useless for people in Laashekoh, but I had my own reasons for coveting paper. Surely whoever had left the documents on our remote hillside wouldn't miss one.

So I took one, folded it several times, and tucked it into my clothing. Resisting the temptation to take more, I returned the box to its hiding place and moved the rock back for cover. I could return later, I promised myself. With any luck, the intruder was merely passing through and wasn't curious about my own activities along this mountainside.

CHAPTER 2

Someone else was keeping watch, but Joey Pearson couldn't help himself. Leaning against a rock wall, he surveyed the scene with field binoculars, patiently following the valley's countless edges and folds. The day was unusually hot, and except for river water trickling along the rocks, nothing moved. No birds, no wood smoke, no breeze. The river didn't roar. The mountains were not the most majestic. But the place was remote, and for Joey, that was beauty. He couldn't wait to leave camp and walk it alone.

But that had to wait until the camp was settled and the contractors left.

Scanning the skyline, he caught movement, a glimpse of a face—a woman laughing. In an instant, the face vanished.

He waited, but there was no other sign. He couldn't get her smile out of his mind.

A loud voice announced from behind: "Captain Cameron Janick, sir, reporting for duty."

Annoyed about the interruption, Joey waved his hand. "At ease," he said tersely. Janick took that as an invitation for an extended conversation.

"So what are you looking for?"

Joey put the glasses down. "The quiet."

The man glanced toward the direction where Joey had aimed the glasses and then turned toward the temporary living unit. Tossing his bag aside and making no secret of his distaste for the flimsy structure with thin aluminum walls, Janick said: "So this is our home for the next three months?"

Inwardly rolling his eyes, Joey thought to himself—a jolly complainer, what every operation needs.

Janick settled in to talk about himself, reciting his résumé. Somewhere in the long list, Joey heard "member of an agribusiness development team," and was tempted to ask if that was a fancy word for *farmer*. But he refrained. Janick wouldn't understand that Joey genuinely preferred farmers over agribusiness developers.

Instead Joey introduced himself as a major on special assignment to organize and secure the outpost and the team of agricultural workers, including civilians. He had to remind himself about his own plan to rely on first names of team members.

Cameron opened the door and tossed his belongings on the cot closest to the doorway and rejoined Joey to gaze at sheer mountain walls exposed by the harsh midday sun. "Hell of a place to call home," he pressed.

Joey offered a noncommittal grunt. He wasn't going to argue. Space was tight at the outpost, and the team was new. Air-conditioning, cots, private bedrooms, cooked meals made the place a five-star resort compared to most accommodations in Afghanistan.

Cameron Janick would find out soon enough.

The two men leaned against the wall, observing the rapid construction underway. Team after team of specialists flew in, each completing their tasks—dropping off housing units, assembling them, hooking up generators, stockpiling food and other supplies, installing fence posts and stringing them with razor wire. The installers would be gone in a week, and the small band of military and agriculture experts would be on their own to patrol the area, offer agriculture assistance to nearby Afghan villages, and prepare a report on whether the area would be suitable for a large training facility for Afghan recruits.

Joey didn't say much, but that didn't stop the man from talking about his home, wife, and two daughters in Janesville, Wisconsin. He grew up on a farm, but left to become a territorial sales manager for a biotech multinational.

"But you know about farming—irrigation systems, crop rotations, fertilizer?" Joey pressed.

"I sell the technology," Cameron boasted. "We have to know more than the farmers do."

"It's primitive out here," Joey warned. "They'll be more than happy with basics."

"Good—our products will look like magic," Cameron said with a laugh.

Joey held his tongue again. The outposts were another experiment in the long, drawn-out war, more than a decade of modern weaponry and Western ideas clashing against a poor and primitive culture. Joey had spent enough time in Afghanistan to know that modern ways did not always win over hearts and minds.

But his mission was support—anything to get cooperation started with the villages. Who knew, maybe Janick's "magic" would win them over. But the task wasn't as easy as presenting good ideas and then waiting for villagers to express gratitude.

Cameron added, "My sales background could help move some ideas. Especially demonstrations."

As Cameron went on about Wisconsin, wheat, and experimental plots, Joey held back on talking about his own background, growing up on a family farm in rural western Maryland and enlisting in the military more than a decade ago to escape a religious mother who rarely smiled and an angry father who drunkenly railed about modern farming and peddlers of "biotech magic." Of course, Maryland was lush compared to Afghanistan, but his family still contended with fickle pricing and weather that defied his mother's desperate prayers.

Every decision Joey made in life, every bit of advice he handed out to others, involved resisting the fear and desperate attempts at self-control that ruled his parents. Over the years, commanders had complained about his playing fast and loose with rules and regs. But they liked the results, and as Special Ops, he had leeway.

Eventually, Cameron asked about Joey's role in the Army Rangers. Joey tersely explained that his assignment as lead military officer and translator was temporary. He'd train a small group of Afghan soldiers who would take over guarding the ag advisors during visits to nearby villages—and then the Afghans would advise the team on approaching villages. That would take no more than eight weeks.

What he didn't mention was that, depending on intelligence reports, Joey and others like him stationed throughout the province could get called out on special missions. With a few hours of notice, he could slip away from the outpost for a deployment anywhere in the world, never seen by Cameron Janick and the rest of the team again.

Joey's schedule and duties were on a need-to-know basis, so he threw out a few standard lines to describe his work to Cameron: He'd train a small group of Afghans in surveillance, combat, and security procedures; collect data for area commanders deciding on a site for a regional training area; and do what he could to help the team build connections with area villages.

It would take months for the Afghans to trust the strangers in their midst—and that was if all went well. In the remote corners of Helmand Province, the team could expect to find three categories of Afghans—hard-core Taliban, moderate Taliban, and skeptical bystanders. Soldiers in Afghanistan had learned the hard way that, depending on day-to-day encounters, news reports, or rumors, any Afghan could slide from one category to another and back again in a week.

Joey was the first to admit that the villagers had good reason to doubt newfangled ideas from the Americans.

"You'll be with us when we go to the villages?" Cameron asked.

"Early on—yes," Joey said.

"So you're the guard dog." Cameron laughed at his own joke and then pointed to Joey's scruffy beard, thick with several weeks of growth. "Should I start in on one of those?"

Beards were common among members of the special forces. But commanders prohibited most other troops from growing them, not that Joey cared. "If you want to," he said.

Cameron stared off toward the river. "And you don't have a problem if I start an experimental plot. Maybe over there by the river." It wasn't a question.

"I don't mind, but don't start projects until the civilian command arrives and gives the go-ahead." Joey was firm. "Setting up the outpost will keep us plenty busy."

Cameron shook his head. "Okay, we can play it by the rules and see if she knows what she's doing. A woman and an academic."

Joey didn't like his tone, but Cameron didn't notice. Instead, he stepped inside and looked around the space—thin walls separating a common area and three closet-sized bedrooms reserved for outpost leaders. "I thought it was just the two of us?"

Joey smiled from the doorway. "No, we'll have the lead Afghan in here, too."

That got Cameron's attention, and he didn't speak for a moment. He looked around at the tight space and then turned to Joey. "An Afghan?"

Joey nodded.

"You think that's a good idea?"

Joey rubbed his chin. "I'll be honest, if the civilian commander was a man, you'd be in the other quarters. We're mixing Afghans with our people, civilians and military."

Cameron shook his head slowly and then muttered, "We'll see if any of them last, especially this civilian commander."

Joey gave a curt nod and stepped away from the door, turning his attention back to the valley and surrounding peaks. Joey had read up on Mita Samuelson and had his own worries about how Afghans would react to the woman. But he wouldn't talk about her with the likes of Cameron. About 15 percent of the troops deployed in Afghanistan were National Guard. On his fifth deployment in the country, Joey had worked with men like Cameron before, eager for fast success, full of ideas that the Afghans would reject or misunderstand—and just as quick with blame and disrespect for the Afghans when the projects didn't pan out.

Time to try something new, he reminded himself. The general had promised that Mita Samuelson was capable, practical, yet innovative.

Joey hoped that was true because he didn't like babysitting dreamers. Strike operations were down, and Joey wasn't thrilled about a shift in strategy that broke up his Special Operations unit. Instead of taking on high-risk missions, his unit was temporarily divided, assigned to securing teams of specialists while training small groups of selected Afghans in reconnaissance and security procedures.

Special Operations troops were flexible, ready to serve under any type of command structure. But if asked, Joey wouldn't lie—he preferred working with other Rangers.

Cameron stepped back out into the sunlight. "We'll know if she's right for this job if she goes for my ideas on wheat," he confided, and kept on talking about statistics and wheat as a global staple.

Joey continued to survey the landscape without responding. Cameron was crazy if he thought he could line others up on his side before even meeting Samuelson.

He'd never tell Cameron, but part of the job in keeping a remote outpost secure was looking for signs that one of their own guys was ready to crack. And it was only the first day.

Joey missed comrades who lived by the same set of rules and habits. He could meet another Ranger for the first time and it wasn't long before they sensed each other's thoughts without a lot of talk about families, homes, or superiors. He reminded himself that Cameron and Mita Samuelson were part of a new strategy from top commanders for the decade-old war. New strategies were in need.

Cameron, trying to be jovial, had moved on to another topic, his dislike for the province. "Helmand," he spat out the name. "All it needs is one more *l*. I never thought I'd miss Kabul."

The joke was old, but Joey nodded and smiled. Anything less would only encourage Cameron to push the issue. The guy was nervous and new and had a lot to learn.

A helicopter swept over the mountains to the east and circled the base, and Joey's radio crackled. "Major Pearson, the Afghan troops are landing." Joey waved to Cameron and started for the field to greet the young commander and his men.

Cameron called out. "Wait a minute—do you trust those guys?"

Joey laughed, ready to start planning for the next eight weeks. "This is their territory. We have no other choice."

CHAPTER 3

The next morning we woke before the sun rose. Ali's clothes were packed, ready for the day-long trip to the maktab where the boy would spend the next several years, reading, studying religion and maybe even mathematics. The boy couldn't be more eager than I was about the opportunities awaiting him.

As my husband went outside to ready the donkey, I stoked the oven's fire, ready to prepare a warm breakfast and pack meals for the two of them, and then paused. The house was too quiet. I had expected Ali to be bursting with anticipation, ready to leave.

I hurried to the dark corner where my boys slept. My eyes adjusted to the darkness and saw four mounds, not five, and I was pleased. Ali was excited and outside, helping his father prepare. Surprised at not hearing him rise, I hurried out to check.

Early-morning mist blurred the outlines of the mountains, homes, fields, and paths in similar shades, like crumpled gray cloth. Parsaa broke through the gray mist, pulling the donkey with twitching ears, close to our entryway. He was alone, and the only sound was invisible birds chattering in the nearby poplars.

Ali is ready? he asked softly, not wanting to disturb nearby villagers. *We can eat our breakfast as we walk.*

He's not inside, I whispered. I felt ill, and joined Parsaa in scanning the courtyard and nearby paths.

But he wouldn't have taken off, my husband murmured, and I nodded, as the fear pricked our hearts. Hurrying inside, I shook awake two of Ali's brothers to search the village. I also went to Gul and Mari, our dearest friends, who lived in the next home.

Mari was delighted. *Don't make him go. He changed his mind about school!*

He wouldn't change his mind, I insisted. Her daughter scolded Mari. Leila looked wretched, as if ill. Irritated, she offered to keep an eye on the children as the rest of us joined the search.

We searched and then we knocked on every door. By afternoon, members of every family in Laashekoh searched for Ali, checking homes, fields, and paths that led away from the compound. Like Mari, others asked questions, laughing at our worry and pointing out that sons naturally resist school. My embarrassment turned into panic. I was desperate to find and hold Ali.

~~~~~

As the sun climbed into the sky, vultures ended their morning ritual of lifted wings and began circling over the ledges that Ali and I had climbed only the day before. My husband, anxious, redirected his search near that precipice and found Ali's battered body on the boulders below. Parsaa embraced the boy with both arms, carrying him like an infant, and once inside, gently placed what was left of our son on a white sheet. The leader of our village and Parsaa's good friend, Gul, stood back.

The boy had taken quite the tumble, his body scraped and broken, his finest clothes for school torn and bloodied. The most severe injury was to the back of his skull.

A horrible accident, Gul said. *Where did you find him?*

Parsaa pointed and described the area just below the ledge and hiding spot I had discovered the day before: *I don't understand why he went there before we were set to leave.*

I didn't understand either, so I remained quiet, too sick to speak about the previous day with others. Questions from others would transform a few moments of joy and beauty into wasted, stolen time, perhaps a reason for the boy's death. Besides, it wasn't a good time to raise worries about foreign troops or papers.

Mari and Leila brought containers of soup and meat, with piles of warm bread, for our family to eat. I ordered my sons to accept the gifts, but to allow no others inside. The women called out for me, and reluctantly I went to the doorway.

You shouldn't be alone, Mari cautioned, offering to help prepare the body for burial.

I shook my head. Like most young men, Ali would want only his parents to see him so vulnerable. I kept thinking of him as a being who could still decide his future—and that led to a rush of hot tears. *This shouldn't have happened. It's not what he deserved.*

The faces of the two women were lined with concern, and Leila's eyes were red from weeping. They hovered close, pressing to enter.

There's nothing you can do to stop this pain, I insisted.

We're here, Mari promised. *Let us know if we can help in any way.*

I thanked her and disappeared inside. Outside our home, other villagers gathered with Gul, Mari, and Leila to cry and pray. Grateful no one expected me to join them, I sat alone and blamed Allah for not protecting us from this death.

~~~~~

Later that evening, the whispers about the odd death of a healthy boy would go silent as my husband came and went. I remained in seclusion, refusing to abandon what was left of my oldest son.

As Parsaa left the village center to oversee the digging of the grave, the questions and opinions took on volume. *The boy should have attended the maktab attended by other children in this village*, one said.

Maybe he didn't want to go, said another.

Allah works in strange ways, Gul concluded. *He gives life and causes death.*

I twisted and squeezed the damp cloth in my hands, until it was tight against my fingers. I wanted nothing to do with Allah if the boy's death was His work.

Parsaa's voice suddenly pierced the conversation. *Ali was attending the same maktab as his father*, my husband insisted, his voice calm and maddening. *He was happy about going. He died in this village. The school had nothing to do with his death—unless others were envious of this choice.*

A woman wailed and Gul quickly shifted the subject, blaming the foreigners gathering by the river. It was the first time I had heard anyone speak about the Americans building near the river. A few men expressed surprise. Parsaa expressed neither fear nor anger about the foreign soldiers, but dismissed the accusations.

They have nothing to do with Ali. It was an accident.

No, I said aloud, closing my eyes and remembering a boy who never had problems scrambling along the rocks and cliffs around our village. *No*.

But no one was inside our home to hear me. I dipped the cloth into water and cleaned the boy's hair, thinking about that last day. I had foolishly suggested that we needed to keep a watchful eye on our part of the mountainside. Or perhaps Ali had watched me find and open the metal box, and then returned to satisfy his own curiosity. Perhaps the owner of the box, following and catching Ali examining something he was not supposed to see, had bashed my son on the head and shoved the body over a cliff.

The owner could come after me next and I'd be waiting.

I studied Ali's face. It appeared younger than it had the day before and offered no clue as to why he had climbed the slope again or who killed him. There was no fear or wonder in his face—no answers. Pressing my hand gently against his neck, I lay my head on his chest, hoping to detect a last bit of warmth leaving his small body.

~~~~~~

We buried Ali that evening. Nothing could ever hurt me so deeply again.

Others tried to help with ablution, but I turned them away. My hot tears mixed with the water used on Ali's hands, his mouth, his face and head, his feet. My hands were shaking, nervous, performing the task dreaded by every mother. My arms felt like heavy logs, and I kept hoping, praying, that the boy would stir and open his eyes. But prayers of the living do not move the dead.

Weary, I helped my husband wrap the final cloth and then nodded for the men to carry his body away. This was a day I didn't want to remember, my son stretched out on our floor. Instead, I wanted to treasure our last climb together. I kept my head down and, throughout the prayers, struggled to focus on memories of Ali jumping, laughing, and talking—so pleasant, yet distant and strange because I'd never know his thoughts again.

CHAPTER 4

The new strategy was to provide security to rural areas and accompany sector teams organized to boost the Afghanistan economy. Military analysts had loaded statistics—education and crime levels, income and other community resources, water, and land features—onto GIS software, creating colorful maps that pinpointed areas of need. Military planners then dispatched teams of teachers, mechanics, healthcare workers, miners, cabinetmakers, construction crews, or engineers to areas with potential, hoping that skills and security would spread. Agriculture teams included academics and professional farmers familiar with chickens, beef, wheat, and other crops; as well as horticulturists, vets, or botanists who could offer specific technical advice. The Afghan soldiers would train with US soldiers and guide teams into area villages to collect requests for projects.

Afghan cooperation was crucial, and Joey warmly greeted the Afghan commander in Dari.

"Major Pearson, I'm honored." Habib Bulaq eagerly shook hands with Joey and then Cameron. Joey felt lucky. He had heard only good reports about this devout Muslim from Kandahar. The father of six was passionate about securing education for his children and resented politicians who used religion to limit dreams and communities. Joey introduced the Afghan, in his early thirties, to Cameron, and repeated sentences in both English and Dari for the two men. Habib politely held up his hand.

"Sir, I understand English," he announced proudly. "I studied for this mission."

Joey flashed a smile. "But I should practice my Dari!" And Habib laughed. Joey showed the man their sleeping quarters, and encouraged him to select one of the two cots left. "In here, we use first names—if that's okay with you?"

Habib nodded. He tentatively opened a small locker, then switched a lamp on and off with admiration. "Very nice . . ."

Joey liked the guy already.

Cameron pointed to a military map of their assigned area in Helmand posted on the wall, and abruptly asked Habib, "Any ideas about which of these places are the most safe?"

"Safe?" The Afghan glanced at Joey. "None of them."

Cameron's eyebrows went up as Joey went to the map. "As soon as troops step into a village, any guarantee of safety vanishes for the people there."

Cameron rubbed his hands and stared at the map. "Once we rip out the opium crops . . ."

"Hold on." Joey held up his hand. "We're not here to destroy livelihoods. Besides, we don't know what they're growing here. Every action we take is to support the villages. That's a direct order from the top."

Relief crossed Habib's face. "Anything else puts us at risk," he said.

Cameron looked puzzled and Joey explained. "We're not here to control. Most people in this area have already ditched opium as a crop. There's too much competition and too much trouble. Even if we find some opium . . ." Joey shook his head. "We don't interfere. We don't push. We wait for their requests."

"Wait?" Cameron protested. "But how do they know what to ask for?"

"You'll work with Mita Samuelson on demonstration projects. And you can join us on scouting missions. We'll get ideas about what the villages want and need, and then Habib and his men will talk it over with them."

Cameron flopped down on his cot. "Wouldn't it be easier to get them going on something reliable, like wheat?"

Joey, realizing Habib still nervously stood at attention, pointed to the cot. "It's fine, Habib." The man carefully stashed a worn backpack underneath the cot. "Look, Cameron, pushing them around is a waste of time. And we don't have a lot of time. And that's the least of our challenges."

Cameron frowned. "What else?"

"Most villages in this valley are relatively new, formed by people who were sick of fighting and relocated. Some estimates suggest that at least seventy-five percent of Helmand is made up of internally displaced people. Some will appreciate the advice. Others will be terrified and refuse to talk with us."

Cameron waved his hand. "They'll get used to us. Once they see what modern agriculture can do, they'll get on board."

Habib glanced at Joey again, as if asking which man would lead the charge in villages. The villages wouldn't like eagerness or control. Unfortunately, Mita Samuelson was an unknown quantity. In Dari, Joey advised Habib that the leader of the ag side had been delayed. "The civilian commander will review and decide on these matters before we head out to the villages," Joey promised the man, before translating a shorter version for Cameron.

"We should get started right away," Cameron pressed.

Joey kept his voice calm. "Don't count on these villagers being keen on a rush of help from outsiders. The country's been at war since 1980—and the villages blame us and the Russians. Not the Taliban."

"Plenty of Taliban sympathies around here," Habib agreed, in English.

"But you'll help us avoid them?" Cameron asked.

"We can't avoid them," Joey said. "Habib's here to help us understand the villagers' point of view. They want no interference. But the good news is they're sick of fighting. The bad news is that some are nostalgic for the days when the Taliban were in control."

Habib nodded, but Cameron was incredulous.

"They want the Taliban back?"

Joey shrugged. "The country wasn't at war throughout the 1990s. For some people, that's good enough."

"You're from California. The give-peace-a-chance crowd can get to you."

"Try again," Joey said flatly. He wasn't about to try to explain what it was like coming from western Maryland and Garrett County. He wasn't going to bring up his farming background in front of Cameron, who would automatically assume he grew up on one of the elite horse or dairy farms dotting the other side of the state. Stereotypes didn't help build assessments. He turned to Habib who listened closely. "Beware of false premises."

"What do you mean?" Cameron asked.

"It's dangerous to jump to conclusions—about me or the Afghans," Joey said.

"So you're from New York or Massachusetts?" Cameron asked. "Vermont?"

Joey groaned. Stereotyping, an inflated sense of superiority—it was why a high-tech military still struggled against insurgents dressed in rags, often going without food or basic supplies, piecing together weapons that were decades old, gathering parts to improvise explosives. The enemy was determined and patient.

Cameron would learn with show, not tell. "After a few tours, it doesn't matter where any of us are from," Joey said. "All I know is that we have one big mess to untangle. But it's like a bunch of kids, using forks to untangle a giant mountain of yarn. If we go too fast, we'll only tangle it more."

Habib spoke up. "The people here don't want to fight. But that doesn't mean they like Americans. They only see Americans and the government in Kabul shoving new laws at them. Out here, it's not a good idea to force new ideas."

"The only chance for success is convincing the villages to approach us," Joey agreed.

"Our survival could depend on it," Habib noted. "I want to get back to my family." An awkward silence followed.

"Okay, okay. You guys understand the place better than I do. All I'm trying to say is if these people are ready to establish some real crops in real quantities, I'm ready to help. And wheat is the way to go."

"And the orders are we wait to be asked, Cameron," Joey repeated.

He stepped away from the map and went to the doorway, studying the surrounding terrain. Joey couldn't see a wheat field popping up anytime soon, not from a guy who was more talk than action. "We've got two months, and we can't blow it." He sighed, removing his cigarette pack.

Habib frowned.

"Don't worry," Joey said. "It's my last one . . ."

"I knew Muslims don't like alcohol," Cameron said. "Smoking, too?"

"The smell," Habib replied.

"If we do surveillance work," Joey said. "The smell carries. Also, remember that we need to finish what we start. If we don't carry through, the villages won't have anything to do with us."

Habib nodded. "Results."

"They can't ask if they don't know," Cameron complained. "Remember that."

"It's up to Samuelson," Joey concluded. "Talk to her about setting up a demonstration. And focus on basic techniques for irrigation, pest control, crop storage." He shook his head. "With luck, the villages won't be stubborn, but some will destroy their fields before taking any advice from us. We can't do enough research or planning."

Habib, eager to learn, repeated what seemed to be a popular phrase for military discussions. "Remember."

There was no escaping pessimism in Afghanistan. Joey threw the newly lit cigarette into the dirt. Twisting his foot hard, he wished that he could stomp away memories so easily.

~~~~~

The team members, eager to get started, were anxious to meet Mita Samuelson. Joey posted a map on the wall and initiated the small group on the region and security concerns, describing the four villages in the outpost's region, all within a hard day's travel of the outpost. "Some villages are more isolated than others, and most don't want to mingle with one another, let alone with us. They want no outside influences— Taliban fighters or NATO forces."

"At least they're honest," Dan, a staff sergeant, offered.

"That they hate us?" asked Cameron, who sat in the front row.

"Telling us what they want," Joey explained. "That's better than the ones who smile and take our information. They hide their feelings and then attack the first chance they get."

"Maybe you've given up on them." Cameron had a haughty way of arguing, even when people might agree with him. Joey stared at the man, deciding he was wrong about the label of Jolly Complainer.

"Hey!" Dan shot back. "Don't say that to a man with as many deployments as Joey Pearson."

"One who has saved other men," Habib said softly.

Cameron held up his arms as if to surrender. "Don't blame me, but this country could use new blood."

"Watch the words, man," Dan retorted. "Blood?"

Joey buried his fury and held his hand up. "That's why Habib and his men are here—to screen proposals—and the team will respond to those proposals."

Cameron looked skeptical. "They do the screening?"

"Requests will be few and small. We expect most to be genuine, but we'll monitor everything, looking for traps."

"Traps?" Cameron blurted out.

"They lure us to a location." Habib spoke slowly, as if interpreting for someone who did not speak English. "Then they attack."

"We'll set up feasible goals," Joey added. He jotted down a note, reminding himself to ask Dan and a few other guys to get to meetings early and take the front-row seats. "We can't rush. Mistakes take months to resolve. The world's most powerful military has worked on this for a decade—it could be another decade before there's real trust."

"What about the women?" Cameron asked. "Why not focus on them?"

"The rules are set up against it," Joey said. "We can't talk with them, we don't know what they want, and they have little power."

"We'll have a woman commander," Cameron pressed. "Maybe we'll find shortcuts."

Joey gave a hard laugh. "The Taliban know plenty of shortcuts. Intimidation, tossing bombs into crowds. A man tossing acid into a woman's face because her family's not ready to marry her off. People out here are tired of shortcuts."

"Some will find a way to blame their problems on the outpost," Habib warned. "I don't know which are worse, the extremists who are impulsive or the ones who wait and plan." He told a story about a translator working with US soldiers in Kandahar hurrying for a fuel purchase from one of the local suppliers. "A new man working there—he didn't like how the translator looked at a woman waiting in the office. She was covered from head to toe, but the fuel guy was looking for an excuse. He didn't say a word and went into a back room. When he returned, he threw kerosene at the translator and lit a match." He closed his eyes. The room was quiet. Every man imagined his own version of flames, screams, and what happened next. "The translator died immediately. The man from the fuel depot was in the hospital for three months before he died. The woman and the troops were burned. Badly."

He concluded. "Shortcuts are not worth it."

For some reason, the memory of the laughing woman on the hillside came to Joey's head. She couldn't have been alone, and he didn't mind that villagers were watching the outpost. The laugh could be a good sign. He hoped that the outpost, Mita Samuelson, and the men in this room weren't going to make her life more difficult.

He tried to forget the face. "This is an isolated area—it hasn't seen a lot of violence," Joey pointed out. "These villages don't have imams, and there are too many opportunities for bullies to lay guilt trips on people. Our success depends on luck and the villagers not feeling threatened. But if someone starts accusing the others of not being religious enough . . ." he shook his head. "People fall for it every time. No matter what we do, we're the infidels."

"And handy targets," Dan said.

"On the other hand, any small improvement will let us make huge strides." Joey went on to explain how every visit, every comment, could send signals to the Afghans. Joey had grown up in a family constantly searching for signs with stoic pessimism, and he had discerned similar tendencies in rural Afghans.

"The rural villages are superstitious," he advised. "They look for signs, and we can anticipate behavior based on how they read us."

"So if there's an attack, we're to blame?" asked Barnaby, a guardsman reporting to Cameron.

"I'm saying be careful with any facial expression, tone, or behavior," Joey said. "It's foolish to threaten or humiliate the villagers in any way. And it's easier to do than you think. No jokes, no laughing, no sarcasm. They might not understand the words, but they can read faces. Don't show frustration. Say what you mean, but keep words to a minimum. Habib will filter comments, but they'll be watching your faces and hearing your voices. Building a relationship takes time."

"Do I hear a 'but'?" asked Cameron.

Joey paused—how to explain the fast-changing emotions in villages lacking schools and Internet, let alone electricity and running water? "We can't expect miracles. Say we meet a friendly guy who listens and wants to work with us," Joey said. "If we go too fast, others could move in and intimidate his family. The extremists could destroy his home or his fields—a year's worth of work. They threaten his wife or snatch his kids. He despises himself for even thinking of working with us. And if we're lucky, he won't hate us. But he's ruined."

Dan nodded and summed it up: "They're doing us favors, not the other way around."

"They're people," Cameron insisted to no one in particular. "They must want what we want."

"Agreed," Joey said gently. "But it's news to them that we see their lives as miserable. Look at it his way—every idea we bring is radical and terrifying."

"Waiting is tough," Cameron said. "I worry patience is a way to keep old ideas in place."

Joey felt sorry for Cameron. He was more afraid of rejected ideas than bullets. The man expected appreciation, and that was a dangerous form of extremism in itself. It happened with every rotation, every new set of people coming into the country.

He kept the session on preparations going, but knew inside that the operation depended on luck.

~~~~~~~

Orders had been issued long before the AH-64 Apache landed, delivering the civilian ag leader: She had free rein, yet all assigned troops had to watch her back and keep her out of trouble. "Mita Samuelson is talented, tireless, and fearless," noted one confidential briefing. "Her past work has attracted media attention and support at the national level, including profiles in the *New York Times*, *Barron's*, *Self*, and *Glamour* magazines. Any missteps or accidents are anticipated to attract negative publicity for the International Security Assistance Force. Don't let anything happen to her."

She was not only a retired general's daughter and active-duty general's pet project, but a media star. She was the reason why a seasoned Special Ops leader was stationed at the outpost, not just to secure the civilian, but to anticipate problems. "Let her get some projects done, but protect her," Joey's commander had ordered. "That's the mission. To be honest, I don't care if nothing else happens out there...."

The Apache landed after midnight, and Joey was waiting. The tiny, bundled woman didn't object as Joey stepped forward to carry the four bags.

Smiling, she waved to the pilot as he took off, and then turned to Joey. "I was hoping to arrive in the daylight and scan the countryside by air," she shouted.

He assured her that reconnaissance photos were on file and more from the ground were coming in. She flashed a smile and said, "But there's nothing like seeing it for yourself."

Joey didn't answer. He liked that she was ready to work, but there wouldn't be any unnecessary flyovers. No point in alarming villages in the area—or arguing about such details late at night. "We pushed the first planning session back tomorrow until 1100 hours. Give you time for sleep!"

"How thoughtful," she said. "But my late arrival has caused enough delays. If it's not too late, can we stay on schedule?" She didn't wait for his answer. "Or I can meet with my team early."

"That's great," he agreed. "You're on." They reached the door to her quarters and he handed over a small handheld radio. "It's on all night at the main station. Press this button and speak if there's any problem at all."

They quickly bid each other good night, and Joey waited to hear the click of her lock before heading for the computer station, checking in with the Army PFC overseeing the outpost's security cameras. He checked the monitors, adjusted a few camera angles, and ordered the young soldier to keep at least one lens trained on the ag leader's door until further notice.

"Does she know?" the soldier asked, staring at the screen.

"Not yet," Joey said. "She just got in. If anything moves near that door, let me know."

Joey sat at another computer, checking e-mail and reports and then reading more about Mita Samuelson. Born to a Bangladeshi immigrant mother and a military father, she grew up in Loudoun County, an all-American girl accustomed to all the privileges in genteel horse country. At Cornell's College of Agriculture and Life Sciences, her interests shifted from the leisurely concerns of horse farms to agriculture in developing nations. Studying applied economics, she became convinced that agricultural exports were key to promoting property and gender rights, if not peace in the developing world. During two summer breaks, she led teams of students to villages in Colombia to work with small coffee cooperatives, composting and tending soils, experimenting with shade, and developing aromatic varieties. The marketing team emphasized the regional character of the specialty coffees, and these became more lucrative than coca.

Graduating with honors, she organized a nonprofit venture in Colombia. Devastated by drug trafficking and eradication of crops by officers on the hunt for coca—three villages signed on for her cooperative specializing in horticulture. The women studied magazines like

Brides, *Vogue*, and *Martha Stewart Living* to anticipate home, wedding, and fashion trends in the countries to the north and then nurtured exotic blooms in custom colors and sizes to suit the styles. The wildly successful nonprofit venture caught the attention of the *New York Times*, and overnight a rich girl fascinated with agriculture in poor lands became a media darling.

From there, she completed an agriculture policy fellowship at Yale and interned with a microfinance program in Bangladesh, before joining the US government as an agriculture economist.

Reading between the lines, Joey realized that Mita Samuelson was not a typical media hound. In every article he had found, she was pleasant and brief—bursting with ideas and generous with crediting her professors and coworkers at every level.

Cameron and the others didn't realize how many journalists had clamored to embed with this team. The DoD public-affairs office would have approved the requests, but Mita had requested that the journalists be kept at bay. The woman had earned the trust of top commanders and held top clearance for releasing public-affairs reports.

It was a solid, strategic move to include women soldiers and civilians on the teams for connecting with villagers. It might just work if the villagers let Mita get anywhere close to the women.

He remembered the woman on the hill and thought that happy people could connect. Tired, he shook his head and looked forward to heading out into the night for surveillance.

CHAPTER 5

After the burial, the other women tried to talk to me, but I refused to dwell on the loss of my oldest child, except to stubbornly repeat sentiments of which I had no doubt: Ali had donned his travel clothes and looked forward to attending school. The boy was curious and a sure climber.

Shaking my head, I went to work with the pomegranates.

Others heard accusation in my voice and could see the fury of suspicion in my eyes, and found it easy to leave me alone with my grief. My other sons scattered, prepared to take over Ali's tasks. With women delivering lots of food, most from Leila and Mari, I didn't have to cook much for my family.

The next morning before sunrise, I ran up the hill that Ali and I had last climbed together. My lungs burned and my hands clawed among the rocks, reaching for the metal box. But of course the box was gone, and I stood on the cliff's edge, looking at the rocks below.

Allah, you should have taken me instead.

~~~~~

Ali's fall was no accident, I insisted to my husband, as we lay together in darkness. Neither of us could sleep.

The man shook his head, but asked questions: *Could he have gone up to check on our plants? Was the saffron a reason for anyone to kill Ali?*

His questions startled me, and it took a moment for me to respond. I had started the secret field, yet never thought that our saffron could be a reason for Ali's death. Parsaa was just as angry, hunting for an explanation. He had a sharp mind, and I felt guilty keeping the box and papers a secret. But maybe it could have been the saffron. *We'll keep watch*, I whispered. *How others prepare their meals, what they say about us, where they go at night. The boys can help—*

Clasping his hand over my mouth, Parsaa let out a cry, breaking off my words before I could vow vengeance against Ali's death. *We cannot think this way*, he ordered. *We don't involve the other boys.*

Without other words, he took me roughly, his strong arms like a trap. So soon after a child's death, I was unwilling and protested. It didn't matter that I felt his hot tears against my face. Afterward, I turned away, shaking off his arm and refusing to speak. He left the bed and headed out into the night.

Our children were the only ones who slept that night. I kept still, but my thoughts raced. Parsaa was right about not involving the boys, but I wouldn't stop hunting. If I saw someone with our saffron, that might provide a clue. I decided against telling anyone, even Parsaa, about the box, the money, and the papers I could not read or explain. If I showed him the paper and he didn't understand, his questions to other men might drive the killer to destroy the other papers.

I had to wait and watch for someone with those papers.

~~~~~~

Over the next week, villagers brought us many meals. None contained the golden spice. Three days after no words between us, Parsaa tried to return to our conversation from that horrible night. *Only a fool would show off the find so soon. We'll keep watching.*

I did not reply, going about my work, mourning, and refusing to talk. Other villagers did not disturb me, and Parsaa stayed away, too. I was angry and hurt. At odd times of the day, I wrapped my arms around my remaining sons, grieving and silently trying to understand how much they, too, felt their brother's loss. Ali had been kind to them. As parents, we never had to convince him to be generous and loving with them.

It bothered me that Ali never had his chance to attend school to learn about reading, solving problems, and talking with others. It pained me not to know what the words on those papers meant.

~~~~~

Before Ali's death, I had often picked up my husband's copy of the Koran and examined the pages. It was difficult to think of the strange marks, with no meaning, as sacred. I scratched the few simple words I had figured out into the dirt, and felt no awe.

Days of mourning transformed into days of planning, as I became determined to learn to read the Koran on my own and keep a record of my thoughts. Not that anyone in Laashekoh cared about what I had to say. This project was for me alone. I didn't want to explain my reasons. I didn't want to fret about losing good ideas. I didn't want to worry about memories of Ali fading over time, much like the memories of my childhood. I wanted to preserve the fondest memories of all my children and not just Ali.

I became convinced that if I knew how to read, then I would have understood those papers hidden away on the hillside. I might have known to warn Ali to stay away.

Uncertain whether such learning was possible, I intended to keep my reasons to myself. No one I knew had learned to read on his own, and finding a patient teacher is difficult for boys, let alone women. But then, teachers don't always realize when or how much they are teaching.

Only a few men in our village could read, and I was certain that my husband was the best of these. I had also observed that the men who could read were better at making decisions. They organized their arguments and didn't worry about losing track of details.

So I hoped that reading and writing would help me think clearly, too.

Like many men, my husband owned a copy of the Koran and read from it most evenings after dinner. He was fortunate to be his family's oldest son. Just before his adolescence, two younger brothers were prepared to take over his tasks, so he left home to attend the maktab for four years. The school was run by an elderly imam, whose followers had turned against him for refusing to join a group of imams eager to denounce capitalists, communists, Americans, Europeans, Indians, and the Jews. The imam had rejected the notion of keeping a list of enemies that was too long or lacking in specific crimes.

Solve the problems that are under our noses, the old man had explained to the boys. *No list of enemies should be longer than my nose.*

Those in charge of that village took his comment as criticism, and the imam was forced to leave his post at the mosque and open a school in a smaller village. He didn't have much education himself, and not many parents were willing to send their boys to the new school run by the strange old man who enjoyed quarreling with authorities.

But the imam knew enough to teach the boys how to read, recite verses from the Koran, apply lessons to daily life, and never stop learning about something, anything. He taught the boys how to farm and raise their own food and use mathematics for transactions. Because he didn't charge much, his school was preferred by rural people who could not afford expensive lessons and did not mind if their sons returned home more freethinking than most young men.

After the war with the Russians began, the man closed the school and encouraged the boys to join their fathers in defending their villages. Not long afterward, the imam was hit by a shell, lost a leg, and died of an infection.

My husband admired his old teacher and had long regretted not having the chance to thank the man for the lessons. After a hiatus of a few years, the imam's son and Parsaa's classmate returned to the area. He had spent several years in a refugee camp, and took lessons provided by teachers from northern Europe. Scholarships were arranged for him to study math at a foreign university, but he decided to continue with his father's dream, reopening the maktab and taking his father's place.

That was the school Ali was to attend.

To prepare Ali for school, Parsaa had read aloud for hours from our copy of the Koran, the translation in Dari that accompanied the

Arabic. Like many men in our village, he had memorized long passages, and it didn't take long before I realized that I, too, could memorize the verses, especially those he read immediately after turning a page. I listened closely to phrases and sounds, and when Parsaa was not home, I opened the Koran, studying the shape and order of characters while reciting the verse. Slowly, I began detecting a few words and searched for them to repeat elsewhere in the book.

Occasionally, after a struggle with a particularly difficult phrase, I stopped my husband during his reading and asked him to point to the word. Parsaa was surprised, but complied. The boys listened to their father, but showed no eagerness to pose such questions themselves.

Why don't you teach the boys more about letters and words? I questioned.

He hesitated, suggesting the boys would appreciate the task more if they traveled and learned from a proper teacher. *It needs to be combined with work or prayer. Recitation is not enough.*

There's no good reason to delay worthy tasks or desires, I advised. With the more lyrical verses, Parsaa encouraged the boys to pick out and repeat phrases, and this lent speed to my own understanding.

By that time, I had calculated that there had to be nearly one hundred letters. Only later did I discover that Dari had thirty-two letters, which took on three forms depending on their position—the start, middle, or end—in any word. Despite early frustrations, I refused to give up. Sadly, I only understood a handful of phrases, not nearly enough to draft a history of Ali's short life or a brief description of my dreams. Our lives were too rich, and I was missing too many words.

~~~~~

Practicing words, trying to learn more, distracted me from Ali's death. Ali didn't have his chance to head to school, and I was determined to read and write before another one of my children vanished from this earth.

Of course, I had our Koran to read, but to write, I needed other supplies. The document from the hill was good for a week of practice. But with Ali's death, it was no longer a scrap. I decided to save that document until I understood what it meant.

My son's death had delayed the men's regular trip to the market, a trip that kept them away a full day. Only the men of Laashekoh went to the market, at least four hours from our village. The women sent lists along with husbands, sons, or brothers. Others grumbled about the inconvenience, but I didn't mind. With the men away, I'd find more time to practice. Like the hawk that silently waits for the squawking flocks to devour seeds in the fields, I let others complain.

As I made breakfast, my husband prepared to leave a day earlier than the other men. I spoke to him for the first time in days and asked him to make a purchase for me. *If we have paper and a pencil, I can better organize our plantings*, I explained. *I can draw plots and plan our harvests.*

It was the first time I had spoken about anything besides Ali's death in days, and he laughed, relieved to have a simple way to distract us from the darkness of our child's death. *Yes, it's a good idea*, he said. *I can help with the numbers.*

He didn't realize how much I already knew. Because of the careful ordering of the verses in the Koran, it hadn't taken long to figure out numbers. With the few pieces of paper and old pencils that came our way, I kept notes. Using words repeated in the Koran or my own symbols, I logged a few observations about the plants, the weather, and the seasons. Just a few words—*garden*, *child*, *running*—could provoke a torrent of memories and feelings. I had much to say and not enough words.

Before Ali's death, building a collection of words was like a child's game. At first, I focused on the easiest of words, oft repeated, that I later learned were nouns—*Allah*, *love*, *land*, and *pomegranate*. But many words were not in the book—*seb*, *gol*, *bara*, and more. So I said words aloud, compared their sounds with the ones I knew and devised my own spelling. As long as this small collection belonged only to me, spelling did not matter.

After Ali's death, the game turned into urgent need, and I hurried to expand my skill. To write about my children, I had to understand words of action, more challenging to discern. The Koran had plenty of verbs: *to follow* and *forsake*; to *waste, submit,* and *forget*; to *doubt, warn,* and *forgive*—but these did not describe my children or the best parts of life. Writing my thoughts was a bridge to others. To write for my children, I needed to know more words of action.

I couldn't understand why others in the village lacked this desire. Did they not share the same sensations? Or was the problem with me, an inability to sort ideas in my head without the benefit of reminders on paper? I didn't dare ask questions, giving others reason to stop the endeavor.

After Ali's death, I had more time alone. Parsaa left our home at night, a habit that normally hinted of dark affairs. But I understood that he missed Ali, too, and grief can take strange turns. Writing and reading organized my thinking. In mastering my feelings, I had more influence over Parsaa, the boys, and others.

I came to realize that writers can control assessment of their ideas, especially if they keep the words hidden away from others.

CHAPTER 6

"The corporate ag types won't like her," Cameron confided the next morning before heading into the first district-reconstruction team meeting led by Mita Samuelson.

"She's not going away," Joey countered.

"She's Muslim," Cameron added. "From around here, I heard. . . ."

"Try Northern Virginia."

"Before that . . .," Cameron said, flustered.

"Bangladesh, on her mother's side," Joey noted. "Not close and nothing like Afghanistan. You have nothing to fear."

Cameron looked relieved and headed for the second row of seats.

"Give her a chance," Joey said. "Listen to her. And no chatter."

Joey shook his head. He had issued orders—no gossip, especially around the Afghan troops. Gossip signaled division and arguments and the notion that the Americans couldn't maintain order. He didn't know why people didn't look her up on Google, but he wasn't about to give them the idea and spur more gossip.

Unfortunately, Cameron wasn't alone. Rumors about one of the few women leading teams, and the only civilian leader, swirled throughout the outpost and beyond. The general had already promised politicians and the Pentagon that he counted on academic go-getters like Mita to stabilize the region and reignite international donor interest in Afghan projects. An avalanche of funding tumbled into Afghanistan following the 2008 US election, but the money didn't last long, not when the bulk had to go for security. Voters in the United States, Europe, and other far-off places were weary of never-ending war in Afghanistan.

The regional military commander was keen on fixing Afghanistan's agriculture industry as quickly as possible, and he counted on Mita and other specialists to spread ideas to convince one of the poorest countries in the world to play catch-up. A charming Muslim, with a Jewish father who had served as a US Army general, she was knowledgeable about military eccentricities and eager for dispatch to volatile Helmand, the largest province in Afghanistan and one of the most sparsely populated. The region had long relied on growing poppy or joining insurgencies for income.

Journalists, generals, politicians, professors, donors raved about her. Joey had his doubts, and there was no point speculating, but media coverage about projects in South America would impress few Afghans.

Mita Samuelson hurried into the room full of men on folding plastic chairs and started speaking, not waiting to reach the desk or board: "Great to see you all here today."

As her large, dark, happy eyes darted about the room, Joey glanced down at his watch. Two minutes before the meeting was scheduled to start, yet she didn't wait. Friendly, warm, she showed no sign of operating on less than eight hours of sleep after concluding seven thousand miles of air travel. "Our goal is to move into the villages, listen to people, and find out what they need." She introduced Joey as the lead on security and strategy and Habib Bulaq as the lead Afghan who would collect requests from the villagers.

Quickly, she went through the background summary: 80 percent of Afghans relied on agriculture for a living, and the nation supplied close to 90 percent of the world's opium. The country grew more wheat than opium, but the opium had brought in more revenues. Troops just barely managed to keep up with destroying poppy fields. The population was young, with 75 percent under the age of twenty-five and looking for ways to earn money and help their tribes, if not their country.

The introduction was modest and brief. She dove into the work, not boring the group with her résumé or reminders that she had the full support of top generals. She was determined and prepared—her voice a soft alto, its tone as sure as a chisel, splitting through any dissension, not matching her tiny stature or dark curls that refused to be tamed by a casual headscarf in lavender. The dozen men might have more military and agriculture experience, but she wasn't intimidated. Joey could not help admire her efficiency and enthusiasm for farming, more carefree than Cameron's.

She then sat down and asked Joey to review security.

He explained that provincial reconstruction teams were not new. Specialists had filed into the cities not long after the United States invaded the country in the fall of 2001. As the war dragged on, US commanders recognized the value of having tested and trusted Afghans lead interactions and any training. Major Habib Bulaq would search for viable proposals that would busy villagers of all ages into the future. At the same time, commanders would decide if this location was appropriate for a regional training center.

"My initial assessment: The area is more sustainable than many in Afghanistan." A few eyebrows went up. Even men who had previous rotations in Afghanistan were impressed by the rugged mountains emerging abruptly like some imposing wall from what looked like a dull desert surface, cracked and interrupted by occasional rocks and stray patches of grass. But a healthy river and a manageable population would support development. "There are some good working farms in these villages," he added.

"Maybe they'd be willing to focus on a big project—close to the river?" Cameron asked. "A joint venture for these villages—one that's highly visible."

Joey was blunt. "That would look like we're taking over the area's major water supply." A few laughed, annoying Cameron. "We don't need that kind of visibility."

"I thought the idea was to do high-profile projects and grab attention," Cameron said.

Mita broke in.

"True, but we need to entice the Afghans first." Rather than detail her own experiences, Mita talked about traditional Afghan families and the difficulties of getting villages to work as cooperatives. Wind came up outside, lashing bits of sand at the thin walls, as she proceeded to distribute research reports on the region's history.

One of the men spoke up sharply, asking Mita to raise her voice, and the question snapped Joey back to attention. The ag specialists peppered her with questions about demonstration projects around the compound, protocol for visiting villages, and her priorities. Wind battering the walls added to tension.

Mita remained calm, inviting Habib to describe the types of requests he anticipated from nearby villages. He distributed a list about general interests among villages—seed programs, veterinary advice on disease prevention, pumping for irrigation and drinking water, soil testing, and erosion control—all straightforward.

"We're relying on Major Bulaq to guide us on viability," Mita noted. "Everything goes through his group—and he'll advise on avoiding hurt feelings or unfair competition. The early projects will be QIPs—quick impact projects—small and doable."

Cameron studied the list. "Nothing here follows the wheat model tried by teams up north. I think Habib should understand all the available opportunities."

Joey waited for Mita's response. The briefest check of her background revealed that she was big on local control and would resist mega projects with corporate sponsors.

She nodded slowly. "I understand that several of you posted here had hoped to work on the wheat projects."

She asked his name and then quickly followed by asking for Cameron's opinion on the wheat cooperatives.

He flushed. "The Afghans rely on wheat, there's plenty of suitable land," he replied. "The crop would reduce reliance on Pakistan for imports."

"True." She started pacing. "But the Afghans lack storage capability for a larger crop. The big boosts in harvests in recent years reduced prices for the small farms. That's compounded by other inefficiencies of the small farms in terms of irrigation, crop rotation." She turned and shot a disarming smile at Cameron. "And I don't even have to go into the messy corporate prohibitions on seed gathering and selling."

She had done her research and knew that Cameron was not merely a member of the Wisconsin National Guard, but also employed by TopSeed International, a biotech multinational.

"It's way too early to introduce Afghans to the ways of big corporations." She fired questions at Cameron, getting him to admit that while his company distributed plenty of free grain seed, there was a catch: The small village farmers were prohibited from selling or giving away extra seed—a confusing regulation for rural farmers in the States, let alone those in Afghanistan.

"You don't want to rush these farmers," Mita concluded. "Any problems and they'll be turned off from biotech for decades."

Joey was relieved. She had taken the time to research her personnel and the nuances of Afghan culture.

Mita moved ahead. "At this point, we have limited funding and patience from the American people. The wheat projects are fine, but won't produce much before the deadline for making a decision on this location. Rest assured, this team and Major Bulaq are flexible. We're not focusing on any one crop or technique. The key words are *fast*, *manageable*, *useful*, and *sustainable*."

Another man asked about processing and export markets. "Only for non-food products," Mita said. "Afghanistan is primitive and most of these villages lack electricity or refrigeration. Besides, news reports coming out of this region have been extremely negative. Let's be honest—consumers in India, Europe, or the US are not ready to rush out and buy Afghanistan jams or cookies. Markets won't materialize in the next few months, and villages don't need false hopes on that front."

More questions followed, and Mita didn't hesitate to turn to Habib or Joey for answers. At one point, Habib discouraged rapid investments in road construction, and some in the group groaned.

"How do we reach these places without equipment?" Barnaby howled.

"If they don't have roads, it means they don't want to be bothered," countered Chuck Greely, another Guard member.

Habib waited for the grumbling to play out. "The lack of roads has also reduced the influence of al Qaeda and other extremists in many regions."

Cameron shook his head, disgusted. "They're stopping progress."

"If the villagers don't set the agenda, we risk increasing resentment," Mita warned.

"We know what works," Cameron fired back with a smile. "You want fast improvements, but reject state-of-the-art techniques. As long as we all see the contradiction."

"There's no contradiction," Mita said, lifting her head. "We're out to help people. Turn their ideas into fast improvements. Not do everything for them."

Cameron turned and muttered to one of his men. Despite the shaking walls, Joey heard the words, "She wants to look good for journalists." Mita heard, too.

She approached Cameron's table and tapped the edge. "The only way we look good for television producers or bloggers is if the villages look good. And we have to plan carefully. No doubt you're aware that journalists are getting wary of corporate charity and the motivations."

A few team members applauded, and Cameron looked uncomfortable. She took a kinder turn.

"Captain Janick is on the right track. We want improvements that are highly visible for the Afghan people and then journalists. We can't keep them out forever, and when they do get out here, we want success stories—not boondoggles."

The room went silent. "It's happened too often here. Roads get constructed between two villages and are used for fighting rather than trade. Schools and hospitals and police stations become traps for those seeking services. I feel fortunate to be part of the ag team. Agriculture offers great potential for this region. Once Afghans see small, manageable projects up and running, they'll be ready to try more substantial projects."

"The big security-training facility—do we mention this area is being considered?" Cameron asked.

"No," Joey said. "This is one of many sites under consideration." He explained how the facility review was supplemental to the ag mission. "We'll be offering advice on farming and security while gauging connections with extremists, as determined by the amount of fuel in the village, the percentage of poppies as a crop, treatment of women and children. There's no need to confuse the two projects this early."

Cameron had made his point and smiled—team leaders were not ready to give local Afghans control in all areas.

Thunder cracked nearby and the lights went out, saving Joey from other questions. One of the tech crew ran out to check the generator. A few started to stand, and a flashlight went on. Mita pointed to the seats. "No reason we can't finish this meeting."

The man with the flashlight directed it at her face. She did not look away or complain. Another man sitting next to Cameron spoke up, and the flashlight shifted in that direction. "Can we expect the Afghans to handle multiple projects? Some specializing could make it easier for us to assign staff to the compound."

"Nobody promised this would be easy," she said to wry laughter. "Major Bulaq wants to hear all your ideas, but listen to him carefully. The people in this area have been displaced multiple times. They struggle to feed their children. The benefits of trade, schools, or a limited family size aren't immediately apparent.

"The nearest school is almost fifty miles away. Virtually none of these families can read, they don't have a clue about the outside markets. They've been taught that singing, art, any kind of fun, is sin. So many are bored to tears, and too many are addicted to opium or find trouble in other ways."

"That's patronizing," Cameron shot back, and Mita looked as if she had been slapped. The room went silent. Joey glared at the man, but Cameron didn't look his way. A poem by Kipling ran through Joey's head: "Take up the White Man's burden . . . Your new-caught, sullen peoples, Half-devil and half-child." Cameron had a problem being supervised by a woman, and that was a bigger problem than Joey had anticipated. He almost spoke up, but Cameron was an agriculture man. Mita had to frame the goals and lead him if she was going to last at this outpost.

"Starting out, most won't trust us," she said quietly. "There are reasons why fear and terrorism whip through Afghanistan. That doesn't mean Afghans are stupid. They have every reason to suspect our motivations and the programs of people from the other side of the world. Why wouldn't they?"

Most people nodded, already tired of Cameron's overbearing ways.

Joey spoke up. "It's basic security. We can't give them any reason to think we're here to disrupt their lives or that we're here to boost our own careers, Captain Janick."

Cameron was chastened by the lack of support, and Mita turned to the board, proceeding to outline the schedule as if the exchange hadn't happened. The team would split up, visiting nearby villages and talking with elders. Basic assistance would be offered. The teams might offer to assess soil samples, water resources, and farming techniques. Any requests for work would be reviewed by the security unit. "It's a client-based system. We help." She paused and turned around the room. "We can't afford failures," she concluded. "Any unnecessary failure will result in immediate reassignment."

One of the men raised his hand and asked about initiatives on women's rights and other services.

Mita shook her head, surprising the group, discouraging what she called "romantic notions" about family farms, tribes, women's rights, or traditions. "Our work is limited to farming improvements."

She held up a hand to stop the murmurs. "Some teams have been on the ground in Afghanistan for five years. Most people—at home and in this room even—are doubtful we can bring about real change. But a pragmatic approach, a few improvements in one area, might nudge a village into a new direction," she explained. "We need to convince Afghans that we're capable, and so are they.

"Fast ag successes first—we can worry about cultural factors later."

~~~~~~

The power was out while a crew worked on repairing the generator. Joey assigned a guard to the team leader's hut. "It's just until the cameras come back on line," Joey advised. "And don't be obvious."

Later that evening, another one of his men, Dan, noticed a dark cloth hanging from the door of the unit where Mita slept—and ordered it carried to headquarters. Joey joined him, and Dan stretched it out on the desk.

"A hood?" Dan asked. "There was a question. I looked away for less than a minute and when I turned back, I noticed it hanging there."

Scowling, Joey folded the cloth in half, and put his hand through the opening. "It's what women wear in Saudi Arabia—there are different kinds, but this is a one-piece niqab. Covers a woman's face in public."

"How the hell did that get in camp?" Dan asked. "The Afghans?"

Joey shook his head. "They don't wear them around here."

"So the ass-hat is one of us."

"The question came from one of the Guard?"

Dan nodded. "Cameron."

Joey stuffed it in a drawer. "We're going to pretend this didn't happen. And don't take your eyes off her goddamn door."

~~~~~

Over the next few nights, surveillance equipment showed that a few curious Afghans ventured close to the outpost late after darkness fell, examining the razor-wire fencing and testing the motion lights. But there were no attacks or niqabs left at doorways.

Mita pressed Joey to begin trips to the villages. "Otherwise, they'll wonder what we're doing here."

"Curiosity is good. We'll understand each other's patterns before we barge in."

He promised that the ag team would soon get the go-ahead to visit the villages, but later that day a radio call came in from Ron, an analyst and friend stationed near Kandahar. "You've got a problem," he explained. "A patrol stopped a shipment of drugs not far from your area." He read the coordinates.

"You've seen the surveillance docs," Joey replied. "The farms around here are clean."

"The drugs aren't from your area," Ron said. "The problem is the guys with the shipment—three scared teenagers. All three were using the same name and carried what looked like new birth certificates."

"They're from around here?"

"We don't think so. The clowns managed to get through at least two road checks with matching names on birth certificates. The place of birth says Laashekoh."

Laashekoh—it was the nearest village to the outpost and the smallest one. Less than 1 percent of the Afghan population had birth certificates or identity papers. It was hard convincing villagers they were useful. Most people in rural Afghanistan didn't know how old they were, and many rural women didn't know where they'd been born. Parents and husbands didn't want them running off.

The government didn't have an exact population count, and so the United Nations began a program to register newborns to help organize vaccines, census, education levels, and other data. Analysts had warned that the literacy rate in Helmand was about 20 percent for men, 10 percent for women, and probably close to zero for Laashekoh's twenty or so families. The place was too backward for organizing a program on birth certificates.

Joey mulled the implications. "Everyone here is an unknown. But that's what we expected when we arrived."

"We see no immediate threat. Someone's passing out phony birth certificates—but why? It's not like they're tickets for anything good. The biometric scans and ID cards are more useful."

"Would you have caught it if the names weren't the same?" Joey pressed. He knew that, unless they had spent time in prison, most rural villagers had not been subjected to the biometric scans yet.

"No," Ron admitted. "But they're in the database now. So keep a close eye on the village, look for anyone using certificates listing Laashekoh as their place of birth or any phony documents."

"This place is off the map. People using Laashekoh certificates—doesn't mean they're from Laashekoh."

"Our thought exactly. The writing was shaky, as if someone struggled to copy the words. We're putting out an alert—hoping someone has an idea about what these guys are up to."

"Corruption by illiterates," Joey noted. "I thought the birth certificates were for newborns."

"That was the plan. Maybe someone in the bureaucracy made a mistake, a few stray certificates getting passed around."

"And the worst-case scenario?" Joey asked. He had been in Afghanistan long enough to expect the worst.

"You got me—maybe use a phony certificate to harass a future president?" Ron joked.

Joey laughed, and then swore. "Maybe they need us more at home, but I'm not sure anyone can stop that bickering."

"Don't sell yourself short," Ron said. "Civilians getting to you?"

"No. The Guard. One jackass in particular."

"He'll figure it out. Or he won't. Seriously, though, I'm hoping there's no good use for these birth certificates."

"As if IUDs, snipers, and trafficking aren't enough."

"Hmm, it could be drug gangs, evading authorities by using different names and villages. Maybe we'll spot more certificates and figure it out. Our team is stretched thin."

"I can't see career criminals in Laashekoh," Joey concluded. "How much difference is there between a phony Afghan certificate and no birth certificate at all?"

"Not much," Ron admitted. "Technically, they're supposed to have passports and visas to cross into Pakistan, but they bribe guards and find unsecured routes. These days they need serious documentation to get into India or Iran."

"Your people working these three guys over?"

"Killing them with kindness. Unlike the rest of us, they love the cooking here. But they look like lost kids and don't know much. We have to find the people calling the shots. Hey, when's your next leave?"

Joey couldn't leave the camp for long, not with Cameron acting out. "It's going to take a while before we're settled here."

"Be sure to give me a ring. We'll go out on the town. Kandahar-style."

~~~~~~

After midnight, Joey wrapped himself in dirty gray and tan cotton—clothes of an Afghan migrant in search of work. To minimize detection, he went alone, moving freely in the night, wearing what special forces called a nonstandard uniform. Along with an old pack, he had purchased the payraan and pants from a merchant in Kandahar who had learned that US soldiers were fussy, preferring used clothing that was worn, with dust and stains from the previous owner.

From afar, with beard and worn clothes, Joey might pass as an Afghan as long as he stood still. But when he moved, Afghans recognized the stranger in their land: His gait was too sure, and his hands, shoulders, and head could not disguise years spent in a more confident land with a faster pace. Up close he fooled no one: His skin and light brown hair were too clean and nourished. His leather boots fit well.

NGO workers howled about any break in the rules of engagement, so after sunset, Joey slipped away and changed, not mentioning his patrols to Mita or other civilians at the outpost. Habib and Mita had the final word for all agriculture decisions, but Joey was in charge of security, and he interpreted that mission broadly. Besides translating for the team, he researched regional activity, designed scouting missions before the team visited any village, and advised on schedules. He ran checks on village leaders for previous anti-military activity, checking out any odd behavior or movements that could signal drug trafficking or other illegal activities.

The split in the team's leadership had its benefits. Joey didn't relay security findings that might unnerve the specialists.

The teams expected smooth operations with minimal interference from the military—of course, until disaster struck and the military had to swoop in for rescues. Joey agreed that soldiers with armored vehicles, flak jackets, and weapons could complicate messages of goodwill. But after a decade, soldiers had a range of experiences all over the country and a feel for Afghans defending their territory. The work of civilians was spotty. They didn't know what questions to ask and didn't realize Afghans already knew the answers.

So for security planning, military personnel often found it easier to leave contractors and NGO types out of the loop as local conditions changed. Once an area was secured, the soldiers no longer searched homes, set up roadblocks, or used drones for surveillance. They became security guards, providing occasional expertise in other areas and letting the civilians take the good results for granted.

~~~~~~

The village was a refuge amid the slopes with treacherous cliffs and passages. At night, the homes looked like plain wooden blocks. Dark, low clouds promised rain. He couldn't see the fields or gardens. People were indoors. Fires were dying down, no longer tended, and dust suspended in the air added to their eerie glow. The American soldier approached cautiously, until he was close enough to smell the wood smoke, maintaining the same distance as the Afghans who had examined the outpost earlier in the week.

Joey carried minimum equipment. He had decided against bringing along his pack, the tripod, or a long-range-laser listening device. He didn't even take the night-vision glasses. Joey didn't want to display any technological advantage, other than his M16.

He put the weapon to the side. Stretching out in a comfortable place, leaning against a rock, he studied the sturdy homes of Laashekoh, all similar in size with no embellishments. Windows were small, and candlelight from lanterns flickered from a few. He waited patiently, hoping to detect shadows moving among the buildings, perhaps even catch the tenor of conversations.

But the place was still. There was more noise from insects rattling in the nearby brush.

He couldn't imagine living in such a place—with no televisions, music, or arguing. He recalled his own home as a child—the quarrels and rowdy fighting interspersed with harsh indifference. More gentle sounds came from the homes in Afghanistan, but those could be deceiving. Adults spoke to children in whispers, and were attuned to listen for any hint of anger or disrespect. Over time he had observed that the behavior of children did not necessarily reflect their parents' character—a discovery that was a relief in a way. Vicious terrorists could have lovely children.

Plenty of cover was nearby, and he listened for sounds of alarm that suggested he had been spotted. He was comfortable, more relaxed than he'd ever be in an enclosed room. It didn't matter if the sleep hut had cool air or not. It didn't matter if he was in Helmand or the States—Joey felt more comfortable outdoors in the fresh night air. Alone.

Content, he remembered a quote from some class long ago, *Nemo malus felix*. No evil man is happy. Not that unhappy people are evil. Most of his fellow soldiers would disagree with him, but Joey thought of evil as rare and war, politics, and religion as imperfect methods for finding or eliminating evil. More often than not, evil was linked with fear.

Footsteps moving through the dry grass interrupted his thoughts. Holding his breath, Joey slowly sat up and glanced toward the village. He didn't reach for his gun. Moments later, a soft cough broke through the night.

Joey slowly turned in that direction and a villager stood close, with a Type 56, the Chinese version of the AK-47 in his hands. A scarf covered his nose and mouth, protecting his face from desert winds or an opponent's eyes. The man's eyes were stern, but his weapon was pointed toward the ground.

"*Salaam*," Joey said.

The man returned the greeting and continued in cordial Dari. "What do you want to find?"

"What I hope Afghans find when they check on our outpost," Joey said. "Except that you probably see and hear more."

The other man smiled. "Who knows if people in any home speak the truth to one another." He studied Joey. "You're an American." It wasn't a question, but Joey nodded. "You must have a plan for this area."

Joey swallowed. "We're part of a team to help villages in this area with farming projects—the villages that want help."

The man gestured toward Joey's weapon. "A useful tool for farming. Even around here, you should keep your weapon ready."

Joey glanced at the M16 leaning against his pack, but made no move. The man walked over to Joey's gun, picked it up, and gently placed it within Joey's reach. "We may not be alone out here," he commented, before squatting and placing his own rifle on the ground, close at hand. "Our village has done everything in our power to separate ourselves from the fighting. We can't be careless."

"The Americans won't start a fight here."

"But the Americans attract outsiders and extremists to this area."

Joey sighed and agreed. "Some Afghans want us to keep the extremists at bay."

"In the cities." The man gazed at the rectangle homes on the mountainside, the smooth mud walls in bright contrast against dark trees and green fields. "We have more control here. We don't want the crime, the greed."

"We don't either. If you—"

The man put his hand up. "Soldiers bring fighting. Our village does not want to relocate. Some will blame you for every problem in this area, even those that developed before your arrival."

"We don't want to interfere."

"I have seen your outpost. There's a lot of equipment."

"It can be moved out as quickly as it was moved in," Joey offered. "We're here to share agricultural advice. And defend against the few who don't want farmers to succeed."

The man waved his arm. "A few will be receptive and others will despise you," he noted. "Most will change their minds. Are your people afraid—or will others wander about?"

"So far, just me. The others are farmers."

The man rubbed his beard and gazed at Joey. "Would any of your people have reason to walk these hills and kill a member of our village?"

The phrasing was odd, and Joey wondered if he misunderstood the Dari. He tried to be as direct as possible. "This team just arrived and is not prepared for fighting. If fighting starts, our group will leave this area."

"It doesn't take much to kill a child," the man said, cryptically.

Joey was unnerved, wondering if extremists were already wreaking havoc in Laashekoh, pinning blame on Americans. "A child was killed?"

"A strange death." The man pointed toward the outpost. "Soon after your arrival."

Joey thought back to the hectic early days. He would have noticed anyone wandering off. Besides, the crew was too timid. "No one left the outpost. They wouldn't have ventured out on their own. I would have seen them."

"Others blame the Americans, but. . . ." Pain crossed the man's face and he stopped. "It was a strange death." They sat in silence, and Joey waited for the man to speak again. "Some will want to hear what you have to say about agriculture."

"Then we can visit your village soon?"

"My village?" The man laughed. "No village belongs to one man." He turned serious again and stood. "In the meantime, keep this meeting between the two of us. Perhaps we meet again some night? *Khuda hafiz.*" Bending his head, he ducked under a low-hanging branch and disappeared into the shadows.

Joey waited, but didn't hear the man or see him return to the village. For all he knew, the man could be bluffing about keeping the meeting a secret and warn his fellow villagers.

Joey wasn't worried. The conversation suggested that people in the region were not outright hostile to the Americans, at least on this night. The guy passed a test by returning the rifle and not pushing him around. The fact that the Afghan had talked so candidly was a good sign. But the man didn't lower the scarf to show his face. Joey couldn't help but sense that the man knew he had not caught an American soldier by surprise.

Alert, Joey hiked quickly back to the outpost in the dark. He didn't want to answer questions about the outing or mention the encounter with the villager. During previous rotations, he would have told fellow soldiers. But this group wouldn't understand.

Going out at night, luring the Afghan villager, broke the rules that

Joey had imposed on the rest of the ag team: Travel in a group while away from the base. Meet with villagers in a group rather than alone. "Together, we're more secure," he had assured the team. In truth, he felt more secure alone.

Before heading to the hut, Joey changed his clothing and took one last look at the sky. The clouds had moved away, exposing a brilliant array of stars. No rain had fallen.

Cameron stood outside, as if he were waiting for Joey. He noted that Joey had not come from the headquarters hut. When Joey didn't answer, he whispered, "Is there something we should know about?"

"Not at all," Joey replied. "Routine patrol."

"Around here? With all the surveillance cameras?" He waited a moment and then pressed. "You told us absolutely no leaving the outpost at night."

"That order stands." Joey kept his voice flat. Answering the questions would lead to gossip. "Perimeter patrol. So far, we've spotted nothing."

"We," Cameron commented.

Eager to crawl into his bed, Joey aimed for ambiguity. "We," he repeated.

"The rest of us need to know what's going on," Cameron griped.

Joey held the door open. "Not when you can't do anything to help."

CHAPTER 7

With the men gone, I had more time alone but could not raise the suspicions of the other women. Every day, I inspected our orchard, impatiently pinching at aphids or weeds. Tending the pomegranates had been a favorite task, until reading came along. I had never imagined finding such joy sitting still, and eager to spend more time with the Koran, I hurried my work in the orchard.

A few years back, after a particularly good season, the men of the village had purchased the large rooted cuttings at the market. They were from Iran, and pushing the sale, the dealer had promised that they would provide ample fruit and screen village homes from prying eyes. *Very easy,* he pressed, holding the cuttings out. *In time, they will make you rich.*

So the village had planted the pomegranates, about twenty in all, in a semi-circle, on the slope flanking our compound. Unfortunately, the dealer had offered minimal instructions.

Looking forward to the tart fruit, I nurtured the plants and their soil, lugging water, using blankets to shield them from wind or cold. I was pleased when all of our family's trees survived into the following year and the next with a show of coral blossoms. Other families lost plants and turned to me for advice.

To replace the failed plants, I removed young branches from the hardiest trees, soaked them in water steeped with compost, and waited for the roots to arrive. Once planted in the orchard, the trees grew fast, and I ruthlessly pruned them, preventing them from growing higher than my arms could reach.

The trees produced ample fruit and resentment. A few women

shrugged, no longer willing to help in the orchard. That was when I learned to hide exactly what I knew and how I knew it. Instead, I asked questions rather than show off my skills. I found other reasons to praise Allah, besides the pomegranates or other crops, never suggesting that He favored me more than others. The women preferred to think of my success as luck, or taale.

At times, I neglected my plantings just enough to allow others to catch up and produce more fruit. After a few seasons, the resentment faded, and the pomegranates required less care. I taught my children how to handle the fruit, scolding them when they wandered off the paths between the rows, compacting the soil and endangering the roots. I saved old tea leaves and regularly mixed that loamy mess into the sandy soil at the base of every tree. As the fruit took on a blush, I scanned the skies for any sign of rain, anxious to prevent the balls from ripening too quickly, cracking, and falling to the ground.

Other women helped with the harvest, plucking the pomegranates and arranging them in crates, loaded by the children into carts, for delivery by our men to the nearest towns. The men were cautious, dividing the produce among villages because they didn't want others to realize our small village's wealth.

In recent years, each tree produced two hundred pieces of fruit or more, earning the village enough to buy supplies that carried us through the winter. We did the same with our grains, apricots, turnips, and other vegetables, and of course, stored plenty for our own use.

That soil and water and sunlight could produce such delicate colors and textures—the ruby globes of pomegranates, apricots with velvet skin, and the golden threads of saffron—astounded me. Pride is evil, but surely appreciating the products of one's labor is not the same as admiring one's self.

Eventually, other women offered to cook and provide meals in exchange for my time in the fields, and I declined, laughing as if they were mad. Instead, I lowered my head and urged them to thank Allah. I do not pray as much as the men do, but my constant gratitude is genuine.

~~~~~~

A steady hum competed with the locusts. Children ran to the compound walls, pointing, before women hurried to doorways, sternly calling children inside. Two young men who stayed behind to guard the village reached for weapons always kept nearby.

The engine slowed and then stopped at a pile of boulders.

From the other side of the orchard, my children looked at me—but I shook my head, signaling them to remain quiet.

Ducking behind a shrub, hiding from villagers and visitors both, I peered at the road for our village that started far below. Three soldiers with large packs trudged away from a large truck that then roared away. Memories of Ali's warning reverberated. *The Americans.*

One man carried a large weapon, strapped to his back like an afterthought. This group was more nuisance than danger, I decided, wondering what the fools wanted from us.

About an hour later, the men took the final steep climb in the approach to our compound. One of the three men glanced upward, with curiosity and expectation. Such a hopeful face was difficult to hate or ignore, and I jerked backwards into the leathery leaves. Unnerved, I gathered my boys and ran for home in a village that had gone silent.

~~~~~~

A few children, chattering and leaping, gathered around the two men and their translator. The visitors nodded to the children, saying salaam, but they did not toss around candy or trinkets as other foreign visitors had tried in the past. Instead, this group was deferential, ready to ask for permission or favors rather than control. The subdued demeanor was more disarming than arrogant, but I wondered if it wasn't an act to gain trust. I had heard the warnings: The Americans could be so appealing, but so unreliable and inconsistent.

The young men left behind to guard the village acted like fools, arguing about inviting the men for tea in front of an Afghan translator who understood every word. The Afghan awkwardly broke into the argument, introducing himself and asking to speak with an elder.

The men are at the market, one of the boys explained. *But we can . . .*

Frustrated, Mari stepped into the sunlight, waved the youth away, and confronted the soldiers. *You are not from these parts. Our men do not want to speak with you.*

Our outpost is near, the translator said softly, introducing the other two with a jumble of names. *They're Americans—trying to help get the country settled.*

We cannot help you, and you cannot help us. Mari's voice was shrill. The translator looked relieved about ending the conversation. But another man, the observant one, pressed the translator to continue. I watched his face, certain that he could understand what the Afghan soldier and Mari were saying.

We want to leave a small gift. The Afghan handed over a tube. *And also some containers of cooking oil.*

Leila, Mari's daughter, moved close behind her mother, curious and staring at the items. If the rest of us needed any reminder of Leila's beauty, we only had to glance at the eyes of our visitors. We were accustomed to her, but these men were mesmerized by waves of dark hair, green eyes, and skin as smooth as an almond petal.

Mari didn't notice, instead directing the men to place the items to the side on a stone bench. With rude silence, she then pointed to the path leading away from the village. As the translator glanced at his colleagues, the tallest man nodded and turned away. Children and women remained in the doorways, waiting for the sound of the men's footsteps to disappear.

But the Americans didn't leave. A third American, with pale hair and face, waved his arm, arguing with the translator, while the tall man shook his head. The pale man was annoyed with his colleagues, not us, but it was still strange. Stepping back, the tall man rolled his eyes and held out his hand as if offering the man to us. A few children laughed.

The Afghan translated. *We came all this way, and Captain Janick wants you to know he's a grain specialist. If you have any questions about growing wheat, he can give advice.*

We have more grain than we need, Mari snapped. The other villagers snickered, and she included them in her scolding. *Allah multiplies for whom He pleases.*

The translator looked embarrassed, repeating the words, bowing his head like the villagers. At last, the group of men said farewell and headed out the gate.

Mari's glare followed them until they were out of sight. *Excess brings injury*, she murmured. Then she turned and snapped at the young men in a low voice. *That is how you handle strangers. Arguing about tea? Telling them our men are gone?*

One of her daughters reached for the tube. *Leave it alone*, Mari snapped. *It could be dangerous. No one touch that until our fathers return.*

The other mothers repeated Mari's order. Flushed with fear or power, Mari collected the containers of oil and stormed into her home, missing the resentment crossing the faces of the young men left to protect the village.

~~~~~~

Joey had ordered the men against loud assessments on Laashekoh until they reached the outpost. The climb down away from the village was treacherous, over piles of unstable rubble, and it would take more than an hour for the men to reach the waiting vehicle.

The narrow pass—the entire route—was probably watched around the clock.

But Cameron didn't wait to let loose with his complaints. "They weren't interested. I don't think they can understand."

"Rushing didn't help," Joey retorted. "With luck, we didn't frighten them."

"Surveillance would have helped," Cameron griped. "We should have known the men were gone."

"Keep the chatter down," Joey reminded. He hated to admit it, but Cameron was right. The trip was a waste. Joey quickened the pace, hoping to wear the other man out and end the conversation.

"We're far enough away . . ." Cameron looked behind.

"Far enough from the village," Joey warned. "If they want, they hear us here. They hear us at the outpost . . ."

Habib nodded, and Cameron's laugh was nervous. "You're trying to spook us." He glanced up at the rocky cliffs protecting Laashekoh from unexpected visitors. "They're not going to head up or down this hill any more than necessary."

Habib and Joey kept a steady pace, and Cameron managed to keep up. "There's got to be a better way into this village," he muttered, squeezing between two boulders. "They couldn't move any big loads of crops out of here if they wanted."

With every step, rocks cracked and crumbled. Steady footing was impossible on the layers of broken rock, and sometimes the men slid along, using the edges of their boots to dig in and brake.

"If the women don't want our help, then none of them do." Cameron panted as he scaled a boulder. "We can scratch this place. It's a lousy location—no decent fields—and the people are out of touch."

Joey was tired of the griping, but waited for the group to hit secure ground. He stopped, facing Cameron. "Keep it down," he ordered. "I doubt anyone in that village understands English. But they pick up on the tone of our voices."

Cameron checked the path and the slope rising above them. "You think the women and kids would follow us?"

Habib shrugged. "Anything is possible."

They walked in silence for a few more moments. Cameron's pace was anxious, and he moved close behind Joey. At one twisted turn, Cameron's foot slipped on loose rocks and he pitched forward. At the sound of clattering rocks, Joey spun and used his body to push the man back into the cliff wall, blocking him from a drop-off of several hundred feet. The three stared at one another.

"Take a deep breath," Joey said. "No rush."

Cameron nodded. Single file, the three men stepped side by side around the curve to safer terrain.

Joey had to talk to distract Cameron, keep him calm. "Laashekoh has potential," Joey said. "Excellent orchards. The women are confident."

Habib nodded. "Rural Afghanistan can be more relaxed than the cities. It depends on who's in charge. The village looks capable."

"They're not ready to work with us," Cameron whispered. "No one reached for that solar flashlight."

Conversation was better than panic, and Joey kept his tone friendly. "They'll come around. We spoke to one woman."

"But Mita wants fast success," Cameron explained. "We need to get these people dependent on us and wanting wheat."

Joey cringed, speaking in English, then Dari, to emphasize the point. "That's not what she wants. She ordered the team to listen, not push projects."

The Afghan nodded, but Cameron did not acknowledge the comment, rushing ahead toward the Humvee's purr. "I've met my first wheat extremist," Habib murmured in Dari.

As they turned the corner, a young girl emerged from the brush, unnoticed by the driver or Cameron. Joey gripped his M16, and Habib's hand covered his side arm. The beautiful girl from the village was not alarmed and waited, a loosely draped blue chaadar framing dark hair and delicate skin. She was the only one who had showed interest in the solar light.

Smiling, she approached the Humvee, running her hand along the side and letting it rest there, as if posing for a photo. "It's okay," Joey croaked, not having the presence of mind to greet her in Dari. Of course, the girl couldn't know what he meant.

Startled, the driver turned. A more skittish soldier might have shot her—fulfilling the fervent wish of every extremist.

"What's she doing here?" Cameron shouted, looking back at Habib and Joey.

Habib took over. "*Bekhatar ast.*"

The girl nodded shyly and stepped closer, a younger, softer version of the one who had just scolded them back in the village. Her eyes were bright, curious, and she held her head high. "I have questions," she said.

Joey took a deep breath, ignoring the other men and his embarrassment. Despite her slight frame and horrible shoes, she had negotiated the rough terrain, managing to beat three trained soldiers down the hill. Not even breathing hard, she looked as though she'd have no problem sprinting another mile.

Habib nodded and waited.

"Why didn't you attack us today?" Her puzzlement was genuine.

Habib didn't take time to translate, following Joey's directions on not breaking the rhythm of initial one-to-one conversations. "We're not here to attack—there are no plans for us to attack. These men will fire only if fired on first." Joey let out a nervous breath, and she glanced his way even as Habib pointed back to the village. "Is that what the others think?" Habib pressed.

She nodded. "Laashekoh is an important place for America?"

Habib's reply could have come out of a recruiting manual. "The US cares about all of Afghanistan. You're doing good things with agriculture here, and the soldiers want to help Afghanistan get its markets going again. *Hamkari. Sheraakat.* If people have good harvests and products to sell, that would slow the fighting and bring prosperity."

She thought about that. "Only if we have goods to sell," she said. "But you must come back when the men are here. Talk with my father. When will you come back?"

Her tone was demure, but Joey didn't like the question—too damn convenient, requesting a schedule. The answer could go back to any Taliban in the area. But Habib was doing a good job, not releasing specifics, so Joey didn't interrupt or confront her directly—no point in letting her know that at least one of the Americans understood Dari. Not yet.

"That's up to our commanding officers. Who wants to know?"

Habib was good, Joey thought. She murmured more about her father, and then mentioned that Taliban were in the area. Unfortunately, Cameron picked up on the word. He hopped out of the truck, startling the girl, and she scurried toward the trees.

"Did you hear that, Joe? What's she talking about?"

Annoyed, Joey curtly nodded and kept his face blank. "Let them continue." Joey spoke gently. Like Habib, he did not break eye contact with the girl from Laashekoh. "Cameron, get back in the truck and shut up. Now."

Leaning against a tree, she watched as Cameron complied. "The Taliban. They're watching you," she warned. "And they watch us."

"Do you feel threatened?" Habib questioned. Sweat dripped from his hair.

"Who doesn't feel threatened anymore?" She shrugged. "There are more ways to threaten a village than ways to stop the threats. All we can do is ignore them or attack, join a more powerful village or run away."

"And which will your village choose?"

She smiled at Habib as if he were foolish. "We won't run away."

"Our team only wants to provide assistance. Help with jobs or money or schools. The same cannot be said about the Taliban."

She dismissed the comparison. "But the Taliban can help. They can pay us and help with supplies." She sighed. "We work in the fields and in our homes. The boys leave for maktab and the girls leave for marriage. Nothing changes. And it's no secret the Taliban will be here long after the Americans tire of this place and return home. But you promise no attacks?"

Joey wanted to defend his entire nation to this one person, beautiful and willing to talk with three foreign soldiers alone, and explain what troops were trying to achieve in Afghanistan. This girl, her mother, and maybe others in the village had spunk. They were not afraid of arguing with men. Maybe they wouldn't mind more education, healthcare, and connections with the modern world. Yet he remained quiet and waited for Habib.

"No attacks." The man was firm. "Are there Taliban in Laashekoh now?"

"They come and go," she said cryptically, tilting her head in a calculating way. With that, she turned and darted away, rushing straight up the mountainside, not bothering with the path. The sounds of running feet and sliding rocks were gone in minutes.

Habib pulled out a cloth and wiped his brow and neck. Joey leaned against the side of the truck and stared after her, relieved that the men followed standing orders—weapons aimed only for active defense.

"You did good," he said to Habib.

The Afghan shook his head and looked uphill. "I don't like it. She's young. She's breaking rules. It puts us in danger."

Habib was right. The three of them would have been goners if a male had startled them. The rules of engagement were stressful when one side didn't know or care. Joey tried not to think about it—and climbed into the back of the truck.

~~~~~

Mita was waiting to hear their report. Though the group had dispensed no agriculture advice in Laashekoh, Cameron did most of the talking. That was fine by Joey, who wanted to hear the man's take on the afternoon and the strange encounter.

"You should have been with us," Cameron complained. "The men were away."

But Mita was impatient to hear about Laashekoh's status as a farming community. Cameron shrugged. "There wasn't much," he said. "We weren't there long..."

"What crops did you see?" she pressed. "What tools or equipment?" The man was flustered.

Joey took over, listing off the observations on structures, size of fields, water supply, the general heath of villagers. "The children and women we saw looked healthier than most," Habib added. "Normal weights. Beautiful hair, clear and healthy skin."

Cameron cut the Afghan off. "Laashekoh is a waste of our time. The bottom line is they don't want our help."

Joey coughed. "On wheat..."

"We had to bring some idea forward," Cameron protested. He thought a minute, and then deftly shifted the topic. "They were upset we arrived when the men weren't there. With better scouting, we could have chosen a better day."

"The women were not afraid," Habib noted.

Mita looked at Joey for his assessment. She encouraged debate and, normally, Joey expected her to give more weight to Cameron's expertise in agriculture, so Joey was careful with his words. "The women were quiet, but not afraid. The village has potential, but they'll need time."

"We can't force ourselves on them." Mita didn't hide her disappointment. So far, all the villages in their target area had been unresponsive, not suggesting projects to the team—even basics like drip irrigation or secure storage facilities. She sighed. "They get enough intimidation from the Taliban."

"Speaking of the Taliban," Cameron broke in. "Habib had a detailed conversation with a young woman who left the village to meet with us alone. She mentioned the Taliban, and it might help if he and Joey share the details?"

"You met with someone alone?" Mita frowned.

Habib looked uncomfortable. "A young adult, no more than sixteen. She followed us to the Humvee. She asked about fighting in the area and our plans." As directed by Joey, Habib didn't go into detail.

Cameron pressed on. "And the Taliban came up."

Joey didn't like going on the defensive, but Cameron was intent on playing team members off one another. "The girl worries about us attracting Taliban to the area." Joey struggled to hold his temper. "It's a common concern. Major Bulaq did an excellent job."

Cameron launched into a long explanation about his need to have more specific translations about any Taliban activities in the area. Looking for attention, Cameron found endless reasons to back away from challenges, delaying work, when his ideas weren't in play.

A report about the girl would be filed with military analysts, though Joey and Habib had already resolved to keep the specifics to a minimum and avoid putting a spotlight on Laashekoh. They both agreed the village was not dangerous. But understanding the village and earning trust would take time. Cameron was right that some Afghans provided their own slant to translations, but that wasn't the case with Habib. Constant criticisms and questions would only make the translators more cautious. And Joey already had enough problems encouraging Afghans to take a lead in encounters, let alone managing Cameron.

~~~~~

The next day Cameron caught Mita waiting in line for the evening's meal of hamburgers and baked beans. "We need to talk," he said.

"Sure, let's eat together?" The outpost, too remote for food-service contractors, did have one cook and a tight schedule for the two prepared meals each day—breakfast was dehydrated MREs, the ready-to-eats. So the dining area was typically crowded during lunch and dinner.

She pointed to two empty chairs, but he suggested they head outside to talk alone. She headed for the exit with him. Stares from others in the mess area followed, and she regretted not just sitting at the table. With a busy schedule seven days a week, the dinner hour was the only time for socializing and listening to team members.

She suspected this meeting wasn't social.

An overcast sky made it seem late, and she sat at a rickety table near the doorway. Before long, a breeze would pick up and chill the night. Once seated, he stared at her tray—with a cup of tea, a slice of cheese, and a small serving of the vegetarian baked beans. "Don't like the meat?" Cameron asked.

She cocked her head. "Not every night."

"You didn't take a roll either," he observed.

"My loss is your gain." She used both hands to point at four hamburgers on his tray, along with an ample serving of fries and beans, and teased, "I was going to suggest this base set up an herb and vegetable garden. But guys like you might go hungry."

He laughed. "I'm not a salad eater. I doubt most Afghans are either." He popped a fry into his mouth. "I want to talk about the wheat program."

"Go on." She wondered why he couldn't admit that the Afghans might have an idea or two about farming the area, that there were reasons they hadn't covered the countryside in wheat. But she kept the thought to herself.

"The villages aren't jumping on the wheat ideas yet. They don't have a lot of interest in anything."

She cut him off. "We've been through this."

He leaned forward to whisper. "It's because of security glitches."

"It's one village, Cameron. To be fair to Major Pearson, you didn't run into that problem at the other villages. The men were in those villages, and the reaction was the same as Laashekoh's." Mita was feeling worn down. Cameron wanted the teams to head into villages with magic tricks.

"My company wants to do more. They're ready to donate plenty of seeds, technology, and equipment to the Afghan farmers. If we could get it going in just one village, the rest would beg for these products."

"Biotechnology," she repeated. "They cannot afford it—and I'm surprised you think that farmers out here can handle it."

"Granted, these farmers are still in the Stone Age," he admitted, missing her sarcasm. "But donors are coming through with funds. The government wants something to succeed out here. And our company is ready to get a village started."

She raised her eyebrows. "I assume you mean modified seeds, integrated pesticides, genetic engineering?"

"Why not? State-of-the-art farming! Give them a shortcut to farming's future."

"Shortcuts have complications."

"Now who's patronizing the Afghans?" His smile didn't soften his criticism.

"It's more practical to introduce technology gradually. Crop diversity is in their best interest. Focusing on any one crop—including wheat—could be a huge disaster."

"So you're not saying no to villages that want to increase drought-resistant wheat production."

"We're not going to force anything on them."

"And that means?"

"Cameron, you can't just brag about the benefits of biotech products and ignore the problems." Mita couldn't help but chastise him. "The high-yield wheat and rice have a price. The water table is dropping fast. Farmers are in debt. I don't know if you read anything coming out of India, but at the community level, the so-called Green Revolution is becoming a public-relations disaster."

"Something that technology can fix."

She leaned forward. "These people don't know that. And do you really think it's a promise you can keep? No." She was firm. "We can't keep making mistakes and pushing costs into the future. Not while I'm on this team. Some assistance on wheat is fine—but on their terms. And I insist on complete disclosure of all possible complications—for the team and the villages."

"What kind of complications?" Cameron shoved his final hamburger to the side, running a hand over his new beard.

She took a sip of tea before answering. "The farmers need to know any repercussions. What will they think when they hear Europe won't touch that wheat? And then there's price volatility. They're not economists, but they know that increased supply of anything will lower prices."

He shook his head. "I was misled. I thought this team wanted expertise."

"Diversity and gradual introduction of new crops will work better. They may not credit us with every little success, but I sure don't want big failures. How many villages are importing wheat around here anyway?"

"A few—not as many as in the city," he admitted. "Look, Mita, some of us worry that the focus on specialty fruits and vegetables is limiting. We could be thinking big."

"Thinking too big, too soon, could lead to big failure. They're not ready to handle big crop loads, trading with other communities. The level of cooperation is not there."

"And that's because security is not getting in there and doing the job," he grumbled.

"Patience," she cautioned. "Baby steps are not a bad thing for Afghanistan right now. Build some trust first. It's not fair to use uneducated people as guinea pigs."

His face flushed. "Hey, I'm here to help, too. A company doesn't get as big as TopSeed by hurting people."

"I know that, Cameron." She tried to soothe him. "And we appreciate that the big companies want to help. But starting programs that can't be sustained after we leave—it's a waste of everyone's time. These farmers don't have the tools to deal with seed licenses, weed resistance, and bureaucracy. Biotech is not exactly a word-of-mouth job. The Afghans need more skills, like how to read basic directions—programs like seed banks that build cooperation."

"I hope you're not shutting out the big players?"

She put her tea down. The breeze kept whipping her hair, interfering with her meal, but she didn't want to change seats. "What's the big rush, Cameron?"

For once, he didn't answer quickly. "Some of us are worried. If we go too slowly, the villages could turn against us."

She didn't want to know more, and didn't tell him her fears— that moving too quickly could put lives at risk. "Is it they don't like the plan—or they don't like taking orders from a woman?" She studied him. "Or a woman with a South Asian background?"

"For some people, it could be all of the above."

She didn't want to admit it, his honesty hurt. But criticism and games wouldn't make her rush into inappropriate projects. It would be better for the villagers if they did nothing, and that would be a depressing waste of effort.

"You want to get them to grow wheat? We need friendly relations and that means pleasant interactions with every person we meet. Show me you can turn opinions around—here and in the villages—and then we'll talk about wheat again." She finished the tea and looked forward to pouring another to enjoy inside. Alone.

"You don't want to know who's criticizing you?"

Instead of showing irritation, she smiled. "That's not going to change our strategy."

"There's something else we need to talk about," he pressed. "I'm hearing rumors. If you find yourself in a firefight—either here on the base or out in one of the villages, I'd stay away from the guys who have been here for a few years."

She stabbed her last few beans one at a time with a fork. "You heard a threat?"

"Not directly, but . . ."

"About the program or me specifically?" she interrupted.

Cameron lowered his voice. "Joey Pearson. You sure he's on board with the ag mission?" She put her fork down, not hiding her surprise. "He didn't help at the village," Cameron added quickly. "And he leaves the camp at night on his own."

She dropped her voice to a whisper. "He's our lead man on security. We have no control over that. Are you implying he's hurting the team in some way?"

"No-oo." The word came out in a drawl. "But he's secretive—doing his own patrols and talking a lot with Habib in Dari."

She shook her head impatiently. "He wants to make Habib and the other Afghans feel welcome. We need that, Cameron. These outposts cannot function without trust between the Afghans and us."

"Pearson isn't straight with you. Did you know about the Islamic scarf tied to your doorway?" Mita didn't answer, but her mouth tightened. It was the first she had heard about it. "Information is power, so why would he keep that from you?"

She kept her voice cool. "I'm not afraid."

"Good," he said. "Most people here won't be as up-front as I am. Members of the team are unhappy, everyone's not on board with civilians, splitting military units, the rules of engagement. I wonder what else he's keeping from us."

"Damn, Cameron, the team has hardly been here a week and you're finding a lot of trouble."

Cool air had congealed the grease around his last hamburger. Cameron shoved his plate to the side. The waste, small as it was, bothered her. She didn't understand people who took more than they could eat, but she forced herself to focus on his string of complaints.

"After a decade, there's confusion. Too many mixed messages. Some people want to get projects going, and some soldiers are too ready for a fight. . . ." His voice drifted off.

She thought about Joey. He had been in Afghanistan for a long time, yet didn't talk much about previous deployments. He never spoke about his personal life. And his commanders had extended a deployment so that he could provide security for Mita's team. "He was highly recommended," she tried to reassure herself as much as Cameron. "They told me we're lucky to have him."

"Put it this way," he said. "Major Pearson could be keeping our side at bay just to make his side look good. He doesn't trust any of us on the ag side."

Cameron's complaints were vague, but the discord bothered her. "We're trying to help people who don't trust us," she murmured. "It's not going to work if we can't get along ourselves."

"The corporations want to help regardless of conditions on the ground," he countered. "There's less bureaucracy. They get jobs done quickly."

"This country needs so much—there's plenty to do for all of us," Mita replied. "Don't forget the Afghans hate interference. Assistance can be humiliating. They're suspicious."

"If we wait too long, team members will get nervous," he replied. "He's slowing us down."

"I'll talk with Major Pearson," she promised.

Cameron frowned. "Don't mention me. We don't want him to turn on us."

She challenged him. "Are you suggesting he could sabotage the program?"

"No," Cameron paused. "I don't know. He's not telling us everything."

He was putting her on notice. She stood, ending the conversation. "We need him here. Losing a translator would result in delays. I'll observe for a few days, keeping in mind what you've told me. Let me know if there are any real problems. Immediately."

Cameron smiled and stood. "Good. And think about who's on your side. Good rule for war and everyday life."

She thanked him curtly, dismissing him, and looked at her empty plate. After so many accolades over the years, she couldn't be surprised about obstacles. She had not accepted the assignment because it was easy. Joey was too quiet, and Cameron complained too much. She felt alone. The team didn't trust her. Some members might give up, letting their projects flop to prove a point.

Or did they want to see her fail?

CHAPTER 8

In a village as small as Laashekoh, families avoided public quarrels. When arguments did burst out, other families got out of the way, but lurked around corners to listen and cringe at the bitter observations. We didn't intervene in arguments of other families, and instead quietly speculated how they might influence our own interactions.

Mari and Gul rarely argued publicly, and perhaps that's why the quarrel over their daughter became so heated. It started outside, behind their home, where they could retreat and talk away from their children. The disagreement quickly swelled into frustration about their oldest daughter, Leila, and her marital status. The two parents lost control. Mari was first to raise her voice. *Delay brings our family shame!*

Gul tried to reason. *You act as if she can stay here . . .*

I held my breath to listen. Our village, like others, had a tradition of sending women to other communities for marriage. The groom provided gifts, based on a daughter's beauty and skill, in exchange for a bride, and paid for the wedding. The system worked and kept families stable. Sending us off alone, to adjust in far-off villages, increased a young woman's dependence on her husband. The system reduced gossip about the prices paid for women, and men understood from the start that the women of their own village were out of reach.

Some women talked about Mari's attachment with her daughter—and I always came to my friend's defense, about how she had no sons and those of us who did could not imagine confronting old age alone, with no children or grandchildren.

I was in the minority. Others insisted that Mari was too attached to her oldest child. No one could remember a young woman staying in the village as long as Leila had.

Gul understood his wife's concern, but the potential problems of delayed marriage made him nervous. Allowing one woman to stay in the village might disrupt other marriage negotiations. Other families wondered why their favorite daughters could not stay, too. Newcomer brides were at a disadvantage with girls raised in this village, and mothers like me worried for sons. Husbands were better than fathers at watching women.

Perhaps it was Leila, and not marriage, that unnerved her father. I wasn't sure if it was her beauty or personality, but in many ways, Gul and Leila were tighter than most fathers and daughters.

At times, that bothered Mari.

Pausing outside near the wall that divided my home from Mari's, I had no trouble overhearing the argument. Even as I listened, my eyes were drawn to a crack where a dark spider rappelled its way down the mud wall. The creature, with its brown and hairy head, leaped about in its own world, oblivious to giant forces nearby. Gently, I poked its strand, wondering if the spider was male or female. With a delicate leap, the spider escaped, finding a new attachment, undaunted in going about its task.

Mari snapped. *She's too good to follow the path of others in this village!*

I heard the sound of a slap and a shout from Gul. *We live in this village. I'm of this village. How can she be better than what produced her?* Anger shifted to sternness, as he lowered his voice. *You can't refuse every man who asks. It causes hard feelings, and that's dangerous.*

Go ahead, let others know your shame. The delay is not my fault. You expect me to find a willing family in this village—it's impossible. Soon marriage will be impossible.

Better not to marry at all than to marry into disaster, Gul concluded.

Glancing around, I checked that no one watched me. Too much curiosity in a small town was among the worst of crimes. Then I leaned my face to the crevice offering a narrow view of their garden. Mari stared at her husband with fury, a reddened check, and tears in her eyes. I turned away, burning with shame for my friend and stared at the spider again, stalking a gnat.

We must begin negotiations, soon, with someone outside this village. Gul's voice was so low that only Mari and I could hear. *Too many people ask questions.*

Let them ask! She is desired by many. That should increase the price for her and make you happy. Sounding more panicked than confident. Mari knew older brides could expect many more restrictions, and Leila would find it hard to make friends in a new village. Other women might taunt her. The conversation continued with whispers, and I pressed my ear against the wall, not daring to move.

The spider took a turn and crept toward my face—close enough that I could count its eyes—two beads in front and three arched on top of its head on either side. I slowly raised my hand, adding a shadow to its world and encouraging it to take a detour. Cocking a rear leg, the spider changed direction, throwing off another line and leaping sideways to snare the gnat.

Mari whispered, and I could make out eagerness, not words. Gul gasped. *You know he's a fool. Why do you suggest such a match?*

We're running out of time. Then her words tumbled, aiming to convince him of an idea that I could not hear.

Have you spoken with him about this? Gul demanded in fury.

No! Mari exclaimed. *I promise! But you could do it tonight.*

Hmm . . . you'd risk marriage to an unknown, so she can stay near home.

I care for her. I want what's best. Think of how she's helped you.

He cut her off. *Because you did not bear sons.* Mari sobbed, but Gul rushed, talking over her noise. *Speak with her before this evening. Make sure this is what she wants before I move forward with an offer.* His voice went into a hush, *And pray nothing happens to her while we dawdle.*

The conversation ended with the sound of footsteps. Suddenly Gul called back, almost as if he wanted the rest of us to hear that Leila's fate would be decided soon. *We decide before the next moon.*

I'm not keen on following every rule. But there's danger in bla-
tantly breaking rules that others must follow. And there's tragedy in
marrying someone for the wrong reasons. I wondered which village
man would be approached and how Gul could possibly arrange such a
marriage, breaking all traditions and allowing Leila to stay near home.
The other families of Laashekoh wouldn't be happy.

Joey took yet another route to Laashekoh, indirect and obstructed by
brush. Starting out as the sun went down with a quick ruby burst, he
stayed just close enough to the river so that the steady, rushing water
covered the sound of his footsteps and perhaps distracted anyone
waiting for movements near the village.

Joey was determined not to be surprised by any villagers. Of course,
intimate with the terrain, they had an advantage. But Joey was skilled,
more than once approaching the compound wall in the middle of the
night without incident. The team—Mita, in particular—was anxious
for another visit to Laashekoh, and Joey wanted to ensure that the men
were there, with no surprises.

He moved carefully, with the same crouching night walk used by
Afghans who occasionally ventured near the outpost. Like the Afghans,
Joey left no footprints or other traces. By now, he was confident the one
villager had not revealed their chance meeting to others.

Suddenly a roar sounded from over the ridge. Joey dropped, rolling to
the nearest boulder. Headlights soon followed, performing a zigzag dance
along the rugged landscape. He looked up only after the headlights passed.
Two dirty, dented ATVs ripped through brush along a ridge lining the one
side of the river. Crossing the river less than thirty meters away from him,
the vehicles aimed directly for the footpath that pointed to Laashekoh.

He didn't get a good look at the drivers. But the route they took
clearly avoided an easier route past the outpost, not a coincidence. Joey
had to assume they couldn't be helpful to the Americans. The visitors
would ask questions about the outpost and how the village planned

to deal with the Americans. If the outpost was perceived as interfering with any Taliban operations in the area, questions would quickly turn into intimidation. The only release from the pressure would be for villagers to join in launching attacks on the outpost, intensifying until either the Taliban or the Americans left the region.

Joey swore and hoped he was wrong.

Moving cautiously, Joey continued to the village. He had no evidence of danger, and didn't want to curtail the ag program. He had to hear more before giving Mita his assessment. He enjoyed working with her more than he had anticipated and didn't want security concerns to cut the program short.

She didn't know it, but helping the villagers was secondary. His mission was to keep her safe.

But during the last few days, she was cool, not chatting much. He wondered how much she trusted him.

~~~~~

The red sun hovered low in the sky, translucent and brilliant, like the plump flesh covering a pomegranate seed. Red light spilled over the fields, the forest, mountains, giving an illusion of warmth. Typically, the women of our village didn't work this late at night, but as the day progressed, winds came in from the mountains, bringing a chill.

We didn't know what temperatures to expect once the sun disappeared, and our weather had been volatile in recent years. An unexpected frost could put a season of hard work to waste. No family member was too young or too old to help strip the pomegranates from their branches, both the ripe and near ripe. If there was time, we'd gather the late beans. The cabbage and root crops could wait.

The coral glow of a setting sun did not last long. I kept a steady pace, snatching glances while placing the fruit in my bag. I counted: Nine fast glimpses, and the red vanished. Twilight's gray blanket smothered the edges of the fields. As darkness fell, some pickers moved quickly, and others slacked.

Anxious to rescue every pomegranate, I focused on slashing the stems quickly with my knife, before gently placing the fruit in a bag slung across my shoulder. When the bag was full, I carried it to the edge of the orchard, where young boys scurried to retrieve them, walking back and forth to a nearby cave that served as our village's cold storage. Inside, small children stacked the pomegranates, and the fruit would keep until our men headed to the market.

Mama, we're doing well, Saddiq whispered. *We're ahead of everyone.*

And what does that mean? That we are better? Cross and tired, I glared, pointing out that his father would not be pleased to see him puffed with pride. Scolding the children came easily, because I still ached for my oldest son and wanted to protect the others. Getting close with the younger ones was painful. I did not want to replace Ali or contemplate the loss of another child.

The boy looked hurt, and I checked the others' positions in the orchard. *Keep working*, I added kindly. *We could lose what's left of this harvest.*

He nodded and ran off, lugging another bag that was half his weight. Ashamed of my harshness, I wondered if I'd forever think of Saddiq as a second son. Hard work made their mother happy, but scolding didn't let my children know that.

Shame and pride were a strange mixture, pushing me to move faster and talk less. Pride couldn't be so harmful, I hoped, if kept to oneself.

A growling overcame the sounds of wind shaking the leathery leaves and chatting pickers. A vehicle approached, struggling to climb our hill in fits and starts over the rocks. Others paused to listen, but I didn't stop.

The blocked pathway wouldn't allow even a small off-road vehicle close to our village, and I guessed it had to be a new set of visitors, not the Americans who had already figured out they must stop and walk the rest of the way.

Tires grinded at the rocks. The visitors would not arrive for at least another forty minutes, but others took the noise as an excuse for ending work.

My fingers hurt, but I pushed on. The timing was not the best, and I found myself hoping it was the Americans. Our men would chase them away. If the visitors were from nearby villages, the late hour would mean they'd stay the night.

Women scurried to Mari's kitchen to heat more nān and āsh soup. Mari had left the fields earlier to cook enough for all, directing children to serve bread and warm water to the crews throughout the afternoon, and preparing a rich stew for the evening. Unlike the others, I refused to take breaks, and instead kept cutting at the pomegranate stems, gathering the globes into my basket for Saddiq to take load after load to the edge of the orchard.

Though it didn't seem possible, I moved faster, hoping others might do the same. My back ached, my headscarf fell to my shoulders, and still I didn't pause.

Take some breaks, my husband had urged earlier.

I accepted water to sip, but stayed in the orchard. *Not until we're through with this harvest*, I insisted.

As women drifted inside, the older children ran to the compound wall. My sons didn't pause, picking furiously and carrying crates to the cave, but remained alert, ready to respond if their father called. I smiled. There was no excuse for any family to stop working as long as fruit waited.

Filling one basket, I stayed in an area cloaked in darkness. I approached the last tree in that row, and a head popped out and startled me. Leila stretched out her hand, as if to ward off an attack. I had startled her, too. Holding my hand to my chest, laughing, I dropped my basket.

She smiled. *I follow your example, auntie, and don't stop working.*

I can see, Leila. The words were gentler than those for Saddiq, as I was a parent who readily ignored foibles of others' children and practiced fierce honesty with my own.

She stood, empty-handed and ready to walk away. Without thinking, I asked about her basket.

But I had another errand, she replied smoothly. *I know you came to ask about the package.* The darkness added to my confusion. Without waiting for an answer, she extracted a gray sack from underneath her garments and placed it on the ground between the two of us, almost as if she challenged me to examine the contents. Leila understood how minds worked in our village.

I refused to challenge her.

I must hide it, she explained. She asked to borrow the spade hanging from a rope at my side. I untied it and tossed it to her—and watched as she dropped to her knees and dug a shallow hole at the base of the one tree.

Not there, I cautioned. *It's not good for the roots.* But she was frantic. *Leila, are you hiding this from your parents or the visitors?* She didn't look up.

I'm doing this for my father. She spoke with self-importance and then chastened me indirectly. *I don't ask questions.*

Of course. And I turned to strip fruit away from another tree— even as I heard my shovel clinking against the rocks.

Darkness disguised our exchange, and the wind eased its pace. My hand reached into dark thick leaves, grasping for heavy globes. The long, hard day was coming to a close, and I was thankful.

My mind raced. The package could be part of her dowry for marriage, something Gul was keeping from Mari. Or was it something to hide from the visitors?

I shook my head, thinking it didn't matter what Gul did. He was the leader of our village, but an insecure man who didn't understand why Parsaa had no desire for power. It was best not to know. Leila had a right to her secrets and so did Gul.

Leila came up next to me and slipped the spade into my basket. Then she went to work beside me—her young eyes quickly spotting the pomegranates among the leaves. Once the stems were cut, she placed them in my basket.

We didn't speak and finished quickly. No boys were left to retrieve the baskets, and so we each took a handle—carrying our load across the orchard.

You don't ask questions, auntie, she teased. *We trust you, because you never ask questions.*

The comment was a strange assessment, and I bristled at her teasing tone. *The braying donkey doesn't hear much*, I retorted. In the darkness, I couldn't see her eyes or mouth, but noticed her shoulders twitch and felt a hard stare.

She didn't respond and, instead, removed her scarf, tossed her hair back, and secured it again tightly. Then she ran through the orchard toward her parents' home.

I was annoyed about her acting as though a grown woman was her equal. My silence drew little information from Leila. I left the orchard, knowing that questions would not reveal what Leila was thinking. Questions were for fools and children.

~~~~~

Three men stepped into our compound, their dark clothing and black turbans blending with the night. Scarves covered their faces against dust and curious eyes. Their assault rifles were on display, slung casually across their backs. Ahmed greeted them, with a few men standing behind, rifles on display and ready. Parsaa and Gul stood in the background without weapons.

As darkness cloaked the fields, most villagers had already returned to their homes, and I wanted to be near my fire, too. But I hesitated to walk past these strangers who moved with arrogance, as if they knew more about our compound than any of its inhabitants. And so I squatted and waited at the orchard's edge.

The tallest man barked commands, as if the village should have prepared for his arrival and dropped whatever else we had been doing. He introduced himself as Jahangir. *We're here to eliminate the infidels.*

Ahmed stepped forward, and the visitor knew the younger man spoke for leaders who remained in the background. *There's been no contact*, Ahmed explained, though the rest of us knew a few Americans had visited and Mari had easily chased them off. He could count on us not to contradict him.

It's not what I've heard . . .

Ahmed shrugged. *We've heard that these Americans don't seem dangerous.*

Give them time, the man in black said with a flat voice. *This is our territory, and that's problem enough.*

We'll have no trouble handling the Americans on our territory, Ahmed scoffed. *Allah is on our side.*

Jahangir smiled. *Not when they meet with your women while the men are away.* Ahmed could not help himself, directing a nervous glance toward Gul and Mari. And Mari looked nervous, too.

We have eyes in many places. If you lie about the Americans in this village, or don't know about their visits, then how can we believe that you can handle them on your own?

Gul nodded, and Ahmed replied defensively. *The men were not here.*

Jahangir walked over to one of the bins holding pomegranates and selected one to examine. *This fruit provides little in the way of sustenance. Do the Americans want your fruit?*

Ahmed did not understand the question and looked puzzled. *We have not talked to the Americans.*

Gul intervened. *They know nothing about what we grow.*

Jahangir reached out and tipped one large basket and then another. Red balls rolled and bounced down the slope, bruising and cracking.

Perhaps it's time you consider growing other crops, ones less pleasing for the Americans, Jahangir said.

The insult was too much, and from the dark shadows of the house came the sound of a man deliberately snapping the clip into his rifle. Our men stood ready to fire, and Jahangir wrapped his hands around his own weapon.

Parsaa stepped forward, to express displeasure. *Our pomegranates have nothing to do with Americans. We have no need for advice—about working our farms or defending this village.*

All right, Jahangir said after a long pause. *Together we'll plan how to get rid of these Americans who dare set up in our midst.*

The men of our village stared at Jahangir and then at one another. I knew my husband's thoughts. After years of fighting Russians and then Americans, no one in our village was in the mood for offensive action. Most of our weapons were decades old. Ammunition was hard to come by. Parsaa had pointed out that the American structures could vanish as quickly as they had appeared. As long as the Americans were passing through and did not interfere with village routines, we didn't anticipate problems.

Gul spoke up nervously. *We're willing to listen.*

Jahangir nodded and looked around at the villagers finishing with the pomegranates. *Why do your women mix with men?*

In our village, women were not compelled to wear the burqa or other clothes that might interfere with chores. During the day we moved about as we pleased, as long as we covered our heads and used the ends of our scarves to cover our mouths around strangers.

Gul was firm. *We're ending the day's work in the field, before the first frost arrives.*

You work at night and don't trust Allah? Jahangir queried.

Gul was stymied, and Parsaa pointed to the piles of fruit. *Delay would waste the crop.*

Only if you defy Allah's will, Jahangir insisted.

Wasting the harvest is wrong, Parsaa countered with a tone that was stern, but pleasant. He cocked his head toward the entrance to Gul's home. *Let's go inside, so you need not look at our wives.*

The man shrugged. *You know God's book, and that is good. These days, we can't be too good. Allah is watching.* Closing his eyes, he bowed his head, his hand still ready on his weapon. Then he added, *These are tense times.*

At last, everyone could agree. Gul insisted the men join him, Parsaa, Ahmed, and a few others for a meal. The men would stay the night and devour food prepared for the village. As always, I thanked Allah—and Parsaa—that Gul was leader and hosted such events in his larger home.

Jahangir looked pleased, looking around, as if trying to determine who wielded the most power in our village. Our men stood in a tight, calm cluster, practiced at showing agreement before any outsiders. The group would eat together, while the rest of us would make do or go to bed hungry.

As Gul directed the men into his home, other villagers slipped inside their homes, and women nervously adjusted scarves to cover hair, keeping our heads down. The men capitalized on our confusion and shame, and I wanted to scream out to everyone—*We have done nothing wrong!*

But instead I hurried home, and was surprised to see Mari near my doorway, frantically searching for Leila. The girl darted out from behind me, offering to assist in serving the meal. Mari shook her head and turned to me. *Can she stay in your home for the night?*

I nodded and didn't ask questions. Leila kept her eyes to the ground, so I couldn't see her face, and I wondered about the hidden sack. I couldn't blame her mother for worrying about her beautiful and headstrong daughter. The girl's loose scarf did not hide the dark, shiny hair, and I said another prayer of thanks for not having the worries that accompany a daughter.

Older boys, including my own Saddiq, remained outside, standing at the compound walls, letting the men know that this village kept watch over its harvest and people.

By then, I was sure that the gray clouds were passing by to the north without releasing heavy freezing rain. Weariness mixed with relief, and I entered my home hungry, though I did not mind missing the meal prepared by Mari.

Without a word, Leila helped me pass out bread and goat's milk to the boys, then clean and ready the kitchen for the next morning. I arranged some blankets for her not far from the hearth, before slipping outside to ask Saddiq and another boy to help in retrieving the spilled pomegranates. *Check them carefully*, I warned in a whisper, reminding him to rinse and dry the intact fruit before storing it in the cave. *We can squeeze juice from the others.*

As I tossed cracked ones into a container, tears came to my eyes about the wasted work and men who shamed women for helping with the harvest. The visitors were dangerous. My husband would not distract them long with sayings from the Koran.

A few of our men urged me to return inside, promising to oversee the task. I complied, grateful until I realized that they did not want the visitors to see a woman.

The sun was but a few hours from rising. My home was dark, only a few embers left in the hearth. Leila's dark hair gleamed in the low light. I quietly crawled underneath a pile of wool blankets near my sleeping sons.

Saddiq came in soon and lay with me. My arms and legs ached from the long day of collecting pomegranates, and I could not sleep. Shouts and bursts of laughter still came from Gul's home as the meeting went on through the night.

A thought pricked at me. My husband left so often in the middle of the night, and I wondered if he had already met these strangers. Twisting, I lay on my back, and Saddiq wrapped his arms around me. He whispered. *Leila was looking around the rooms. She thought I was asleep and came in here. I chased her, and she scolded me.*

I gently shushed him, but held him close. *There's nothing to find, but you did the right thing.*

The boy's breathing relaxed, but I could not sleep. My back ached. The insides of my fingers were raw from pushing aside tough leaves and pinching stems. But the sensations felt good, reminding me how much effort went into saving the crop. I didn't mind the strange men's taunts. A frosty rain might be close, and I shivered.

Eventually I fell into a troubled sleep, thanking Allah for not making me a man. Men were too worried about control and easily haunted by shame. Women's quiet resilience goes unnoticed.

~~~~~

Mama. At dawn, my youngest pulled on my arm. I turned and found that Parsaa had not joined us for sleep. A neat pile of folded blankets were left by the hearth where Leila had slept. Jumping up, I cracked open our door. No voices, only the distant mutter of departing vehicles.

Closing the door, I leaned against it. I'd have to wait for scraps of information from Mari or my husband. It wasn't a good sign that the meeting lasted so long into the morning. I worried for Mari, Gul, and Parsaa. I firmly believed that every encounter shaped our personalities, and wondered how these men might influence our village.

But then, Parsaa would influence them, too.

~~~~~~

Like the other women in the village, Mari rose with the sun and immediately set out with buckets to bring water back to her home. She never had to coax her oldest daughter, Leila, to help, and Mari appreciated that the girl cherished spending time with her mother, away from the younger sisters. Leila knew that she was her mother's favorite and worked hard to maintain that status.

The morning was cold, damp, and rather than linger at the stream, the two women hurried home. The other children waited for their meal with their father, grumpy and tired. No one in the family had slept well.

The stove was hot and waiting; the bread cooked quickly. Gul did not talk, and Mari hurried to set out the morning meal—rice, yogurt, spinach, and lots of warm bread. Finally she commented. *Our visitors are gone.*

They'll be back. Gul was curt, as he glanced toward a small shelf in the corner, at a small plastic box, green and white.

Mari continued working and didn't ask questions. Too often, he treated her as if she were one of the children. She had to wait for him to drop hints about what the visit might hold for the village. Likewise, the other women in the village would have to wait for her. Mari had heard enough to know the men resented the Americans and had many ideas for attack. Gul would never admit as much, but he had a habit of presenting his concerns to her, then scoffing at her advice. Somehow her ideas melded with his as soon as he gathered with other village men. He wasn't the only man in the village to harvest ideas from his wife. Women shaped the village, but only through their men.

Mari noticed that Gul did the same with Parsaa's ideas, and she preferred when her husband favored hers.

Gul moved some bread into his mouth methodically and then spoke. *They want us to resist the foreign soldiers.*

But the village has not mixed with the Americans. Mari was puzzled. *They left the torch, but we gave nothing in return.*

They will want more. Gul was blunt.

Maybe they'll forget, she said.

But Gul scowled and shook his head, as if the suggestion was ridiculous. *Do any of the others in Laashekoh know that Jahangir has been through this area with his shipments?*

Mari shook her head. *None of the women know. I would have heard.*

It's one thing giving them supplies as they travel through this region. But they can't tell us how to live, what to grow. He shook his head. *We can't let the other villagers know, or they will blame us.* He paused and looked at his children.

Leila spoke up. *Why did I have to stay away from Jahangir last night?*

He does not like women who don't know their place, Gul snapped. *Our meeting was for men.*

Mari frowned. She did not like him scolding Leila. The girl worked so hard to help at home and with her sisters. Every year, she took on more responsibilities, and Mari wasn't sure how she would handle the house without her oldest daughter. Leila was more adult than child, but to say as much would rile Gul. Mari dreaded the thought of Leila marrying a stranger who might not appreciate her. She had often daydreamed about Leila with young Ali, but such a match was no longer possible.

Allah would provide a good husband and soon, but only if Gul and Mari would stop arguing. Mari smiled to herself. She had planted the idea of Jahangir as a prospect into Gul's head. She allowed Jahangir a quick glimpse of her daughter, and then kept the girl away. The man could not help but want what was kept away from him.

Mari asked questions, but Gul looked at the children again and refused to talk. Only after Mari sent the younger girls for more water did he continue. *They say they want to give us protection.*

Maybe they know something we don't, Mari offered eagerly.

Then they should tell us, her husband snapped. *Some protections can attract new enemies.* He slammed his fist to the floor. *This village is gone the day we cannot protect ourselves.* He paused, as his wife delivered more bread and poured boiling water into their cups. Only then did she sit.

They want us to take photographs of the youngest girls.

Leila turned her full attention to her father at the comment, and Mari was troubled.

What? she questioned. *We can't do that.*

He wants the girls to help with some task. He shrugged. *He promises the images will be destroyed.*

Mari paused, surprised at how she suddenly liked the idea of keeping a photo of Leila and her other daughters hidden away. *Is this for marriage? For Leila?*

No, not Leila, he said, shooting a worried look at his daughter before looking down. *The other girls. Jahangir wants girls before they're ready to marry. More of his foolishness.*

Mari pondered the details. The village was small. At least twenty girls were that age, and Leila was the most stunning. But recently, the girl stood out for her age and not her beauty. Other girls her age had already left the village for marriages. The only other girls near her age in Laashekoh were the new brides.

Leila stood to examine the box that could capture photographs, her long fingers twisting and poking it. *We can take a photograph of me so we can see what it looks like?*

Put that down, her father snapped.

The Americans do not frighten me, she countered. *Neither does Jahangir.*

Do not say that in front of Jahangir, he warned. *Ever.* Then he ordered Leila outside, to join her siblings in retrieving water. Leila handed the box to Mari, and her husband didn't talk until the girl closed the door.

How does this box work? Mari asked.

The box is of no use to us, he explained. *Jahangir gave directions. It works like a gun scope—we capture the images.* He took the box from his wife. *I can do it, but I don't want to.*

We can examine them before handing them over?

Gul raised his eyebrows. *Jahangir is the only one who can see or remove the pictures.*

Mari could tell her husband was displeased, not wanting to participate in a process he didn't understand. She didn't understand the need for taking photographs either.

So they won't show the images to us, Mari pressed. Her husband, nervous, didn't answer. *If you don't like it, if you don't know about this, you should not have taken the box,* Mari countered. For the first time, she worried that the family had waited too long to arrange marriage for Leila. She worried about the photographs being used to plan some important marriage—and Leila would miss out.

How she dreaded a marriage that would take away her helper and friend. During times like this she was thankful the village had no mirrors. Her oldest daughter had a haunting beauty, long, dark waves framing sweet green eyes against skin that was softer than an almond blossom. Mari had last seen a mirror some years ago, and suspected that after bearing children and working years in the fields that she would no longer recognize herself. Though there were some, like Sofi, who still moved like a young girl and gained a certain grace with age.

But Sofi didn't know, and it was better that women did not know their beauty.

Witnessing the slow deterioration of other women, after difficult births and unstopping work, Mari was thankful to avoid reminders of her own aging and decline. Admittedly, it would be painful to watch her beautiful daughter age, too. As far as Mari knew, Leila had never held a mirror, but the child had long ago sensed the admiration she stirred in others.

The eyes of men were a dangerous mirror.

We need to know if this has anything to do with a good marriage, Mari insisted, torn between Leila leaving the village or marrying into a powerful family. *If this is about marriage, Leila deserves a place. She is beautiful, hardworking, the best this village has to offer.*

Gul nodded slowly, having heard these sentiments repeated many times by his wife. *I want Leila to be happy, too.*

Mari nodded and thanked him. Happiness for her depended on Leila's security and contentment. *No one around here is good enough for her.* Mari's fretting had long annoyed her husband, but she didn't care. Anything repeated enough could take on the aura of truth.

The man chewed slowly and refused to speak.

If you take photographs, they would choose Leila, Mari said with confidence. *Take one of her. But for what man?* She frowned. *Others in the village won't allow photographs of their children. Not if the plan is vague.*

I will take care of it, Gul promised. *They're coming back in a few days. We'll know more then.*

PART 2

2-1. Mission tactics can be viewed as freedom of action for the leader to execute his mission in the way he sees fit, rather than being told how to do it. Execution of mission tactics requires initiative, resourcefulness, and imagination.

—Ranger Handbook

Read your book; your own self is sufficient as a reckoner against you this day.

—Koran 17:14

CHAPTER 9

Mita worried about the team's slow pace in their part of Helmand. She received a daily bulletin that listed cautionary notes and success stories for the district teams. So far her team had multiple visits with villages in their area, but none expressed interest in workshops or demonstrations. In other provinces, villages had filed requests for specialists and advice. One of the teams farther north had found success by convincing a village to set up demonstration projects and hiring Afghans to work as extension agents.

"What about Laashekoh?" she asked about the only good candidate in the area for such a project. The other villages struggled to farm, and many relied on generosity from Laashekoh. They could learn much from the village closest to the outpost.

"They pushed those boulders into the path," Cameron said. "They don't want people coming in."

"That also means that they don't get visits from roving Taliban, trying to stir up trouble," Mita countered. She asked Joey about another visit to Laashekoh. It was time to see the village herself.

He nodded. "We can handle it," he replied. "The only action we should see there is the pomegranate harvest." The other team members laughed. "We need to stay visible—send the signal that these village programs are a priority for us," he continued. "Convince people this outpost is about farming and only farming."

"Good," Mita agreed. "Let's give Laashekoh another try. And I'll go along."

~~~~~~~

The meeting broke up and Cameron caught up with Joey outside. "We'll need extra security for that trip."

"Extra?" Joey was surprised. "I don't anticipate problems."

"Not for us," he said. "But for Mita . . . these villages won't be comfortable with a woman telling them what to do."

Joey frowned. "She wants to observe. A woman could mitigate hard feelings after the last visit. . . ."

Cameron lifted his eyebrows. "I don't have good feelings about this. A woman tagging along puts us at risk."

"She's smart. She knows how to dress and will let Habib do the talking." Unlike some others, Joey thought to himself.

"If something should happen, I'll cover her."

Joey didn't like the comments. Ratcheting up the fear could jinx the visit before it began. "Nothing will happen." His curt reply did nothing to boost his own confidence.

Joey knew what he had to do, but wouldn't let Cameron know until the next day. He was tired of hidden agendas and promises of a magic bullet. In the end, the field was not much different than the policymaking offices of Washington—when it came to taking risks or playing it safe, too many people were out to promote their own careers. Helping Afghans was not a priority. Cameron fell into that group. Joey wasn't sure yet about Mita.

He had to keep reminding himself that, more often than not, the ambitious could have good ideas, too.

In the end, Joey believed that the military could make life better for ordinary Afghans without a lot of money and technology. But then he was just a guy who could shoot well, follow tracks, and guide others through rough terrain. Out here his degree in history from the state university seemed irrelevant with so many experts running around.

So he didn't rush to give opinions, though he had been in Afghanistan long enough to watch a decade of history unfold. In the fight against the Taliban's controlling ways, he couldn't help but notice how others tended to take on those ways. Using control to fight control was a terrible idea.

Before leaving headquarters later that evening, he left a page from command on his desk—and he counted on Cameron stopping by and reading over the page:

"Our strategy cannot be focused on seizing terrain or destroying insurgent forces; our objective must be the population. In the struggle to gain the support of the people, every action we take must enable this effort. . . . Gaining their support will require a better understanding of the people's choices and needs . . . perceptions derive from actions."

It was a good reminder. Too often, personal goals interfered with the big picture. Joey was determined not to fall into the same trap.

~~~~~

Carrying water across our courtyard, my two boys stared at the four visitors. *Keep walking and finish our work*, I murmured.

The boys were not alone in staring at a rare group of visitors, particularly the one woman standing with the American soldiers. Our men were surprised, but gracious hosts. Ahmed held out his arm, welcoming the group and guiding them to sets of benches underneath two apricot trees. Parsaa, Gul, and the others sat on pillows arranged on the ground. Mari and Leila stood near their doorway, glaring, making no effort to hide their annoyance about this visit. And that only made an obstinate Gul more gracious.

Like others, my attention was caught by the small, dark woman. She bore a resemblance to the traders from India who had occasionally passed through Afghanistan villages long ago. I had not seen an Indian in years and was surprised to see her with the Americans. I recalled a whispered warning from a cleric long ago: *The Americans are tricky about enticing people who belong to other countries. They're impure, mixing tribes and races.*

The tiny woman didn't seem to care about working alongside men. Her eyes were alert, and when she spoke, I detected a firm tone, respectful, but still an equal. She was not a woman accustomed to being treated as a servant or a child.

She dressed to blend with other women in our area, wearing a traditional tombaan and perahaan in dark colors of the earth, modest and loose-fitting, the cloth clean and stiff. Dark hair peeked from a chaadar embroidered with slender willow leaves. Unlike the male soldiers, she carried no obvious weapon. Accepting a pillow, she sat behind her men, folding her hands and leaning forward. The soldiers sat on benches, after handing over a sack of flour and more cooking oil as gifts for the village.

Two of the Americans carried weapons and put them to the side, to signal trust. Gul, Parsaa, and the others sat in a line behind Ahmed to observe while he spoke. Parsaa tried to hide a smile, knowing that the women of the village were fascinated by the guests, especially the woman. This visit would feed family conversations for days.

Ahmed snapped his fingers, and several young boys emerged from Mari's house bearing hot water, mugs, tea, as well as the flat bread and thin slices of dried fruit. The woman's eyes darted about, admiring the fruit. It wasn't my imagination. She held it up and closed her eyes for the taste, appreciating the beauty from our orchard.

The Afghan took charge of the conversation, and as he spoke, the Americans remained disciplined, keeping eye contact with Ahmed. A common complaint about the Americans was that they spoke too quickly, firing off lists of questions without really listening—but not this group. They allowed Ahmed to take the lead. He asked if any others at the base spoke Dari.

They're still learning, the Afghan soldier noted. *Some are better than others.* Our men and the Afghan soldier laughed.

The soldier explained that the Americans brought another gift. Unlike Mari, the men gave the translator a chance to turn the light tube on and explain. He pointed to the sky, then to a small silver panel on the tube's side, and explained: *It absorbs the sun's rays. Leave it outside for eight hours and you get four hours of light at night.*

Ahh, we thought the other one stopped working.

No, the Afghan soldier said. *Bring it into the open, and it will work again.* The village men passed the tube around, each pressing the switch on and off a few times, testing the flash of light.

Gul approved. *It's small—easy to hide. Some in these parts do not appreciate toys from the West.*

The translator nodded. *Those who prefer darkness to light?* Our men looked thoughtful, and no one spoke up to disagree. How much harm could come in a tool that brought light into a home?

We do not want to put you in any danger, the visitor assured the villagers. *But someday, you must decide which groups have your best interests in mind. Who respects this village and who wants to control you? Is it us or those who fight us?*

Our village was safe before you and the other foreign soldiers arrived, Ahmed noted.

He turned to Gul, who was blunt: *What do you expect from us?*

The Afghan soldier was ready. *Let us know about any threats against the outpost or other villages in the area,* he explained. *And resist joining in any fighting.*

That is all? Gul questioned.

The visitor nodded. *We don't expect you to fight for us. But do not help them. In exchange, we can provide some tools to help you increase the crop levels. You can give us project ideas, say farming, and then our men will come and help you with tasks that you assign.*

What type of tasks? Ahmed questioned.

The visitor was ready with a list: planting, planning irrigation ditches, installing water pumps, checking livestock for disease. *The crew will follow your wishes and nothing more. If we set you up with a solar oven, you can dry fruits and grain and cook more with less firewood. We can help in clearing out mines along the roads, so you can get your crops out to market quickly. Or more. We want your ideas.*

Ahmed leaned forward. *Many in this country resent any cooperation with the foreigners. Accepting your gifts will invite attacks. And then there would be no people left to harvest the crops, or bring them to market.*

The group did not argue. The Americans had been in the country long enough to understand the dilemma for small villages.

Like others, I listened anxiously. This offer would divide our village. For a few among us, fear led to constant public demonstration of religious beliefs. They'd warn about the dangers of working with the infidels, listening to their flattery. They would call the gifts bribes. In the end, the religious arguments would sway.

Listening closely, I noticed that the translator did not repeat all of Ahmed's or Gul's responses to the group, and I didn't like this. Either they understood, or the Afghan would explain later, though I doubted anyone was capable of understanding our village or conveying our feelings to strangers from another country.

The visitor continued, *Most of these Americans have been here long enough to understand the dilemma for the villages. I am Muslim. Mita is Muslim. Muslims live and practice in the United States. It's a government that tries to respect all religions.*

The men murmured and shook their heads in disbelief. It was an impossible task to protect all religions. There was but one way. The Prophet had warned about the loss of power that comes from arguing with those weak in heart.

Gul directed Ahmed to offer more fruit and turned his attention back to the Americans. *Good Muslims don't mix with the infidels.*

I was sure the woman didn't understand or she would have been insulted. Instead, she took another apricot slice. A smile accompanied her bite, and I felt triumph.

She was so exotic next to the Afghans and the Americans, more comfortable and relaxed. My eyes could not stray from her for long, and I wondered how she kept her composure among men and strangers. It was hard to believe she could participate in the debauchery whispered to be practiced by Americans. I looked down at my own patched perahaan, the colors worn to a soft gray, and reminded myself that it revealed a woman who worked hard.

Anyone can don a chaadar, bow her head while speaking in soft and pleasant ways. But the woman had a grace that had nothing to do with clothes or hair. The way she studied and admired the fruit, she knew such a harvest required more work than the men let on. And she cared about others. It didn't matter if they were strangers. Such grace was possible only after years of practice and not the work of deception.

After the group was silent for a few moments, the woman quietly pointed to the tray of fruit, then to the orchards behind the mud brick homes, before asking a question of the Afghan soldier. He translated, and it was as though she had read my thoughts. I leaned forward to catch every word.

Mita asks me to relay that this is the most productive village she's seen in Afghanistan. The apricots are the most beautiful. Such sweet fruit is the product of long hours.

Gul shrugged at the compliment. The orchard and fields were not a priority for him. *We make do*, Ahmed said.

The woman spoke quickly and the Afghan nodded. *The Americans could learn from you.*

You flatter us, Ahmed said. *But hard work is the only ingredient we know.*

Of course, the Afghan replied. *Allah extends rewards on those who work hard.* The men bowed their heads in Allah's praise. *If you like, we can we leave some papers with you? About projects you could work on.*

Ahmed glanced around, and Gul gave a nod that was barely perceptible. Mita opened her pack slowly to expose its contents, but Gul waved his arm to hurry her along. Suicide attacks were not part of the American arsenal. Americans had more reason to fear the afterlife, or so the imams said.

Ahmed accepted the folder, giving the contents a cursory glance, before passing them to Gul.

The rest of us stretched our necks, curious about colorful images of trees, seeds, leaves, and roots.

I suppose you will give these to other villages, too, Gul said. *And lower prices at the market.*

Not all villages want to grow the same crops, the Afghan soldier assured Gul. *Everyone doesn't have rich soil or ready supplies of water. And if the harvests increase, plenty of people in the cities would appreciate your fruits and nuts.*

Gul flatly dismissed the idea. *We have no time to travel to the cities. But others do have time, and you could sell to them.*

Not without roads. Gul was curt. *Blocked roads protect our village. Otherwise unwanted visitors show up.*

The group of Americans started murmuring among themselves, almost like arguing. The woman was earnest with the Afghan soldier, and the others seemed to defer to her. He addressed our group of men: *Your area is fertile and rich, and you could teach techniques to other villages.*

The women handle the fields, Gul interrupted. *We do not need help in these areas and have little time to help others who might hurt us.* He pushed the papers near the fire, to show his disinterest. Our men looked like fools, I thought to myself. Stern fools who regarded flimsy paper as threats.

Watching from the doorway, visible to all the other villagers, I dared not express my own eagerness. If I were lucky, the papers might make the rounds in our village, eventually passed on to Parsaa. I might get my chance to unfold the papers, crumpled and worn, and study the details.

But that wouldn't happen if I showed how much I cared.

The group asked about purchasing vegetables, and Ahmed quickly agreed, directing boys to carry the sacks to the cave and load them with crops. *Choose the best and pack carefully*, Gul ordered. The Afghan handed over Afghan currency.

Parsaa and others stole looks for my reaction. Unsure whether they expected anger or pride, I tightened my jaw, determined to show nothing.

The group said their farewells and agreed to another meeting in the future. As they stood, the woman turned and smiled shyly at the female audience gathered in nearby doorways. Surprised, we stood there gaping like old wooden dolls, surprised by her acknowledgement, as if it were wrong for us to smile.

At that moment, my own anger at the Americans seemed pointless, reminding me what Parsaa's teacher had told him long ago: We cannot let our list of enemies get too long.

The Americans could sit, talk, and eat in our village and offer advice, but they couldn't understand the divide between our way of life and theirs. That alone was enough to trigger fear.

As people separated and went about their way, Ahmed bent and looked over the papers. He looked towards Gul, who shook his head, and Ahmed tossed them into the fire.

~~~~~

Trees with their dark leaves filtered the late afternoon sun and the quivering, mottled light was hypnotic, belying any sense of harm. Not far from the village, with its cool mountain streams and trees, the landscape abruptly changed to harsh and barren folds of dirt and rocks in browns and grays.

Joey led the group downhill, and it didn't take long before he sensed they were being followed. He listened closely, but heard only their trudging feet, the whispers of rustling dry leaves, and the nagging questions inside him.

Walking slowly, he scanned either side of the trail, as well as ahead and behind, checking for any signs of trouble. More than once, he paused abruptly to catch the tracker off-guard. He was alert, his weapon ready with safety off.

It could be the girl following again, he tried to tell himself.

He signaled Habib, but didn't tell the others. No point in alarming them. Habib nodded and relied on the same cautious approach, taking the lead and forcing the others to pick up the pace, while leaving Joey in the rear.

The visit to Laashekoh had gone better than the first: Mita, more attentive and respectful than Cameron, had intrigued the villagers. Cameron, left behind, had smugly announced he couldn't wait for her report.

Now Joey had to make sure she made it back to give that report.

A branch cracked behind them, and Joey paused, first retying a boot and, moments later, adjusting his pack. Better to get a confrontation over with quickly.

But the follower had no intention of catching up.

Joey couldn't wait to get off the desolate, steep path and reach the

Humvee, returning to the familiar and secure outpost. The wind picked up, kicking up dust, jerking the treetops, and flattening the tall grass.

Every move made him jump inside.

The most time-consuming part of the trail was covered with tons of sliding broken rocks, overlooking a drop-off. They had to move one at a time—flattening their chests against the slope, digging the boots into the side, inching along—utterly exposing themselves to anyone watching the trail from above or below. They stared straight ahead at the wall of rock and dirt, not looking down.

Habib went first while Joey provided cover. As Mita approached the stretch, she tripped on a root. Joey lunged, grabbing her arm to break the fall.

Her laughter sounded like birdsong. Joey cringed, not wanting villagers to think the laugh was directed at them, and automatically put his finger to his mouth. "Take it easy," he said, nervously. "We're far enough from the village, but we shouldn't take chances."

Nodding, she crossed the rock pile without a problem. Barnaby followed, and then Joey, as Habib eyed the surrounding area and provided cover.

After the rock fall, the path widened and passed through a rocky meadow. Mita waited for Joey to catch up. "You seem nervous," she said in a low voice. "I thought the visit went well. That village is . . ."

He wanted to hear her reaction to the meeting. He wanted to talk and laugh with her. But that had to wait. Joey put his finger to his mouth: "Wait until we get back to the base."

She looked around, sensing his problem was immediate. "What's wrong?" Mita whispered.

Joey shook his head, but the question alerted Barnaby. Time to put the group to work. "Keep moving," he ordered. "If you see anything, call out a description and a position. Hear a noise—hit the ground and find cover." Barnaby looked like he was going to get sick. "We're fine, we're near the Humvee. If they wanted to hurt us, they would have done it where we were exposed."

"They want to make sure we're taking off," Habib added.

The other two nodded, but looked worried. The price of striving for predictability, Joey thought to himself, the price of not knowing one's enemies. A visit in open daylight might reassure villagers who wanted to cooperate, but could make the team a target for the resentful.

On the way back to the outpost in the Humvee, though, they would drive off-road.

As they rounded one of the last switchbacks in the meadow, a lone shot blasted, skipping in the dirt in front of Habib. The group froze, just for a moment, before Barnaby and Mita took off in a wild run.

"Cover!" Joey shouted, as he and Habib rolled into a stand of tall grass. Mita crouched and scrambled to reach some inadequate rocks. "Lower!" he screamed.

Furious, Joey thought about spraying the hillside with a round, but waited. He scanned the rocky slope, but could not determine the number of shooters or intent. The slope was still except for grass swaying in the fickle breeze. He reached around and found a rock that fit into the palm of his hand. He swung his left arm back and heaved. It landed along the edge of the path, bouncing in the dust.

No response.

He glanced at Mita crouching by the pile of three rocks, each barely larger than her head. A serious shooter could have easily picked her off. Habib had already climbed to a more secure position, covering both Mita and Joey. Still, Joey signaled her to lower her head.

They waited, watching the hillside. Sweat made the bullet-proof vest and heavy pack more uncomfortable than usual, and Joey was ready to take off. But Habib shook his head firmly, lifting his left palm, the signal for them to hold. The translator was right. Afghans had infinite patience.

~~~~~~

After a half hour, Joey tightened his helmet, determined to flush the shooter out and get Mita off the hillside. The Afghan circled his fingers and held them to his forehead, then pointed toward the top of the slope. Joey crawled to get a better view.

The man holding an assault rifle was backing away over the ridge, no more than fifty meters away.

No point rushing into a trap. The driver had radioed. The Humvee was near the pickup point and reported no action. Someone was taunting the Americans, reminding them who controlled this territory—or forcing a delay, to give time for planting an explosive for the Humvee's trip back to the outpost.

Darkness was at least three hours away. But that wouldn't help with the ride back to the outpost. IEDs would be hard to spot.

Joey didn't want to wait for darkness. "I'm going to try the path," he shouted. "Habib, shoot at anything that moves."

Barnaby howled. "If you're shot, what the hell happens to us?"

Joey sternly held his palm out flat, and then stood. Barnaby clung to his cover, as Mita stared, squeezing one of the rocks. Habib shifted position to provide coverage.

Joey stood and moved slowly, testing the shooter. Nothing happened. He slowly headed for Mita. It took at least a minute before he was close enough to reach for her hand. "You okay?" he asked gently.

"I just want us to stay together," Mita said.

"Good plan," Joey agreed.

Staying close to her, he walked backwards until the path dropped away from the meadow into a thick stand of trees. With every step, he made sure he was between her and where they had last seen the shooter. He positioned her behind a huge boulder. "Move, Barnaby," he shouted. "Habib has you covered!"

Barnaby jogged toward them, and only then did Habib back away to join the other three. "Let's get out of here," Joey said.

"We're pushing our luck, going to villages where we're not wanted," Barnaby noted.

Joey sighed. "That bullet didn't come from the people we just met with—I'd lay my life on it."

"They're not down here helping us either," Barnaby pointed out.

"Keep moving," Joey said. "And be ready to fire."

The rest of the way, the group kept to the one edge of the pathway, maintaining a pattern of pauses and moves as Joey stepped out ahead, testing the shooter before directing the other three to the best cover. Over and over, they paused, waited, then moved.

It was still light when they reached the Humvee. Joey ordered all packs off once the vehicle was in sight, and Dan was ready with the doors and single-movement lock. Joey advised Dan against using the road and easiest way back to the outpost. The driver took a hard left over rugged terrain.

In the rear, Barnaby checked the packs. "The fruit is bruised."

"Be grateful it's not you!" Dan teased.

Joey scowled. "Enough. A shot was fired at us."

The two men in the Humvee were surprised. "We didn't hear anything," Dan said.

"Why shoot one bullet?" Mita added. "Could it have been a mistake?"

"Maybe." Joey tried to keep his voice light. "Or they wanted to test our panic level." He didn't say it out loud, but if the shooter had been serious or brought a friend, the four team members would be dead, stretched out along the meadow's path.

Mita leaned back and stripped away the scarf, shaking her hair loose. "They were so friendly in the village," she murmured.

"They are," Joey added. "Problem is someone else doesn't want them to be."

~~~~~~

The strangers in black returned minutes after the Americans trudged away. This time, Jahangir and his men arrived by foot, slipping over the compound wall. Approaching the bench where our men had sat and drank tea with the Americans under the afternoon sun, they were prepared to judge the exchange.

Some men looked surprised, but not Parsaa or Gul.

Jahangir spoke for his band of men. *Did you enjoy hearing the Americans praise your fruit? Have you forgotten that they are the foreign invaders?*

There's no harm, Ahmed responded. *We need to know their plans.*

What did you give to them? Jahangir questioned.

We gave them nothing, Ahmed said. *They paid for fruit and vegetables.*

Supplying them aids their cause. Jahangir directed his comments at Gul. My eyes stayed on Parsaa who stared hard at the man. *Do you think the Americans want to help you?* Jahangir spoke as if puzzled or disappointed with a child. *Is that how Allah expects you to meet the infidels?*

Gul did not answer. To his credit, he did not divert his gaze from the inquisitor. *We can use payments from the Americans to banish them from our land*, Jahangir said. *You will help.*

We decide how to protect Laashekoh, Gul insisted.

Jahangir jerked his head, shifting the target of his ire to the gawking crowd, and snapped, *Why are these women listening to us? Did the Americans see them?* The man's bullying fury made us behave like slithering insects. Most backed away, including me. *Are they foolish enough to get ideas from the American woman?*

His shift in mood was frightening, and I felt an urge to escape the fury. Mari's doorway was the closest, and pulling my youngest son, I joined her. She draped her arm around the boy as we listened from around the corner. *I told my husband not to have anything to do with the Americans*, she whispered. *I chased them away, and he should have done the same.*

I wondered how she could be more alarmed about the Americans than Jahangir and his men. But it wasn't the time to argue.

Outside, Jahangir's voice softened again. *What bribe did they bring you?*

No bribes, Gul protested. *A small token—a torch.* Jahangir held his hand out, and Ahmed reluctantly turned it over. The man twisted the tube in his hands, switching the light on and off.

Allah does not provide enough light? Such gadgets don't feed your families . . .

The Americans will get suspicious if we evade them.

So you take their toys?

This catches the power of the sun and gives us more time to read the Koran. Gul aimed for the logical tone employed by Parsaa.

You know what Allah wants? Jahangir screamed. Gripping the light, he swung quickly, knocking it against the older man's head. Gul staggered, dropping to his knees.

It doesn't provide enough light for you to see the sins of invaders. Jahangir addressed the others. *No light can match the power of Allah. You have no use for these tools.* He smashed the tube against the nearest rock.

Saddiq and two other boys, loyal to their uncle, lifted their rifles. But they were trained to wait for a signal from the older men. Their eyes shifted between Jahangir and Parsaa.

Jahangir's men aimed their weapons at Gul.

Shrieking and rushing to her father's side, Leila broke the standoff. Glaring at Jahangir, she wrapped her arms around her father and struggled to help him stand. Only then did Mari break away from our shelter to assist. Before reaching for Gul, she tugged at Leila's scarf, which had slid away from her long hair.

Stepping forward, Parsaa shook his head at our young shooters. *We have more reason to be upset about the Americans than you do.*

Jahangir ignored him, turning on Mari and Leila. *I pity the man who relies on the protection of women,* he scoffed. *Do not touch him.*

My husband is a good man, Mari protested.

You cannot know what good means, woman! Jahangir laughed and looked out over our men, who watched helplessly. After putting weapons aside earlier, the men were forced to rely on our youngest shooters. Except for Leila and Mari, the women had all but disappeared.

These arguments weaken us, Parsaa interjected.

Jahangir accepted the comment as a peace offering and stepped away from Gul. *The infidels bring out hard feelings,* he muttered. He turned to Leila. *And why does this one care so much?*

This is my father, Leila retorted. *By talking with the Americans, he learns their plans.*

Jahangir laughed, and then taunted her. *So much for the strategy of women. You still live with your father, as old as you are? Not married?*

Jahangir spoke to his men. *There are reasons men keep daughters around. You'll be lucky to be a fourth wife.*

Jahangir's men laughed, while Mari gasped, her eyes dark and calculating. Gul's eyes were dazed, distraught about being shamed before the entire village.

The rest of us hesitated to step forward and defend them. Not even Parsaa, who looked stunned. I wanted to vanish. At last my husband moved, grabbing Mari and Leila and roughly pulling them to the doorway where I waited.

Keep them inside, he ordered me. *We'll take care of this, Mari.*

I reached for each woman's hand, as my husband returned to stand next to Gul. *We cannot interfere,* I whispered. *Our husbands are doing what they can to keep this village safe from fighting.*

Jahangir continued with his sly comments, something about Leila and the Americans. Mari seethed as his men railed with laughter and snapped, *My husband is a fool.*

There is no reasoning with that type of man, I protested.

Gul tries to act too much like Parsaa. She pulled her hand away angrily.

I tried to soothe her, but wondered why she was angrier with Gul and Parsaa than Jahangir. She scolded me to be quiet, so that she could overhear the conversation outside. Not that women could act. More often than not, we stood back and watched as fellow villagers were bullied, hoping to avoid such encounters. Ashamed, I didn't blame Mari and Leila for resenting the rest of us.

Jahangir continued to interrogate our men, asking what the Americans said.

You heard! Gul protested. *They talked about farming, and we promised them nothing.*

Have you told them about us? Jahangir pressed.

My husband laughed. My hand reached for Mari's and squeezed. I couldn't bear it if the man lashed out at Parsaa. But the laughter broke the tension. *As if that mattered.* Parsaa put his hand on his friend's shoulder. *The Americans are not a problem, and Gul handles our affairs well.*

Some better than others, muttered Jahangir.

Mari tightened her grip on my hand, and Parsaa frowned. *You make a mistake not trusting Laashekoh. You misunderstood.*

The sound of a bullet in the distance interrupted the confrontation before our eyes. Heads turned, staring toward the path leading away from our village. Surprise and worry crossed most of the men's faces. But Jahangir and his men smiled. The Americans either shot or were shot, and we knew they would blame our village.

We waited for more gunfire. But none came.

Did your men shoot at the Americans? My husband was incredulous. *You'd bring their wrath on us?*

This is a small village. You have no idea how complex these matters can be. Jahangir glanced around at those who stared at him, hiding fear or fury. *You will need our help in the days ahead.*

~~~~~~

Throughout the night, Joey reviewed the topography of the area surrounding Laashekoh and other reports. There was no logical reason for anyone in the village to antagonize his team. The single shot was a test, gauging intimidation levels and whether the team would avoid Laashekoh.

Joey's announcement the following morning that the visits to villages would continue set off a buzz.

"Laashekoh included?" Cameron asked.

"The shot was far from the village. No one was hit."

Cameron shook his head warily.

"One shot, from a sniper close enough for a hit," Joey said. "This village doesn't want a battle. It was a warning."

"A warning?" Cameron questioned. "So what happens next? There might not be a next time."

Mita shook her head hard. "The village welcomed us," Mita added. "That bullet was a stray. The precautions may have made the incident seem worse than it really was."

"We need more security," Cameron said stubbornly.

Mita shook her head. "It's a mistake going in with too many guards or guns. That overshadows the ag mission."

"You're both right," Joey said, shutting down the argument. He then announced a mandatory weapons review that afternoon. Directing trained soldiers through any hostile territory was hard enough without unpredictable civilians. "We'll go in with the same numbers, but more of us will be armed."

"Did you run the shooting incident by analysts in Kabul?" Cameron questioned.

Joey crossed his arms and stared at Cameron. The question was a challenge. "The command unit is aware," Joey said. "Mita remains in charge of scheduling."

"There will be no delays in these projects," she said. "Both military and civilian specialists—this is what we signed up for. And Cameron, you don't need to worry about Laashekoh, I'll take the next visit."

At last, Cameron stopped asking questions, but a new round of nervous looks went around the room.

~~~~~

The team headed to a canyon with a dry river bed and plenty of cover and also used suppressors so as not to alarm local Afghans. The security side of the team observed the ag side taking practice shots throughout the afternoon. Most of the ag specialists, even the civilians, had handled weapons before—but this wasn't simply target practice, and Joey wasn't taking chances. He personally checked each team member for follow-through—steady position, aim, trigger touch, fire. They practiced team coverage and shot from crouching, standing, sitting; long range and short range. He even improvised a moving target, a life-sized paper man pulled back and forth with a rope. He wanted every team member to walk away from the practice session with more confidence.

Mita was the worst shot of the group, and Joey spent extra time on her flinch that produced wild shots. He removed the magazine from her M9 and sat cross-legged next to her.

"You need to practice breathing." He advised her against holding her breath. "Close your eyes and work on slowing your breathing down." As she closed her eyes and took long, slow breaths, he gently placed his hand on her back, to guide her rhythm. "Slower," he murmured. "Slower."

He urged her to relax her eyes, neck, arms, every part of her, practicing another twenty minutes before he was satisfied, and then he wrapped her hand around his, as if it were a gun. "My finger is your trigger. Keep breathing, but get ready to press." He timed her breaths, and told her when to fire. "Gentle," he advised. "Fire . . . fire . . . fire." She squeezed his finger more than a hundred times before he was satisfied. "Doesn't take a lot of pressure to release the trigger," he noted, before handing over her M9 to practice dry firing.

He pointed to the target and told her to use both hands. Again, he directed her breathing and a light touch on the trigger, all the while watching her eyes, muscles, and hands.

She looked almost disappointed when he stood and told her to keep dry firing. "No ammunition?" she asked, surprised.

He smiled. "You're going to be fine if you stay calm, keep your breathing steady, and stay ahead of the target."

She looked down at the M9, oversized in her hands. "I couldn't shoot a person anyway," she admitted. Patting her shoulder, he understood.

~~~~~

The session went well and the group returned for dinner, pleased with their results. Fortunately, no one asked why they had practiced shooting at such short ranges.

Even after sundown, the teams drifted off to finish tasks and prepare for the next day. After checking the preparations, Joey walked the perimeter of the outpost. Just beyond the barriers protecting the outpost, Cameron fiercely tackled the beginnings of his experimental wheat plot, plowing furrows and arranging plastic tubes for drip irrigation.

Cameron worked tirelessly, intent on proving his point. The flurry of field activity so late in the day attracted attention. Joey was on his way to check the nightly reports waiting in the admin office when he spotted Mita on a slope, screened by low branches of a pine tree. She was watching Cameron, Barnaby, and others move a boulder from the field. He circled around the building's rear to walk her way. "What do you think?" he asked.

"Too soon to tell," she said. "We're not going to be here long enough for wheat, but it gives Cameron something to do." She stood and brushed off her pants. "Mind if I join you?"

He nodded and they walked away from the trees. "He's working hard. You've got to give him that."

Mita raised her eyebrows. "And making the rest of us feel guilty for not helping him."

"He's chafing under our leadership and out to prove something. But it's not just me or you. He'd butt heads with anyone."

"I noticed," Mita said wryly. "I wish I could get him to understand that we're here for Afghans. Not our careers."

"He wants to be right." Joey looked back out over the field at Cameron, using a shovel to loosen another boulder. The man was sweaty. "His plot's not a problem, is it?"

"No," she admitted. Colors of the land darkened with the dropping sun, and Joey relaxed as she continued. "He's going to plant a special variety that develops rapidly and resists drought. Its genetic structure includes biopesticides. But there are other problems here, fungus and Sunn pests—that's a relative to the stink bugs we have back at home. It's risky to specialize too quickly on any one crop."

"So it's only a problem if the Afghans follow his lead?" She nodded in response. "I don't see that happening," Joey said. "So let him go. The field keeps him out of trouble. All of us avoid going stir crazy by him stepping out, even if it's only a few yards away."

She laughed, and he slowed his pace, happy to walk with her and eliminate reasons for worry. "We may disagree," she said. "But at least he cares."

"And who knows what will break the ice with these villagers?" he said. "Maybe they'll take pity on us." Mita sighed, looking out over the distant mountains. "Something is bothering you," Joey observed.

"I'm frustrated," she admitted. "I hate to waste the time. Cameron doesn't know it and the villagers probably don't either, but Asians started growing wheat thousands of years before it was cultivated in America. It's an insult to hand over hybrid seeds or tell them what to do. But it's hard to wait, too."

"It's a good idea to keep him busy and away from the villagers," Joey said.

"But what if the villages don't want anything we offer? Are we any better than Cameron?"

"We work with what we have," Joey said. "Get rest—something will break our way. I feel it."

CHAPTER 10

Our compound was quiet at night. Most villagers went to sleep soon after sundown.

After Ali's death, I didn't sleep well. With every passing night, my worries for the boy, alone in the afterlife, intensified. Parsaa often slipped away from our bed at night, and I assumed that he had trouble sleeping and escaped our village walls to think about Ali, too. I understood. The dead keep their distance, until we're alone with our thoughts.

I crept away from the covers where our family slept and draped a blanket around my shoulders. Outside, I stared upward, feeling one with the night sky. A cool breeze kissed my hair, and in the distance, tiny stars sparkled with greetings. Tears came to my eyes as I wondered if Ali could see them.

A sound of footsteps startled me, until I realized they came from behind Gul's home. Moving slowly, I went to the wall to check and held my breath, wanting to avoid explanations about why I stood outside in night clothes, with no headscarf and a blanket for my cloak. Inching close to the crack, I peered, but saw only darkness. Suddenly, a shape emerged, and I recognized Gul filling a pack in his courtyard. Fortunately, his attention was focused on his doorway and not my direction at all. Adjusting the pack on his back, he turned and disappeared.

I backed away and sat on a bench, mulling the nighttime habits of men. Did Parsaa and Gul meet or go their separate ways?

And then it hit me. On Ali's last night, he might have left our home in darkness, too. Maybe he wasn't restless, thinking about the upcoming journey to the maktab. Instead, he may have helped Parsaa or Gul in some way or followed them.

If the two men knew more, they wouldn't tell me or the other women. Not knowing became a fire in my chest.

I sat alone in the chilly night, wrapping my blanket tight around me, trying to think of how to learn more about Ali's last night. But my mind was too angry and afraid. Shaking my head, I hurried back to a warm bed with four sleeping sons, but no husband.

~~~~~

The next morning, I tried to learn more, asking Parsaa in a roundabout way about Gul. *Mari's husband is too easy with the visitors.*

He wants to get along. Parsaa did not look up from his meal. *It won't be for long.*

They want more from us than simply chasing the Americans away, I said. He didn't respond and he stared at our two youngest tumbling about on the floor. *How do you know what they want?* My voice dropped to the softest whisper, trying to show more concern for Parsaa than curiosity. *Are Gul and Jahangir involved in something that we do not know about?*

That is Gul's affair, Sofi, Parsaa admonished. *Do not question him, and he won't question you.*

I frowned. *But he doesn't stop the questions from Jahangir.*

Parsaa knew I was right, but he walked away. That infuriated me, though there was no use letting him know how I felt. It bothered me that my husband might work with Gul and Jahangir in the night. I wondered how much Mari or Leila knew. Maybe everyone knew but me.

Leaning against the wall, I watched the children play and quarrel among themselves, and thought about Ali. I missed his questions and intelligent ideas about village life and how to get along. If he had thought the men were doing wrong, he might have followed.

His death lurked in the back of my mind, troubling me more and more, as I tugged at weeds, washed clothes at the river, or prepared our meals. Horrible thoughts tainted every routine as I imagined his fall from every possible angle, his flailing hands, the open mouth and eyes, the long scream. I resented that I could not talk about these thoughts with my husband. I despised that he didn't question the notion that a strong boy, one who had long chased the goats on the hills, had taken an accidental fall.

Any other suggestion would strain relationships in our village, and that was an inconvenience for Parsaa and other men.

~~~~~~

My curiosity about what the men did at night should have waned after a few days. Maybe it was the lack of sleep or trust since Ali's death, but my need to know strengthened with every passing day.

Why didn't Parsaa tell me more? I had understood him taking off during the nights soon after Ali's death. But why did Gul slip away, too? Men kept too many secrets, and women didn't have a clue until fighting broke out.

I did not want to lose another son. But there was no use asking Parsaa questions that he'd refuse to answer. So I took to listening for men stepping away from the village late at night. Every night I put the children to bed and waited, listening and ready to follow. Parsaa left before the children went to sleep. After the evening meal, he sat outside, drinking tea with the other men for a short while until they drifted off to their homes. Then he vanished, and for all I knew, the others assumed he was at home in his bed.

I couldn't risk getting caught.

Over the next few nights, I waited for the children to fall asleep, and then slipped from the room and donned my darkest clothes. I went to our bench and waited. For three nights, the village was quiet. On the fourth night, a door opened and the sound of quiet footsteps came from Gul's home.

The sky was overcast, and the only sounds were rustling leaves and furtive footsteps. I wore a pair of Ali's shoes that I had saved for the younger boys. They fit well and would help on rocky terrain. Waiting until the sound of the walker faded, I hurried around the corner and watched Gul head for a small trail toward the river—the opposite direction from where Ali had died. It was tempting to use that as an excuse to return home. But curiosity pushed me on, and I kept a safe distance, focusing every thought and motion on not getting caught.

Once away from the compound, Gul picked up the pace as he moved downhill.

After heading away from our gate, I glanced up and down the path, checking for followers. But the village was a silent refuge. Before I became afraid and changed my mind, I darted off, staying close to trees and brush.

The biggest risk for getting caught was near or inside our compound. I tried to think of excuses for why I walked outside our compound in the middle of the night—with no gun, escort, bundle, or reason to leave. Gul or other men could always claim to be hunting, relieving themselves, or checking on intruders, but such excuses were not available for women.

If caught, I worried about putting my family in danger. People had left me alone since Ali had died and didn't ask questions. But wandering around the countryside on my own went beyond eccentricity. It was unforgivable.

Several days earlier, I had left a water bucket hidden in the bushes along the way to the stream. If caught near the compound, I was prepared to explain we needed water and that I had to retrieve our forgotten bucket. Not the best excuse, but it would have to do. And a bucket wouldn't help if Gul caught me far from the compound and stream. All I could claim was that I got lost, very lost. Then I'd force tears and feign relief at being found.

I hurried after Gul, pausing only occasionally to check his direction. I knew these trails well, better than most women, and that helped in the darkness. Gradually, the distance between us spread. Hearing the thuds and crunching sounds of his feet hitting rocks was unnerving, and the silence was awful, too. He could easily lie in wait to trick and catch a follower.

Once our village was out of sight, a light suddenly flashed on ahead, swinging back and forth—the torch provided by the Americans.

Light that sped his way also made him easy to follow.

Gul went farther than I had expected, but he was easier to follow than Parsaa would have been. Maybe the two took turns meeting Jahangir. I was suspicious of secret business our village might have with Jahangir and his men who called themselves students of Allah, endless travelers who talked more than worked, relying on an ability to wheedle supplies from villages and get their way.

A sheep wailed nearby, and that gave me an idea for another excuse. I could claim to be worried about a lost sheep, one who was pregnant. If need be, my son would find the sheep in question, and use a knife on the top inner fold of her thigh. My mother often said women's secrets brought suffering to other women.

Before long, I tripped over a root—and fell with hands out and a hard thump. Stones scattered and slid down the hill with a noisy clatter. My palm was scraped and both wrists were sore, but I forced myself to roll into the grass and remain still, holding my breath, listening for Gul to turn around and confront his follower.

I stretched out to check on the location of Gul's light, and panicked when I didn't see it.

Then my eyes caught the moving speck of light bobbing ahead. His pace was brisk, and he was far ahead, so the light flickered on and off with every curve of the trail.

When the light was no longer in sight, I moved on, pausing regularly, making sure there was no sound or movement ahead or behind me. He took a trail that led to a mountain pass not far from our village, and I didn't worry about losing him. The bigger worry for me was running into one of Jahangir's men.

Beyond the pass, well out of sight of our village or the American outpost, Gul's light merged with a large campfire and vanished. Moving deliberately, I kept my breath in check, grateful about not carrying a pack.

Staying off the path, edging my way in the darkness, I approached close enough to hide behind a boulder and overhear the conversation. A large wagon was nearby, and the night was dark. Still, I had an excellent view of the clearing and the silhouettes of two men standing near the fire and warming their hands. Crouching to the ground, I took a deep breath and pointed my head downward, hardly believing that I was so far from my bed and family.

It's not easy to leave a home and small village in the middle of the night, Gul snapped. *We don't need questions.*

Train your wife not to ask so many questions, Jahangir taunted.

My wife has nothing to do with this. We need to worry about questions from others. How many do you need?

Jahangir mumbled, and Gul exclaimed, *Eight! Where are they from?*

From the north—Ghōr. But why do you care?

The only reason I have a part in this business is to help the poorest families. Gul spoke with lofty sternness. *Ghōr is in a terrible way . . .*

But not Herat or Laashekoh? Jahangir countered. *Rest assured, we help the poorest of families, and they are grateful to be rid of the responsibility.* Gul waved his hand, insisting that he had no need for details. *Come with me, you can inspect them yourself.*

Jahangir tossed the contents of a cup into the fire, and smoke soared. Gul backed away. *That's not necessary. No one needs to know about my involvement.*

Jahangir laughed. *You can thank me for that. No one in your village suspects a thing after I struck you.* Gul mumbled a protest. *You are too fond of secrets, my friend. Of course, you're here to help the children—not for the money that passes your way.* He laughed again. *Don't worry—if they behave, the best could go to the richest families in Pakistan.*

I shivered at his use of the words *children* and *money*, how his silky voice soothed Mari's husband before tightening into a tricky cord that strangled reason and left only shame. This business was evil, and I had to think about my own exit—not fear about capture and what either man might do. Gul was a fool. Jahangir terrified me, and I prayed that Parsaa and Ali had nothing to do with such evil.

A whimpering sound came from the wagon. *Help us!* called a child, far too young to be alone with any man not a parent or an uncle. *We are thirsty.*

The two men turned to look in my direction. I cringed, not knowing if the girl cried out to me or Gul, and flattened myself to the ground.

Gul pointed to the pack. *I brought supplies for the children.*

You would give her water? Be her servant? That's not how to teach children control.

Pressing my face into the grass, I refused to look up as one of them stepped beyond the circle of firelight and approached the wagon, standing but a few meters away. Jahangir's slippery male voice taunted the child. *We protect you from the Americans, and that's the thanks you give? Ask again, and you will wait that much longer.*

More than one child sobbed, yet my fear won out over compassion. Sliding backward, flattened to the ground, I hoped the sharper eyes of children had not spotted me, expecting rescue. My stomach was sick. Heartless thugs could act as though they had nothing to hide while I crawled away like an insect.

Jahangir strode away from a rickety wagon, surrounded by crates and blankets haphazardly strewn about the ground. I didn't know the number of children, but realized the men were transporting them, hiding them amid crates covered by tarps. What must be hidden must be wrong, I thought to myself. As Jahangir laughed at the crying children, I remembered Ali's still body. Gratitude replaced my fear. There were worse fates for children than death. Shaking my head, I begged for forgiveness from Allah.

There's no reason to mistreat the children, Gul nagged.

Jahangir stepped through the darkness to the wagon—close enough that I could hear his heavy breathing—and he dragged a child away, shoving the boy at Gul's feet. The child's hands were tied. *Let's see how you discipline them.*

Gul turned his head and pulled his scarf to cover more of his face.

You promised to help these children, Gul accused.

We are, Jahangir promised. *We have parents pleading for our help.*

So many children . . ., Gul murmured.

Jahangir shrugged. *Families cannot afford to feed their children.*

He lifted the boy back into the wagon and returned to the fire, where they spoke about logistics. Gul asked him about the next trip and the fighting to the north, adding, *Our village is in no mood for fighting.*

The fighting will come your way.

We can outlast the Americans.

There was a long silence. I pressed my face against the cold ground, looking away from the camp.

Your village could do more, but you'd rather leave the fight to the parents of these children?

The Americans have not lifted a finger against us. I'm helping you with these transports. Others in Laashekoh would be less accommodating.

So you admit you have no control over this village? Jahangir scoffed. *Do not talk about these matters with others. I will handle that.*

I had heard enough. Their bickering would cover any noise of my backing away, and time was running out. Keeping my eyes on them, making sure their heads did not turn my way, I crawled backward until the fire was a distant glow, taking time with every move.

I remembered how Gul had outpaced me earlier, and I couldn't take a chance that he might catch up, especially in the fields just outside our village gate. Once the fire was no longer in sight, I took off running, aiming for a hiding place among the brush overlooking the path. Clutching roots, I climbed toward my perch. Pulling my scarf over my eyes and wrapping my arms tight around my knees to keep still, I waited for Gul to pass.

Alone in the darkness, I tried to imagine what would compel me to turn my children over to the likes of Jahangir. He was only transporting them, I tried to tell myself. He claimed to have their parents' approval. That didn't keep guilt from stabbing at my heart.

A light eventually came bouncing along, and I held my breath as Gul passed, so close he could have stretched out an arm and touched me.

In seconds, he was gone, yet I waited to make sure no one followed him. After Gul's light was no longer visible and a long silence passed, I climbed down the slope and continued on the trail.

Walking away from horror wasn't so easy. Every step away said *Kharaab, kharaab, kharaab* to me. Wrong, wrong, wrong, to leave the children behind, to worry the little ones had spotted me, to allow evil to win over courage.

My logical side responded. If I had spoken out, Jahangir could have easily cut my throat and hidden the body. Parsaa would have never known. And accusing Jahangir in the village wasn't an option. No one would believe a woman.

I could tell Parsaa, but I no longer trusted him after he failed to press for the reasons behind Ali's death.

Shaking my head, I tried to focus on remaining quiet. From the river valley, along the last stretch, I could make out the rooftops of our village along the mountainside. Near the gate, Gul's light was extinguished. Cautious, I did not hurry to my home and instead went off-trail, heading for a small stream and collapsing near the bucket I had left behind. The urge to check my children was strong, but I dared not risk letting anyone see me slinking into the compound just before sunrise, close on Gul's heels.

Avoiding Mari was essential. She'd never stop pressing for a reason, and there was no acceptable explanation—either I suspected her husband of wrongdoing or I was trying to lure him away. She wouldn't accept coincidence and would seek vengeance.

Shivering and sad, I leaned my head against a tree and waited for sunrise, wishing that the stream's song could erase a child's cry from my head.

CHAPTER 11

Jahangir and two other men, on horseback, stormed through the compound gate.

The older children gathered to hold and watch the horses, while younger ones kept their distance. The poor animals gasped for breath, lifting and lowering their heads, desperate for water. Unlike the others, our family did not gawk. My sons ran to search for their father while I hurried to my stove, annoyed about the interruption.

Grabbing a clay pot, I angrily chopped carrots and cabbage, as Leila called softly from the rear entryway and then slipped inside.

What do you think of these men? she asked.

We do not need more men telling us what to do, I snapped.

They said there's fighting to the north. They need a place to stay for a few days.

She knew about these plans before the men had arrived, but I didn't comment. Maybe Parsaa did not tell his wife as much as Gul told his daughter. Fuming, I turned away from her to select potatoes from a basket. Then I snatched another knife and handed it to Leila with an onion. *Work as you talk. Who will they stay with?*

It hasn't been decided. She kept her eyes on the vegetable. *It's only for a few days.*

I hope they do not bring the fighting here. I chopped furiously. *They resent the women because we resent their fighting.* I checked her work, but noticed the pieces were mismatched and would not cook evenly. Her hands were shaking, and I took pity on her.

Your father is kind to them, I continued. *Even though they have odd ideas about how this village should behave.*

They will be busy, and come and go.
We can't work the fields that way. We'll go hungry.
Auntie, you'd never let us go hungry. Ali said that you work magic in
the fields.

It hurt to hear my son's name mentioned so casually. Tears stung
my eyes, and I put the knife down to check my other sons. My response
was harsh. *There's no magic. If I knew of any, he'd be standing here.*

~~~~~~

More than once, villagers have asked my husband to be a prayer leader
and he declined. *But he knows the Koran better than any of us*, others
admonished. Parsaa shook his head, explaining he had more to learn.
He was a hard worker, motivating others to do the same. He categorized
verses from the Koran, ready to use any that suited his arguments.

The Koran backed every decision we made, and Parsaa was skilled
at using the good book's verses to get his way. I wondered if the reason
he studied the book so closely was to understand the unanswered mys-
teries: Does a lack of sustenance and favors in this world reveal Allah's
displeasure? Which sins are forgivable? Do believers have choices?
How does one guard against evil, and can individuals determine the
essence of evil on their own?

The emphasis of a word or phrase over another created dilemmas
for alert students. My husband often repeated the phrase "I do not
control you for evil or good." A statement, simple on the surface, does
not clarify whether he cannot control us at all—or whether he controls
us for other purposes.

The Koran repeatedly cautions against "evil," but the emphasis is
on guarding against it, joining against it, and not repelling, forbid-
ding, or fighting it. Some may blame their evil acts on the jinn and evil
spirits. Yet in the Koran and our village, the evildoers are in control,
often more intent than those who believe.

I cannot shed my guilt after witnessing Jahangir with the children
and walking away. One would think that people could readily agree

on the worst evils and how to avoid them. Yet as Parsaa could wrap the Koran's verses to justify any opinion, others were equally skilled at twisting reasons and shedding responsibility. Before Ali's death, I had always agreed with Parsaa's interpretations, but since I've wondered why he didn't do more to expose the evil in our midst.

Gul and the others were not as adept with the Koran, and I pitied them. Yet I was relieved that Parsaa was not a leader. We never spoke about it. As a family, we refrained from talking in public or displaying our emotions, and when Parsaa did speak to me or the children in front of others, it was rough and brief. I kept quiet, limiting eye contact or smiles. Sadly, the public persona worked its way into our private lives. My studies helped with loneliness.

A serious husband was better than a pompous fool. We worked hard and saved, making do without many items from the market. Parsaa didn't have to convince me to do everything in our power to avoid courting envy.

I listened closely to our family's readings of the Koran. The sound of children's voices reading, halting, not understanding everything they heard, brought me comfort—even as I discovered that the messages for me were not the same as those heard by my husband or the children. That did not make the words less powerful.

Allah insists we have choices. I believe it's left to us to decide which choices work to His liking. Each time I tried to read the Koran, thrilling thoughts jumped into my head. I yearned to find more to read and wondered if power would come with other words.

~~~~~~

It's easy to cast a spell over a hungry man, with the aroma of a luscious lamb stew and baking bread. I stirred the stew slowly, adding more fragrance to the room. My sons hovered as I placed the pot on a mat in the center of the carpet where we ate our meals. Then the boys sat on the floor, backs straight and legs crossed, waiting for me to serve their father first.

When I wanted to speak to my husband about any pressing matter, I served dinner earlier than usual, providing him with a small portion that lasted until the children ate and wandered off. Then I gave him another serving. No longer hungry or distracted, we talked.

Despite many sleepless nights, I decided against revealing what I had seen in the middle of the night. An accusation from any of us would put my family in danger. Still, I tried to plant distrust about Jahangir and Gul. I kept my voice low. *Jahangir and his men could break this village apart*, I commented. *If he stays, he will try to take control.*

Parsaa dismissed my concern. *Better he's in our sight.*

I refused to give up easily. *He pretends to be devout, but he knows less than you do about the Koran.*

Not in front of the children, he murmured.

The children should know our thoughts on whom to trust. How can they learn if not from their father? It was a phrase he had used on others. Parsaa scowled, checked the two youngest boys, busy with a game in the corner, and then closed his eyes. *You can ward him off with verses from the Koran*, I insisted. *You should know his activities and tell him we won't join with his evil—*

He slapped his hand to the floor. *Enough!* he shouted.

That day eroded my certainty about the Koran's power—not if it taught us to fear and hide from evil. Parsaa and I did not understand the book the same way.

Not long ago, a friend—Karimah—had talked about the drought in our area and suggested that the cause was unseen evils. I laughed and she asked, *You do not believe?*

I'm old enough to know that neither good nor evil is linked with nature. Fear crossed her face, and I tried to assure her. *It doesn't matter what I believe. We're alone with our thoughts.*

It's dangerous to think too much on your own, she cautioned, one of the regular reminders that I had to pretend to think like everyone else, keeping questions and arguments to myself.

Too many assume that certainty is strength and uncertainty is weakness. Unlike others, I did not fear doubt. Of course, worries about Parsaa's commitment to me and his priorities were like a heavy sack on my shoulder, yet other doubts, like the questions of faith, are like fluttering wings of moths, lifting my thoughts to new heights and leading to other possibilities. Doubt and new ideas cannot weaken me.

I did not think like others.

~~~~~~

I resented Jahangir lingering around our village, but hoped that Parsaa was right, that in plain sight, the man could not commit evil.

Jahangir joined the sessions of village men reading the Koran. I listened from inside and soon realized that he only pretended that he could read. Parsaa and the others read along, acting as if nothing was amiss.

And men pretended to know great truths just as easily. Any man could scratch words on paper and insist his words are truth. If we cannot read, compare, and test ourselves, how do we trust any words on paper or from the mouths of men? How can we trust others' instincts? After Ali's death, there was but one certainty. Regardless of good or evil, Allah does not watch us all.

I loved my family, and kept such thoughts to myself. Reading and other secrets added to my distance with Parsaa. The two of us had to grapple with our fears alone.

My favorite time of day shifted away from the dinner hour and time with my family to any hours spent alone, working in the fields, studying the soil and sky, recording my observations as I could with numbers and a few words. Our village shared the work of tending the fields, and I remembered the history of previous seasons well. Alone, I could test new ideas—giving the seedlings more space, trimming new shoots from plants until the fruit appeared, digging troughs around roots to direct the rainwater. Noticing the rich soil under rocks, I ordered my sons to build three small rock walls to store and shelter old leaves and wasted vegetable scraps that in time would turn to soil.

When others praised our harvests, I credited my husband's daily prayers. More than once, travelers like Jahangir complained about Laashekoh women working in the fields, stressing that other villages did not allow such indignities. *Without you, our fields would not produce half as much*, Parsaa had admitted. *We would have to depend on men like Jahangir.*

But even hard work was no match for droughts lingering for months, insects devouring crops, or soldiers demanding supplies. Until Jahangir's arrival, the families of our village had banded together, refusing to compete or prick the envy of others. Accomplishments belonged to the village, not individuals. Otherwise, Laashekoh could not have survived.

My husband claimed to trust Allah, but I lacked such certainty and refused to be ashamed. Uncertainty and curiosity are intertwined. Those who are certain lack the urge to learn more.

~~~~~~

The visitors complained that women and girls moved too freely throughout our compound, that we didn't cover ourselves appropriately. Most of Jahangir's outbursts, though, took place when Parsaa was not around. And Parsaa and the other men left our village too often.

Women started to worry after one of Jahangir's men shoved a young girl to the ground, calling her a *sag*—dog—for dashing about with her brothers. Then another man threatened to shoot a young wife for laughing at a joke made by her husband.

Resenting being watched and judged, we complained to our husbands and insisted that at least a few men stay in the village at all times and accompany the women as we worked in the orchards or gardens.

We're afraid to work, one young wife protested.

The hihab is not enough for them!

It's only temporary, the men promised. They procrastinated out of fear, and that added to our resentment. Mari was willing to rationalize the visitors' contempt.

It's a sign from Allah, Mari insisted. *We could do more to follow the ways of the Koran.* A few women scowled at her, but none responded. The women whose daughters were insulted became cool, staying away as long as Mari intended to defend the strangers.

Women could no longer trust their husbands or friends.

CHAPTER 12

Cameron had spooked more than one member of the team about any visit to Laashekoh. That didn't deter Mita. Joey had suggested that it was better to test the village mood sooner than later—and collect information on what the village knew about the gunshot. She was ready to take off, in kalaa Afghani that was old and worn.

Joey, Habib, Dan, and Mita took on the assignment of hiking to Laashekoh. They carried pamphlets and empty packs to bring back whatever fresh vegetables they could buy. Joey also presented Mita a holster for her Beretta M9. "How do you want to reach for it, side or front?" he asked. She held her right hand over her chest, and he placed the holster over her shoulders, sizing it and cutting the straps. "It's like fitting a little kid," he teased.

She didn't laugh and avoided touching the firearm. "I worry about showing a lack of trust."

"The villagers carry guns, too. It's not them I worry about." He stood back. "There. . . . With your jacket, they won't see it. We have to be ready for anything."

The morning air was crisp, cool, the sky was clear. The four climbed out of the Humvee and hiked without pause. Past the avalanche section, the narrow stretch forced visitors to move single-file the last few kilometers to the village. Joey took the lead, and as he shoved branches aside to round a sharp curve, the shooting began.

One of the first bullets ricocheted off Joey's helmet, stunning him. Knocked to the ground, flat on his back, he automatically pressed the trigger to his M16, spraying the hillside and the source of the shots. Then he rolled for cover.

Head pounding from the hit, or maybe from the blasts chipping at nearby rocks, Joey checked the others. All were safe—Habib hovering over Mita after shoving her to the ground, Dan crawling to join Joey. While Joey reloaded, Dan took aim at a man in black, dodging in and out of sight around the brush overhead. The shooting was steady, almost mechanical, keeping up with the pounding pain in Joey's head.

Dan didn't take his eyes off the hill. "You okay?"

"Stunned, but I'll get that bastard. I'm sure it's one shooter." Joey held his hand up, the signal to stop shooting. Silence descended on the hillside. "Let's see what he does," Joey murmured. He glanced back at Mita. Her gun was not even out. "Did you get a look at the guy?"

Dan narrowed his gaze. "He's in black."

"Keep an eye on him—we'll trap him." Joey signaled Habib to climb the hill and get the advantage of higher ground. Using the curve of the mountainside to stay out of sight, Habib moved quietly. Joey and Dan kept crawling uphill, deliberately moving slowly, to distract the sniper.

"Come on baby, four against one," Dan crowed.

"Try three against one." Joey countered.

The shooter suddenly dodged backward out of sight, and Dan swore. A few rocks suddenly fell onto the path, directly in front of Joey. Too close to come from Habib. The sniper knew the terrain.

"Get him," Joey said, more to himself than to Dan. "Get him. If he makes it to that ridge, he'll pick us off . . ."

They sprayed shots just above the guy, trying to prevent him from climbing higher. But he was out of sight and had stopped shooting. Joey held his hand up to stop firing from his side. He wanted to see the sniper and know once and for all if the shooter was from Laashekoh.

Joey also wished that he could have stayed closer to Mita. But the shooter would have a tough time getting to her, past three opponents. "Is visiting this village worth it?" Dan called out.

Joey scowled. "Since when do we let one clown stop us?"

"Could be a good idea if a general's daughter is tagging along," Dan teased. "Why don't those women like to shoot?"

"She'll shoot if she has to." Joey scanned the hillside. "But she doesn't have to. I'm sure there's just one shooter."

Dan nodded. "That's all I've heard."

Joey lowered his voice. "I don't want him to spot Habib, so I'll move ahead to get his attention. You cover. Unless he starts descending, and then get closer to Mita."

As Joey started, shots rained down on the sniper from above. Habib had reached the top.

Taking advantage of the barrage, Joey held his chin to the ground and crawled upward, taking advantage of every boulder and blade of grass for cover. Dan and Habib did not let up with the fire.

For a few moments, no gunfire came from above. The sniper must have found cover for reloading. Then suddenly rounds started biting the dust at Joey's feet. He dove behind a boulder.

The sniper didn't have the best aim. But with an automatic rifle and plenty of ammunition, he didn't need it.

Joey checked the positions. Nearby, Dan was stretched out, firing away. The only sign of the sniper was the rifle's barrel poking from a vertical crack in the hillside, close to the ground. No cover was nearby, and the guy stayed in place, shooting wildly. Overhead Habib steadily crept along the ridge. They were close to trapping the sniper.

But Mita was out of sight.

Joey was too damn far from her. He wanted to call out, but couldn't risk drawing attention to her. Joey was in better position to hit the sniper, so he signaled Dan to head back to the path. As Dan tried to move, the shooter let loose with steady fire, chipping away at nearby rocks and boulders.

Let the guy spend his ammunition, Joey thought.

Joey and Dan had little choice but to be patient, aiming the M16s in single-shot mode for accuracy, keeping their eyes on the rifle barrel. One of Joey's shots even hit the barrel. The sniper pulled back.

"He's stuck," Dan said.

There was a long pause, as the two men stared at the gun barrel resting on the ground, just barely visible.

"Maybe we got him?" Dan asked.

Joey shook his head and checked below. "I'll wait. You check on Mita."

Dan took off, sliding downhill toward the path where Mita waited. *She's carrying the Beretta*, Joey tried to reassure himself. *She'd holler if anyone approached.*

Suddenly, a single shot landed just to the left of Joey's head—and he scrambled along the side of the boulder and then glanced up toward the crack. The gun barrel had not moved.

Damn, Joey thought to himself. The sniper had tricked them into thinking he was stuck. But the vertical crack must have led to a passage, and, leaving one gun as a decoy, the sniper used the time to make his move. He had a new position with plenty of cover, and Joey had no idea where the man was at.

Shaken, Joey realized that the single shot probably didn't alert Dan and Habib to the sniper's new position—and he couldn't see them to signal. "Shooter moving!" he shouted, along with the code that the position was unknown.

Leaning against the rock, Joey waited a moment before checking the terrain. He couldn't see Habib, and the Afghan couldn't see his signals. Joey eyed a pile of rocks a few meters away. He wanted to signal Habib to suspend his part of the operation and back away. The team had to move quickly, increasing their distance from the shooter, returning to the path, and reorganizing.

Dropping into a crouch, Joey took a zigzag run before diving for the next cover.

But the sniper had lost interest in Joey, and no shots came his way. Breathing hard, Joey heard footsteps scrambling above. Habib stepped along the ridge to avoid entering what he assumed to be the sniper's sightline. Exposed to the upper reaches of the hillside, pressing against a crumbling dirt wall, Habib approached the crack from overhead, never realizing that the sniper had moved away from the opening where the rifle barrel still waited.

Joey shouted, pointed, to warn Habib to pull back. But the Afghan had already jumped down to the ledge, blasting the opening and stray rifle.

High above, the sniper was ready, firing one shot that slammed Habib. Didn't matter that the Afghan wore a vest—he went down hard, blood splattering over the dirt and rocks.

Furious, Joey stretched atop the boulder and sprayed the hill nonstop. There was a scream, before the sniper took off and fled over the ridge. A hit. At such close range, the guy would likely die without immediate medical attention.

Joey raced toward Habib, not taking his eyes away from where he had last seen the sniper. Habib's eyes were closed and his neck was half gone. There was no point in checking for a pulse, but Joey put a hand to the man's shoulder. Dan scrambled back uphill, and Joey stood, providing cover. But no more shots came their way.

"You got him," Dan said.

"Not in time for Habib." Joey was bitter about not taking more caution about a motionless rifle barrel. After straightening Habib's arms and legs, Joey stood and murmured a prayer: "He belongs to Allah, to Allah he returns."

Dan solemnly crossed himself.

"He saved my life." Joey stared up the hill, as he removed his jacket for an impromptu stretcher. "We'll carry him back to the truck—then hurry back to Laashekoh."

"We're still going?" Dan asked, incredulous.

"Hell, yes," Joey snapped. "We'll check if they have a wounded sniper on their hands." He scanned the hillside again, but the sniper was long gone. Each man held his rifle with one arm, using the other free hand to heft Habib, preparing to trudge back to where the Humvee would pick them up.

"The villagers had to have heard this," Dan complained.

"It was one guy. We can't expect them to come to our rescue."

"They may know more than they're telling us, have you thought of that?"

"We'll follow his trail . . ." They reached the path, and Joey suddenly lowered his rifle, twisting to check both directions. "Where the hell is Mita?"

~~~~~~

After Joey radioed for assistance, it didn't take long for others to arrive. He and Dan lifted Habib's body into a truck for transfer to the outpost. From there, the Afghan's body would be whisked by helicopter to his family later that day for an immediate burial.

Joey and Dan had already paced the pathway and found Mita's empty pack next to the tree where they had left her. But there was no other sign. Joey asked Dan if he had heard gunfire coming from the path.

"Absolutely not," Dan insisted. "I would have never moved forward. And she didn't shoot either. There was one shooter . . ."

"That's what I thought, too," Joey said. He worried the shooter was a distraction for a kidnapping. "I hope she still has the gun."

~~~~~~

An hour later, more than a dozen searchers joined the two men, spreading out and systematically circling out from the tree where Mita had last been seen. About two hours later, on a ledge below, Joey frightened a flurry of birds feeding on berries and found Mita's mobile radio unit and weapon. He checked the unit. It was still on. Moments later, Dan found her helmet on the rocks below.

"She didn't try to make a transmission," he noted. He looked up, certain the three objects had not been tossed by Mita or tumbled off the cliff alone.

Joey checked the area, finding no sign of ambush or trauma other than some crushed branches—almost like a hole in the brush, as though something hard had fallen from the path above. He pointed out the damaged brush to the others. "She was here when the gunfire broke out. She might have been changing her position, and had an accident backing away."

Dan winced and looked up. "Hard fall."

"At least ten meters . . ." Cameron said. "She'd be hurt."

"She's tiny, and the undergrowth is thick. It might have cushioned the fall."

"Then where is she?" Cameron asked, looking around. "She'd be waiting with a broken neck or leg. Or she'd head back for the path."

"Damn it, yes," Joey said. Holding onto a slender branch, he clambered down from the ledge and detected what could be a rough trail carved into the hillside, barely noticeable and overgrown with brush. A berry was on the ground, perhaps dropped by a bird. He knelt to examine what looked like the mulberries back home. Pushing his way through more brush, he checked the way for another fifty meters, but saw no sign that anyone had passed along the way—no broken branches, scattered leaves, or footprints. Below was a steeper drop, with more rocks than vegetation. They conducted a thorough search, and Joey was relieved about not finding Mita's body.

Joey couldn't imagine a reason for Mita to move far from her position, leaving her radio behind. Unless she had been abducted.

He climbed up to the ledge again. Pressing against the cliff wall, Dan looked out over the valley, checking for sign of movement in the area thick with forest, the river area, and the desert beyond. "It's odd she left the radio and gun behind," Joey said.

Dan shrugged. "She either dropped them in a hurry to get away— or someone took them away from her."

More than three hours had passed, and that could mean Mita was already miles away.

A black bulbul scolded him from a nearby bush stripped of berries. Hopping from branch to branch, the bird dipped its head, searching in vain for ripe fruit. Surely, there'd be signs of a struggle if Mita had been taken against her will. Frowning, Joey returned to the path and met with other searchers.

"Anything?" Cameron asked, and Joey shook his head.

"Maybe the gunfire was a diversion for taking her hostage?" Barnaby noted.

"She would have struggled and yelled." Joey shook his head. "There would be signs." Suddenly a sliver of hope went through him. "Maybe she went back to the path, and instead of heading toward the Humvee, she went ahead to the village." He turned and looked in that direction, studying the path for some sign.

"To the village?" Cameron questioned. "Alone? That would be crazy!"

"It's worth a look," Joey snapped. "Who wants to come?"

Dan nodded, and the two hurried away, leaving the others to keep searching for a body or a clue.

~~~~~

Sweating, visibly upset, the two men reached the village, entering its main gate without relaxing the grip on their weapons.

The villagers should understand—they couldn't have missed the earlier gunfire.

The midday sun was warm. The scene was peaceful. Men and women sat in their doorways, engaged in chores, chopping vegetables or cleaning tools. Children broke away from a game that involved jumping over a stick. A few recognized the Americans and smiled. No one reached for guns.

It wasn't the scene for a wounded sniper seeking treatment or kidnappers hiding their prey. There was also no indication of a surprise visit from a lone American woman. Joey felt ill and was anxious to get his questions out of the way. Even if Mita wasn't in the village, the villagers might have an idea about her location. "Did one of our colleagues, a woman, arrive this afternoon?" he questioned in Dari.

The adults looked at one another, genuinely blank, and shook their heads. Panic swept through Joey. It would have been so easy if she had somehow wandered into the village—totally against the rules, but a huge relief. He could only fear the worst had happened—and felt the urge to run back downhill to join the search, to order surveillance drones and search details to the valley.

Ahmed, Gul, and other men gathered at the village center under the trees. The group was puzzled, willing to hear him out. Joey had his answer. Laashekoh was not behind Mita's disappearance, yet Joey had to be patient if he wanted their help.

"Thank you for seeing us again." Joey tried to both hurry and be polite. "We were attacked as we approached the village—one of our colleagues, the woman with us before, is missing." The villagers seemed upset and groups started chattering in fast Dari. "Please, did she come here?"

"The little one?" Gul asked. Joey nodded, and Gul sternly looked around. The group shook their heads, looking at him with concern. There was no anger or hatred. Joey worried more. The villagers didn't have a clue.

"Did you hear the shots?" Joey asked.

"It wasn't us." Ahmed was firm.

Having no clue to her whereabouts was excruciating. Joey was tempted to rush off, return to the ground search, send in fresh pleas for an immediate delivery of high-tech tracking equipment that could help in scouting the region and finding any encampments. The earliest equipment could arrive was the following morning. He forced himself to stay calm and ask more questions.

"Do you know who would shoot at us?"

Ahmed paused a few seconds. "I can only guess. There are some who don't want Americans in this area. They're worried about foreign fighters. But we did not shoot anyone."

"Would they take the woman away?"

Ahmed looked at the men behind. All shook their heads. "We'd know if someone had kidnapped your woman," Ahmed replied.

She's a team leader, Joey wanted to scream. But he nodded and listened. There was no time for unnecessary comments. If anything, the villagers of Laashekoh represented the best chance of finding Mita.

"Could you check with others or help with the search?" Joey asked. "She's not part of the military. The only reason she's out here is to help with farming projects. It would be terrible if something happened to someone who only wants to help people in this area."

Ahmed frowned. "We would know." Again, he glanced at the group of men. Joey couldn't tell if one man or all were sending signals.

"I promise you, this woman would not hurt anyone." Joey came close to pleading with the group. "Please, let us know if you hear where she is. Anything."

"Of course," Ahmed assured him. "We can do that. This should not have happened near Laashekoh. If we hear, we'll send a messenger to your camp?"

"Thank you." Joey lowered his head, and closed his eyes. He couldn't think of more. He asked again if a few villagers would join the search. "You know this area better than we do."

"Our village cannot get involved in your fight," Ahmed said.

"I worry, too" Joey spoke softly, so they wouldn't take his words as a threat. "The fighting will be terrible if harm comes to that woman."

Another man spoke up from behind. "We will look for her in our own way."

Joey recognized the voice. It belonged to the stranger who had found Joey watching Laashekoh in the middle of the night. Joey made no other response than to nod with gratitude. Trying to hide his frustration, Joey gestured for Dan to exit the compound. Visiting the village was a waste of time. His priority was finding Mita.

CHAPTER 13

During this troubling time for our village, I preferred being alone, rising before dawn to do chores, making up excuses to spend time alone in the fields or hillside. I cautioned my sons to stay away from the visitors and any who defended them: *Then they can say nothing about you.*

The youngest shrugged. *They do not bother with us. The boys are not the problem.*

Only a fool expects such patterns to stay contained, I snapped. *Once these strangers chase the girls into hiding, they will have more time to watch you.*

That frightened the boy—better my sons feared the men than become their cohorts.

Taking a basket, I asked Saddiq to keep a close watch on his brothers, especially the youngest. *I'm collecting walnuts and their skins for making dye.*

Can we come, Mama? The youngest pleaded.

Not with those snakes poking around our village. Better I'm alone and make no noise.

I headed for the orchard early, when the men were prostrate with morning prayers. Quickly, I slipped behind the wall and hurried straight down the hill, ignoring the brambles catching at my oldest clothes. I waited behind a tall oak on the slope, tying my basket to my side, and patiently listening to make sure no one else wandered in the area. Not far from the wall, I ran across the main path that twisted its way to our village and descended downhill, directly into the tree cover draping the hillside.

It was exhilarating to dash down the smoother grades, holding my hands out like springs, catching myself against the tallest trees. Along steeper parts, I curled my toes, pressing my shoes into the soil and avoiding roots and rocks jutting out from the hillside.

Walnut trees near the village had already been stripped, but I knew of a healthy tree along a slope not far from the main path. The steep approach promised solitude and extra nuts. To get there, I had to walk downhill, then climb back up, and along the path, I searched for soft patches of dirt to quiet the noise of my footsteps and avoid alerting the visitors. I didn't worry much—few would choose the twisting, treacherous way to gather charmarghz, the four-brains.

Occasionally, I paused to listen. As long as the birds chattered, I was safe.

Before long, I took a detour around an exposed rocky area and moved through brush underneath the rocky ledges just below the path leading to our village.

So close to the path, I used every caution. Rather than roughly shove branches aside or break them, I avoided lifting them and bent low to move underneath. Along the ridge, I stayed close to trees, creeping slowly, so passersby would not spot my movements. I used both hands and feet to test sturdy branches or embedded rocks for support.

Ahead, I saw birds darting in and out of a large green tangle, and I approached to see what they were after. Mountain berries were hidden among the heart-shaped leaves. I picked gently, to avoid crushing the ripe, black beads.

Pleased to have found a treat for my children, I pushed my way deeper into the tangle, relishing the mottled light from the leaves shuddering in the breeze. The birds scolded as I plucked away.

Above me, a sudden burst of gunfire interrupted my solitude.

At first I almost dropped my basket and ran. But good thinking prevailed, and I crouched low along the ledge, pressing my back against the cliff. Unless the shooters climbed down this way, I was out of sight, out of the line of fire.

Above, a man shouted foreign words, abrupt and hard. The Americans had returned.

Terrified about getting caught, I forced myself to crawl slowly into the middle of the berry thicket. The shooting moved away from me. I had no choice but to wait for it to stop. Then I'd sneak away from a fight that had nothing to do with me.

A rustling sound could be heard from the footpath directly overhead, and I avoided the temptation to peak upward.

Suddenly, a body came crashing down the cliff, landing with a hard thump where I had stood picking berries only a few moments earlier.

Without thinking, I reached out and grasped a handful of cloth. Any wrong move and the person would have fallen from the precarious ledge, tumbling to the rocks far below. I didn't think that the person would panic, or attack and push me from the ledge. On my knees, I leaned over the pile of cloth covering a crumpled form, a person smaller than Saddiq. Pulling the cloth away from the head, I uncovered the American woman who had visited our village.

I swallowed, unable to decide which was worse, getting caught by my fellow villagers or by the foreigners. Looking upward, I thought about copying the birds that had long escaped—diving over the body and darting down the hillside, anything to get away.

Shots still fired, though farther away. Feeling sorry for the woman, I pulled her away from the edge, before gently lifting her head and examining her. She was groaning as if barely conscious. She wore a helmet and thick vest underneath her perahaan, but not the rest of the uniform worn by American soldiers.

The men had left her behind. As she moaned in pain, I wanted to protect her against the shooting or anyone chasing after her. I removed and smoothed the hair away from her face and rubbed my hand along her neck and arms to stir her blood flow. Underneath the vest, I felt a hard object—a gun.

I closed the vest and sat back, less sure about reviving her.

Not long after the shooting ended, shouts came from above. Cradling the woman, I pressed us both tight against the wall of the cliff. Shifting my foot, I accidentally knocked the helmet off the ledge, and it fell without sound in the brush below. I forced myself to take a deep breath, remembering that tree limbs and berry brambles shielded us from the men above.

Mita! Mita! Frantic men called over and over. *Mita!*

I remained quiet. Of course, I could not get involved. She may have had her own reasons for escaping them, I told myself.

Their efforts focused farther downhill along the path. I could hear shouts, branches being broken, and rocks rolling as they shoved aside brush. Once, they called from directly overhead, and my chest pounded. I closed my eyes.

If their calls had roused her, she could have decided whether it was safe to respond. I refused to turn an unconscious woman over to men I did not know or trust. Fortunately, the men did not spot us on the ledge. Like the shots earlier, the shouts became more distant.

Quiet returned to the hillside, and the only sound was that of two women breathing. Gently touching her skull, I felt a lump on the side of her head. But there was no bleeding.

She moaned again and stirred. I had so many questions, and she might know the answers. She could explain why the Americans were so interested in our fields and crops, and if fighting was going to start again in our valley and take my sons. Before Ali's death I would have fought to stay. Now, I'd find a way to talk Parsaa into leaving.

It was time to move the woman away from the ledge. I couldn't leave her alone and return to the village for help, not with Jahangir lurking around. Better to move her away from the precarious trail and find a secure, comfortable hiding place for her until she could assure me that she was safe and ready to leave.

A small box was strapped to a belt around the woman's waist, and it had a blinking light. And just like that blink of light, a selfish idea leaped into my head. Removing the box from the belt and the gun from underneath her vest, I left both on the ledge.

Maybe she knew if the Americans had any reason to kill my son— and maybe I could show her the paper I had found that horrible day. Maybe she knew how to read.

~~~~~

Not long after the shooting, the woman groggily shook her head and tried to stand. She was weak, and I encouraged her to lean against me even as she asked questions, a few Dari words mixed with her foreign tongue.

I put my finger to her lips. *We must get away*, I whispered. *There was shooting.*

Moving slowly, with my hand draped around her waist I guided her downhill, away from the ledge, the path, and another dangerous fall. Not far away was one of the many caves hidden underneath the mountains.

Unsure about how much to trust her, I didn't want to talk about myself. Oddly, though, the woman seemed to trust me and followed my directions like an obedient child.

Once in the smoother terrain of the valley, far from the roaming shooters, we tried talking. She knew a few Dari words, and we managed to exchange other details with gestures, facial expressions, and patience. She said the word *American*, and I understood. But she didn't understand after I tried to ask why she looked so much like the Indians who had once passed through our cities from the south.

Tofang. She pointed to her side. *You took my gun away.*

I left it behind—too heavy to carry.

Along the way, she paused a few times and looked backward. *Why do we walk away from the village?*

Your life is in danger. You must hide. Even if she didn't understand, she could not miss the warning. I stopped. My question was abrupt as we neared the cave. *Can you read?*

Puzzled, she shook her head. I cupped my hands as if they held the Koran, moving my head slowly back and forth. Still, she did not understand, so I cupped my left hand and bent my head, pointing a finger as though reading words. Excited, she nodded.

I hurried to explain how she must hide until the danger ended. *It won't be long.*

But how? The woman was unaccustomed to Dari, her phrases choppy with missing words. *Shots. I fell.* She asked what had happened to the men with her.

I hesitated, and then whispered. *They may be dead.* The woman choked back a cry. *We'll find out . . .* My promise was vague. Taking her by the hand, I led her toward the cave, with a narrow entrance accessible only to children or small women. The only clue to the opening was the sinkhole, obscured by years of falling rocks and spreading brush. Rolling aside the large rocks scattered in front, I then used my hand to brush away smaller rocks to clear the entrance. I pointed. *We can go in here and be safe.*

The American looked at me as if I were crazy.

All right, I'll go first. You follow. And I removed my perahaan to keep it free from dust, placing it inside the basket. I gestured for her to do the same before shoving the basket inside the tunnel.

Lying flat on my stomach, using my elbows to reach out and my toes to push against the walls and gain leverage, I entered the tunnel. Wriggling and pushing my way through the narrow space, I poked the basket ahead of me. Only one section was especially tight: There I stretched my arms completely forward and tucked my head, squirming with my hands, knees, and feet to guide my way through.

The cave's entrance was hardly the worst in our area. Some openings took terrible downhill slides, with tighter squeezes for longer stretches. In all, the tightest part of the tunnel, just barely accommodating my head and shoulders, was not long at all, about the length of three legs stretched end to end. After that tight portion, the tunnel expanded and dropped off to a smooth, sloping wall and a comfortable chamber where we could easily stand, sit, and talk without worrying about others catching us.

After wiggling my way through, I stood inside. Brushing the dust from my clothing, I poked my head back inside the tunnel section and called out to her, my voice echoing against the cave walls. *Come! You're so tiny you'll have no trouble.*

Slowly, she lowered herself and tucked her head into the tunnel, blocking most of the light entering the chamber. *Come,* I encouraged and stretched out my hand. A slight bend in the tunnel stopped her head, and I reached with my hand, guiding her to twist more to the left and tuck her chin tighter to her chest.

It took her about four times as long, but after a few groans, she stood next to me.

It's so dark, she whispered.

The next chamber has an opening and more light, I said. *Follow . . .*

The cave had smooth rocks for sitting. She pointed at her chest and said, *Mita*. I copied her gesture and said, *Sofi*. *Sofi*, she repeated and nodded. *Thank you, Sofi*.

Our hiding spot was dry, cool, and deserted, one in a chain of many long-forgotten caves used as hiding places during the Soviet invasion. A few were still used for contemplation during times of mourning, sickness, or anger, but this cave was small and inconvenient for people in our village, making it ideal for my purposes.

I checked around and saw no sign that anyone had used the space recently. The remains of an old fire pit were in the next section—dangerous because fires eat away the air in such enclosed places. The fire pit looked the same as it had during a previous visit, more than four seasons earlier. No one had been in the cave since my last visit.

The cave was nestled at the base of a cliff that blocked views of the Americans or villagers. The secluded cave would serve for a long stay, with a nearby small spring trickling from the side of the cliff, landing in a small pool behind an outcrop of rocks.

The American woman could hide indefinitely, as long as she was agreeable. *Wait inside here, and do not make noise*, I advised. *You'll be safe until I return with food.*

~~~~~

The visitors constantly scolded our women for stepping out in public, distracting the men, or gathering in groups of our own. So most of us stayed inside or wandered off alone to the fields. No one asked questions about my whereabouts.

Smiling, I handed my sons the basket half filled with berries, and ordered them to start an array of chores. After preparing my family's dinner, I crept back to the cave and the mysterious woman known as Mita.

As I walked back to the cave, carrying a small pack of food, I said earnest prayers that she was safe, that she had not tried to make her way back to her camp. I believed what I told her—with the visitors and soldiers, the area surrounding our village was no longer safe.

In a small pack, I carried cooked lamb, yogurt, fresh fruit, and a container of water that could be refilled at the spring. I also brought a notebook and pen. Outside the cave, I paused. The surrounding scene was so peaceful—the clearing with young trees, a magnificent view of a pleasing corner of the valley.

Bending toward the hole, I whispered. *Mita?* I felt trepidation but had no choice but to crawl inside. The cavern was dry, comfortable, with no occupant or sign of a struggle.

She had left, and I didn't know whether to be relieved or worried.

Opening the pack, I reached for a plum and took small, fast bites. What had I been thinking? That I could hide a woman without anyone finding out? That she might not have a family of her own and better things to do? There were so many rumors about American women— that they preferred prostitution to caring for families, they were bossy and abused, forced to do the work of men. Spending too much time with an American could only put me in danger.

I finished the plum, gnawing fibers from the pit, retrieved my pack, and pushed my way back to the open air.

Before pushing the pack outside, I peered outside to check for unwelcome surprises.

And there was Mita, not far from the opening to the cave, leaning against a tree. Weary and nervous, she stared toward the path leading to Laashekoh. I called out.

You're back. She smiled with relief.

With a meal for you. She wasn't anxious to escape, and I felt a thrill as I removed items from the pack, handing them to her. I also gave her soap, a tarp, and a blanket. It had been so long since I had tried to start a new friendship. Only the very young were new to Laashekoh.

Water never tasted so good, she said. Mita sank her teeth into a plum and smiled. *And this is the sweetest plum I'll ever eat. You are my Kabuliwala.* Uncertain about what she meant, I shook my head vigorously, but sensed a compliment and was pleased.

Where are we? Mita looked out over the view, pointed toward the Americans' camp, and asked another question.

I pretended not to understand and pointed to the meal.

Laashekoh? Is that where you're from? I nodded.

Anxiety replaced her happiness. *I need to get back*, Mita said. *The others will worry.*

You came to our village with men. Are you married to one of them?

She shook her head, and I bowed my head. *That's not good for you.*

She looked alarmed. *My Dari is not good.* She hurried to reassure me. *They're like brothers. Did the men come looking for me?*

I did not see them, I said. True, I had not seen the Americans, though Gul and the others were asking questions about the missing woman and an attack so close to our village. But they wouldn't ask the village's women. Men assumed that women didn't know about such matters. *It's best if you wait here awhile.*

Mita sighed. *I'm not sure what happened. There was shooting and then I fell.*

You need to rest.

She held her hands, pointing one finger as if holding a weapon. *Did you see who was shooting?*

I shook my head hard. *Until we know more, it's not safe for you to return.*

Mita frowned. *I worry my colleagues will blame your village.*

I thought a moment. The shooting had to come from Jahangir, and Parsaa and Gul would make it clear to the Americans that the man had nothing to do with Laashekoh. They might even force him to leave. *I don't think so. Our village won't like a shooting so close to the village. Only after we know what happened and why, only then will it be safe for you to return. Eat more while you can. And then we will figure out whom we can trust.*

She daintily used her fingers to scoop the lamb and yogurt and smiled. *Americans use . . .* She pointed three fingers downward and jabbed at the food, but I didn't understand. *I'm out of practice. . . . Do other villagers know that I'm here?*

No.

Not even your family?

I shook my head. *Men have strange ideas about what women shouldn't do. And there are other men watching our village.*

Your husband? She pressed.

He's not one of those men. It was embarrassing to admit how men controlled us.

She asked how many children I had and their ages. It didn't seem right to say I had four sons, and I included Ali in my count. *I'm lucky you helped me,* Mita said.

The warm food was gone and all that was left was more plums, apricots, and bread. I asked if she really was an American, and she nodded.

But you look like the people who live in the south and west.

Mita laughed. *My mother grew up in Bangladesh. I was born in America and went to school there. She's Muslim and so am I.*

Muslims in America? You hide your faith?

She laughed, and in awkward Dari, talked about Muslims mixing with others in villages, schools, and business. They worked as doctors, teachers, and bankers. It was hard to believe. *You like it there?*

Mita smiled. *Very much, it's open and free. People work hard and love the land.*

It's that way here, too. She looked startled and I explained. *We're free to grow what we want. We work hard, and our families are comfortable.*

Mita reached for an apricot, touching the soft skin with her fingertip. *What you grow is . . .* She held the golden fruit as if it were treasure. *Perfect.*

Perfect, I repeated the foreign word.

Mita laughed and added, *Exquisite.*

Ex-qui-site, I repeated. Confused, I pointed to the apricot. *Perfect? Or exquisite?*

No, apricot, she said, as if scolding herself, followed by another laugh. *What kind of English teacher starts with adjectives? A perfect apricot. The apricot is exquisite.* Then she explained that the apricot was good, or *khoob*. Stretching her arms out higher with each word, she repeated: *Good, perfect, exquisite. Ta-shar-koor.*

Understanding only her gratitude, I repeated the string of words.

The apricot is good. She smacked her lips. I laughed and repeated her sentence.

Yum. Mita returned to Dari and pointed at me. *You could teach others to farm. You could teach others how to grow these.*

I smiled and shrugged: *Everyone knows. It's not something to be taught.*

Mita explained that she had studied farming in school. *Only a few farmers grow such special fruit.*

It was my turn to laugh. She dropped the endings of some words, though I caught the words *farm* and *school*—ideas that did not necessarily go together for me. I didn't understand what she was trying to tell me. *Farmaan-bardaari?* I asked, but she didn't understand. I folded my hands and nodded slowly, mimicking one who showed obedience. *Baleh, baleh, baleh.* But Mita looked puzzled, too, and pointed to the apricot once more.

Only those who care can produce such beauty, she said. Her Dari was stilted, but the praise was sincere. I fought the pride surging inside. Caution was required for one regarded an enemy by so many in my village, even if she was a woman. Trust took time to grow. Fast sparks could destroy a friendship. Still, I was fascinated. I had never met anyone so different from myself and the other women I knew. We had heard rumors that American women tried to act like men, and this woman was assertive about what she knew. We'd heard that American women spoke too much, and I could recall never conversing so long with anyone in my village.

But nothing about the afternoon seemed wrong. I had an exotic creature to myself, and I wanted to ask my questions before she found the cave or me dreary.

She enjoyed talking about farming and schools. *In the school where you learned about farming, did you learn to read?*

That school was for farming and science, ilm va daanesh. We learned to read before that school. Then she said a string of words in English that I didn't understand at the time, but eventually became clear later, thanks to her gestures and odd mixture of English and Dari. For soil composition, she fingered a small handful of dirt; for genetics, she plucked two blue sage flowers, gently rubbing the insides together and then pointing to a group of flowers.

I had not expected such complicated ideas. *Do you read Dari?*

She frowned and explained how she spoke little Dari, but was picking up more every day. *Especially with you,* she added. *I read English and my mother's language, Bengali.*

Disappointment tore inside me, and she reached for my hand. *What is wrong?* I explained my desire to read and asked if she could teach the little that she knew. Rather than look sad, she eagerly offered suggestions: *We can study Dari together. Or, I could teach you English?* She pulled a small bundle of papers, lashed together, from a pocket.

A friend gave this to me before I traveled here, she explained. *I love wildflowers and he pulled together descriptions and photos of plants from an old Iranian field guide and added English translations.*

I studied the script. *It looks like Dari.*

It's Farsi. Dari and Farsi are close. And Bengali and Farsi rely on some of the same words. Why don't we see what we can do?

I sat by her side, and she pointed to photos, asking me to identify them. She showed me the words in English, and we located the Farsi words on the paper. From my studies of words in the Koran, I was pleased to discover that I already knew many words—*land, sun, green, branch, fruit,* and others.

You learn so quickly, she commented. *You must have been working on this for a long time.* I nodded, in a hurry to absorb more words.

CHAPTER 14

A helicopter buzzed overhead, moving fast over the mountains and desert in search of vehicles, camps, guards—any signs of insurgents guarding a captured woman. But the searchers did not look for a cave at the bottom of a cliff or two women huddled under a leafy tree with papers and notebook.

The first time Mita saw the searchers, she stood, using her hand to shield her eyes from the sun. *They're looking for me.*

I frowned. *Yes. But they're not alone. The men from the north planned to attack your outpost. This area has become very dangerous.*

But my friends must be worried. If there was a way to let them know . . . Perhaps if I gave a letter to you?

I cannot admit to seeing you. I'd be in grave danger. Mita frowned, and I hurried on. *No one knows where you're at, and this confuses the attackers from the north. It also is saving children. We must wait.*

I don't understand, she admitted, but she returned to her seat.

She handled time alone in the cave better than most women of my village would. She didn't complain about the food and spent most of her time writing in the notebook. She wore my clothing, but her skin was smooth, protected from sun and wind over the years, and so even from a long distance, she wouldn't pass for an Afghan woman. More than our differences though, we were surprised by how many interests and ideas we shared.

She sighed. *My parents will be frantic.*

You still see your parents? I asked.

I'm their only child. I must find some way to get back. Can you help?

When the time is right, I promised and took a deep breath. *The men from the north will leave soon. Then it will be safe to return.*

Mita was unsure but didn't argue. We resumed our lessons, and I vowed to bring her the finest fruit the next day.

There was truth in what I told Mita. The visitors from the north were close. As soon as the alarm was raised about a missing American woman, they appeared, climbing over the wall behind Mari's home and watching our men conclude evening prayers. The strangers stood back, guns in hand, not waiting for the men to finish.

Where is the American woman? one of Jahangir's men asked.

Our men stared at him in disbelief. *She's not here*, Ahmed insisted.

She didn't go far, Jahangir countered. *Not without help. Did you kill her?*

Of course not, Gul replied. *We assumed she was with you.*

We would not be here asking questions. Jahangir was impatient. *This disrupts our plans.*

Gul glared at him. *We have no plans that include the woman.*

The Americans will ask questions, Jahangir pressed.

They already have, Ahmed said. *And if it wasn't us and it wasn't you, then—*

They'll give up, Gul broke in.

The dogs won't give up! Jahangir paced back and forth. *You don't know them. They were headed to this village. Someone in this village must have seen something.*

We've told you all we know. Parsaa broke in, irritated. *We cannot keep watch over the unseen. The rest is Allah's will.*

That comment irritated Jahangir. One of the younger men handed him a mug with tea, and he flung it into the fire. *We must find her first. The Americans won't leave until she is found.*

We do what we can, Gul said cryptically

The Americans will blame Laashekoh. I promise. Jahangir pointed out that his own encampment would attract attention, and Gul begrudgingly gave permission for the group to camp inside the compound.

The strangers came and went as they pleased and could startle us at any moment, suddenly stepping out from behind a tree or climbing over a wall. Typically, they joined the conversations of our men and offered strong opinions, revealing that they had been listening all along.

Other women complained bitterly. The eyes of Jahangir and his men followed us as we worked the fields, retrieved water, or gathered wood. The men claimed to watch the Americans, but we were also targets of their scrutiny. They watched our children at play. Villagers remained quiet and kept to themselves, taking fewer breaks. Some made an elaborate show of their prayers. When the young laughed or spoke too loudly, older villagers scolded and reminded them of the strangers, taking nervous glances at the surrounding walls and trees.

These activities complicated my ability to move freely about the fields and into the hills or valley.

I spent long hours with Mita, careful about retrieving a pack that had been hidden in the orchard early in the day and leaving while the men were talking or praying. Every day, besides extra clothes and meals, I packed a few comforts for her, including knives, a brush, our finest soap with oils from nuts and spices.

I wanted her to stay a long time—though anxiety was a constant. At home, I worried about Mita, and in the cave, I worried about Parsaa and the children. So many were searching for her, and I worried about Jahangir finding her first.

All eyes were on the men in the village center, as I slipped out a rear doorway and headed for the orchard and the wall. I pulled my chaadar tight. If anyone asked, I'd simply say that I had work to do and that was under Allah's control. But with so many women staying out of sight, no one noticed my absences and I quickly became accustomed to the new patterns.

Hurrying away from Laashekoh, I should have worried more, thinking about the many difficulties associated with hiding Mita. But a deep gratitude pushed such thoughts aside. Allah had provided a way to stop Jahangir from moving children.

I was determined to keep it that way and wondered why others in my village were so complacent. Reading and talking with Mita had pushed me to question others' decisions to control or remain quiet.

She had changed my way of thinking, but not as others had long warned. Instead, I had more to think about. More opinions came from having more to compare, and too often we fear our preferences. People in our village constantly compared, assessing this day against the previous, one child with another child, one year's crop with that of the previous year. Our minds constantly assess, determining which ways work better and which do not. So much depends on the point of comparison. One person might prefer the sour taste of an unripe plum over the liquid sweetness that precedes decay. Others prefer laughter over serenity, contentment before perfection.

Those who prefer continuity avoid comparisons and regard any hint of choice as criticism. New interpretations from others might twist their own opinions in unknown ways.

Our village frowns upon too many opinions.

Reading expanded the meaning of words for me, empowering me to think on my own. When the Koran says, "the good women are therefore obedient, guarding the unseen as Allah has guarded," *obedient* takes on new meaning: Women can judge their own behavior. If husbands or fathers do wrong, if our men lie, steal, or kill—then of course we must ignore the men and obey Allah and the way we know is right.

I had no doubt that obeying a tyrant like Jahangir, his evil plans and ruthless control of others, is as much a crime as devising those plans. Jahangir and others had terrible reasons for insisting on dull obedience from women. Men do not want women to compare.

Comparisons can establish ideals or form the basis of sins like jealousy, greed, pride, or sloth. Religion can label an action as right or wrong, with adherents arguing the reasons for centuries.

Our daily routines influence how we hear another's words and view their behavior. There's no reason to fear comparisons and inquiries that come with good intentions. Mita said aloud what I had always known: Believers cannot fear the nonbelievers. Those who resist questions or comparisons lack true faith.

The Koran cautions that our time is brief and not to be wasted. Reading the Koran, studying its passages closely, made me more devout.

Distorting the Koran for evil purposes is more sinful than rejecting the book.

My village would ostracize me if I admitted to preferring some of Mita's ways. Yes, some American ways were better than ours. Learning is not evil. Refusing to acknowledge truths is evil. Developing my own thoughts is more valid than blindly quoting the thoughts of others. Examples are better than sermons for teaching.

Living in a small village, I must keep my comparisons to myself.

~~~~~~

With Mita hidden away, I planned my days with care. I didn't talk much, and my family and other villagers assumed that I remained distraught about Ali's death. Of course, I grieved. But my grief had ushered in a new purpose. I was determined to push myself to read and write, and a patient teacher lent efficiency and joy to the process. Every moment not spent on that task was a waste of time.

Our men kept an eye out, speculating about Mita, but they had no interest in taking time from other tasks for a search. My biggest worry was that Mita might wander away from the cave and encounter one of many searchers patrolling the area. She resented sitting in the cave for long periods and, when I arrived, often insisted on walking about, what she called stretching her legs.

Over and over, I cautioned that discovery would bring catastrophe for both her camp and my village. She promised to remain quiet, leave no signs, and stay close to trees, shielded by their canopy, while taking any steps beyond the cave.

Eventually a routine emerged, with us spending early mornings and late afternoons together. I slept less than half the night, adding to my irritability.

Of course, I longed to make excuses and hurry off to meet with Mita. But that would raise suspicions among Laashekoh women, and make me the subject of their gossip. To snatch extra time with Mita, I had to join others in noticeable ways and made a point of spending a few hours each day with Mari, Talibah, Karimah, and the others. We worked in the fields, prepared meals, washed clothes, or tended the children, and I was quiet, dependable, intent on not mentioning my new activities.

I was accustomed to keeping secrets about what I like to do. That way, no one knew what to take away from me.

As long as I showed no eagerness to escape for a secret task, the other women asked no questions.

~~~~~~

Every few days, when the sun was strong and the air dry, the women carried a load of clothing, bed linens, and rags to the river. Young girls and their mothers took more care with the textiles and colors, dipping the items carefully, while older women beat the clothes, ignoring fading patterns or worn spots.

The conversations could be as dreary as those clothes—women comparing thoughts about illnesses, quarrelsome children, cooking, and other chores. When the young girls were not around, the women whispered about how to conceive sons, prevent pregnancies, or keep men away altogether, fooling inconsiderate husbands into thinking a woman's time of month could last fourteen nights or more with the help of lamb's blood.

I hid my impatience for lessons, listening to the conversations, agreeing with others on innocuous details of cooking, planting, or weather. Most of my life had been spent in Laashekoh, yet still I felt out of place. My secret lessons alienated me even more.

We carried our clothes to the river, filling pots with water and then building a fire, letting the clothes soak until the water cooled. We stayed close, hoping the visitors would not scold such a large group. With the village under stress, the women whispered about the visitors and the Americans.

Even as we worked, noisy machines buzzed overhead, flying back and forth over the river, and Leila complained. *So much noise, when will it stop?* She was impatient because she and Mari had to wash clothes for Jahangir and his men, too. Of course, the rest of us pitched in.

Her willingness to talk prompted other women to open up about Jahangir and his group and plead for details.

Yesterday, dozens of men hunted for her along the lower path and river, Talibah added. *So close. They're not giving up.*

They don't believe us . . .

The visitors are convinced that the Americans are really after them. Mari shook her head.

The visitors are fools, muttered another.

All men are fools. Leila repeated an old and useless complaint.

Jahangir and his men want our men to join in fighting the infidels, Mari added.

The group mulled that disturbing news. As a teenager, my husband had fought in the final days of war against the Soviet invaders. In nearby villages, women a few years older than us had lost husbands in that war and were grateful for marriages as second or third wives. Bile seeped into my throat at the thought of my sons leaving to fight.

We did not want another war.

Jahangir says the Americans will demand food from us and not pay, Leila spoke up. *The strangers from the north promise to protect us.*

The Americans have paid us, Karimah snapped. *How do the strangers know more about what happens near our village than we do?*

Shhh, Mari cautioned. She and Leila stood, twisting and squeezing water from a heavy wool blanket, before carrying it to a nearby tree. Silence fell over the group. Mari was nervous and so was I, because listening to gossip could get any of us into trouble.

Methodically dipping clothing into a pool of flowing cold water, I let the others think of me as fearful or stupid. My fingers ached, gripping the heavy pieces and swirling them in the water, before lifting, wringing, and hanging them to dry.

Karimah dropped her voice to a whisper, so only a small group nearby could hear. *My son told me that Jahangir is looking for someone to send in for an attack. He wants to frighten the soldiers away.*

Why involve us? Talibah was alarmed. *He can send his own men.*

Karimah hushed the younger woman, glancing toward Mari and Leila. *My son could get in trouble.*

The whispering stopped as Mari and Leila returned from draping the blanket over the branches, so the sun could bake the moisture away. The two women wanted to talk more about the attacks. *Our village is closest to this outpost,* Leila began. *Jahangir says it's our responsibility to stop them.*

Hafa shook her head. *It makes sense to wait until the Americans bother us.* Just then, a helicopter buzzed low over the stream, with a deafening roar of spinning blades. The women stared at the noisy contraption, a reminder about how little our village controlled.

They aren't looking for the woman. Leila stood as if to confront the machines. She explained that her father didn't think the woman was missing. *It's a ruse. The Americans are watching us.*

Sometimes it's best to attack before being attacked, Mari added.

And Jahangir says it's better to attack while the Americans are new to the area. Leila smiled.

Talk is easy for those who have no sons to lose, Talibah said. Even as she spoke, the helicopter dipped around the nearby mountains and moved out of sight.

Mari flinched at the comment, but responded quickly. *War is hard for women, too,* she snapped. She was irritated and tired, too, and I sympathized with her. Jahangir and his men went to Gul's home for many meals and talked long into the night. Mari and Leila had undoubtedly overheard many plans.

Attacking the Americans is not all they want, Karimah spoke up. *Jahangir complains about us working in the fields. The strangers say the soldiers will take the girls away from us to work as slaves . . .* Her voice drifted off. She did not have to explain.

Jahangir should know, I thought to myself. Even proof would not save me from his wrath.

Do you think Jahangir knows where the American woman is at? Hafa whispered.

Mari glared. *He would tell us.*

Leila smiled. *The Americans could be hiding her to cause trouble.*

The conversation shifted to the American woman working with men so far away from her home. I was nervous as the others whispered about Mita, wondering if she had special powers. There was so much to learn from Mita, but I dared not hide her for much longer.

The clothes, including some worn by Mita, were rinsed clean. Taking a bundle at a time, I placed them on a large, smooth rock and pushed at them with my hands to press more water away, before carrying the pieces to the nearby trees.

Jahangir wanted to scare the Americans and make them go away, but it didn't work, Talibah warned. *They may blame us and attack our village.*

Jahangir promises that won't happen, Leila said.

The women and girls who finished quickly helped the others, so that we could return to the village together. As we gathered our piles, I fought my eagerness to hurry away from the village and meet the subject of the massive search.

The women disappeared into their homes, and once again it was easy to slip away. I had more secrets than friends, and sadness overwhelmed me that my closest friend would soon leave.

~~~~~

Mita's patience amazed me. Early on we talked about reading and agriculture. Our conversations—rushed and packed with words, a stilted combination of Dari and English—naturally tumbled toward history, religion, politics, health, markets, and something she called economics. We spoke about the differences between our cultures. My curiosity knew no bounds, and Mita gave like a gushing rain, so many drops of knowledge that could merge in ways I had never imagined.

She asked questions about my childhood and our daily life. She wanted to know about farming and religious practices, how children played, what women talked about, what families did with their free time. She asked how the village handled disturbances or crimes. She was curious for my opinions about the oddest characters in our village and how others regarded them.

She was shy about describing her parents and her home, and it seemed more fantasy than real. Her father was in the military and once flew planes. Everyone in the family had a vehicle and computer. Machines washed clothes, did dishes, and delivered water. Some mothers with young children stayed home and others went to work, but all could read. Her mother had a degree in math and taught at a university. After marriage, women and men visited parents often. Children, even the girls, traveled to other countries to study and stay with friends. Her family lived on a farm with horses that weren't used for work.

She was embarrassed by my eagerness to hear about such riches, and I wondered why the Americans came to Afghanistan. "To help," she said. "To counter the extremists who believe that freedom and the human spirit are a threat to Islam."

Mita never complained about the hiding place, and was grateful for the supplies I brought each day—ties for her hair, tools, a hairbrush. She was neither spoiled nor helpless as others claimed Americans to be.

Unlike others, she did not laugh about my fascination with composting and worms that made new soil and instead was excited about my idea to mix special rocks to speed the process. Together, we found a shady place underneath a berry bush and dug a deep hole with straight sides. Gently, we rescued worms that might get in the shovel's way and lined the hole with large rocks. We argued about which mixtures of leaves, grasses, or foodstuff might create the best compost for certain plants, and developed experiments to test which of us was right.

It made me sad to think that we might not have ever met—or never talk again. The power of chance and the pressures of time weighed heavily on us.

CHAPTER 15

Joey ached every time he returned to the outpost without Mita. He didn't want to eat or sleep or talk, though he knew that heading back provided a fresh start and resources. An elite search unit was dispatched to the base, and all agricultural work was postponed indefinitely, with resources diverted to the search.

Cameron had protested when Joey put a hold on MWDs—the dogs used for searches. "But her trail will go cold!"

"We tried the one, and there was nothing."

"You didn't take it into the village!"

"We know she's not in the village. We have plenty of equipment."

More people and equipment for searching didn't turn up any sign of Mita. At meetings, Cameron tried to dominate the discussions, insisting that Laashekoh was a problem and should be searched. Joey took no joy that others quickly shut him down.

"No one listens," Cameron complained, once they had returned to the bunk.

"It's obvious Laashekoh is not involved," Joey fired back.

"Mita should not have gone into Laashekoh." The tone was light, but the words hurt. "It was asking for trouble."

"She wanted to go," Joey replied.

"You should have known better. Her involvement turned an agriculture mission into conflict."

But there was no conflict. Joey packed gear to head out for another search in the night. He didn't need Cameron—he blamed himself for Mita going missing. Joey didn't care if Cameron thought he could run the team better. Ass-hats had their way of seeing the world and then wondered why others avoided them.

The trouble was Joey wasn't so sure she was abducted. No one else had raised that possibility, and none of the signs were there, but that didn't stop his worry. The rest of the team was sure that the project was jinxed. Joey had sent Mita's radio, Beretta, and helmet off for fingerprint testing. Not that the databases would include many fingerprints of rural Afghans.

All Joey could do was get away from the outpost and search.

~~~~~~

The outpost's headquarters had no offices, no dividers, yet Cameron took it upon himself to check Mita's desk for clues and then made it a habit to sit at the desk regularly. Joey was short with others who complained about Cameron going through her work and asking so many questions. "He's second-in-command on agriculture planning," he said.

Reports about Mita, the terrain, the search efforts were piling up. Search teams for Mita were still dispatched daily. The terrain was tough, but most trips covered old ground with hikes and flyovers. There were no more attacks. Others expressed surprise, but not Joey. The kidnapping wasn't typical.

Cameron and IT security accessed her computer files and e-mails, and found no hint of fears or anxiety. Her notes were professional and detailed, documenting the visits to Laashekoh and other villages, describing the region as resistant, yet full of potential. "An independent streak bodes well for women's rights, controlling extremism, and establishing agricultural markets," one of her draft reports noted.

Sifting through her notes, Cameron scoffed, "It doesn't sound like we went to the same village!" He was irritated when others did not share his point of view.

"The second visit went better than the first meeting," Joey maintained.

"And on the third, you lost Mita." Cameron's tone was matter-of-fact, not sarcastic.

Joey wanted to keep Cameron busy and didn't argue as the man typed in furious additions on Mita's notes: Mixed results were coming in from the fields. The villages were polite, accepting free seeds and small gadgets, but they refused large equipment, solar ovens, technical support—anything that signaled cooperation with the Americans. The program was not moving fast enough.

Joey advised Cameron to review Mita's notes with others. Joey also gave the go-ahead to Cameron on organizing a meeting with the ag specialists to discuss any factors even remotely related to her disappearance. But it quickly turned into a gripe session. "If this program gets up and running again, we need to change how we run projects and focus on crops that matter," Cameron drawled.

"The ag side of this program is on hold until we get Mita back," Dan snapped, furious that resources might be diverted away from the search for Mita. He turned to Joey. "I thought this was supposed to give us insights into Mita's thoughts? This is a waste of time." He slammed a notebook against the table and stormed out of the room.

"Fine—don't listen to the one person who warned everyone about Laashekoh," Cameron shouted to Dan's back. Joey slipped out of the room, too.

〜〜〜〜

As Joey headed off to prepare for yet another ground search, Dan stopped him. "What the hell was that about? Your job is to keep people like that on a leash."

"It's a circus," Joey admitted. Dan followed him on a path that led away from the structures. "But he's not all wrong."

"What do you mean?" Dan lowered his voice.

"He's annoying as hell. But someone should go through her notes. And we're just security. The generals like Mita's ideas today, but they're part of a revolving door. The next set could like Cameron's ideas. The specialists have to get their act together. Giving him free rein and a platform exposes the tension. We get an idea about who resents her or why she might want to get the hell out of here."

Dan lifted his eyebrows. "You don't think he had anything to do with her disappearance?"

"Honestly, no. But she wasn't snatched by the village. Maybe her vanishing has more to do with personnel here . . ."

Dan promised to keep his ears open. "But that clown spouting off—it's not good for morale."

"There's no morale here until we get her back," Joey conceded.

~~~~~~

Joey almost felt sorry for Cameron, trying to wrest control over the projects while few paid attention. The military strategy for this region, supporting and defending economic-development efforts, required a patience that the man lacked.

Mita had not explicitly complained about Cameron or anyone else. Rushing into the villages with projects that didn't improve daily life would not support the overall strategy. Cameron was a man with many defense mechanisms, yet was astounded when others pushed back. Joey didn't want to add to a pileup. He had to trust subordinates and get them to trust one another—despite the constant annoyances and bickering.

After dinner, Joey found Cameron leaning against the fence, looking out over his unfinished wheat plot under the stars. "I'm heading out to check the path and surrounding area again." Joey was blunt. "Did you find anything in her notes? Any reason Laashekoh or anyone on this team might have something to do with Mita?"

"Nothing," Cameron admitted. His voice was calm under the cover of darkness. He appreciated being consulted. "She liked the villagers. She enjoyed running the team. She has good ideas. But something odd's going on. I warned you. I warned her. You didn't listen."

"Cam, we're in a war zone. It has risks. If we backed away from villages like that, nothing would get done."

"They had their chance." Cameron crossed his arms. "They don't want improvements." Joey remained quiet, no point arguing until hearing him out.

"The people of that village remind me of insects mindlessly building mounds, living separate lives, eating, and reproducing with no thought for the future. They don't want help. They don't care about potential. And I resent it . . ." Joey couldn't see the man's face in the dark, but his voice was intense. There was no arguing with such bitterness.

"We're risking our lives, and they don't give a damn. Dan says I waste time? This whole mission is a waste of time. How do we proceed if we don't find Mita?"

Joey felt sick. He wasn't ready to think that way. "It's too soon . . ."

"What are you waiting for? You need to order a sweep of that village. Someone there knows something."

Joey shook his head. Such a search would kill relations before they began. Just what the extremists wanted. "Whoever's holding her could panic," Joey said. "It could end up getting her killed." And he wasn't sure she was being held. Attacks on foreign women in Afghanistan were rare, and there had been no ransom demand, no threats or attacks since.

"They're making us look like fools."

"That doesn't bother me," Joey insisted. "We can get more from them by being cordial."

Cameron laughed. "You're thinking like an American, not an Afghan."

Think like an Afghan, Joey thought to himself ruefully. That meant hitting Laashekoh hard.

Cameron went on as if he had read Joey's mind. "They'd attack, without waiting to find out who's at fault. They don't know what they want except to aggravate us."

Joey leaned his head against the wall. Cameron didn't realize it, but he triggered an idea. If Mita had been kidnapped, the kidnappers wanted something. Maybe someone wanted to panic Americans and Laashekoh. Maybe a warning about a village search could trick the kidnappers into revealing their location. So many "ifs" kept leaping to mind.

"That gives me an idea . . ." Joey surprised Cameron by thanking him and hurrying away.

~~~~~

The army wanted to keep the case of a missing aid worker low profile. Mita's father had made calls and asked that Major Pearson be kept on the investigation into his daughter's disappearance. A high-level representative from Central Command arrived for a status report on Mita's disappearance. While sympathetic to the outpost's dilemma, he wanted results. He offered resources, investigators, equipment, cash rewards. He expedited the fingerprint analysis. The radio, gun, and helmet carried Mita's prints. But two other prints were found that didn't match those of outpost personnel. "With a high-ridge density, the prints likely belong to a woman," the analyst's report noted. Most of the search team dismissed the finding as nothing special and assumed a woman had accompanied the kidnappers. Of course, Afghanistan did not have a central database for fingerprints. There was no way to make comparisons.

The outpost had plenty of support and nothing but dead leads.

No one said it aloud, but searching for a single human in the Afghan wilderness was an impossible task. Teams had searched the area around the path to Laashekoh repeatedly and agreed—she could not have gone far and survived in the remote area on her own.

Dan gave daily reports on area surveillance. "The chance of villagers holding her is slim. She would be too hard to hide there. She was probably moved the first day—and far away."

Cameron made a case for sending a unit to the village and tossing homes. "Too much time has passed," he insisted. "They're not cooperating."

"Antagonizing them won't help Mita," Dan insisted.

"It's the price of war," Cameron dismissed the concerns. "Someone in that village knows something."

"We'd find the weak link if we show them we're serious," Barnaby added. "Someone will talk."

Joey listened even though he had made up his mind about the next step. Forcing the village to submit to a search would end the mission.

Mita would be displeased by failure. Joey wondered if Cameron would be so adamant if the ag side of the mission had gone along with his wheat plans.

"Not yet. A rough search gives her captors an excuse to take it out on her." He didn't say that Mita would have wanted the mission to continue without her.

"She wants to get away and live, too," Cameron concluded. "How will we feel if we don't try a raid?"

~~~~~

Joey needed sleep, but anxiety took over. Restful sleep would not come until Mita was found.

He had few options left to try. The days were long, the searchers were frustrated. No ransom request had emerged. Mita had vanished from an access route between a river valley and an isolated village. Commanders had approved pushing the search out hundreds of kilometers away.

But she was near. Closing his eyes, he felt that. A generator fan whirled outside and played with his head, carrying a hint of Mita talking somewhere near. Since he was a child, he was sensitive to any background noise—the vibrations of insects, morning bird chatter, his mother's muttered prayers about sons who did not share her fears.

His parents did not believe in confronting fears. They told their children to forget much of what they learned in school. As a child, he checked library books out in secret, keeping them hidden in his desk in school. His mother despised Atwood, Bradbury, Ellison, Orwell, Twain, Shakespeare, anything with violence or sex and anything by blacks, Jews, or foreigners. She knew what Jesus wanted, and she didn't want her children wasting time by reading books she didn't understand.

He stayed after school to read. At night, alone in bed, he thought about what he read and imagined conversations with characters and authors. The refrigerator's motor, passing cars on a highway, pattering rain, any of these could transform into voices that cared what he thought. Later, he realized that it was a form of self-hypnosis to get through difficult times. The habit stuck, listening for sounds, imagining conversations that offered clues to his state of mind.

That night, he heard Mita, as if she were participating in an earnest lecture. He didn't catch all her words, but she was happy and hopeful. Hugging his pillow, he laughed and closed his eyes, then fell into a deep sleep. Mita was somewhere close and in good hands.

CHAPTER 16

To save paper and do drills, I had covered sand under the trees with a layer of dark soil. Typically Mita spoke quietly and I gave her my full attention, but today she was restless. We didn't hear the helicopters moving back and forth overhead. After scratching short sentences into the dirt, she leaned against a towering pine, hugging her knees. *Surely it must be safe for me to return to the base now.*

I was troubled that they had given up searching, but Mita was confident the search wasn't over. She warned that it had just entered another phase. *I'm afraid of what the soldiers might do.*

I was running out of time. If she wandered away or met with Americans, she would discover my lie. I could not help but frown. *The men from the north don't know who has you. It's the only reason they hold off from attacking the post.*

But the outpost could hide me, too, she countered. *And I could warn them.*

I shuddered. *Men watch Laashekoh and the outpost. We must wait for the right time.* Her restlessness did not help our lessons.

I brought something for you. And I reached into my old pack, handing over a gun, an old one that I had removed from Mari's house when she wasn't looking. If any of our men found the American woman, I didn't want her holding a weapon that belonged to Parsaa. Besides Gul had more pistols and rifles than he needed.

She held the pistol as if it were a dead animal. *Do I need this?*

Getting you back will have its dangers. We'll leave soon.

She smiled and that broke my heart. *I'll miss the lessons and talking with you. Promise me you'll keep on reading and writing—and not lose your skills.*

Nodding, I thought of all I needed to ask before she left. She had already taught me so much of what she remembered from classes—crop rotations, pest management, planting and harvesting techniques, composting, and the balance between food supply and population. I had learned new words in English, like *agronomy* and *management*, for tasks I already knew.

Embarrassed, I reached into the folds of my clothes for the document I had found long ago. *I must show you something.* She had admitted to not reading Dari well, but I handed over the piece of paper found hidden on our mountain.

Mita examined the stiff paper. *It looks like a blank government document.* She pointed. *That's the seal for Afghanistan, a garland around a mosque.*

And what does it mean?

I don't know. Maybe to mark a birth or death. The government uses these to track people.

That doesn't sound good. I frowned.

I'm not explaining it well. Birth certificates help with identification and enrolling children in schools and planning other services. Governments and parents have a copy the day a baby is born. Death certificates explain how and when a person died.

I was puzzled. People live and die without paper. Babies are born. They sleep and cry and eat whether they have a certificate or not. The old die. Family members remember as long as it matters. Such a paper could not have kept Ali alive. *Is it valuable?*

She studied the paper again. *Not really, only to the person to whom it belongs. And if they get lost, people can get replacements. You don't have one?*

I shook my head, taking the certificate from her and staring at it, wondering why a worthless certificate seemed so connected to Ali's death. Refolding it, I tucked it close to my heart, and thanked her.

There was much more to ask—about Ali, Jahangir, the caravan of children. But I didn't want her to think badly about our village and be afraid to return. Besides, no woman, not even an American, could do much on her own.

We'll leave in a few days, I repeated. *When the men of our village travel to the market. We cannot be too careful.*

She took both my hands and looked me in the eye. *I trust you with my life, Sofi.*

~~~~~~

The night was cool, the sun had set, and a fire glowed in the compound's center, turning slow movements into leaping shadows. After sharing the work of cooking a lamb dinner, the women cleaned pots, softly comparing how their children ate. The men laughed about a young chicken that had attached itself to a young boy, following him about. The men drank tea and talked, keeping an eye on the children not ready for sleep.

A stick snapped in the night and uneasiness swept over the camp. The men stopped talking and reached for their weapons. Barely visible in the firelight was a tall figure, in dark clothes, standing still near our stone wall. He could study us, but we could not read the emotions on his face.

Jahangir. Holding a container at arm's length, he slowly approached, a long shadow stretching behind. Fear was his way to catch our attention. I was grateful to sit far from the fire so he could not see my face.

Where is the American woman? he demanded.

She's not been found, Ahmed replied.

There has been no sign of her. Gul spoke quickly. *It's an excuse for Americans to move through this area. There's nothing to find.*

Dismissing Jahangir's concern was a mistake.

How can you be sure?

No one answered, and Jahangir held out the metal canister, pouring liquid in a circle beyond the edge of the fire. Hurrying, he splashed another circle around that one. Far from the fire, I caught a whiff of fuel, and anger mixed with fear. Men and boys moved away from the fire.

You don't understand the Americans, Jahangir said. *They don't care about land or the village. They'll get more anxious with every passing day.*

In their culture, the leaf matters more than the tree or the sky. They won't rest until they find her.

She's not here to find, Ahmed said. *There's nothing we can do.*

There is always more you can do, Jahangir scolded. He tossed the can low into the fire, and the nearest onlookers jumped away, trampling others sitting behind them. The flames flared high in the air, flashing out in circles. Mothers, horrified, hurried away with their children, several wailing. A few stared with fascination.

You must find her. Furious, Jahangir stepped back and took his anger out on the nearest object—one of the twin apricot trees that graced the center of our compound. Using both hands, he ripped off a limb and tossed the leafy branch into the fire, then he broke another.

My husband lunged, gripping Jahangir's forearm, his voice low and calm. *It's time you and your men leave this village. We will take care of the Americans.*

Jahangir looked at my husband with disdain. *This is how you treat a traveler who has offered his assistance?*

Parsaa placed his hand on the apricot tree and didn't respond.

I do this to show you what the Americans intend for our country. They've been in this country for years, and what have they accomplished? Jahangir turned to the other men and spoke as if preaching. *Their women run away. When they leave, the chaos will end.*

Parsaa did not flinch. *We'll give you what you need to move on. We can handle them and do not want to trouble you.* I cringed. A volatile man who trafficked in children could make any wild request. None of us wanted to contribute food or daughters to the brutal man's cause.

We need nothing from this village, Jahangir said with scorn. *Be sure the others want us to leave.* With a smile, he stalked away.

The men were annoyed. The village of Laashekoh resented interference, whether it came from Jahangir or the Americans, and Jahangir sensed our resentment.

Leaning against my doorway, I was sickened by the broken tree, no longer graceful and full like its twin. It would be a permanent reminder for our village of a brutal man who could not appreciate beauty and sustenance.

Taking anger out on plants that belonged to an entire community was a sign of weakness, and I wondered if the man would really leave. If he didn't and presented unpleasant bargains, the villagers would eventually resent Parsaa, too.

Alone, I retrieved the broken limb, its leaves already wilting. Snapping the branches into smaller pieces, I arranged them crisscross on the compost pile, so that their death could someday nourish seeds of other fruit.

~~~~~~~

Because of the lessons with Mita, I missed the morning's whispers. Soon after Parsaa demanded that the visitors leave the village, Jahangir had met with Gul and proposed taking Leila as a bride. He offered plenty of money, horses, and blankets—far more than men in neighboring villages could afford—and then he took off. The marriage would take place after his return in a week or two.

The news bothered me. Mari, a good friend, wanted what was best for her daughter, and I had not forgotten Jahangir's cruelties with moving children in the middle of the night. No one would believe me though, and I still had not described the scene for anyone, including Parsaa or Mita. I could not admit to following Gul to Jahangir, or taking care of Mita in a cave. That would end my freedoms. I could go as I pleased, as long as I moved in secret.

Parsaa was angry but refused to talk about Jahangir. Other women murmured about the arrangement, describing it as a mistake—but not around Leila or Mari. The biggest obstacle, according to the whisperers, was that Jahangir belonged to no village. Young, beautiful women were safer in small villages.

Later that night, when the children and my husband were asleep, I heard low voices, and slipped out my back entrance to listen. Mari and Gul argued. To my surprise, Mari favored the marriage.

The girl doesn't know what she's getting into, Gul complained. *She won't be safe with that band of men.*

He promises a comfortable life, Mari said.

There's still time to find another prospect, one who lives closer.

Hah! Mari snapped. *There is no time! You heard Jahangir—when others hear about his choice, there will be no other offers.*

I thought you wanted her to stay here, Gul countered.

There was a long pause, so long I thought the couple must have walked away. But then Mari spoke eagerly. *We have no son. Jahangir has no village. Why can't he stay here?*

Gul heaved a sigh. *But the others . . .*

I don't care, Mari insisted. *Jahangir is young, strong. He can help this village. Those who deny that are jealous!*

I'm not sure he can abide by our rules and ways of doing business. Gul's voice shook with hesitation. *How dare he complain that she's old? That she is spoiled and soft?*

Men don't say what they mean, Mari noted. *We can't miss an opportunity . . .*

He should be grateful, not telling us, her parents, what to do! And how do we convince the rest of our village that it's a good idea? His voice dropped low and I could not hear their murmurs. *I hope you know what you're doing*, Gul warned. *He means it when he says he doesn't want American eyes on her.*

She has no objections. Mari was frantic for Leila's marriage, and I wondered if the girl knew about her mother's promises. *She can handle Jahangir.*

I regret doing business with the man. He's not the best husband for my daughter.

Hush, Mari interrupted. *The children will hear. Not so long ago, you were worried about her not finding a husband . . .*

I'm less certain that a terrible husband is better than no husband at all.

You're not a woman. Mari spoke so softly, I had to press my ear to the wall.

You mistake his volatility for strength.

Leila is clever . . .

She may be able to manipulate me or other village men. She doesn't know about men like Jahangir.

Be jahanam! Mari retorted.

I heard running and a slamming sound.

Left alone, Gul sighed and spoke to himself. *It's why women should not be included in these negotiations.*

~~~~~

A piercing shriek broke the night, and my youngest boy clutched me tight. I stroked his hair and pressed close against my husband's side. *No!* came shrieks of one or more women. *No, no, no.*

I sat up and heard scuffling noises, followed by sounds of sobbing, splashing water, and running footsteps. Parsaa was awake, but still. *Do something*, I urged. Without a word, he stumbled from our bed and went to the doorway to peer into the darkness.

Stay here, I ordered the youngest and joined Parsaa. The moon was not out, silence mixed with complete darkness, as if the screams had never happened. Not even the light from a tiny candle pierced the night. Still, Parsaa waited.

Other men must have done the same throughout the village, and maybe some other women, too. *It was close*, I whispered.

Leila and Mari, Parsaa replied, his voice flat.

I urged him to check on them, but he did not respond.

And apparently no one else responded, as silence took over the village, replacing the screams. In our village, it's rude to interfere with, let alone witness, the problems of other families.

The youngest whimpered, and I returned to the bed, pulling a cover over our heads, a poor attempt to chase away worries. The silence remained unbroken, yet Parsaa waited by the window. My thoughts refused to give way to sleep.

~~~~~

No one talked about the burst of screams that erupted in the middle of the night. Living in a small village, we knew that we'd learn the reasons soon enough. Often, only parts of the story made it through the village. Complete stories were disturbing.

Later that morning, I saw Leila. Once the most beautiful in our village, she was burned, the right side of her face raw and red. Her chaadar was draped loosely, defiantly, as she made no attempt to cover the horrible mark. Mari's eyes seethed, watching the other women gather to walk to the river for washing clothes.

More than one woman touched their forehead, lips, and heart, with quick prayers asking for Allah's mercy. Many looked away and then returned their stares. The wounds, horrible to our eyes, had to be painful.

She didn't deserve this, Mari hissed. *None of us deserve this.*

Standing under the trees, most of us stood frozen, mouths gaping. It was impossible to proceed with daily affairs. I panicked, my insides churning, selfishly wondering how to escape for my next meeting with Mita.

Only a few dared talk about the travesty. *Auntie, what happened?* asked one woman.

Mari explained that a masked man entered the home in the middle of the night, as the family slept, and tossed acid onto the girl's bed. *She did not turn away suitors, she didn't insult any men.* Mari started to sob and reached out, tugging at her daughter's scarf. Leila tossed her head and slapped her mother's hand away.

I wasn't alone wondering if Jahangir was insulted by Gul's hesitation in accepting the marriage proposal. Or was someone else upset that Jahangir had asked? One of Jahangir's men?

One cannot invite Shaitan and not expect attack.

As was her way, Mari blamed the Americans. Sobbing, she shoved to escape the crowd, pulling her daughter back inside their home. We stood in silence, listening to Mari's cries.

Many wanted to think of the culprit as a stranger to our village. But how would a stranger know the exact location of the girl's home and bed, without alerting the mother, father, or others in the village?

Our village was new to such an attack, and the women were terrified. Carrying rugs to beat, an excuse to talk, we moved quickly to the
water, an open area with no walls or trees to hide curious ears waiting
for our reactions. The youngest girls, terrified, huddled close to their
mothers or sisters.

Our group diverged along two lines—one set wanting retribution,
and the other hoping to forget the night and shove it into the past.

Will the men do something? One woman asked, not addressing any
of us in particular.

What can they do?

Mari doesn't know the attacker, retorted another woman.

Besides, the girl is still alive, said Karimah.

The injury could have been worse, said Talibah, whose younger sister
had suffered a similar attack long ago in another village. *They put cold
water on it quickly and stopped the damage. Praise Allah.*

The rest of us automatically repeated praise for Allah, while pri-
vately wondering why a powerful being could allow such attacks to
happen.

*It's odd how a stranger could quickly make his way through the house
and find his target*, offered Hafa.

He may have had help, said another.

Who in our village would help with such a vicious attack? Talibah
exclaimed.

Hafa stared at the group of women, and even Karimah, pounding a
small rug against a large smooth rock, lifted her head. *Perhaps someone
in her family did not want her to marry*, Hafa murmured.

Nervous about the direction of the conversation, we moved our
hands quickly, tightening our grips on the rugs, beating away dust,
anger, and fear.

A father would attack his own daughter? Talibah countered, after a
few moments of vicious pounding on one large rug.

Hafa shrugged. *How else to prevent a marriage to someone he
despises? To someone in need of a home.* She looked around at the circle
of women, challenging us to contradict her.

I thought about Mari and Gul arguing in the night. Jahangir had no reason to be angry with Gul just yet. The family had not refused him. But Gul had every reason to prevent his daughter from marrying an angry nomad who brought criminal activity close to the village late at night.

Of course, all of us expected Jahangir to withdraw his marriage request. *She'll find someone else*, Talibah said. *Some men don't mind scars.*

It's better for a woman to find a man who doesn't mind a scar than live with a man who despises her beauty, Hafa conceded.

Quietly, we pondered these thoughts. Villages and parents struggled to protect their children from evil. Women were covered, separated, guarded, and reprimanded for protection. Some may scorn Leila and Mari, blaming them, casting the scars as punishment from Allah. Evil was random. All parents could do was embrace a child after the harm was done.

The conversation drifted away from Leila, about other villages and attacks on women, the reactions from fathers. . . . Someone called out my name, asking about my father. The question stabbed me and I shook my head, pounding at the rugs with all my strength.

~~~~~~

My father had delivered me to Laashekoh years ago. I lost exact count. My mother and the other women in the family dressed me in colorful clothes and arranged my hair with a pretty veil saved for my special day. The family laughed and cheered, praising my strength, disposition, and good fortune.

I was the oldest of my siblings, and the memories feel odd with every passing year as my parents remain young and healthy. During that happy celebration, it had never occurred to me that it would be my last memory of them.

With tears in her eyes, my mother embraced me and my father lifted me gently to our donkey. The younger children danced and waved, and I waved in return as my father and I set off on a grand adventure.

At some point during the trip, my father assured me that I was one of the lucky ones, moving on to a village with good farmland. My male cousin was only six years older and his family promised that they would wait at least a few months before we began our life together or thought about having children. And I smiled with joy because time with my father was all that mattered to me.

The trip took more than two full days, with only a few stops. The last stop was not far from the tight trio of mountains my father had pointed to as our destination. Always thoughtful, he chose the beautiful scene as a place to sit, drink water, and have one last talk alone.

I have something to give you, and you must tuck it away until you can find the right place for planting. He pulled a package from his pocket and slowly unwrapped it. *These are yours, to remind you of home.*

Inside were tiny corms that burst into the flowers and cloaked a nearby hill in purple every autumn. With every year, the cloak expanded, as my parents dug up the green strands and separated the corms, spreading them into other nooks. In the fall, the children helped my mother pluck the golden threads from delicate blossoms that emerged only for a day. I accepted the packet and should have been delighted. But I sensed a serious break in the life I had always known. There was no talk of my returning home, and I dreaded not seeing the cloak of purple near my home again.

My father put his hand to my chin and gave directions: *They're not many, and they are our secret. Tuck them in your bundle. That's a good girl. Keep them until you find a good place away from other people. Plant them wisely, and remember how we took care of them together as a family.*

Dread of the future filled me, and I could not speak.

The family we are meeting. They are kind people. In a few years the threads will help your family.

Then he followed my mother's directions, smoothing my hair, brushing dust away from the shalwar, adjusting my chaadar. My happiness returned, and I smiled at him, because fathers did not typically bother with such details. As he returned me to the donkey, tears showed in his eyes. At that moment, I hoped he might change his mind and decide to take me home. But with nothing more to say, we continued on our way.

As we rode into the village, the donkey was weary, and my father was quiet. We stopped at a large house, and women immediately pulled me inside and covered me in new clothes that were big, soft, and warm. Someone showed me the kitchen where I would work and the bed that I'd share with my cousin's sisters.

Shhh, one of the younger girls whispered and pulled me close to the window where we could watch my father talking with her father and Parsaa's, too. My father handed over some bills and a bundle of embroidered sashes, in the fiery colors of gold, orange, red. The two men held each other's shoulders and kissed.

She's a good girl, my father said, *the most intelligent of my children, and you know me well enough that this praise is not false.* I had never heard my father express such an opinion before and dipped my head to hide my pride.

Parsaa's father offered mutual assurances. *She'll be a great help. The other women in the village will help her get settled.*

I must leave before sunrise. Should I say farewell to her tonight?

Let us explain, the older man said. *She is with the other girls, so why upset her? She fits in well already and will forget her old life soon enough.* Upset, my father looked toward the house, but did not see us peering into the dark. *You're young.* Parsaa's father laughed and put a hand to my father's shoulder. *This is your first daughter. The other men in your village should have warned you.*

Pressing my hands against the mud and rock walls, I yearned for my father to change his mind, furious he didn't retort that his daughter would never forget. But he nodded slowly and walked away, the sweet donkey nudging at his shoulder. To think I'd never pat that animal's head again or chase our chickens or sit at my mother's feet stung at me. I wondered if the donkey would forget about me, too. Would my father ride home, and forget, enjoying life with my mother and younger brothers and sisters?

I could not help feeling resentment, but turned to my new friend, pretending not to care. Girls had always left our village, and the boys stayed. That was the village's custom, and I knew that I would not have this friend for long.

At that moment, I realized that the men had no more control than the women do.

CHAPTER 17

Joey climbed the hill to the village directly up the mountain, through the forest, avoiding the footpath. As he approached the compound walls, he waited among the trees and listened. The place was quiet, no sounds of animals or children pestering for attention and food. Mita was resourceful—she'd find a way to make noise if she were awaiting rescue somewhere inside the walls.

He wondered how a group of people lived with such quiet. Perhaps they knew that he was approaching and waited for him.

He couldn't rest since Mita's disappearance and couldn't bear the growing despondence among the team's members. So he conducted his own searches, checking on Laashekoh and other villages. He heard plenty of conversations, none about the missing American woman.

Joey doubted that, since going missing, Mita had passed through this village. If she had, she'd been moved long ago. Air patrols hunted for signs of movement in the region every day that weather allowed—and patrols stopped every truck and caravan. None included the woman.

He crept toward the stone wall and dislodged a rock to observe the goings-on and listen to voices before entering the village gate. He had nothing better to do.

A woman suddenly emerged from the woods on the far side of the orchard. Nervous, she looked around, not wanting to be seen. Then she slipped through some brush near the stone wall. She tossed her basket over the wall, and then hoisted herself. She pulled what looked like a pile of clothing from the basket and hid it in the tall grass, before reaching for a rake.

Standing on her tiptoes, she aimed high, combing the branches of a stone pine, bringing cones to the ground. She worked at a furious pace, and it wasn't long before she returned the clothes to the basket and covered them with cones. Another woman approached the stand of trees. "There you are," the older woman called out. "Your sons are waiting for you."

"Ahh," the other woman responded, as she tossed more cones into the basket. "Saddiq was supposed to watch his younger brothers."

"Hah!" exclaimed the other woman. "He said he talked with you. Jahangir is returning today with horses, and he promised to teach the boys to ride. The older ones went to the river to meet him. The younger ones are at my house." She shook her head, critical of a mother who did not know the location of her children.

The younger woman looked startled, but she moved swiftly without break. "If you'd like pine nuts, bring another basket. The boys will strip the cones." Not one mention of the woman returning from a walk in the woods, with a bundle of clothes—the older woman either hadn't seen or didn't care.

A thrill went through Joey. He slowly backed away and headed downhill for the regular path, so that he could enter the village properly.

~~~~~

The American soldier came alone to our village. Once again, he sat for tea and put his gun aside, and again he waited politely, not pressing with demands. Speaking Dari, he listened more than he talked. Parsaa, Ahmed, Gul, and the other men appreciated that he was patient despite his obvious desperation and fatigue.

Eventually they asked the purpose of his visit. He asked if they had heard reports on Mita's whereabouts.

Nothing, Ahmed said with a frown. He glanced at Gul and Parsaa, who signaled for the younger man to explain. Ahmed lowered his voice, *Some in this area are annoyed about the search. They assume we helped her move.* Ahmed, sincere, held out his hands helplessly. *But that's not true. I wish we could help.*

You can help. The soldier looked distraught for a moment and closed his eyes, before repeating, *You can help.* He surprised our men by asking them to gather as many villagers as possible to discuss the disappearance of the American woman. *Some Americans are getting angry and want a search that will disturb your village. I need to find her soon.*

Men and women? Gul questioned. The man nodded. *As many as possible*, the American replied earnestly.

Gul nodded, and the boys called all the villagers they could find to the courtyard, to gather around the American.

Nearly eighty people gathered. The soldier's message would travel quickly. I stood back, but sensed the man's eyes bouncing about, and his gaze landed on me more than I liked. The soldier was sure that one of us knew Mita's whereabouts. He wanted to find her, and I was determined not to feel sorry for him. I moved closer to Mari, using her as a shield, as the soldier spoke of concern for the missing woman and a need to protect the village from false accusations from the Americans or others.

She may have formed a friendship with one of you, the man said.

I avoided looking at him and instead glanced at Parsaa. His suspicious stare, already directed my way, was enough to twist my stomach. Keeping my face blank, I looked downward. When I checked again, Parsaa had returned his attention back to the soldier, who spoke about Mita's generosity, tireless work in agriculture, and other qualities that I had discovered firsthand.

Standing next to me, Mari was agitated, shaking, as Leila slowly approached the gathering, and this attracted the soldier's attention. Since the accident, Mari had been seething, ready to explode—storming away from any conversation that focused on concerns other than her daughter's mistreatment. Gul tried to convince her to forget the attack, but nothing else mattered for her. Mari was furious with all men.

The soldier stumbled and stopped speaking altogether.

Leila's head cover was loose, and lovely dark curls swirled from underneath, a smooth frame that contrasted with her face—one side showed raw burns and pus, her left eye and mouth twisted into a gruesome grimace; the other side was flawless and smooth like cream and bore a trace of a smile. The memory of her beauty seared.

What happened? The soldier gasped.

An attack, Mari blurted out. *In our home.*

Here? He looked around at the group as though expecting to see a monster. He stood alone in a world he didn't understand. A stranger's fresh wound distracted him from the hunt for Mita. *Who would do such a thing?*

We'll find out, Mari snapped.

The man sighed, staring at Leila with sympathy and guilt. *We, we . . . the doctors at our camp could examine your wound. Or we can send the doctor here, though it's better if you and family members travel to a base with equipment. We can make arrangements.*

The offer intrigued Leila, but Mari blasted the soldier.

To fix? Scowling, Mari looked around at the other villagers and spat her words. *There would be no scars to fix if the Americans were not here.*

Suddenly, Jahangir stormed into the courtyard, followed by a group of our boys, demanding to know why the crowd had gathered. He spotted Mari and Leila with the soldier. *Why does my wife-to-be stand before this man?*

Leila turned slowly, and Jahangir was visibly startled. Approaching her, he reached for her chin to examine the damage. His puzzlement was genuine. He had not seen the disfigurement before. She bowed her head, and Mari hurried her back to their home. The man turned to Gul and roared. *You allow this? You parade your women before a dog? Allah punishes you with a daughter whose face is ruined!* Gul was rattled, as though he had been slapped.

The soldier stood and responded in near-perfect Dari. *A dog wouldn't offer medical care.*

Jahangir recovered immediately and lowered his voice. *Understand, our custom does not allow our women to associate with strange men, foreigners or Afghans.* Jahangir's voice was smooth, but the soldier did not relax. *Why are you in Laashekoh?*

I'm searching for a woman who went missing near here.

If she was near, we'd know. She must be dead.

There would be a body, the soldier countered. *Others are losing patience, the searches will become more intense.*

Jahangir laughed. *Do not test our patience. Your women would be safe if they stayed at home.*

Safe. The frustrated American pointed to the door where Leila had disappeared. *Like her?*

Jahangir's eyes flashed. *The men of this village don't do their duty. Women*—he waved his hand. *They are unpredictable and best kept at home, unless they're under the close supervision of a husband or father.* He looked around, expecting support from the others. But Parsaa and the other men frowned about Jahangir taking over the conversation with the foreigner. Most women slipped away to escape judgment. As the two men argued in Dari, my curiosity melted away and I lost the thread of the conversation—until Jahangir turned to my son Saddiq and asked him to bring drinking water. The boy raced to our home, and my stomach turned. The man knew Parsaa's weakness.

Shaking, I backed away, joining Mari behind her wall and started to whisper, but she shook her head in a daze.

I must think, she snapped, not bothering to keep her voice down. *Leave me alone!*

Embarrassed, I took the rear path to my home and realized Mari fretted about Jahangir's reaction to the scar. The man was ruthless, but he was truly surprised by Leila's face. He had every reason to back away from the marriage agreement. Yet from all appearances, he did not loathe his bride-to-be. Mari had reasons to worry, but the family might not suffer the embarrassment of a marriage partner changing his mind.

I glanced out on the scene. Our men, especially Gul, were troubled. Scolding the American, Jahangir talked not like a newcomer, but as if he controlled the territory surrounding our village. Our village was helpless.

The humiliation and anxiety of men are dangerous for women. For their own reasons, Jahangir and the Americans would monitor movements near our village. I had to return Mita to her outpost soon.

~~~~~~

Usually he sat for these meetings, but this time he remained standing, arms crossed, mouth set. Joey defended the villages at the team meeting, but kept it to himself that he suspected a woman in Laashekoh was hiding Mita and caring for her. He wondered if Mita could walk away and hoped that he wasn't taking a reckless chance.

He wanted to keep his people away from Laashekoh, and he knew only one way. "We're postponing the search," Joey announced. "We're pulling back on the pressure."

Except for the members of the elite search unit, the room went into an uproar. "One week," he added. But no one heard the last part.

Questions came fast. "What reports are you getting from the field?" "Won't they pull the search unit if you don't use it?"

"What about Mita?" Dan asked, upset.

Joey held his hands up for silence and referred the questions to the unit leader, another Army Ranger. The man explained that a group of extremists were moving through the area.

"They're all extremists!" Cameron interrupted.

The unit's captain kept going as if Cameron had not spoken, explaining that most of the people just wanted to raise their families, grow some crops, not get involved with criminal activities and regional or national politics. He chose his words carefully. "The villages are struggling over whom to trust. If we relieve the pressure, we might get her back."

"We need to hit them hard!" Cameron exclaimed. "Now, or risk not seeing Mita again."

"We're monitoring the movements of the extremists," Joey reported. The room broke out in nervous chatter and questions, especially among the civilians, as if an electric switch went on. He waited for the room to go silent. "The villages in this area are small," he continued. "Hitting hard would endanger civilians and Mita. They're taking advantage of the divisions and actively working against us in these villages. Our surveillance will continue."

Joey didn't go into detail, but the team assumed any search parties were at risk for immediate danger.

"How close are they to the outpost?" Barnaby asked.

"They're near the villages, trying to gather support for an attack. We don't want to give the villagers any reason to join."

"Extremists are moving in and we're letting Mita down," Cameron said, glancing at the search specialists, who reported daily to commanders in contact with Mita's father. "That's how I see it."

Joey was ready. "This delay's been approved from above."

"Doesn't matter if she's already dead." The comment came from the back of the room.

"We didn't use dogs. We didn't do a raid." Cameron's tone was patronizing. "Joey, these extremists have to be working hand in hand with the villages."

"Too many raids end up with a dead prisoner," Joey fired back. "No raid until we have a location. And for now, we know she's nowhere near Laashekoh." He crossed the room, lowered his voice, and addressed the rest of the group. "The villages are divided, assessing us and comparing us with the extremists. It's not the time for a raid."

"The villages better decide which side they want to be on." Cameron shook his head. "We're losing valuable time."

"The delay is one week," one of the specialists repeated. "After that we look at other options."

CHAPTER 18

Between visits to the fields or cave, while waiting for bread to bake or rice to boil, every free moment, I sat near the fireplace and opened my husband's Koran to practice reading. *Practice daily*, Mita had urged, and I followed her advice. Murmuring the words aloud, I didn't hear the cruel winds whip the trees outside until the door burst open and Saddiq entered, pushing his younger brothers inside.

I closed the book quickly and stood, returning it to its special shelf. The younger boys did not notice, but Saddiq gave me a strange look.

When did you return? He held the door open. *Father was looking for you.* Outside, the wind was accusing, whipping up whirls of dust that looked copper in the sun's glare. Stalks of grain were beaten flat. Mita was all right, I thought to myself. She never went far from the cave.

I needed solace. Without another word, I poured the boys warm tea.

The wind kept us inside. The house was well stocked with wood and water, and a stew bubbled on the fire. The children were quiet, waiting for their father to return and sit for the evening meal. I took the youngest into my arms and rocked him, using this as an excuse to relax, to be a mother, to present an image that might counter whatever Saddiq might tell Parsaa.

When my husband entered, my ability to control the children vanished. The four turned full attention and questions on Parsaa. He avoided looking at me or speaking, and without a word, I stood by and piled his outer garments by the doorway, where they would wait until the winds died down and I could shake them outside.

I quietly went about my tasks for preparing dinner, occasionally glancing his way, trying to discern his mood. I added more wood to the fire and flames teased the sides of the large pot of stew. As I stirred rapidly, Parsaa moved close, grasping my elbow and bending his head toward my shoulder.

The time for mourning has ended. The children need you. Parsaa's voice was so low, I wasn't sure I heard all his words. His tone was cold, firm, as if he had to deal with a stranger. He quickly turned before I could respond. He knelt on the floor, wrapping his arms around the three younger boys as they demanded a story.

Only Saddiq was quiet, so serious, glancing back and forth between us, studying our reactions. I wondered if he'd mention finding his mother looking through the Koran, if my husband would think of such behavior as strange or evil.

Since Ali's death, since Mita's arrival, no one in the house had mentioned my long absences. The work was done, but they couldn't guess how little I slept, how quickly I moved my legs and hands throughout the day, constantly thinking of ways to add speed to my tasks before slipping away from the compound when my family and others were occupied.

No one dared ask me to account for my time. No one asked about the small bundles tucked behind the folds of my clothing. Over time I had moved containers of food, water, and other items to the hiding place. I had thought about every step and avoided patterns that could be detected by others. The midday meal was my excuse—no one noticed extra portions carried into the field. In the orchard, I sat and waited on the wall, using one hand to sort fruit and the other to slip items intended for Mita into the crevice. The right hand never stopped moving, almost as if it were under its own control. Once the meal or clothes or tools were tucked away in a crevice, wrapped in old gray clothes indistinguishable from the stone wall, I worked awhile.

When ready to meet Mita, I retrieved the items and ran to the cave, careful to repeat the steps on my return.

So much went into rushing through work, hiding and feeding a teacher, and keeping what had to be a thousand new concepts from my family. Yet there was no relief that the lessons with Mita were coming to an end.

~~~~~~

No rain had fallen since the last full moon. Mari approached as I used a shovel to shape small ridges around the base of sensitive fruit trees, hoping to guide more rain to their roots. Annoyed, I slowed my jabs into the soil. Of late, Mari had been preoccupied with Leila's difficulties, and while I was sympathetic, she didn't want advice. She only wanted to scold, and I did not appreciate conversations that took time away from work with Mita.

Can I help? she asked. Hiding my irritation, I nodded, and she pulled a small shovel from a bag and hacked at the soil.

Don't make the sides so steep, I suggested. She studied my work before continuing.

After a few minutes of digging furiously, she brought up Leila. *Jahangir wants to finalize the contract.*

That's good news . . .

Many men would have rejected her. But he's a strange one. He laughed and said he likes her better this way! Gul, the stupid man, wants to delay.

She was so moody about Leila, as if every detail of any day could influence the girl's destiny. I stopped digging. So much agitation in one family could hurt our village, and I had to broach this carefully. *Gul wants what's best for his daughter.*

We won't find anyone else willing to marry her! But Gul's unhappy and wants to know where she will live.

It was a relief that Gul did not welcome Jahangir to our village. All along I had suspected that without Jahangir the transports wouldn't happen. But if he moved here, they would continue.

They could stay here until Jahangir is settled! Mari exclaimed. *But Gul won't talk to Parsaa or the others.* She stopped working and continued complaining, not realizing that I understood Gul's unhappiness. His daughter's loyalty would be divided, and she'd help her husband interfere with village politics. Surely Mari already knew and I did not have to tell her.

She paused and asked, *Do you think the Americans can fix the scar?*

I told her I didn't know. It seemed unbelievable.

Jahangir fights with Gul about Leila entering the American outpost. Gul doesn't want her to go?

Not with lies.

What kind of lies? I asked.

That people in this village attacked her with acid. That this village is hiding the American woman. Foolish lies.

Stabbing my shovel into the earth, I pulled Mari to sit with me on the nearby wall and spill her anger. Jahangir was obsessed with the Americans. He was trying to provoke them into leaving. One of his men had shot at the Americans as they approached our village. Now he wanted Leila to blame her injury on villagers.

Mari was more upset about Leila's difficulties, explaining that Jahangir had brought new clothes for Leila to wear. *The burqa—and that made Gul angry, too. I fear the marriage won't take place.*

She was angrier with Gul than with Jahangir. I was annoyed she'd put up with such rules from Jahangir, and she failed to realize that he intended to control our village.

Mari enjoyed the superiority lent by rules and order that she could control. She tried to be devout, more than any other woman in our village. Despite a shallow understanding of the Koran, she was constantly on the hunt for those who did not follow its teachings. The Koran made no mention of the burqa, clothing our village couldn't afford. Women had too much work to do. Besides, such clothing did little to protect women from men intent on detecting every misstep. The burqa hides a woman's look, but does not disguise what catches a woman's attention. A woman must remain alert, tilting her head in one direction and shifting eyes in the other to keep prying eyes from knowing what tempts her gaze.

Headstrong Leila would not do well in such a garment.

If Jahangir stayed in our village, Gul had to realize that such demands wouldn't stop with one woman. Or maybe he suspected that Jahangir had plans to use Leila to attack the outpost. At last, I voiced my speculation.

No! Mari tossed her shovel aside. *Leila gives him too many good ideas.*

This surprised me. So worried about my own secrets, I forgot that others had them, too. I doubted that Mari knew about her husband helping Jahangir with the children. *If Jahangir wants to stay here, he must listen to Gul,* I insisted.

But she was bitter and frantic. *The delay, the arguing, is Gul's fault. He resents Jahangir. Parsaa and the others resent him, too. Gul thought her scars would keep Jahangir away.*

Thoughts rushed in my mind, ones I could not share. I didn't want Mita at the outpost if Jahangir planned an attack, yet knew that one of us had to warn the Americans. I took Mari's hand. *If Jahangir attacks the outpost, the Americans will lash out at us.*

That's why our men do not want Jahangir to stay in this village—they fear him, Mari said. Distraught, she dropped her face into her hands. *Nothing can stop this marriage.*

It's wrong you should feel this way. I placed my hand on her shoulder and tried to soothe her.

It's not! I blame our men. They don't protect the village. Since the Americans arrived, evil has afflicted this village.

I didn't dare defend the Americans or call her superstitious. All she cared about was rushing a marriage for her flawed daughter, but for the rest of Laashekoh, the strangers from the north were more alarming than the Americans. *Don't blame our men . . .* I said weakly. *They do what they think is best.*

They're afraid and useless . . . She checked the perimeter of the orchard to ensure we were alone. *We have a plan.*

I don't understand . . . I was nervous and tried to sound agreeable, to learn what Jahangir was up to.

She dropped her voice to a low whisper. *We could easily remove the men who mistreat women, like those who hurt Leila.* Stunned, I couldn't speak and she moved closer, peering to read my eyes. *You're troubled.*

The other men . . . would never forgive . . . My voice broke. She sensed my fear and that emboldened her.

Then we could take care of them, too.

But you don't know who attacked Leila . . .

I blame them all, she said bitterly. *Life has been terrible since the Americans arrived. Our men do nothing, and Gul is the worst.*

The hatred for her husband was chilling. I shook my head, feigning puzzlement. The strangers had arrived soon after the Americans, and I wondered at how two women in our village could disagree so fiercely about the source of our problems. *Does Leila know about this plan?*

She cocked her head in a strange way, studying me, and I hurried to remind her that the Americans, Jahangir's men, and others would ask questions.

We won't be caught, she scoffed. *It will be an accident, nothing more. One we can blame on the Americans.*

Other villages will ask questions. The Americans, too.

It's wrong to befriend the unbelievers, she warned me sharply. *By talking to them, letting them inside our gates, our men have put us in danger.*

I gently stroked her back. *You're tired. There's much to prepare for Leila.*

How do you know what I feel? she asked warily.

Your eyes, your voice. Her question was strange, and the desperation of my old friend scared me.

Will you tell Parsaa?

The plan was impossible. How could I tell anyone? No one would believe it. Of course, I shook my head and frowned. *Promise to wait and think this through. How will you . . . ?*

She put her hand to my lips. *I'm not ready to let anyone know.*

What about the children? Of course, I thought of my sons.

She was gruff. *It's not good for boys to grow up this way. Older men criticize them into taking actions they do not want. Men who treat women with respect are scorned by others. We won't hurt them, and perhaps it's not too late. We'll mourn their fathers, and they'll forget.*

Mari, we could help Leila in other ways.

This is not about Leila! They don't listen to us, Sofi.

I chewed my finger, trying to talk her out of such foolishness. *Mari, how do you know other men won't come and take over our village?*

She shrugged. *If they do, we'll take care of them. Aren't you tired of being blamed for problems caused by men?*

I only nodded, trying to calm her, hoping that she'd be embarrassed about the conversation after a night of sleep. *Leila did nothing wrong.*

Women set themselves on fire, take poison, anything to escape this life. Her eyes gleamed.

Yes, ideas about how to kill travel far. I closed my eyes. *Not Parsaa though?* I asked. *Or Gul?*

She smiled. *Some say Gul arranged the attack on his own daughter.*

Nervous, I glanced away, confirmation that I had heard the same. The conversation was bizarre, though the two of us had every reason to trust the other. Mari had arrived at the village before me. She had befriended me and assisted in the birth of my sons, holding my hand, alternating orders with words of comfort. And I had assisted her during childbirth, for all her children except Leila, her oldest. Our bond was strong, and I had no choice but to keep the secret and protect Mari from herself.

Gul loves her, I insisted, then whispered. *If only there was another way . . .*

She smiled. *If you find one, let me know. I'm not afraid to die.*

I sighed because she was right. Death was the only way for women to convince men of their wrongdoing.

~~~~~~

Mari had thought she was safe telling me about her plan. She sensed my resentment about men refusing to work hard in the fields, while taking credit for the best harvests. She may have noticed the distance between me and Parsaa, but Mari didn't know about Mita.

Waiting for the men to leave for market, Mita and I knew our time was dwindling. Rather than focus on our lesson, we talked about our lives and hopes. At one point, she urged me to think about writing an article for others about replenishing sandy soil. I laughed. *Others would have no interest in my words.* But she insisted they would.

She asked me to plan a study of my system, planting crops with varying mixes of compost and sand. *You must give the crops the same care and water. Keep notes on exactly what you do and how the plants respond.*

But why try a way that I know doesn't work? I protested. *The one set won't grow as well as the other set!*

You want a sample for comparison. She explained the scientific method and control samples—keeping all other factors equal provided proof that adding my mixture to sand was the reason for better growth. *Then you write the article.*

I laughed again. *I don't know anyone who would care.*

She shook her head. *People who care about farming. Putting words to paper teaches other people,* she explained. She repeated her warning about treating the crops alike, except for the one condition—the soil mixture. I promised to comply.

We also talked about Jahangir's threats against the base. *I have heard about his plan to attack, and you can warn the others.*

The outpost security would check any visitors closely. Mita was trying to convince herself.

One of your soldiers already invited a woman. Her face was scarred with acid. They're making arrangements for her to meet with a doctor.

How horrible. Upset, Mita paced in a tight circle and then pointed to the sky. *The search has stopped.*

They have given up? I asked.

She shook her head with a confident smile. *They may have ideas about where I am. Have you seen American soldiers—especially the man who can speak Dari?*

He came to our village yesterday. I recalled the discomfort at his many glances directed my way.

Joey. . . . She smiled and sat cross-legged in front of me. *He must be so worried. But he'll help your village.* She paused and reached for my hands. *I wasn't in real danger from anyone in your village, was I?*

I owed her the truth, but that was so uncertain. *Everyone's in danger here. The dangers change every day. But you can't tell your American friends that you were with me. No one from my village can know that I spent this time with you.*

She nodded. *If that's what you prefer. But they spent a long time searching, and I must give some reason. I'm afraid what they'll do if they think I was held prisoner.* She looked down at her clothes. *And they'll know someone helped with clothing and food—that we didn't try to signal the searchers.* She swallowed nervously. *Why didn't we?*

I thought you were in danger. The shooting. You fell from the cliff, and I didn't know who was shooting. I dipped my head. *Later, I was selfish. I wanted to learn from you.*

Have there been other attacks? I shook my head. Mita nodded again slowly. *You don't want your village to know about us, and I face serious trouble for disappearing for no good reason. They'll have questions. And Sofi, how do I know about plans for an attack on the outpost?*

I had not anticipated so many questions, and assumed that the men at the outpost would simply be grateful for her return. *I'm not sure . . .*

Seeing my fear, she gave me a hug. *I must tell Joey the truth. I was unconscious. Someone helped me to a cave. I wasn't sure how far. There was a gun. I wasn't sure how many people were around. Someone told me there would be an attack.* She paused and thought. *And I'll ask that he keep the details from others.*

Thank you. I closed my eyes. *Our village has so much turmoil.* I hesitated to give Mita too much information from Laashekoh that could get us both in trouble. But she was so helpful with advice. So I told her about the uncertain marriage for Leila, Mari's anger, and the plan.

She's angry and wants to kill the men in our village. Aloud, the words sounded strange. She doesn't believe that Jahangir might use Leila in an attack.

Why now?

She says it's the only way life can change for women in our village.

There are other ways . . .

Sighing, I explained how women had little choice but to hide feelings and wait for men to control their lives. *She wants my help.*

Mita had many questions, if Mari had trouble sleeping, or if she was depressed or manic, but I didn't know the answers. *She won't do it, not unless she is ill.* Mita's voice lacked confidence.

Mari is sure that Allah agrees with whatever she decides. It may be why she told me.

Can she carry out the plan?

I thought a moment. *She's capable. Leila's accident has changed her. And she talks about finding a way to blame the deaths on the Americans.*

Mita was distraught and bit her lip. I remained quiet, waiting for her, though I had already asked too much of her. *I cannot withhold information about a plan to kill so many people*, Mita said. *I have to warn the outpost.*

There was no going back. Unlike the women of Laashekoh, Mita was not keen on keeping secrets. She saw my despair and tried to assure me. *I'll be careful. It will be difficult because I can't explain to others how much you helped me.*

We went over specific details about her return, and she was thoughtful. We agreed it was best that she return to the outpost and not the village, which didn't need such attention.

The area surrounding the village is not safe with Jahangir. We must move with care. We decided that I would accompany her most of the way. She would wear old clothes of mine that blended with the arid landscape. Once we parted, she'd change into her own clothes.

We went over her story once again—that she had fallen downhill during the firefight and went unconscious. She awoke inside a cave. She was lost, and did not understand the rescuer's language. The rescuer was terrified of being blamed. Her recovery and determining her location took time. When ready, she hiked alone to the outpost.

It was the best we could do.

~~~~~~

A strong whiff of spices and garlic simmering in oil drifted into the orchard, making me hungry. Someone cooked over a fire, not far from the path I traveled after meetings with Mita. Curious, I followed the smell, acrid smoke mixed with sizzling oil, mint, garlic, and cilantro— and could imagine biting into grilled lamb, moist and tender with a spicy crust. One of the women must have planned a special dinner, wanting to keep the concoction a surprise.

The pungent smell came from the far end of the orchard, beyond the wall. Hidden among the trees, Mari was on her knees, slowly stirring herbs into a pan of hot oil. When flames leaped against the pan, she used a rag to grasp the handle, tilting the pot and letting the oil smoke. Old corks and empty jugs waited nearby.

Overhead the tallest branches of the needle trees swayed in the wind and she didn't hear my approach. *Mari, it smells so wonderful!*

She jerked around, startled, and oil sloshed onto her foot. Crying out in pain, she returned the pan to the stones. *You should not have crept up on me!*

Her fierce anger startled me and I apologized, explaining how the smell had taken over the orchard. She waved her hand at the smoke and complained about the messy work. *Will you use it tonight?*

No, it needs time to sit. She watched the flames. *It's the oil from the Americans. Try some if you like.*

She dipped a cup into the oil and filtered it into one of the containers. *Be sure to use it right away, no later than tonight, and let me know how it tastes.* She turned back to the fire. *Now let me finish . . .*

Without another word, I hurried away, carrying the jug with two hands. Up close, the odor was choking, no longer tempting. The bottle was dirty, with remnants of old, unrecognizable foods inside. Disgusted, I walked faster, wondering if she had even washed the containers. Mari was typically so meticulous.

After crossing the orchard, I took another sniff and looked around. Leaning over the wall, I drained the jug's contents into the tall grass, watching the oil glisten and mix with the soil.

~~~~~

The men departed for the market before dawn. I was ready before them, but waited until their voices faded. I shook my sons awake and whispered about an urge to go alone and pray. I made Saddiq sit up. "You must watch your brothers," I ordered. He was not to abandon his brothers or leave them with Mari. *There is no need to bother her today.* I made the sleepy child repeat my directions.

For the last time, I hurried to meet Mita at the cave. She had brushed away our footprints with a branch thick with needles. I had already carried home most containers, articles of clothing and papers, and we stashed the few remaining items in hiding places far from the cave so I could retrieve them later.

The team could still search for evidence of abduction, she warned. We checked inside the cave and the surrounding area, careful to remove any trace of her presence.

Once satisfied, we set off for the outpost, taking an indirect route, approaching a way that was opposite from Laashekoh. That meant moving extra miles along the foothills, more than four hours of steady hiking, more than twice as long as the direct route. Traveling as two lone women added complications. We stayed off-trail and listened for sounds of other passersby.

Our clothes were worn, blending with the bleak landscape away from the river.

If all went well, I'd return to the village before our men. I had left plenty of food for my boys. I had worked tirelessly in the field the day before, missing a lesson with Mita, so there could be no complaints about work that needed to be done. The boys would be irritated, but I was prepared to be moody, too, and refuse to answer their questions. It was unbearable to think of no more lessons with Mita.

No lesson lasts forever, Mita gently told me.

That does not stop a student's ache about the end, I cried. She just smiled.

Once the sun threw out its early sheer veil in pink and lavender over the sky, we kept to the edge of forests and fields, pausing before every rise. We were intent on avoiding the men of my village, the American soldiers, and especially Jahangir and his likes. Men had many advantages—vehicles, binoculars, and the ability to move freely without question.

We didn't have a plan if we got caught, other than trying to attract the attention of Americans still searching for Mita.

But the helicopters no longer patrolled low overhead.

I tried not to worry. To enjoy the outdoors as much as I did, I had long practiced blending with the landscape, moving cautiously, constantly scanning my surroundings for any sign of movement. We rubbed dirt on our faces, and I trained Mita to look ahead, constantly selecting a rock or stand of brush for her next shield. More than once, I warned her to step on bare soil, to avoid snapping leaves and twigs that could leave a trail.

By midday, the sun was hot and we were far from my village. The outpost was a small smudge in the distance. Breathing hard, Mita and I stopped, sitting side by side on a fallen tree. We shared bread and water, and spoke in whispers. And when the bread was gone, still we talked.

You must be the best teacher in the world, I said.

She laughed softly. *You can teach, too*, she reminded me. *One person's pursuit of education improves life for many. And a parent's education helps her children more than herself.*

I thought about this. *How would I start?*

Sadness crept into her eyes. *We're trying to get books and teachers here.*

It would frighten the other villagers. Education is admitting what we don't know.

It takes courage to admit that you don't know, Mita said. *Too many people equate education with others controlling us rather than controlling ourselves. Adults in my country have the same problem.*

I laughed. *My secret is blending in, attracting no attention at all.*

That makes it difficult to share what you know, she noted. *Keep thinking. You might find a way to show children and adults how education can help a community. Especially if we can send books.*

I could not admit to the other villagers that I knew how to read. I didn't want Mita to leave, thinking that her time spent on lessons was useless. *Many people here don't want life to change. They fear new ideas.*

It's not only Laashekoh—many fear change. Work with your children.

Maybe. . . . I nodded, upset to admit that I could not even teach my sons. *It's a struggle to argue with those who are sure. Like convincing Mari not to try her plan.*

The woman who wants to kill the men? Her mouth tightened with worry, and I nodded. *She hasn't changed her mind?*

She hasn't talked about it since . . . but I see the determination in her eyes. I explained how Mari took charge of cooking during the busiest times of year. *She used the oil your men brought—cooked it with garlic and herbs and . . .* Mita looked puzzled, and so I told her, *It could be poisoned.*

Our oil? Mita cried out.

She could blame the Americans.

If you told your husband or others, what would happen?

I will tell him not to eat her food, but she will be impossible. I keep hoping she changes her mind. I stared at ants moving away from some tunnel underneath our log. *Contemplating such an act is a crime, and the men will consider all the women guilty.*

It doesn't make sense. Mita was morose, leaning forward, her elbows on her knees. Arguing about Mari and Leila was not how I wanted to spend our last hour together.

I'm sorry, it's best to wait for events to unfold. I will find a way to stop it, Allah willing.

Mita twisted her head to study my face. *Resisting change leads to extreme acts—and that will destroy the village.* She reached for my hand and stared. *You must stop her. Talk to her, steal the containers, but don't let anyone use that oil.*

I'm ashamed, I said, covering my eyes. *I give you only problems.*

I'm glad you told me, she said firmly.

No one else can know, I pleaded. *If you talk about the plan, Mari will know it was me.*

Are you sure others are not pushing her?

I had not thought of that. Jahangir. *I promise I'll watch closely.*

If you need help, come to the outpost. Or, do you remember where you found me, along the path? Just before the cliff with the ledges, there's a flat rock that overlooks the valley. I knew the rock and nodded.

We can leave notes for each other there. Place them under a small rock next to the flat one, on the side closest to Laashekoh. And if you hear something and need to let me know right away, you could send a signal. I can leave a note for you. The largest hill that stands behind your village—do you go there often?

Gul and his wife use those pastures. We sometimes help tend their sheep.

So you could climb the side looking out over the outpost, just at the tree line. If Mari is ready to act on her plan—or you need us—attach a white cloth to a tree there. We could try and help.

I hesitated. *If Mari notices, she'll never stop asking questions.*

The cloth does not have to be there long. Tie it loosely, and you can say it was tossed in the wind.

So many were angry in our village—Leila, Jahangir, Mari, and probably others. But I smiled. Anything could happen in the next few days, and it was comforting not to feel alone.

There was a long pause. I didn't want to admit it, but we had to leave if I wanted to return before our men. We checked the desolate horizon and saw no sign of patrols or caravans. Other than the outpost, there was no sign of humans. I pointed to a nearby stand of trees and a rock. *Wait until their shadows touch the rock. That will give me time. Make sure no other travelers are in sight and then hurry. Someone from the outpost will spot you.*

Her smile was sad. *Don't worry about me—I'm almost home. You hurry and get back before dark, and hide if you hear the helicopters.* Her voice shook. We both expected the American soldiers to ask a lot of questions and start looking for those who hid Mita.

Then she hugged me, urging me to practice writing every day. Tears flowed from our eyes. I had no way of stating in a few words how much the lessons had meant.

She stood, watching me hurry away. We returned to our old, separate paths, but our lives would never be the same.

PART 3

*11-2. With training, equipment, and the WILL
TO SURVIVE, you will find you can overcome any
obstacle you may face. You will survive. You must
understand the emotional states associated with survival, "knowing thyself" is extremely important in a
survival situation.*

—Ranger Handbook

*Your Lord has not forsaken you, nor has He become
    displeased,
And surely what comes after is better for you than that
    which has gone before.*

—Koran 93:3–4

CHAPTER 19

I returned as the sun set—relieved that I didn't have to use Mari's gun and defiant about showing remorse for being away the entire day. First, I stopped by the fields, walking briskly and retrieving a basket of potatoes and turnips gathered and hidden the day before. Then I deliberately crossed the village center, empty because the men were still at market. To avoid suspicions or questions, I moved quickly, as if hard at work all day, without stopping to shake the dust from the clothes.

The most difficult part, returning after a day-long absence, was the angry reaction from Saddiq. He turned away—no greeting or smile. Stepping into the back courtyard, where no one could see, I beat the dust from the clothes with angry swings of a stick.

In the cold kitchen, Saddiq waited, sullen. I fired up the oven and then bustled about, as if I had not abandoned my family. The home felt strange, a single day away had reduced my sense of belonging.

I didn't want to ask a string of questions that would only emphasize my long absence. But the boy didn't talk much. Annoyed, fretting about the other boys, I gave in.

Standing in front of him, I snapped, *I trust the other children behaved? They helped you with the herd?*

They were not much help. He looked away.

It's your job to teach them as Ali taught you. I pounded flour, oil, and water for bread.

The boy lashed out. *And who taught Ali? You walked the hills with him. You showed him the favorite grasses, the spring for water, the best places for keeping watch. You showed us how to move the animals along the hillside and play games to use our minds. But you don't care anymore....* He covered his eyes with his arm.

We miss Ali, too, his voice broke. *But we miss you more.*

Shame swept through me, though it wasn't the boy's purpose. Walking the hills had lost all joy since Ali's death, and I cringed at remembering how little I had thought about the children during the trek with Mita.

Since Ali's passing, I should have tried walking and working more with the other boys instead of clinging to grief and memories.

Pounding the bread, I refused to apologize or take the boy into my arms. His hurt had built over a long time. He wasn't in the mood to trust my sincerity with sudden gestures or words. So much more was required to make up for days of neglect. For the time being, it was enough I didn't argue. It was frustrating to feel wrong about hiding Mita and activities that could only improve our lives. Mita's return to the outpost, the end of our lessons, would give me more time with the children. But I was resentful and didn't want to take my feelings out on Saddiq.

It's good to show your brothers. It was all I could say while slapping the dough hard. *Where are they?*

They are at Mari's house. Madar, Hassan got hurt today.

My hands stopped. *What happened?* The boy rushed with an explanation. *He's all right now. It happened when I handed the gun to Zalmai. We dropped it and ...*

What? I screamed.

It fired and hit him in the leg.

Saddiq, why didn't you tell me immediately? Such a fool I was, hurrying with ordinary tasks, trying to hide dust and bake bread, while a son was hurt. The neighbors should have heard my howls of anger long ago. My voice was too weak. *How is he? Can he walk?*

It was no more than a scrape. I tied a cloth to stop the blood.

I dropped to the ground in relief, giving thanks to Allah that the boy was all right and promising to devote more care to my sons. My bitterness about saying farewell to Mita was wrong. All I wanted was to get my sons home.

I was upset about my sons spending too much time with Mari. Cleaning my hands of flour and dough, ready to retrieve him, I paused by our doorway. *Saddiq, how long ago?*

After lunch, he said.

I'm not angry with you. Does he need help getting home?

His eyes were wide with responsibility and fear. *No, he can walk, and the wound is clean. I tried to keep him near, but he cried so hard. Mari came inside and wanted to know what happened. She took him away, cleaned it again, and gave him candy.*

No other food or drink?

Some fruit and bread. The question puzzled Saddiq. *That quieted him. But she kept asking questions and blamed me for taking one of their guns.*

Of course, you didn't . . . I murmured.

Hassan fell asleep, and I got tired of her insults.

What did she say? I bit my lip, cringing inside.

That you and father do not keep a good watch over us! I told her that we have enough guns and my parents work hard. She told me I was disrespectful, like the Americans. The boy frowned. *She also asked if you and father talk about Jahangir.*

And?

I told her no.

Of course not . . . The question was odd. But my children had long been taught the dangers of divulging details about what went on inside our home.

Mari's question revealed how much she didn't trust us. Suddenly, I dreaded facing her, so soon after talking about her plan with Mita. She'd look into my eyes and guess that I had revealed her secret. I turned and faced Saddiq. *You are a big boy . . . can you carry Hassan home? Without waking him. Please?*

The boy leaped up, ready, almost as if he felt guilty and wanted to please me. I touched his shoulder. *What's wrong?* he asked.

Nothing. Hurry. Give her no time for questions. I turned back to the dough.

She's busy—Uncle Gul fell ill during the night and didn't go to market.

My fingernails clawed into the dough. *Only Gul?*

He gave me another puzzled look. *I suppose . . . the pain worsened throughout the day. She is sitting with him.*

Hurry, hurry, and get your brother! Panic swept me that Mari had packed a meal that went off with the other men. That the men passed around her oil and Parsaa tried some with his bread. He could be clutching his stomach, writhing in pain, somewhere along the trail.

I didn't know what else to say, rushing to bake my bread and deliver some to my friend. Mari either assumed that I didn't care about her or my children, or guessed that I had been away from the village for the entire day.

My resentment returned. Men did not have to explain their whereabouts. Little boys could interrogate their mothers. A friend could talk about killing her husband and get upset that I left my sons alone.

At least I didn't have girls and didn't have to force restrictions on them. My boys had enough secrets. Someday, before they took wives, I'd explain to them that women were just as curious as men and had ideas, too. Maybe when I understood myself . . .

The bread went into the oven before it was ready, and I stirred the pot of stew and hung it over the fire—barely enough for two families. I would not eat, and the boys could go and collect more carrots.

I slapped and flattened the bread. Of course, I'd refuse to talk about my whereabouts. The truth was impossible, that I had left the entire day, accompanying an American woman who had been hunted for many days. Travel for two women beyond the boundaries of their village, without male relatives as escorts, was dangerous. Inside, I trembled with thrill at the feat—hiding Mita and then returning her safely.

I'd refuse to explain—let Parsaa guess that I went off and prayed for Ali. In death, the child protected my lies more than I had protected him in life.

The meal was almost done, and I readied myself to carry it over, forcing Mita and the long walk out of my mind. Maybe I'd hand the meal to Leila and not see Mari. She wouldn't realize that I had contacted the Americans and that her plan was no longer a secret.

Then I chided myself for being foolish, collecting rags for carrying the pot away. Gul's illness had nothing to do with her plan.

Or maybe she'd stop with Gul.

Still, I prayed that I wouldn't see Mari who had a knack for seeing what others did not want her to see.

~~~~~~

Word quickly went through the village about Gul's illness. One family after another knocked on the door of Gul's home. Mari simply shook her head and explained it was a stomach virus. The man couldn't eat or take liquids, and Mari and Leila handled his care with efficient serenity.

I delivered warm bread and a pot of stew with a small group, and Mari's eyes locked on mine. I stared over the top of her head into the room and caught my last glimpse of her husband. Gul was still, his eyes barely open as he moaned softly, his wide eyes suggesting that he wanted to writhe and scream in pain. Mari refused to allow anyone to join her or the children in the vigil over her husband.

He cannot swallow or speak, Mari said, as she took the bread. Then, she slowly closed the door, her eyes still on me. In them, I could read no sadness or revenge, though I was thankful she did not want to spend much time with me.

Returning to my home, I had to pass by the group of young men at prayer near Gul's doorway. I could not forget Mari's gaze and was nervous to know her thoughts and if she suspected that I told others. My moods shifted from feeling guilty for not telling Parsaa to scolding myself for thinking that she had hurt Gul.

If she were behind this strange illness, more men would have suffered, I told myself.

From inside my kitchen, I heard the men taking turns reading from the Koran. Not long ago, I would have followed along, and tried to pick up new phrases. But I was familiar with these passages and now could read better than the youngest men. Listening to the readings, I realized how often the word "care"—*ehtiyaat-kar*—was used to mean warn or guard against. Such was the nature of our village.

After darkness fell, I tossed Mari's gun over the wall, close to the rear entry of her home, and would not argue if she accused the boys of playing with it. I did not want it in our home.

The other men returned from market, but Parsaa was not with them.

I crawled into the bed. A weary Saddiq draped his arm around me on one side, and the youngest pressed against me on the other. I was in a bed with four children and should have felt relief after the long day. But I had never felt so alone.

Of course, I couldn't sleep. Long hours of steady walking, the fear of getting caught, the agony of saying farewell to Mita, and the thought that we might not ever talk again—too many racing thoughts interfered with sleep.

I turned from one side to the other, bothered that Parsaa was not around. Fear about explaining my absence that day mixed with relief and sadness. Maybe I wouldn't have to explain to Parsaa at all. With Gul's illness, my husband would be busy and might not hear about my long absence. Or, perhaps he'd already heard and was out searching for me. Or maybe he prowled for a second wife. Either way, blame for the day's problems could slide my way.

A few hours later, after midnight, I heard greetings for Parsaa from the other men gathered outside Gul's home. It was too late for Parsaa to knock on his friend's door and visit, and the others updated him.

He didn't enter our home, instead joining the other men with their prayers. Throughout the night, Mari and the daughters took turns holding Gul's hand, comforting him. In the end, paralysis took control of his limbs, and Gul died before dawn.

CHAPTER 20

A guard radioed Joey about a small figure approaching the outpost from the east. Joey reached for the binoculars and sprinted for the barricades. Someone in dusty clothes emerged from rocks and forest edging the base of the nearest mountain just before sunset—and walked in a direct line toward the base. A woman.

Moments later, two Humvees exited the outpost gate—and the woman whipped away her head cover, waving it like a flag. The vehicles encircled her, creating a cloud of dust, and then braked. Recognizing Mita, the men let loose with ecstatic hoots. Joey hopped out of the back of the nearest vehicle and ran to her, wrapping his arms around her, lifting and twirling her with joy, squeezing as if never to let her go.

Exhausted from walking all day in the sun, she leaned against him and could not speak. Her eyes and skin were crusted with dust, exposed to blowing sand, and her feet burned. But she beamed a weary smile.

"Where were you?" "How did you get away?" "Are you all right?" The questions came fast and she let loose a happy laugh, unaccustomed to dealing with so many people at once. "That day . . . ," she started to reply. "I fell . . ."

"Give her a break everyone," Joey ordered. He handed her a bottle of cool water, urging her to drink. "Small sips." She happily obeyed, and he wondered if she was more grateful for the water or the delay in having to explain what she had been through during the past two weeks. It didn't matter. Relief exploded inside him, and he wasn't ready to handle the tumbling emotions, not in front of a group. He also didn't want Mita locking herself into statements in front of so many witnesses.

Wrapping his arm around her shoulder, he guided her to a Humvee. "Get her back to the base!"

"But I don't . . ."

"Quiet, and that's an order," he whispered as he squeezed her. "I'm so damn happy to see you." As the vehicle sped back to the outpost, Joey didn't miss her wistful glimpse toward the craggy stretch near Laashekoh.

~~~~~~

Time stretched out in the hours after midnight. The night Mita returned, Joey went out to wait and sleep within sight of Laashekoh. She had managed to convince him that she was fine, not hurt, though somehow spirited away the day Habib had died.

She didn't provide specifics and, in dealing with a retired general's daughter, some of his commanding officers didn't want many details either. Everyone was ready to take her at her word, and the meetings were perfunctory. A specialist would fly in later in the week to conduct a routine assessment.

She didn't talk much, and it didn't take long before Joey guessed she was disturbed by her time away, worrying about Laashekoh and its problems.

So he planned on observing both her and the village—and hoped to confirm his suspicion. From a distance, the place appeared serene, no arguing or suspicious, defensive, or paranoid activity. The place had fewer conflicts than the outpost did.

He enjoyed time alone away from the outpost. Leaning against the tree, he listened to the sharp insect noises and tried to imitate them. He thought about the war that had consumed a decade of his life and the thankless task of trying to undo centuries of wrongdoing. He thought about time and how creatures, young or old, small or large, experienced it differently depending on the content of their memories. He wondered if adding clocks and watches, heightening the perception of time, would change Afghan attitudes.

The Afghanistan nights, the landscape, reminded him of a poem memorized long ago:

> Knowing that Nature never did betray
> The heart that loved her; 'tis her privilege
> Through all the years of this our life, to lead
> From joy to joy: for she can so inform
> The mind that is within us, so impress
> With quietness and beauty . . .

He couldn't remember all the verses or the poet's name, and he reminded himself to look up the poem the next time he was online. Watching the village wall, he remembered fragments of other poems and thought about writing his own before he fell asleep.

~~~~~~

He awoke to find a man in gray waiting patiently in the nearby shadows. Once again, the Afghan draped a scarf around his face, revealing only his eyes. Joey sat up slowly. "*Salaam aalaikum.*"

"*Wa'alaikum salaam,*" the stranger said. "You're too trusting."

"Trust breeds more trust, no?"

The man cocked his head. "It's common for men to act—and then reconsider."

"Everything you've told me so far has been true."

"You stopped the searches, and the woman came back."

"She is back," Joey admitted.

"She was never in Laashekoh." The man looked away. "But someone there may have known her whereabouts."

"A woman . . ." Joey said.

The Afghan studied Joey's face. He picked up a small pebble and tossed it, watching it land. "Will you pursue the matter?"

Joey couldn't make promises, but his interests aligned with those of the village. So far, questions were few because of Mita's status as star.

But that could change. "She is safe. She was injured and not abducted. Of course, some of our people don't believe her."

"It's best not to pursue the details." He tossed the pebble again. "Outsiders are furious at us for letting her return. They want to cause trouble and control this area."

"The man who called me a dog?" Joey smiled.

"He does not realize that calling a man a dog does not turn him into a dog."

"Not the worst insult where I come from."

But the villager was less sanguine. "This man is dangerous for us and you. He wants to use this area for illegal activities, and that's the only reason he goads our men into fighting the Americans." The man kept his voice low and gruff, his face covered, but it didn't matter. Joey felt comfortable with him. "The Americans slowed the drug trade, and now he finds it easier to sell children. His excuse is the funds go toward fighting the foreigners. But his activities won't stop if you leave."

"Have you seen these transports?"

"I've heard from other villages."

"Nobody around here wants checkpoints and us stopping caravans. To take action, I have to witness an actual transport. I need proof."

"That could come soon," the man explained. "He wants the village to ready supplies of food and water for a group traveling through in the next few days. That could be your chance."

Joey frowned. "You're sure it's not a school or a family moving through . . ." The man glared and didn't answer. "How many men with them?"

"Based on what I've heard about previous trips—only one or two men travel with the children. They'll meet up with one or two from our village. Understand, I have no direct knowledge."

Joey looked up at the sky and thought. He didn't like an operation involving kids. The possibility of a firefight meant dead kids and an end to any American goodwill in the area. Efforts to stop trafficking operations had a way of backfiring on Americans.

"Can you help me act on this?" the man pleaded. His voice and eyes were earnest, but others could have plans to lure both him and the Americans into a trap.

"I'll need your advice on the best places to keep a lookout," Joey said. "I'll need details about what weapons they might have."

"We can do that."

"And you've got to let me know if you figure out who in your village is involved."

Families had so many children in Afghanistan—sometimes ten or more. Men moved truckloads of poor, rural children through the area, pretending they were orphans. Using a series of lies about communities attacked by foreign forces, the traffickers pretended to take them to refugee camps. The men starved, drugged, or terrified the children—convincing them that their parents no longer cared, that names and memories of their family no longer mattered. Desperate parents sometimes cooperated, handing off children, especially girls they could no longer afford to feed.

The most appealing children were adopted, married, or sold to sex traders. The others worked long hours as servants or apprentices for carpet makers, stone quarries, or farms. Which group was more fortunate was debatable.

"The traffickers are typically secretive and change their routes frequently," Joey said.

"Increased patrols have pushed them our way, away from main routes. If anything goes wrong in this area, they will blame your outpost."

Joey was sickened. "Others must oppose this trafficking. How do they get away with it? And how many believe stories about attacks from Americans?"

The man sighed. "The traffickers find the poorest villages. The parents want to believe them. And sometimes, the Americans do attack."

Touché. "What do you want from me?"

The man had his plan and hurried to explain. "Our men can kill the men who pass through, but the networks that rely on these trips for funds will target us for revenge. We can stop this man, and you could return the children to their villages."

Joey nodded.

"You're fighting the Taliban anyway. If the Americans attack the traffickers near our village, then the ringleaders may leave us alone. Any help from me would be kept secret."

The plan made sense. "Okay. But we need a plan where none of the children get hurt. Not one." The Taliban were too damn clever at luring Americans into attacks and blaming them for civilian deaths.

"Better death than a life of hell," the man said.

Joey wanted to hear more about the ringleader, Jahangir. The Afghan described him as impulsive, angry, and insecure. "He's dangerous. Some of his men have run off—and he's looking to stay in our village."

Joey had to prepare for anything. "Others from your village will help?"

"Not many," the man said, looking away. He pulled out a bottle of warm tea and offered Joey a sip. Thanking him, Joey swallowed the strong tea. The drink was sweet, coating Joey's teeth, and he couldn't wait to sip fresh water to clear the taste out of his mouth. To be hospitable, though, he drank more.

The two quietly passed the bottle back and forth, and Joey thought about how war and crime pushed the need for a secret alliance. "I'm not sure how many men in my village could be helping the traffickers. I worried about one, but he's no longer with us."

"To Allah he belongs, to Allah he returns." The man nodded, and Joey listened to the description of a sudden turn to illness followed by a quick death.

"The flu?" Joey asked, alert about a contagious disease that could rampage through villages and hit the outpost, too.

"Perhaps. He had trouble swallowing, and we could barely understand him."

"Was there coughing or fever?" The man shook his head, and Joey thought the symptoms sounded odd. "This could delay the transport?"

Troubled, the man paused. "Others could take over for him. It was Gul, and I do not know if he was assisting Jahangir. If he was, he may not have known the exact nature of these transports."

"A village leader . . ." A sudden illness, followed by a power shift, was a concern.

"Gul was a friend all my life, and I worry if he was involved . . ." His voice broke. "Or others. I do not know. What will you do with the traffickers?"

"Arrest them," Joey replied. "They'll be sent to Kandahar for trials and then prison."

The man looked down. "If women from my village are there with foolish ideas, you'll let me handle them."

Joey swallowed, wondering what the guy had planned. "A woman would help with such an operation?"

"For the money? Or think they are helping children? Anything's possible." He shook his head and looked down. "Only one is my concern, and she should know that men like Jahangir do not help children."

Joey agreed that the man of Laashekoh would confront the traffickers first and determine the ringleaders before arrests were made. Time was short. There was no time for practice, and the Americans had to avoid the area, so as not to alert the traffickers. "If you're in danger, we need a phrase," Joey noted. "A signal for my men to move in."

"All matters remain with Allah," he said with no hesitation.

Joey nodded, and advised the man to also lift his right arm high especially if he could not speak out. "One signal or the other, we move in," Joey repeated. They sipped tea, exchanging other ideas for an operation only a few nights away.

The Afghan suddenly changed the topic. "Let me ask you? Why are the Americans here? It's not just about the farming or trafficking?"

Joey told the man the truth. "We're scouting the area for locating a base that would train soldiers for the Afghan military." The man asked about how many. "A few hundred. If we can train enough men from this area, your village—the entire country—will be more secure."

The man put his palms together, raised them to his lips, as if in prayer. "Our village is too small. Such a force would overwhelm this area. Do you have a say in the decision?"

"Some," Joey admitted.

"You must let the others know this is not the right place. Do what you can to put it near one of the cities. We're not ready. And if it's not good for us, then it won't be good for you."

"I've had the same thoughts," Joey conceded.

"One or two men can keep a village on the right path." He tightened the cloth around his face. "I must get back."

Joey stood too. "We'll be watching for the caravan."

"Do not let them see you," the man warned. "If I find out more, I'll try to let you know. And I warn you, this man Jahangir will do everything in his power to make the Americans look bad."

"*Khoda hafiz.*" He put his hand over his heart and then raised his hand before disappearing into the brush and darkness.

Joey waited in the darkness, giving his comrade time to separate and get some distance.

~~~~~~

Joey returned to the outpost, retrieved his laptop, and headed to the trailer office with the VSAT modem, used for work by day and contact with friends and family members during off times. Overseeing the outpost's security, Joey had priority. But at 0400 hours the satellite link was free, and he didn't have to chase anyone off.

He logged on to an early-reporting system designed to catch ordinary contagions like the flu or attempts at a biomedical terrorist attack. He typed in the symptoms described by the stranger: slurred speech, difficulty swallowing, and muscle weakness.

Then he did his own Google search, typing in the same symptoms.

The results suggested brain tumor, stroke, ALS, Myasthenia gravis, food poisoning, or botulism.

Joey didn't want to wait for doctors and bureaucracy. Instead, he immediately fired out an e-mail: "Send antidote for botulism to outpost Rockville-628 ASAP. Possible case in nearby village." He added the list of symptoms and then hit "send," before heading back to his room to crash for the night.

CHAPTER 21

A noise outside startled me, and the sunlight was more alarming. After the stress of hiking from the day before, I slept long past my normal time. My husband abruptly stormed into the bedroom, and ignoring the sleeping children, he ripped the covers away from my head and grasped my wrist. With one hard pull, he jerked me away from the room where we had once slept together in peace.

The kitchen carried the night's chill. I longed to start a fire as a way to avoid Parsaa's questions, but he refused to release my wrist.

Where were you? He kept his voice low, so others could not hear. Such control had its own way of terrifying.

A fury went through me that I could not ask the same of him, but I kept my face blank. Thoughts of Ali leaped to my mind, but I refused to use the boy as an excuse. He did not deserve a mother who had to lie to his father. Thoughts of the boy tormented me, as I struggled to remember his eyes and smile. He had joined my parents in a distant part of my mind.

I was walking in the fields.

A good mother does not go off all day and leave her children alone.

It won't happen again, I said softly, bowing my head to keep him from staring into my eyes.

My demeanor threw him off guard. His voice lost its gruffness. *Such wandering is dangerous*, he concluded. *There are men who do terrible things to women.*

The vivid image of Jahangir took over my head, increasing my anger. *And there are men who let them do as they please*, I snapped. Parsaa stared, but I refused to explain. I wasn't sure I could and only repeated my promise.

He flung my arm aside and headed for the bedroom. And then he turned. *There's no need for your promises. I already spoke to Saddiq. He will tell me where you go and what you do, every moment. You're not to go anywhere without him, do you understand?*

I stared at him, furious at a husband who didn't trust me, who shamed me before my son, a step in turning my boys against me. There was no use arguing. I no longer understood a world where women had so few privileges or control.

And if you try to sneak away in the night, the boy knows the reason why he can no longer sleep. This is for your protection. Embarrassed, he grabbed a pack from the bedroom and walked out into a brilliant morning ready to expose our flaws.

~~~~~~

Mari bathed Gul's body alone. He was buried before noon that day.

Many expected my husband to take over Gul's duties, but he refused to discuss the matter, alternately spending his hours praying and assuring Mari that she and her family would be well taken care of in our village. Parsaa and others worked together, cooperating on the burial and other arrangements for Gul's family. Jahangir returned a few hours before the burial and surprised many by insisting on staying in Gul's home.

So the man who detested any freedoms for women lived next to my home. But could I complain if Mari didn't?

Gul's death, painful and sudden, would deliver unavoidable changes. Everyone was anxious, and the other villagers overlooked my eyes burning with shame about my husband teaching our sons to belittle me and treat me like a prisoner. Sadness returned, and I realized it was more about missing Mita than Ali.

~~~~~~

I'd been so content about Saddiq sleeping close throughout the night, and only afterward realized that his motivation was no longer love, but a lack of trust.

I thanked Allah for giving me the wisdom to guide Mita away from a land of such foolishness. No wonder Mari was desperate to devise a plan to end the control of men in Laashekoh. Slapping my cheek, I tried to get my anger under control. I had to think of other ways to escape prying eyes and villagers who believe that women are incapable of thinking on their own.

Parsaa's anger wouldn't last forever, and I was patient. No man, no child, could watch a woman every moment. Women can steal their privacy, claiming it was their time of month. Without hesitating, I went into the kitchen and snatched a knife and copied what other women did when they wanted to avoid intercourse with their husbands. Pulling clothing away, I sliced the inside of the top of my leg. Blood seeped onto a rag, and I left it close to our bed where it would not escape Parsaa's notice.

Pacing, I imagined troubles in the days ahead. I waited for my chance, and while Saddiq slept and Parsaa was in the courtyard, I went to the cabinet where my husband kept an extra pistol and a rifle. In this part of the world, we keep the guns loaded, ready to fire. Men, women, and children know how to handle the weapons, ready to pick them up to defend our families or celebrate.

The village had celebrated little recently, and there wouldn't be many reasons until the Americans and Jahangir moved on their separate ways. Standing before the cabinet, I thought about what to do.

Hurrying, my hands shaking with anger and fear that someone in our family could turn on another, I took each gun and removed the bullets, shaking every last one from its chamber.

Then I gently returned the guns to their place. Tucking the bullets inside a rag, I placed the bundle next to the container for carrying drinking water. I'd hide the bundle later.

I wished that I could unload every gun in our village. In Afghanistan, empty threats or unloaded guns can be lethal in their way, and I would leave the consequences for Allah to decide.

~~~~~

Saddiq kept a distance, but I felt his eyes on me. As long as I was in the house, he and Parsaa left me alone. Inside, I cooked and swept the floor. I organized laundry and sometimes wrote in my notebooks. I expected that, with time, my husband and son would become less vigilant.

Convincing Saddiq to hide anything from his father was not an option. But I didn't blame my son and remained pleasant, as if nothing was horribly amiss in our home. My composure disconcerted them.

After the confrontation with Parsaa, I felt no shame. As far as I was concerned, the men were resentful, suspicious, and strange. I was reasonable, patient, and superior.

Their watchful eyes reminded me of the danger of getting too attached to my own secrets, and I shuddered imagining what might have happened had Parsaa trapped me this way before Mita had returned. Disclosing her location to Parsaa would have been unthinkable and so was the notion of her making the trek back to the base on her own.

Allah smiled on me. Mita was back at the outpost. I had learned much, though the lessons made me long for more. I was certain that Allah didn't frown upon the time spent with Mita. No, Allah had led her to me.

I sighed. Now He wanted me to spend more time with my children.

~~~~~

The morning was cool and I warned the boys to don extra layers. Saddiq and the youngest would help me in the orchard, and the other two would tend the sheep and goats.

We left the house together, and we encountered Mari on the path. She carried a basket and asked if we wanted vegetables. I told the boys to run back and retrieve a basket. Saddiq lingered and stood his ground even after Mari tried to chase him off. I had nothing to hide regarding this encounter, and expected her to tell me more about Gul. *He obeys his father, not women*, I explained to Mari.

Mari glared, and then turned her back on him to whisper, *Leila is ready to go to the Americans. Jahangir has her under a spell.*

Frowning, I questioned how.

They plot together and do not include me. She says she will ask for treatment, but I don't know. I worry they plan an attack.

How can that help? That Leila was willing to go along with such a plan surprised me, though it was a relief that Mari was worried and had come to her senses.

Mari looked toward the village. *Jahangir spins tales of glory and changes his mind about what he wants with every sunset.*

Mari, we must protect her from Jahangir.

We must protect her from herself. Mari's smile was odd, and she plucked a turnip from the basket, twirling it in her hand.

Will they still marry?

They must. She was firm. *The marriage will happen soon.*

I shook my head. *She'd marry a man who wants to kill others?*

Leila matters more than the Americans, Mari retorted. The turnip dropped, and she ignored it.

My youngest ran over and interrupted, handing us a basket. She patted the boy on the head as I bent to retrieve the turnip and waited awkwardly as Mari slowly transferred vegetables from one basket to the other.

I told the boys to run ahead, while I delivered the vegetables to our kitchen. Again, Saddiq hung back and stared. *Jahangir's plans won't help this village.*

Mari glanced at Saddiq and shook her head. *The boy is a nuisance.*

I murmured an apology. *Parsaa worries about my safety.*

Allah has His plan. Mari scowled. *Jahangir promises to help my family.*

But if he makes new promises every day . . . I wanted to warn her. *I don't like to think of him with our children.*

She stared. *Sofi, these are dangerous times. You should not take your eyes away from your children and go off alone.*

I struggled to stay calm and keep my face blank. It was mortifying to think that Mari and others knew that Parsaa had put me under watch. I mumbled about unending grief for Ali, and inside, begged for forgiveness from both him and Allah. My grief was real, and the child was more than a convenient excuse.

Upon our friends, our strength depends, she said with a curt nod.
Then she lowered her voice, *All of them are wrong for how they treat us.
Don't warn any of them, but it will end this week.* With that, she hurried
off toward her home.

~~~~~~

Without explanation, I told the boys we'd climb the opposite hill
to check our animals from a distance. They laughed, but it was easy
convincing the boys about a walk. *Who knows what we'll see if they don't
know we're watching?* I suggested.

I ran home and emptied the basket of vegetables. Lining the basket
with an old white scarf, I added bread and fruit for us. Then we climbed
the hill. Light rain from the night before made the grass soft and lush.
Mari's sheep were content, alert as we first approached. Once they realized we meant no harm, they grazed and ignored us.

Saddiq looked to our hill and shouted with glee. *Our lambs play
more than Mari's!*

That's good to know, I replied.

The boys wanted to climb to the very top, and I told them that I'd
wait for them at the tree line. The sun was bright overhead, and while
they raced to the top, I removed the scarf from the basket and tied it to
a low branch to provide more shade. The boys weren't long, and after
we ate, they wandered about, examining rocks and plants. Questions
tumbled from them, and I answered most, admitting what I did not
know. The day was beautiful, the best since my last walk with Ali, and
the boys didn't want to leave even as a fierce wind arrived.

On the way home, Hassan remembered the forgotten scarf and
offered to run back. *It can wait until tomorrow.* Laughing and agreeing,
the younger boys raced down the hill.

Saddiq and I walked more slowly, and it was then that I murmured
thanks to him for reminding me about the pleasures of the hills. He
smiled, and I did not have to explain further.

CHAPTER 22

Mita's father had thanked the outpost and search team for his daughter's safe return. No one expressed surprise that she was ready to continue with the mission. No one demanded an all-out investigation.

That didn't mean Joey didn't investigate. He spent hours with her, asking questions, and found most of the story, what she was willing to tell, troubling and hard to believe.

During the firefight, she had backed away, fell down a cliff, and went unconscious. An unknown Afghan moved her away from the scene and hid her in a cave, bringing her clothes and food. Another unknown was planning a possible suicide attack on the outpost, but it was postponed after Mita went missing. A third unknown was planning to poison the men of Laashekoh. She couldn't divulge names or details, and warned that revealing the plans would endanger the informant.

"We'll see a signal if something is about to happen," she said, and explained about a white cloth.

He asked if she could guide him back to the hiding place, and she shook her head. "Even if we tried by air?" he pressed. She shook her head again.

It wasn't the first time that Afghan wiliness had withstood state-of-the-art surveillance equipment.

Joey paused. "I know it's a woman who helped you." Mita looked startled but did not confirm or deny. "I almost called in dogs," Joey added. "Cameron wanted to raid Laashekoh. God knows what your father wanted."

"I'm grateful you did what you did," she said quietly.

The details of the briefings sounded less like intelligence or evidence, and more like a mysterious dream. He asked her to let him know immediately if she remembered other details.

~~~~~~

Confirmation of her strange tale came soon. Joey held her arm and helped her to the roof and the surveillance scope. He typed codes into a laptop and then pointed to the hillside that blocked a view of Laashekoh. A thin white cloth was tied or caught in a treetop. "Is that the signal you talked about?"

Mita dipped her head and stared into the scope at a long headscarf, whipped by wind, that was ready to break free from the dark tree. The magnification was strong enough to see the gauzy weave and a knot twisted around a limb.

"The knot—it's deliberate." She pulled her eye away from the scope and was surprised to see him studying her more closely than the scarf.

"Mita, can't you tell me more? Where you stayed?"

Mita hesitated. "It was just one woman, not the village. And she'd be in serious trouble for warning us. Please understand, Joey, I must protect her."

"I don't see how withholding intelligence protects her!"

"They're afraid to talk to us," Mita said. "If you try, they'll guess she was involved. Even her family didn't know." She reached for his arm. "Joey, you had to be there. . . . I was unconscious. She took a risk by helping me. The woman yearns to read and write and study. I would love to give her a book to read, but that alone would mark her as dangerous in her community. If we're not careful, she'll be dead."

Joey went quiet. The story revived memories of growing up with brothers and friends who snickered at a boy who loved reading and school, as if either minimized one's toughness. Extremists had a knack for devising narratives that ensured obedience among the uneducated, raising uncertainty about educators and others unafraid of change. "Could she be a pawn for extremists?"

"Absolutely not," Mita insisted, sitting near the scope. "She begged me not to tell anyone. . . ."

"But how do you know it's not a trap or a game?" he asked.

Mita shook her head. "She's not like that. It was my idea, and she promised to signal if she heard any strange plans."

He talked as he typed away on the computer. "It might not be her fault, but it could be a way to distract us from other activity."

"From what though?" Mita asked. "Laashekoh is one of the more comfortable villages in this area."

"All the more reason for extremists to target them."

"You asked me about other details? I do remember something. . ."

He moved close and got on his knees in front of her. "Every detail is important."

"She wanted to read and write, and had nothing but the family Koran, which I couldn't read. One day she showed me a piece of paper—an Afghan document."

"What kind of document?"

"Just one page—a certificate. Maybe a birth certificate."

That got his attention. "A certificate. One of her children's?"

"No, it was blank."

"Do you remember any numbers, a name of a city or province?"

"Nothing special, but my Dari is not that good," Mita apologized. "She asked me what it said, and I wasn't sure. So we didn't talk much more about it, and she didn't say how she came by it."

"Did she talk about illicit activities—drug or human trafficking? Did you see illegal activity?"

"No." Mita said, frustrated. "I was in a cave, and she was nothing but kind. She did nothing wrong, except help a stranger and try to read."

"Mita, can you find the cave?" he asked again.

She took a breath. "Maybe. . . . But I can't chance betraying her."

"You don't trust that we can help people like her anymore?"

"It's not us," Mita said with a sigh. "It's the endless obstacles in these villages. The men don't agree, and the women don't know what's going on. They have enough problems, with one woman attacked by acid and another woman thinking about mass murder." Mita paused. "Their life is so hard, but this woman never complained. I cannot risk hurting her."

"There are good men in the village, too," Joey noted. "The factions could work for us."

She sighed. "I think so, too, but how many times have we heard there are no moderates here?" she said.

"If one group is a shade friendlier than another, depending on their reasons, they could become our moderates."

"The extremists despise moderates and will attack them with a vengeance. I'm terrified for my friend and others like her."

"Changing minds takes time," Joey said.

"Something we don't have." She returned to the scope and asked to reposition the view.

He nodded. "You won't see the village," he added. "Just sheep and rocks and the waterfall down the south slope." She stared into the scope without talking. Joey watched and wondered what she was thinking.

He didn't blame her for not trusting anyone at the outpost with details about the woman. Hell, he still hadn't told her that he had already guessed which woman had provided the help. Before calling Mita to the platform, he had watched a woman and children descend the slopes. Dressed in dark gray, she had slowly zigzagged down the hill, arms out, latching onto tree trunks to slow her pace and perhaps avoid being seen.

He didn't want to alarm Mita into trying something foolish.

"You arranged a place for dropping off messages with her—let's leave a note and ask her to drop off that paper?"

"Sure, if you think it will help," Mita said.

"Write a note that could only come from you. Tell me where to leave it, and I'll head out tonight."

"If she still has the paper, she'll get it to us." Mita was more confident than he was. The woman may have kept Mita away longer than necessary, and Mita may have provided more information than she realized about the outpost. Fortunately, he was in control of that investigation.

The Laashekoh woman may have already had regrets about

befriending Mita. She could be in trouble with others or frustrated about her reading, forgetting words, and wanting more. She could be angry that Americans didn't stick around villages long enough to ensure that real education took hold.

"The paper? You won't let anyone else know?" Mita asked.

"Only us." It wasn't a good idea, but he wanted to reach out, hold her, kiss her the happy way he had the day she returned.

The many questions about her time away were a constant distraction. She was a Muslim and a civilian. In a strange land, her loyalties could be divided for many reasons.

"Go write that note," he directed. "In your handwriting, as simple as possible."

He stood, ready to log on to a more secure computer and report the birth certificate, if that's what it was, to the intelligence analyst center. Getting his hands on it was another test of whether Mita was telling the truth and whether her contact was reliable.

But he had another problem unfolding fast. A reply to his e-mail about the illness in Laashekoh was waiting:

"Sounds like botulism. Antidotes work best BEFORE poisoning, not after. Only some experimental antidotes are available for actual cases. We put in a request. If the case is botulism, the poor guy's already dead. Wpn dev? Try to get samples. DO NOT eat anything coming out of that village. Specialists on way."

~~~~~~

Joey still moved out for surveillance every night. He felt more secure working alone. Adding others meant more tracks, noise, and complications. The band of traffickers would be ruthless. He wasn't going to try and stop them on his own, but he could prepare. He had to work within the parameters set by the villager—and he had to ensure that no children were hurt in the process.

Joey announced that visits would resume from agriculture specialists. "You've already been shot at once near that village," said a soil scientist.

"The indicators suggest the attack came from an outside force," Joey said. "They asked for these pamphlets, and we're responding."

"You heard from someone in the village?" Cameron questioned. "But how . . . ?"

"A reliable source."

"Maybe we should focus on finding the people who snatched Mita," Cameron grumbled.

"The village didn't take her." Joey said in a firm voice to counter the whining. Others were getting irritated about Cameron constantly questioning orders. With every question, the man managed to spread doubt about the mission, Mita, Joey, Laashekoh, all of Afghanistan.

"We're running out of time, and passing out a few pamphlets isn't worth the risk," Cameron insisted. "There are US companies that would help, but these villages are too ignorant to want that." He shook his head.

"They're doing better than any village around here, without our help," Mita protested. "We should be thrilled. We need to catch up on making contacts with the villages."

"You haven't been around the last few weeks," Cameron accused. "That's why we're behind. An absence still not explained."

"For security reasons," Joey retorted.

Cameron, visibly startled, was at a loss for words and looked about the room. When no one else spoke up, he fired back. "What are you talking about? We deserve full access to any reports on that village and abduction. We're risking our lives out here every day . . ."

"It's enough for you to know that the village had nothing to do with Mita's absence, as you put it. The assailants are unknown. Mita was separated. An unknown civilian assisted her. End of story."

"But who?" Cameron demanded. "The incident compromised our safety. It's your job to find out more."

"We're not talking about this." Joey put his pen on the table. "Not knowing could protect you."

"You don't trust us!" Cameron accused.

Joey didn't answer. It was ridiculous trying to convince a man who had started the pattern of mistrust, who argued with anything that didn't go his narrow way.

"The goal hasn't changed here," Mita said. "We're letting the villages decide their needs, and we're not going to impose our ideas. They're not guinea pigs for our pet projects."

Some people looked down and others nodded. Support for Cameron was fading.

"This is chaos," he concluded. "Waiting for villagers who don't understand their options."

Ending the meeting, Joey asked Dan and a younger soldier to stick around. Cameron was curious, but Joey waved him away. Only after the room emptied out did he explain. "The Taliban are getting money somehow, and we're investigating shipments passing through this area at night."

"I'm game," interrupted Daniel.

"Me, too," said the younger man.

"I'll give you more later. We're tightening the noose."

~~~~~

Joey promised to check for a message from the woman in Laashekoh—and Mita was disappointed when he returned the first night empty-handed and reported that the note still waited underneath the rock. The next night, though, the note was gone. It was after midnight, but he couldn't resist seeing and telling Mita. He tried giving two soft knocks on her door, and the door opened quickly, as if she had been waiting.

The room was dark. Feeling awkward, he waited by the door until she switched on a bedside lamp and gestured for him to sit beside her on the cot.

"Can't sleep?" he whispered.

"So many thoughts racing through my head," she admitted, crossing her legs and facing him. "And I worry about my friend in Laashekoh."

He reached for her hand and held it. "The note's gone," he said. "There's no message."

"You're sure it was the right place?" she pressed.

He went over once again the description of the pile of rocks near a stand of trees, just off the footpath. "Believe me, I didn't forget where we were ambushed. But I worry—it can't be safe for a woman to leave the village."

"But she left to see me for such long periods every day. . . ."

"I found these on top of the rock."

He pulled the wilted sprigs of cumin from a top pocket and placed them into her hand. She sniffed. "*Kala jeera*, the seed that cures every disease but death."

"Powerful stuff."

"Cumin." Mita smiled as she studied the stems, evenly cut. "It's from her."

"I didn't think it was a coincidence. I'll check again tomorrow." Joey leaned back against the wall and took her hand again. "We may have two informants inside that village—if anything, it's more confusing than it was before."

She curled her legs and leaned against his shoulder. "Not in here . . . not with you."

CHAPTER 23

I was pleasant, but stern, keeping Saddiq busy at women's tasks he had never tried before—folding the family's laundry, stirring and watching the stew, and sweeping floors. *My shadow must copy whatever I do*, I pointed out. *Or your father won't be pleased.*

My husband's directive still irritated me, and if anything, Saddiq would learn that women worked as tirelessly as men. Parsaa and the boys could name my many flaws, but the sin of shirk was not among them.

In the fields, I moved at a brisk pace—snipping bare limbs from the trees, tossing the compost, and carrying buckets of rich soil to far ends of the field, stretching to pluck vegetables and then lugging the bins to the cool caves at the base of the mountain.

I wanted the boy to drop with weariness, to fall in bed exhausted and grateful. But Saddiq kept up without complaint. Together, we ate and walked, worked and rested. Eventually my anger subsided, and I found myself enjoying his company. I learned to work and think with my constant and quiet shadow.

Soon I realized that the boy was not sharing my every move with his father. Slowly, my trust in him began to build, and it was less painful to think of him as my oldest son.

A warm breeze lifted the autumn day, and I prepared for a longer walk than usual. Talibah agreed to watch the younger boys. I wrapped some bread in a cloth, added apples to my sack, then poured water into four containers that were easy to carry a distance.

Bring a hat, I advised Saddiq. *We will work in the fields and then climb the hill and check some plants.* Moments later, I set off for the fields, carrying several bags, while he gathered his pack and ran to catch up.

Reaching an area with onions and carrots, I heard his footsteps pounding behind me. I handed over a sack and without a word bent over and started plucking young carrots from the ground, a small variety. Less sweet, they were tangy and wild and delicious with roasted lamb and raisins.

I checked the carrots in his sack. *Do not miss any with tops wider than your thumb. We do not want them to get too tough.* He nodded, but studying the carrot tops slowed his work. By the time I reached the end of the row, I had two bags to his one.

As we passed each other along the rows, he put his hand out to me. *You work so hard for us. Please don't be angry with me.*

I'm not angry, not at all. I stood and stretched.

But you're not talking with father.

It's not easy being treated like a young child who can't take care of herself.

He's only trying to protect you.

My laugh was short. *It's foolish to rely on others for protection.*

Especially those who pretend to protect, the boy muttered. *The Americans.*

His bitterness surprised me. As far as I was concerned, our village had more reason to resent Jahangir than the Americans, and I wondered what Parsaa had told the boy. *The Americans have left us alone. I worry more about those who invent threats to prove their superiority.*

The boy nodded, but I doubted that he understood my reference to Jahangir and others like him. Even with my own family, I had to be careful about defending the Americans. *It's dangerous to talk about these matters. But children your age can handle more than adults imagine.*

He nodded and moved with more speed. We worked more rows, without pause, before I called him to join me to check the steeper slopes.

We'll eat lunch up there, I promised. The climb toward the ridge didn't take long, but I had to stop often, catching my breath and blinking to hold back tears. I had not been to the area since after Ali's death, when I returned for the documents. The days since stretched like years.

I worried about climbing this ridge with another son. But to harvest the crocus, I was left with no choice. I was determined not to let him near the ledge where the documents once waited.

Not many in the village came to this rough area. My husband and I had not been here together in years. Perhaps it was selfish, but we didn't want to attract attention to the tiny plants sprinkled along the roughest side of the mountain.

I had started the field years ago with the handful of corms given to me by my father. Every year, I worked at separating corms and expanding the field, removing weeds and stones, loosening the soil and providing ridges for drainage. I studied the mountainside from afar and was careful about expanding the plots. Every autumn, the flowers burst into bloom against ancient rocks, and all together, from below, they looked like nothing more than a cloud's shadow stretched along the folds of the mountainside.

Early on, I collected only enough saffron for our family meals. After a few years of marriage, Parsaa asked where I had found the cache of crocus. I brought him to the field, and he agreed the place should be kept a secret.

You took a long time to tell me about this, Parsaa had commented only once. *Your secrets can be my secrets.*

Maybe, I had thought to myself. *Maybe.*

He didn't tell the others, and I was relieved. Our secret field expanded every year, and this made explanations to other villagers more difficult. Parsaa and I, and later Ali, worked alone, camping out and ready to pluck stems with blooms that lasted but a single day.

Each year, we faced intense work ten days or so, pinching the blooms soon after they made their appearance and then carrying the flower-heads to a nearby cave where we removed the stigma that provided golden color and flavor. We placed the slender threads on trays so they could dry, before arranging them in small tins that Parsaa carried to market.

Then I'd climb about the hill, checking corms, dividing and spreading more. I always kept a few corms hidden away at home, close at hand, just in case the unthinkable happened, and we were uprooted from this village.

Villagers had no reason to question our activities or climb the twisting paths for this slope. Of course, the young and those who had keen eyesight might spot us. We donned dark gray clothing, and only worked during the early morning hours, when other villagers were busy with tasks. The fold of the mountain shielded us from most onlookers, and as the field expanded, we kept visits to a minimum.

Parsaa made a point of taking the boys on long walks far from Laashekoh, and so a few walks to this area did not seem unusual. I also took the precaution of planting corms on other hills—and shared that saffron with other families.

On this day, I stood at the top of the hill and stared down at the treacherous fold that dropped into a precipice. Dark strands of autumn crocus leaves poked out from behind rocks over the hill, with no sign of purple blooms among the hundreds of plants.

This isn't far from where Ali died, Saddiq noted.

I nodded. Ali had been the only one of our children who knew about the crocus harvest, and he often helped, heading alone to the field before dawn, plucking flowers steadily throughout the day, using our handmade wooden tweezers to gently remove the stigma.

Our family didn't own the slopes of this hill. As a whole, the people of Laashekoh had rights to use the surrounding fields and hills for farming and grazing. Since my arrival, I had assumed we were the only ones who frequented the rougher slopes. The saffron belonged to us as long as we were the only ones who knew about it.

Before Ali's death and after, I had kept an eye out for anyone setting out on the path to undertake the difficult climb—and never saw climbers. I was sure the crocus fields were still our secret. The one who had killed Ali didn't seem to know or care about the flowers and their value.

Maybe Ali's death was an accident. Or maybe someone had returned the documents to their hiding place. Since Mita had left the cave, I yearned to find something new to read, anything, and was curious.

So I used the crocus to distract Saddiq from watching me hunt for the papers again. We walked the ridge, reached the section overlooking the crocus field, and sat on a large rock to eat our lunch. After we finished, we sidestepped down the slope, where I pointed out the spiky leaves that we had planted and explained how we collected the stigma. *We do not tell anyone about the saffron*, I explained. *It would cause too many problems. Of course, your father and I share our wealth in many ways.*

I gently poked with my finger among the folded leaves to show him a bud, and directed him to descend the slope and check the lower parts of the mountain's fold. From there, he would not see the hiding place overhead in the rocks. *See that large rock? Climb carefully. The plants there are in the sun and can bloom a week earlier than those up here. Tell me if you see any hint of color at all.*

As he skipped down the hill, I called out for him to use care on the loose stones. Then I backed away, hurrying to the ledge to remove the rocks and check the hiding place. But there was no point. The metal container and papers had not been returned.

Returning the rocks as cover, I scanned the river valley and wondered about Ali's final thoughts, praying that he was happy and free of evil.

Then I returned to the ridge, and sat, waiting for Saddiq and his assessment. *They're not nearly ready*, the boy reported.

The next rain . . . I said, staring up to the sky and looking forward to the frantic work and deadline. *They will burst into bloom. One of us will be here every day, gathering what is ready.*

And Ali helped with this? he asked with awe. *He never told me.*

He was very good at keeping secrets, I said. *And you are, too.* The compliment pleased the boy, as children always enjoyed being trusted with the secrets of their parents. I gave him advice on taking cautions to prevent others from noticing our harvest. *I always pluck fresh mint or other herbs and keep it in a basket, to cover the saffron, if others ask questions.*

So this is where you went to be alone, he said with a voice of wonder. I didn't correct him. *Mari and the others wonder why you are so good with the crops.*

I just pay attention to what's around us. Someday, your father will show you how he delivers the saffron to market. The saffron allows us to pay for your school . . .

Saddiq bit his lip. *I'm afraid to go to school after what happened to Ali.*

I took him by the shoulders. *Ali did not die at school. He died here, close to home.*

Yes, but Leila and the others didn't want him to leave. I heard Jahangir laughing with Uncle Gul. He says schoolwork makes boys weak.

I dared not criticize the men directly. *Your father respected your uncle, but that's one point they did not agree on. School will make you strong in ways Jahangir doesn't understand. You will solve problems and have ideas.* I looked out over our field. *The beauty of saffron is how much power comes with its slender size.*

~~~~~

We hurried down to the other fields, stored vegetables in the cool caves at the base of the mountain, and then took plenty more back to the village. As was the custom, we left a large basket of carrots for others to take. By evening, the basket would be empty.

Once at home, Saddiq helped me chop carrots and onions, and we used lamb from the previous day, putting the mixture over a low fire. I added raisins and the fragrance filled our home.

I decided the time was right to check the rocks along the path, where Mita had agreed to leave messages. Under the watchful eye of Saddiq, I dared not check too soon. But as days passed, Saddiq no longer stayed so close to my side, staring at me every second. *Saddiq, there's a spice that I'd like to add to this meal,* I noted. *It won't take long for me to get it at all.*

He nodded and stood by the doorway, waiting for me. *Tell me what it looks like,* he offered. *I can go.*

A green plant with white flowers and small, spikey leaves, I said. *Black cumin—it's easy to find.*

I think there's one along the wall not far from the orchard, he exclaimed.

Hmm, I saw a good one not far from the village gate. He didn't ask questions, and we hurried off, climbing over the wall. The trail was empty in both directions, but I didn't worry. Searching for spices around the village was common, and I carried a basket.

Which way? I pointed downhill, and he dashed ahead.

The pile of rocks where we agreed to hide notes wasn't far. With Saddiq busy, I had plenty of time to pause, lift the rock, and check for a message.

A folded piece of thin paper waited in the crevice, and I was delighted to find my first note to read! Looking around, I checked that no one was near before folding my fingers around it and putting the rock back in place. More than anything, I wanted to unfold the paper on the spot and read words from a good friend.

But that had to wait until I was sure I was alone.

And because I had no note with me, I left a few sprigs of cumin on the rock, a way of letting Mita know the note had been received.

CHAPTER 24

Mita's note described waiting near the river before she returned to the outpost; the antics of songbirds; and a reminder about my experiment on mixing compost and sand. The words made me nostalgic for the sound of her voice.

She also asked if I could send the document that she thought was a birth certificate. Excited about receiving another note, I wanted to send my own reply quickly. I snatched a paper from the notebook and wrote a description of the spices that grew along the hills, the taste of wild carrots, the long wait for rain and our saffron to bloom, and the constant help from Saddiq. I was too embarrassed to explain how Parsaa had put me under watch.

My words came quickly and I relished that I could control how an American woman saw my world. Eager for a reply, I retrieved the document, folded it with the note, and hid both inside my tombaan.

It was a relief to dispose of the reminder of an awful day.

But Saddiq might wonder about getting more cumin so quickly. I dipped the leftover cumin in hot water from the stove, and placed the ruined pieces to the side before taking a basket and calling out to him. *I need more cumin. It wilted so quickly. I should have put it in cool water when we returned home.*

He examined the sprigs. *The plant in the orchard is better than the ones along the path*, he offered. *And it's closer.*

The plants along the path get more morning sun.

He shook his head, puzzled, but accompanied me, climbing over the wall and returning to the path. Along the way, I happily pointed plants out to him—one that soothed a burn, another that eased stomach aches, and others that flavored meals. A large array of plants, each with a special purpose, emerged around our village year after year—for me that made a home, along with learning their names and what they could do.

Approaching the hiding place with the tree and the rocks, I slowed. Saddiq pointed to the blunt cuts where we had already removed sprigs. *This is the plant you used.*

Kneeling, I pretended to examine the plants. *I already took the best sprigs, and there are probably more ahead. Can you run and check? Find one that gets more sun and select the youngest leaves.*

He dutifully went ahead. I was impatient and, while he was still in sight, extracted the note from my tombaan.

It was a terrible mistake to focus on Saddiq and not check for others. As I lifted the rock, ready to place my note underneath, Leila stepped out from behind a tree. Startled, I dropped the rock and stepped back. She gave her lopsided smile. Her skin no longer looked raw, but it was stretched and scarred.

Are you waiting for someone? she asked.

Yes, I replied, pointing to Saddiq, and then tugged at a stem. *We're collecting cumin. Would your mother want some?*

She likes spices, but aren't there enough growing near our doorways?

I shrugged, trying not to sound nervous as I put both hands behind my back. *We are hunting a certain kind.*

Yes, you're always so particular. She moved closer and cocked her head, asking about the paper in my hand. Panicked, I glanced down the path. Saddiq heard our voices and hurried to return, to guard my side, as ordered by his father. Trying to think of what to say, I didn't want to connect my son with the paper.

This—it's not mine. I tightened my grip on the papers, distraught that Leila had discovered my hiding place for messages and I could not leave the document for Mita. Upset, I crossed my arms and stuffed the note up one sleeve. Leila could not read, but I felt better with it hidden, pricking my skin. I reminded myself that I was an adult. I did not have to explain to her or Saddiq.

What's wrong? Your hand is shaking.

I lifted my chin, but she was still taller than me. *No need for concern. Let me see what you found,* she demanded.

I took a step back, moving closer to Saddiq, afraid she could grab my arm and insist on seeing the paper. My son was nervous, but he held his ground. Her demand made us stubborn. *What I find must be shown only to Parsaa,* I insisted.

She circled the rock, looking around. *Where did you find the paper?*

Along the path . . . I didn't have to tell her anything, but lies were the natural response to her intrusive way.

It belongs to my father. She reached to tug on my sleeve. Saddiq took a step and blocked her.

Parsaa can decide. My voice was calm, but inside, I was furious about not leaving something for Mita. *It's not for you, a child, to decide.*

Leila glared at Saddiq, tugging at her headscarf to cover more of her cheek.

I'll tell Jahangir about this, she warned, before slipping back into the trees.

She's too bossy for a girl, Saddiq whispered. *Are you all right? You look sick.*

I shook my head, though I did feel sick inside. The boy gave me a questioning look. *What was she talking about?*

Something I found. Nothing important. I can give it to your father.

Neither of them realized I held two papers. Leila would tell others about the paper, and Saddiq would surely tell Parsaa. All would complain if I didn't produce some paper, and that certainly could not be the note to Mita.

I thought about producing a blank piece of notebook paper at home, but Parsaa would be suspicious. I tried to convince Saddiq to go ahead, but he refused, waiting by my side. Lifting the rock again was too risky. Leila could have waited, peering from behind any tree. The note could land in the wrong hands, and the questions about who wrote such a note would never end. The hiding place was ruined and I had no way of warning Mita. I had to hide my note, hand the document to Parsaa, and hope Leila did not cross me again. With luck, he'd show no interest in the document and toss it aside. Perhaps I could retrieve it and find a way to give it to Mita.

And maybe, Allah willing, Parsaa's reaction would provide a clue about Ali's death.

Saddiq waited as I picked through the cumin and gathered more sprigs. Once again, I left a small bouquet behind on the rocks. It was heartbreaking not to leave the note, and I hoped my friend might see the cumin as a message for her not to worry.

More than once during our time in the cave, Mita had suggested that life for women in rural Afghanistan was a trap. She might guess that I had encountered a predicament and not forgotten my teacher and lessons on how to write a note.

We started walking back home, and Saddiq was quiet. I hoped that he and Leila would feel foolish mentioning the paper or quarrel to others.

My life was a prison. The guards were no longer just the men, but neighbors and children, too.

~~~~~

The fragrance of the stew filled our home and the four boys waited eagerly, hands wrapped around the bowls and noses pointed in the air. I put the pot on the carpet—the warm bread was already there—and my husband dished the stew into the bowls.

Raisins! The youngest cried gleefully.

We're lucky, Parsaa said. *Your mother's the best cook in this village.* I could not help but smile. Trust and happiness, an inextricable pair, were slowly, slowly returning to our home.

I filled our mugs with fresh goat's milk. Parsaa filled my bowl with mostly carrots, turnips, and broth, with less meat, as I preferred. Our youngest son babbled about finding rocks and playing a game with friends, and the brother just a year older teased him as if he had countless more years of experience.

As I turned to offer Saddiq more bread—the door to our home burst open. Jahangir stood in the doorway, followed by two of his men. He didn't remove his shoes, and he stared hard at me. *Where is it?*

The boys paused in the dipping of their bread and Parsaa stood. When he spoke, his voice was flat. *What brings you to this home?*

Where is it? Jahangir screamed and came closer, staring down only at me.

Parsaa did not answer and slowly pointed to the door. The younger boys looked terrified. Saddiq's hands were on the floor, ready to leap to his feet and follow his father's orders. *You are not to address my wife. We can discuss this matter later, after this meal is finished.*

Jahangir bent down and swept the nearest bowl of stew against the wall. The bowl broke into pieces. The thick broth oozed down, as if our wall had a wound. Our youngest started crying. *There's no waiting. She has a paper, and I want it now.*

I kept my head down, horrified that Leila had mentioned the document to him and glanced at Saddiq. But he didn't take his eyes off Jahangir, waiting for a signal from his father.

The document was still tucked in my perahaan, within easy reach. Without thinking, my hand went for it. To defuse the tension, to see Jahangir's reaction, I flattened the paper and placed it near Parsaa's feet. Surprise crossed my husband's face, whether because I had the paper or because of what it meant, I wasn't sure. He didn't reach for it.

It's something I found, I said defensively.

Taking advantage of Parsaa's surprise, Jahangir pounced and snatched the paper, staring at it for a long time. I was sure he had no idea what the words on the paper said—and I almost smiled. As the intruder glared at my entire family, I could sense that Parsaa's fury was directed at me for giving Jahangir a reason to enter our home. Of course, I should have waited to show Parsaa the document.

Both men stared hard at me. *Are there more?* Jahangir pressed.

This conversation can wait. Parsaa's voice was cold.

This has nothing to do with you, Jahangir retorted. *These documents come from those who work with the Americans. How well do you know your wife?*

We'll talk later, Parsaa replied stiffly.

Yes, we'll talk later. Jahangir tucked the document away into a pocket. *Before then, figure out how to keep her under control—not meddling with matters that none of you understand.*

He glanced my way. *If you find more papers, bring them to me. Otherwise, I'll search this house until not one wall is left standing.*

He stormed away, leaving the door open. The doors and walls of our home no longer secured us, and I shuddered to think of Leila married to this monster, trying to bend all of us to his will.

I found it today, I murmured nervously. *Leila . . .*

Waving his arm, my husband cut me off. *I will take care of him. And we will talk about this later.* He sharply told Saddiq to finish eating .The two drained their bowls and left our home in silence.

My arms shook as I pressed my own bowl tightly, no longer hungry. Leila must have run straight to Jahangir. Complaining about a villager to an outsider—it meant that she couldn't be trusted by any of us. I should not have been so stunned. A woman's alliance with her husband should be stronger than other relationships or friendships, even if she stayed in her village home. Women had little choice but to depend on their husbands for survival.

Frightened, I could do little to cheer up my sons who worried about parents who couldn't secure their home. It was wrong of Jahangir to bring terror into our home, and I wondered what could make our lives normal again. Was normality simply the lack of problems—daily routines, conversations, meals, and work? Was it wise to avoid any contacts with strangers? I pretended to smile and chat, trying to distract the children. But they sensed my fear.

Your father will handle this, I promised the boys. But would he?

A beautiful meal, a pleasant night with my family, was lost forever. Our religion calls on us to submit, but we must be wary about identifying the authorities to whom we must submit. Every man claims to know the word of Allah. Rather than encourage others to find their own meaning, too many men twist the message, simply trying to impose their will on us for their own devious ends. In the end, we must remain the authority over our own decisions. Blindly following another's authority, without assessing the worthiness or purpose, is cowardice that leads to self-destruction.

CHAPTER 25

Before the firefight and her long absence, Joey had been amazed at how Mita, the tiniest person on base, could charge a room. Optimism and a command of details motivated team members to work on her projects. But enthusiasm had waned since she returned to the outpost. Mita was quiet, distracted. Doubts overshadowed any conversations about projects.

Joey saw her sitting alone in the dining area, eating mechanically. "What's bothering you?" he asked gently.

"Can't talk here," she said with a small shake of the head and a wan smile. "Not now. Meet me in the garden when you're done?"

She hurried away, shoving her cardboard bowl and utensils into the bin for composting material, not stopping to chat with others. Joey collected lunch and carried it with him, leaving the tray behind. He glanced at the others in the room. The mood was hard and impatient. Initial attitudes of setting out on an adventure and accomplishment had long vanished.

Joey headed into the cool, dry air outside and the garden where Mita and others grew tomatoes, squash, and other vegetables that went into outpost meals. Rain had not fallen since they arrived. To grow the few vegetables, staff took turns lugging river water to the garden.

He looked around, wondering if she had changed her mind about the meeting. Then he spotted her under a small overhang that protected a compost pile from the sun's glare.

Wielding a shovel, she stabbed deep into the pile. The pile didn't have enough soil and wasn't ready to turn. Her wrists had to ache.

"Not my specialty, but it's not the best time to turn that pile over,"

Joey teased. Then, he noticed the tears in her eyes and reached out, covering her hand holding the shovel. "Hey, what's wrong?" he pressed.

"How do these villages survive out here?" Mita paused, waving her arm toward the hills. "Could we make it without all the air-drops of food and equipment? Yet they arrange plots in these hills, taking advantage of every microclimate. How dare we try to tell them how to raise crops?"

He crossed his arms. "You're right, but something else is bothering you."

She heaved a sigh and looked down. "You didn't hear? I might be pulled off duty here. A legal team is coming this week to question me and anybody involved with my 'unauthorized absence,' as they call it."

Joey hadn't received notification and wondered what was waiting in his e-mail. "When did you find out?"

"A friend called this morning." She sniffed. "My team members don't know yet, but I needed to talk to someone."

He stepped into the compost pile, under the shelter and away from any prying eyes, and held her close, smoothing the tangle of short curls from her sweaty brow. "Someone here complained to a newspaper reporter, about my going AWOL and getting off light for being a retired general's daughter. It's quite the story—we weren't getting projects up and running so I must have set up the abduction as a ruse, a way to get attention." Her laugh was short. "Going AWOL in Afghanistan? You know that's not what happened, Joey."

"Cameron, damn him." Joey swore, upset about another disruption from a man who worried about anything except the mission at hand.

"What will they ask me?" Mita asked. "How much trouble am I in?"

"They'll ask why you left the outpost without permission, how you survived that long without help from Afghans, and why you didn't issue a thorough report on your return. We can handle it." She wasn't in trouble alone, but he didn't mention that. He took a deep breath. "Look, you told me everything, the woman, the cave, as soon as you returned. I ordered you not to talk about the details with others. I did not want to endanger one, maybe two informants."

His assurances did little to relax her. "Sofi." Mita revealed the woman's name for the first time. "We can't put her in danger."

"Are you sure about her name?" Joey was pointed.

"You don't think they'll try to question people in Laashekoh?" She thought a moment. "We can't mention that name to anyone. Promise me!"

He nodded and, keeping his hands on her shoulders, looked into her eyes. "Is there anything about your time away that I don't know about and should?" Joey asked. "Anything? Tell me now."

"Joey, I probably stayed longer than necessary," Mita admitted. "I could have left on my own, but I didn't know the way back and was afraid of walking alone. Maybe I could have tried to signal for help from a plane. But I learned more from her about that village and Afghans in those two weeks than any of our visits. Look, she didn't hold me against my will. And she kept warning me about a possible attack on the outpost—that the villages were troubled by my kidnapping and factions were blaming one another. And that's why neither of us tried to signal the searchers." She paused. "And she was desperate to learn how to read."

She leaned her head on his shoulder, and he thought as he hugged her tight. "Once you returned, we determined that there was no kidnapping. No one stepped forward to claim responsibility. You didn't divulge security information?"

"Never."

"You made no promises to her?"

"None," Mita replied.

"The woman's not a danger to us—she's an informant who helped the mission. We just need to find a way to prove that without releasing her name." He clapped his hand against a nearby post. "Damn, it would help to get our hands on that birth certificate."

"How would that help?"

"You gathered information while you were away. Made an important contact." He shook his head. "And Cameron, what the hell has he done to help?"

"He's upset that we're not using his ideas. He can't stand giving these villages time to find their own way."

"He's a divider, that one. Any investigation of you is a waste of time. We never sought any publicity over your disappearance. Keeping a lid on abductions is SOP. Only families are notified."

"He's going to tell them about us. . . ."

Joey dismissed that concern. "Let them interrogate. You are the bravest woman I know." He kissed the top of her head. "I have a lot of work to do. We're headed back to the village."

~~~~~~

Joey and Mita walked into Laashekoh alone, determined to prove the village was not a security risk. A security detail waited outside the gate.

The villagers were wary. Most men did not stop working; the others didn't put down their weapons. Most of the women were inside, busy preparing for Leila's wedding. Even the children held back from greeting the team.

I waited in my doorway and stared. Mita did not look well, and I was worried. She was less confident, less in control than she had seemed back inside the cave. She looked more worried than me, a woman who had to live in a village stalked by Jahangir.

I watched their approach, but dared not move about outside, not with Jahangir watching for any misstep. The man did not assume Gul's duties, but he managed to cow an entire village. Still, he remained careful around a few men, including my husband.

But Parsaa was not around. He had left early, and all we knew was that he had promised to return before the wedding meal.

Ahmed was torn about a welcome Jahangir would criticize. But rudeness to visitors before Leila's wedding could be a bad omen for the couple and the village. And none of us wanted the foreigners to see Jahangir bully the village. The young man stepped forward. *We're busy today, preparing for a celebration, and have no time to talk.*

The man named Joey stood back and was polite, but looked surprised. *We are here for several reasons. It won't take much time.* He stumbled over his words, avoiding looking at the blank faces directed his way. He kept his eyes on Ahmed. *First, we're very sorry to learn about the death of Gul. We appreciated his vision.*

Gul told you that we would come to you if we needed help, Ahmed said tersely. *We have not been to your camp to ask for help.*

Mita spoke quickly to Joey and he translated. *My colleague wanted to come in person and thank the village for its understanding and efforts during the search.*

Tashakor, Mita added.

Ahmed's face softened, though he did not invite the pair to sit.

Is it possible we could purchase more fruit?

Jahangir stepped from the threshold of Mari's home—and stared at Ahmed, waiting for his answer. That irritated Ahmed. *You wait here,* the young man quickly replied to Mita. *We'll send the children for the fruit and bring it to you.* He slapped his hands, and two boys ran over. *Enough to fill their packs,* Ahmed ordered.

Joey guided Mita toward a shady area and then he knelt on the ground and extracted pamphlets from his pack—offering them to Ahmed. *We can leave these here, too—guides on predicting weather and planning harvests.*

We have no need for these. Ahmed sounded so nervous. *As you have said, our products are as good as any grown around here.*

Then maybe you can pass them on to others. Joey awkwardly left some of the papers on the bench.

Jahangir approached the group and looked at the pamphlets.

Did you not hear? We have no need of these. He lifted his foot and knocked the pile to the ground. *The only words we need are those from the Koran. We have no need for words of any other man. You do not trust in Allah?*

We are here. We want to buy food from you—we trust both. The village and Allah, Joey countered.

You who must depend on a small village for your supplies? We are not fools and know you have other motives.

Jahangir turned and spoke to the other men. *They have plenty in storage and pretend they don't know how to farm.*

Joey protested. *We could get fruit shipped in, but if the village has extra to sell, we are willing buyers. It saves extra transport to the markets.*

Never satisfied, Jahangir raised his hand as if his patience were taxed. *You do not need products from this village. You are here to spy on us.*

Suddenly he turned and studied the other men. *And I suspect that you have help from this village.*

He stared at our men and they stared back. *How does he know about Gul's death? The Americans have not been here since that day.*

Mita looked surprised, too. Backing away, I pressed my back against the wall, trying to think. I had sent Mita on her way the day Gul died; she had not learned about the death from me. I don't know, I was not involved, I repeated to myself like a prayer.

No one responded, and he raised his voice. *We understand your ways. It's time for the intruders to move on.*

Joey turned to Ahmed. *So, someone new is in charge of the village.* Joey gave a curt nod before signaling to Mita that they should leave. I stepped out into the sunlight, grabbing a bucket as an excuse. She caught my eye, and I dipped my head twice in sad agreement. Catching myself, in case others were watching, I pressed my lips together to hide any hint of emotion.

The American soldier's comment, suggesting that the village had relinquished control to an outsider, startled the other villagers, and there was shame in hearing the words spoken aloud. It was as if the American had held up a big mirror that showed our fear. Most forgot Jahangir's questions—and stared at Ahmed and the other men. Even Jahangir looked startled as the American man stalked toward the gate, with Mita trailing.

I let out my breath slowly, doing all I could to hide how much I cared, how much I wanted to run after them.

~~~~~~

With the sun directly overhead, Mita and Joey trudged down the mountainside, with the security detail taking up the rear. Mita didn't talk until they paused near the rocks where Sofi was supposed to leave the message. It was no surprise that nothing was there.

"You're upset with me," Joey spoke up.

Her lips were tight. "That didn't go well."

"That guy is trouble." Joey had no other explanation.

Mita turned to him, exasperated. "But storming off didn't help, not after a comment that may have humiliated the entire village in front of him. These villages have enough pressure, and all we did was add to it today. Besides, he jumped on the fact that we had word of Gul's death. He'll be looking for who told us."

"It's good for him to worry."

"I worry about the people who informed us," Mita scolded.

"Did you see the woman?"

Mita nodded. "She smiled once, but otherwise she looks terrified and beaten down. Something is going on that she can't even leave a note."

"She didn't get caught or she wouldn't be standing there," Joey replied. "Someone should look into Gul's sudden death. It's not a coincidence." Mita didn't look convinced. "Look, I'm trying to goad Ahmed and the others into taking some control. They need to act like leaders."

She closed her eyes. The comment could have just as easily been directed at her. "Village leaders are not always apparent."

"They're letting a bully get out of hand—and that's not good during a transition." She slowed her gait and he waited. "I want to fix this now, Mita," he implored. "What can I do?"

"I hate to walk away, insulting them," she said. "That's all we accomplished today. . . ."

He balked at the idea of heading back to the village to make amends with Jahangir.

"Not him, but the others," Mita pressed. "We can't abandon people who support us and depend on us. And it's easier not to insult people in the first place." She leaned against him and smiled. "We have to show the few villagers who do trust us that we're different from Jahangir and the Taliban. We have to work with the Camerons and not walk away."

Joey wanted nothing more than to hurry from the village and forget the uncomfortable encounter. But delaying contact with the village would complicate future contacts, not a good scenario with an investigative team arriving soon. Besides, he didn't like arguing with Mita. She was right.

"They're having a wedding," he noted. "What can we bring as a gift?"

~~~~~~

Every girl in our village had one goal, and that was marriage with children. Mari had worked hard for Leila's day, years in the making. Jahangir did not have family in the area to throw the wedding party, but Mari took over. Because she had worked so hard at the cooking and preparations for other families' weddings, all of us stood ready to help.

Of course, this wedding was unusual for our village. Normally we celebrated weddings of our sons and the strangers who were their brides. The women whispered and shook their heads when Mari was not around. As far as anyone could remember, Leila was the first woman to remain in the village and marry.

For the rest of us, including Mari, we had attended our own weddings as timid, lonely, young strangers. Eventually we came to regard this village as our home, but we still could not help but regard Leila with envy. She was the only woman who did not have to find her way in our village.

But then she had to marry abrasive, loud Jahangir. No one looked forward to him making a place in our village.

So a nervous shiver went through Laashekoh about any break in tradition. Some suggested that Leila staying would upend balance; others believed that the wedding would solidify Jahangir's power and that he might invite others to settle in this area. Others insisted that this wedding would make no difference at all. I fell into the latter group, certain that Leila's staying in the village would not change much. Our village adapted to women coming and leaving—and if strangers didn't change the character of the village, then how could one woman remaining behind possibly make a difference?

The threat was Jahangir.

I should have been comforted that Mari was elated. Despite Gul's recent death, she wanted to do most of the cooking, and the rest of us helped in little ways.

Parsaa returned, and I noticed how that lifted the mood of the village. The boys followed him about, and the women chattered more. Everyone expected him to defend us against unreasonable attacks, and inside, I hoped that he was not like Gul. I didn't want my husband to fight, but I also didn't want him to be another willing, complacent partner for Jahangir.

The villagers spread out and worked to hurry the marriage and make it part of the past. Mari talked to Ahmed and other young men to pull Jahangir aside, so he could dress and prepare for the dinner in his honor. He was docile, complying with the minor matters of etiquette urged by Mari, and he didn't mention the burqa.

I gathered the finest vegetables to go with both a goat and young lamb, which had roasted throughout the day. Karimah had moved a small worktable outdoors and I worked beside her, chopping apricots, berries, apples, and other fruit into tiny jewels, before adding pomegranate seeds and heaping mounds into split melons.

The day was brilliant, allowing us to celebrate outside. Men arranged carpets, cushions, and candles in the village center—one large carpet for the men and the other for the women. Piles of bread and small bowls of sauces were arranged. Some of the women worked on arranging one another's hair and all wore their finest clothes.

Jahangir requested that there be no gifts or music and announced that he and Leila would stay in Mari's home for the time being.

The men would eat first and then drink tea, while the women gathered for their part of the meal at their separate area. Jahangir was unhappy about men and women sitting so close, but Parsaa dismissed those complaints, pointing out that the village had made enough changes to accommodate the unusual couple. Leila remained out of sight until the ceremony, and I knew her sisters and friends painted her hands with henna and arranged her hair before adding the shaal. She would be decked in the few old pieces of family jewelry available in our village, shared by women for these special occasions.

There were no guests other than the people of our village and Jahangir, not even the men who traveled with him. As the afternoon unfolded, the women buzzed and laughed with excitement. The change was small, a bride not traveling far away, and yet so easy, exciting—and perhaps not wrong at all. Maybe our ability to adapt to something new made the day happy and relaxed.

Not everyone agreed. Karimah angrily sliced the flat bread into triangles.

Perhaps Jahangir will calm down, I murmured.

She shrugged, refusing to agree or disagree. *My younger son is tight with Jahangir.* She gave a hard, angry shake of the head. *But he doesn't listen and I dare say no more. . . .*

To myself, I wondered how life could go on this way, with so many afraid to voice ideas or concerns because of one man's temper. I wondered how long any of us could possibly withhold our responses to the dark moods without lashing out?

Karimah went around the corner and returned with a bottle of oil and spices that looked familiar. *What is that for?* I asked.

For dipping—Mari asked me to cut the bread into strips, drizzling oil over them and dusting them with more spices. She wants this bottle for the men's meal and this one with less garlic for the women.

One of Karimah's daughters laughed. *She warned it's so spicy that it will boil the men's stomachs!*

I was ready and glanced at the men. *Let me handle this—while you check the children.*

Don't you want to get ready, too? Karimah asked.

I'm fine. No need to bother Mari.

Karimah agreed. *You'll do a better job than I can. She's so particular for someone whose daughter is not going anywhere!*

Smiling, she ran off, and I was sure Karimah had no clue about Mari's plan.

~~~~~

Later, Karimah returned to help pull the bread from the outdoor oven. It was crispy brown, doused with flavored oil outside and fluffy soft on the inside, to join many other delicacies. She tried to chase me home. *Go change!* she scolded. But I shook my head and knew I appeared worried and distracted with hair astray and still in work clothes. Yet I refused to walk away from the area of food preparation.

The men were gathering to take their places as the two Americans returned through the gate. Both stood back, like chastened children, punished while others played. Mita caught my eye, and a tiny smile flashed. An urge to call to her, inviting her to join our preparations, swept through me. Instead, I stood still, feeling dishonest and unkind about my inability to greet this woman, my teacher, openly as a friend. That would raise too many questions that neither of us were ready to answer.

Ahmed and two other young men greeted the pair. *You're back*, he said flatly.

Parsaa frowned—bothered by Ahmed's tone or annoyed about not being told about the earlier visit.

I must apologize for leaving so abruptly. Joey's gaze was direct and warm. *I was wrong and must admit that I don't always understand the ways around here.*

Ahmed thanked him, discomforted about being reminded of the earlier slight. He glanced nervously at Parsaa for direction.

And you mentioned the wedding. We wanted to bring a gift for the couple. He reached into his pack and extracted a pen that worked in all weather and a bag of candy—and asked the group to accept the tokens for the couple.

Ahmed examined both and promised to pass the gifts on to the man and woman. Parsaa coughed and gestured toward the carpets, prompting Ahmed to speak up. *Perhaps you would join our celebration?*

With a smile, Joey glanced at Mita and she nodded. They left their packs by the stone wall, as Ahmed gave rapid orders to others to welcome the newcomers and find them places.

Mari must have heard the noise. Startled, she hurried to Parsaa, whispering. But he shook his head. Mari tried to convince him one more time, but again, Parsaa and Ahmed ignored her. She walked away, muttering about checking Leila.

As I checked the roasts and the vegetables, Jahangir emerged from the building where he had bathed and dressed. Agitated at seeing the American soldier seated on a cushion for a meal, he stopped. *What is he doing back?*

The crowd went quiet. The Americans looked nervous. After a moment, Ahmed replied. *They're our guests. They returned to apologize.*

Jahangir remained standing and glared at Parsaa. *I do not feel comfortable.*

Parsaa studiously ignored the comment and warmly directed everyone to sit. *Yes, sit, sit, and start eating. It's a happy day, there is plenty, and I feel our friend Gul smiling on us.*

The other men of our village cheered the sentiment and took their seats. Ahmed reached for the bread and passed it to Joey, boasting that his wife had baked it.

Everyone sit, please. And Parsaa nodded at the women, too. I guided Mita to a seat close to mine. Still, we could not have spoken freely.

Allah would not approve. Jahangir was stubborn. *I won't sit until they leave and neither will my bride.*

Parsaa stroked his beard with his hand and glanced at Ahmed. *The groom is nervous.* Most of the men chuckled. Then he turned to Jahangir and kept his voice low. *If you want respect, don't ask from others very much.*

The feeling in my heart is in Allah's hands. Jahangir smiled, but his voice was cold. *You will see his power, and then you will believe.* Taking a quick turn, he hurried back to Mari's home.

So we may not celebrate the wedding today. Parsaa shrugged and took a slice of bread. *Such nerves.*

Watching my husband, the American, Ahmed, and the others chew the bread, I felt nauseous to think how close they had come to falling ill. It was enough that I had prevented Mari's oil from being served during the wedding meal, dumping it into weeds beyond the village wall and replacing it with flavored oil from my home.

The incident was over. There was no good reason to tell anyone about my suspicions. Mari could not ask questions, and if she did guess, I'd suggest that Allah had intervened.

Our village acts on crimes and not intentions. If punishment was doled out on suspicions alone, the women would suffer the most. In our village, it was best to remain vigilant and quiet. Once, I might have told Parsaa about Mari's plan, but he had made it clear how little he trusted me.

~~~~~~~

The Americans did not stay long. They ate, they chatted with those sitting nearby, and then they left quietly. The groom was difficult, and the Americans were noticeably embarrassed that they had disrupted a ceremony.

Not long after the Americans departed, we heard shouting from Mari's home. Then, Mari guided Jahangir outside to his place of honor. She looked around at the group relishing her meal and the near-empty baskets of bread before speaking to my husband.

You are right, Parsaa. They are nervous. Jahangir regrets his temper, and the two are ready for you to bless the marriage.

Jahangir nodded politely at Parsaa, but my husband waved his hand. *No need to apologize. Two men who believe can work together.* He stood and a group of young women called excitedly for the bride.

Leila emerged from the home, graceful in shimmering rose folds with detailed embroidery, an exquisite wedding outfit that must have cost Gul more than a few weeks of work. A veil hid her scar and her eyes were bright—and villagers could not help but recall her beauty. I wondered if I was alone remembering Gul's worry about a burqa.

The villagers cheered the couple, and then resumed eating and conversing. Jahangir placed only the goat meat on his plate and glanced at Mari with a smile, as she wept and did not eat. That's when I knew she never intended to kill all the men of our village, but only the men who threatened Jahangir—starting with Gul and moving on to Parsaa, Ahmed, and others.

The children, including my boys, darted about and crawled into the laps of parents. Parsaa handed over some of the bread to Hassan, and Ahmed shared some with his youngest. Mari never spoke up or tried to stop any of them—and my anger built inside, replacing hunger. Moving slowly, I helped clear away the bowls and make room for more courses, watching the others laugh and chew the oily bread with no thought at all.

I wasn't sure which disturbed me more—Mari's callousness or my husband's graciousness with Jahangir.

No doubt, as the celebration lasted through the evening, Mari was surprised that none of the guests complained about stomach pains. I saw her examine one of the baskets, poking at the few golden scraps with her finger.

The men were convivial, speaking and chuckling well into the dark. From my home, I watched Jahangir with disgust, how he raised tension and then smiled and laughed, letting everyone think that his wrath had faded. The speed of his changing moods was most disturbing. The anxiety of waiting for his next eruption was a dark and all-consuming force.

~~~~~~

During the wedding, the man named Parsaa had passed close to Joey and murmured one word. "Tonight."

So Joey had hurried Mita back to the outpost and warned his best fighters to prepare for a raid. Then they returned to the area near the pass, hiking to a small cave not far from the river and the village of Laashekoh.

Taking an indirect route, they reached the cave by midnight. Parsaa had described the place in their earlier meeting—easy to access, secluded, shielded by brush, with multiple exits. "We can confront the traffickers near the village or wait until they're farther away." Joey had explained when they had exchanged ideas during the meeting. "It depends how you want to deal with those from your village."

"I'd like to see how many men from my village are helping Jahangir," Parsaa had explained. "If it's more than one or two . . ."

"Would any of the children help him?"

"Anything's possible," Parsaa admitted.

So Joey relayed the plans to his men: They would identify Parsaa as their village partner and wait until he lured Jahangir and other traffickers away from their cargo. "We don't know how many or whom," he warned. "We won't rush in. We want to be sure what we're dealing with."

Dan ran a hand over the cave's smooth and sandy wall. "It looks like a good place for waiting. They won't see us until the last minute. The informant suggested it?"

Joey nodded. He understood the concern that they could be lulled into an elaborate trap. "I know," he said. "Multiple exits don't mean much in the way of safety, and they could have more men out there than we do. But I trust this guy."

Dan nodded, then sat and opened his pack, ready for final prep. "Then we do, too."

"The traffickers have been spending time in this area," Joey warned the others. "They could know this cave or send a scout in advance. We don't know how careful they'll be. We don't move until our man confronts the group, and we know the exact location of the children."

The younger men understood, after countless warnings that the Taliban loved nothing better than tricking Americans into taking aim at children.

Joey studied the men. "If we don't get a clear separation between our targets and the kids, we'll track them all the way to the Pakistan border."

After the briefing, the soldiers kept talk to a minimum, sleeping while two kept watch outside the entrance. Even in the darkness, they had a good view of the river and the mountain pass through which the caravan—if real—would emerge.

Parsaa had insisted that no more than two villagers besides Jah-angir could be helping with the trafficking operation. The Americans had better weaponry and would have no problem handling up to four men. If there were more than four, Joey would postpone the attack, radio for air support and backup. He refused to take chances with the possibility of any kids in the area. More troops would only increase the confusion and chances of an accident.

Surprise was critical, and Joey looked around again, praying the cave wasn't a trap.

CHAPTER 26

The night's layers of clouds veiled the moon, and a cool breeze quieted the rattling of the season's last insects. My mind could not get past Mari's and Jahangir's treachery or the pleasant reactions of other village women to Mita as they pelted her with questions for the brief time she joined the wedding celebration. Sleep was impossible.

It was late when my husband slipped out of bed. My stomach tightened, and bile seeped into my mouth. Parsaa had taken Gul's place in more ways than one. Fear replaced the other thoughts—fear that Parsaa worked with Jahangir, removing young children from their homes and families, profiting from the pain. Love was impossible without trust. Faith that relied on fear was wrong.

I waited until Parsaa left our home and then I leaped out of bed, too. I had no plan, no idea of how to stop the caravans passing by our village. But maybe I could talk sense into my husband. At the very least, I might convince him not to help by supplying Jahangir food and water for the rest of the journey to the Pak border, and maybe that would force the men to return the children to their homes.

After draping my darkest scarf over my head and around my neck, I sat on the bench and pulled on my shoes. As I stood, Saddiq emerged from the shadows and stared at me. *There is no need for you to follow*, I snapped. *I'm going after your father.*

Saddiq blinked and tightened his lips, but did not respond and kept his hands in his pockets. My husband had trained this boy well, and my disgust spilled out. *Your father's involved in something foolish, and I'm trying to stop him. If you follow, you'll only hurt us. You could get us all killed.*

Saddiq blinked again, showing a hint of fear. *I'm your mother, and I order you to remain here with your brothers.*

I slipped outside our door and headed for the wall, as fast as possible without making noise. As I crawled over the wall, I stared back at my home. The door was closed, and all was quiet. Perhaps I had convinced the boy not to follow.

~~~~~~

With no clue as to which direction Parsaa took or what I would do if I found him, I headed to the same place where Gul had met with Jahangir in the middle of the night. I moved slowly down the hill, pausing to listen for long periods and using boulders as shields. I dared not risk noise, knocking a rock or branch out of place and getting caught. As I neared the river, the sound of women's voices surprised me.

A small fire glowed behind a pile of stones, and I could see three figures moving about, unloading containers and crates from a rickety cart, then hiding them behind the brush, out of sight from the nearby path.

How much longer will they be? Mari called out. *Should we wait here?*

Jahangir spoke in a low voice, directing her to return to the top of the hill and keep watch and warn if any villagers approached. Mari muttered something, and a woman laughed in response. Leila.

Allah was on my side. I had reached the area just in time, while the group talked among themselves. Mari and Leila were far more observant than Gul had been. And I still did not know if Parsaa was near. I held my breath, holding back from approaching too close. Instead, I took a new vantage point, a distance from where the wagon had stopped last time, and remained curled behind a large rock in a grassy section higher on the slope. Mari hurried by, passing so close that I could have touched her fluttering black scarf.

There was no sign of Parsaa.

But then, that bit of relief turned into a nagging worry about the possibility of Saddiq dutifully stepping down the hill, following his father's orders to protect his mother. I wasn't sure whether Parsaa worked with or against Jahangir and the men selling children or how much Saddiq knew.

I wondered if Parsaa waited nearby. And I had been firm with Saddiq. I only hoped the boy had listened to me and stayed away.

Even before the sound of Mari's footsteps faded, Jahangir roughly pulled Leila close, stripping her of her veil. Near the fire, their two shadows became one, writhing in the open grassy patch.

Shivering and afraid, not wanting to hear them, I clutched my arms across my chest and bent my head to my knees, praying for a distraction from Allah. The pair broke apart suddenly and only then I heard a snapping sound, shouts, and crying children. The wagon slowly approached, rumbling over the dry and rocky trail, a lantern dangling back and forth.

May Allah ruin them, Jahangir growled. *The Americans could hear.* He stepped away from the fire, disappearing into the darkness, but his scolding was clear. *I told you to keep them quiet.*

The driver, a lone adult, stopped the wagon and hurried toward the fire as children wailed. *They don't listen.*

Don't speak to ears, Jahangir retorted. With that, he handed a supple branch to Leila and snatched a piece of food from an improvised rack over the fire, before moving toward the wagon's rear. The smell of roast lamb was tantalizing. A few high-pitched voices pleaded for a taste, reminding me of the humiliation of hunger.

Only the quiet get to eat. Jahangir's low voice was ominous in the darkness. *No food for any who make noise.*

Holding a thin branch, Leila latched onto elbows, dragging the dawdlers from the wagon. The children's hands were tied in front, and a long rope connected groups of three or four, looped around their necks to discourage escape. *Hurry*, she admonished. *We don't want to be here all night.*

With that, Jahangir threw a small piece of meat down, and a few boys leapt to the ground, snatching at the food and fighting, pulling others down with them.

Other groups huddled closer together. Leila shook her head and led each small group away, one at a time to another area where they relieved themselves. To hurry them, she whipped the branch against the back of their legs. It was her wedding night, and she was impatient.

The waiting children, more weary than stunned, stared desperately at the fire and sticks with roasted lamb left over from the wedding celebration. The driver shoved pieces down his throat followed by long gulps of water.

This canyon was gloomy, but I could count at least twelve, maybe fifteen, children. Their clothes were soiled, and only a few had shoes. The scene sickened me, yet I could not tear my eyes away.

As Leila led the groups away, Jahangir continued using water and food to turn the children on one another. Teasing them, he tossed a few more scraps and forced them to compete. The ropes tangled, and one thin boy elbowed hard, prompting shoves and a flurry of hands. The child was accustomed to fighting for food.

Jahangir pulled the child aside and held a chunk of lamb high. *These children have not been kind to you*, he said in that low voice. *Tell me, which ones do you think we can trust the most?*

The boy started pointing and blurting out names that had no meaning—and Jahangir held up his hand. *Wait*, he cautioned. *Think about this carefully. Which are the most dangerous? Which have reason to hate me the most?* Jahangir put his hands on the boy's shoulders and smiled. *And let me advise you, there are right answers and wrong answers. The right ones will bring rewards and the wrong ones . . .* The man feigned a grimace, as if fooling around with a friend in a silly game.

The boy was shrewd. *It's easier to show the ones you cannot trust.* He looked over the group of children and quickly pointed out two tall boys who had already handed their snatched portions to younger children in the group. The boy explained in detail how long he knew the various children. He had grown up with some, and others he only knew from a wagon ride of two days. He supplied Jahangir with specific details.

All right. Which children are most likely to scream or make trouble as we move through towns?

The boy stared at Jahangir, who held another stick with a large slice from the roast, and then turned, quickly dismissing the oldest boys and all the girls as untrustworthy. He singled out one of the older boys and a younger girl, who must have been brother and sister: *These two whispered about running away.*

Jahangir extended his hand, and the boy snatched the meat. As the girl cowered, the boy stared defiantly at Jahangir. *Lock those two at opposite ends of the wagon and no food for them tonight,* Jahangir ordered Leila. *We'll sell them in separate places . . . no city life for them, I'm afraid.*

The man ignored the sobbing as Leila separated the pair. He turned to the child pulling at the meat with his teeth and instructed him to dole out flat bread to the rest of the children. The boy followed Jahangir's orders exactly.

Keep a piece for yourself, too. Now tell me, which of the group is the weakest?

The child shook his head and looked at the man as if he had asked a silly question, before pointing to the youngest, so small, sitting on the ground, head down, sobbing. An older girl had her arm draped around the little boy's neck, trying to lift his head and tuck bread into the quivering mouth. The child's eyes were terrified and he had given up.

Of course, Jahangir said. *We will dispose of that one soon, so there's no delay. And you, for helping me, we'll be sure to place you in one of the finer places, where you can use your skills in some trade.*

Jahangir handed over another slice of meat. *I'm important!* The boy piped up, waving his prize and devouring it quickly, unconcerned that hungry children watched. Jahangir didn't respond, turning to consult the driver who had delivered the children. The two men examined the children, pulling headscarves away from the girls, checking the boys' backs, testing arms and legs. With Leila, they discussed the ages and potential of each and, using the information from the boy, redivided the children into several groups.

I tell you again and again—only healthy ones, Jahangir scolded. He looked over the group. *And angry ones, we can break. Compliance is more valuable than cleverness in the markets.*

The men anticipated how much money each child would bring, once they had moved the entire group to a border town in Pakistan. The most attractive girls selected for men seeking young brides would fetch the highest prices, followed by strong boys and girls who could help as skilled or domestic labor. The children who did not fit into those categories would be sold to carpet-makers, brick-kiln operators, and farmers who kept prices low by relying on child labor.

The group selected for Jahangir's trust was small in number and young.

Pulling a carpet from behind his seat on the wagon, the driver talked about sleep.

No time for that, Jahangir countered. *Get them back on the road tonight.*

No need to hurry, the driver protested. *This load is from Ghōr. Their parents were relieved to be rid of them.*

Jahangir shook his head. *American soldiers are in this area and want to look as though they're doing something. Unless you want to land in their jail, you need to move.* Jahangir reached in a pack and handed papers to the driver. *Here is the letter of transport for eighteen orphans and the certificates. Bring back what's left if there's no need for them in Pakistan.*

You never know. Wait—there are no names on these!

Jahangir was irritated. *Give them names—any names you want. You'll find someone in the city who can insert the names later.*

I expected that completed here!

You worry about minor details. We lost the man who could write. Leila scowled behind Jahangir. *Give them new names and carry the documentation if you're stopped . . .*

Suddenly, there was a shriek on the hillside, just behind my hiding place. Then another shriek. *He bit me!* Mari screamed. *I caught him, and he bit me!*

And down the hill she came, dragging Saddiq behind her, even as the boy twisted to get away. I gasped, backing away to another large group of boulders. The others were startled at the interruption, and some of the children called out. *Komak konid.*

No one heard me. Shaking, I dropped to my knees and clung to the rock, trying to think of how to remove Saddiq from this scene and feeling relief that Parsaa, who could write, was not cooperating with Jahangir just yet. But where was Parsaa? Saddiq's best chance was if Parsaa waited nearby.

What did you do? Jahangir snapped.

I was watching on the hilltop as you advised, and found this one approaching, watching the lot of you. The little snake bit me!

Jahangir walked up to Saddiq, lifting his head and stroking him under the chin. *So you'd like to join this group of children? You're lucky. Tonight we have room for you.*

The boy twisted harder, and it hurt not to rush to him. Instead, I bit down hard on my forefinger, forcing myself to remain quiet until I had a viable plan.

Locking Saddiq's wrists together, Jahangir called for Leila.

There was no fear in Saddiq's eyes. His stare was a challenge. But she refused to look at him or connect. He was an annoyance for her.

Ready with rope, she quickly bound the boy's hands, tight, and then for extra measure, wrapping the ends of the rope up to my son's neck. He jerked the rope hard at one point, pulling her down. Leila cursed and turned to Jahangir. *This one cannot be trusted. Get him out of here.*

I don't have space . . . , the driver complained. *You yourself said the letter talks about eighteen children.*

Allah's wrath on you, fool, Leila hissed. *You risk the entire operation. This boy has seen us!* Jahangir dragged my Saddiq close to the wagon, ready to load him.

The driver cursed. *I'm the one in trouble if they misbehave and we get caught. . . . I deserve a higher payment!*

Wait. Mari stepped forward. *Taking him with the rest is a risk. His father and mother will never stop looking.*

Jahangir scoffed. *The parents give up before a week has passed, and they hope for the best.*

The children forget quickly enough, the driver agreed. *Especially if they're young and haven't been to school.*

Be quiet, fool! Jahangir kicked a rock toward the fire and sparks flew.

This one must go. Leila shoved past her mother, and spoke directly to Jahangir. She was not about to let the boy return to the village. *All's lost if he tells his father about our operation.*

Jahangir put his hand up and turned to the driver. *If you must, unload the unruliest along the way. Make it a lesson for the others and leave no trace.*

The man nodded. *Before we cross the border and reach Quetta.*

Push through the night. No more stops.

They talked lightly about killing my son or another child, eliminating an inconvenience. The exchange must have terrified the children, but Saddiq seemed distracted in his struggle against the ropes. Jahangir edged closer to the wagon. Like me, he noticed the boy twisting and trying to reach into the folds of his pants.

Swiftly the man grabbed the rope around Saddiq's neck with a hard, irritated yank—and removed the pistol that Saddiq had tucked away in his pocket. His father's pistol—the one I had unloaded. Parsaa would have checked the gun before leaving our home, but I was less sure about Saddiq. Unless he checked and reloaded the weapon, it was empty of ammunition.

The boy was devastated, as if he had lost his only hope. I closed my eyes, praying that the gun was still unloaded. The boy was better off without such a weapon. Jahangir handed the gun to Leila and murmured, *Only if necessary.*

Noises traveled far in the valley, and Jahangir didn't want the sound of gunshots so close to the village or the outpost.

Leila held the gun with two hands, aiming for Saddiq. *How dare you follow us? Did your parents send you?* He glared, with no answer, and she kicked him, to humiliate rather than hurt him.

I thought my parents worked with you, Saddiq snapped.

That startled her and Leila was indignant. *They should be so smart.*

They are around here, Saddiq warned, defiant. *They are cautious after what happened with Ali.*

Leila went frantic, swinging the gun and screaming, as Saddiq ducked his head behind the wheel. *You creep around in the night like a spider. Your parents know nothing!*

Another firm voice broke out from the shadows. *I know enough.*

Parsaa—it took me a minute to place my husband's outline on the other side of the clearing. Relief swept through me, and I had to lean against the rock, wondering how long he had stood there and how much he had seen. His rifle—the one I had unloaded—was pointed at Jahangir, Parsaa's finger on the trigger.

My son came looking for me. And he will go home with me. Parsaa stepped toward the wagon, as if curious about the huddled children. I wanted to scream out, worried that he had no understanding of what he interrupted or just how dangerous Leila, Jahangir, and Mari were. Jahangir's and the driver's weapons were leaning against rocks, well off to the side. Their only weapon was Parsaa's, in Leila's hand. Jahangir had warned against making noise. But I didn't trust her.

As Parsaa approached the children, Leila backed off a few steps, smiling, alternately aiming the pistol at Parsaa then Saddiq.

Parsaa smiled at our son, and maybe I detected a worried shake of Saddiq's head. Both of them had to wonder about my whereabouts. Shame swept through me about putting my son in such danger, and I wanted to run to him, shield him. But neither husband nor son mentioned my name. Until I had a plan, I had to wait.

Staying low to the ground, I stared. Parsaa was calm. Jahangir and Leila were impatient. Mari was agitated and embarrassed about Parsaa catching her and Leila. Only a few days before my husband had instructed Saddiq to follow me, and I had complained to Mari. I prayed that she did not connect that Saddiq had been ordered to follow me wherever I went.

Do not move closer to him, Leila ordered. As the oldest daughter in a family with no sons, she was a practiced shooter. But her hand shook. Parsaa was a strange man for her, not ambitious, insecure, or fearful like her own father or Jahangir.

Leila couldn't be sure about what the man might do to protect his son.

Suddenly, Jahangir stepped close to her, reaching to cover her hand and point the gun toward the ground. *You startled us.* He spoke up in a friendly way. *We're relocating orphans from the north.*

Orphans whose parents track you down? Parsaa took another step closer to the children. He didn't move his forefinger from the trigger. *No, these children aren't going anywhere.*

Fool! Leila spat with anger and jerked the gun away. *He knows more than he lets on. He always knows more.*

Standing over his son, Parsaa gazed at his old friend's daughter as if she were a stranger. *They can wait in our village for their parents to arrive.*

This has nothing to do with you, Jahangir replied. *This is business between people in the north and contacts of mine in Pakistan. You have no right to interfere.*

If this is a crime against children and families, if it involves Laashekoh, then I must interfere, Parsaa countered.

Jahangir laughed. *Think about it—why do you care about the people of the north?*

Parsaa held the rifle with one hand and used the other to loosen the knot around the boy's neck. *If I stop an injustice against another village, they will do the same for Laashekoh.*

I held my hands to cover my mouth, hoping that Parsaa and Saddiq would simply walk away. Surely, Parsaa had checked his weapon. My throat was dry. The cool night air did not ease its tightness.

Leila edged closer to her mother. *He's not going anywhere. You do not control us anymore. Our village can do better under Jahangir.* Her voice was shrill, and Parsaa stared coolly at her. She was inconsequential to him. He was not afraid, and that unnerved her.

Saddiq stared at his father, waiting for a signal about what to do next. But Parsaa was serene, and I couldn't read his intention. Like my son, I could only wait.

In the firelight, the eyes of the two women glinted. *You are not going to stop us,* Leila warned.

Shh, Mari scolded her daughter, then tried to convince Parsaa to join ranks with Jahangir. *Laashekoh can use the money. Just this once, Parsaa, and then no more. Allah is forgiving.*

Allah knows what is in your mind, he said, shaking his head. *Hurting the weak doesn't give us strength, and His forgiveness is not for those who persist in wrongdoing.*

I couldn't stand another moment of Parsaa wondering if I hid in the shadows, lacking the courage to confront this group. Moving slowly backward, away from the boulders and slipping into the dark shadows of trees, where the firelight could not penetrate. *Mari,* I called out, trying to keep my voice from shaking. *Let them go. You helped me on the day I gave birth to Saddiq. You'd never forgive yourself if something happened. Let them go, and we'll talk about these matters in the morning.*

My voice rolled down the slope, away from the path. But none could see me. Jahangir jerked around in surprise. Leila was enraged, twirling and aiming her weapon into the darkness. For the first time, Parsaa, across the clearing, looked worried. And my old friend Mari was distraught.

All of them are here, Leila protested. *They try to control us.*

Sofi, I promise, there's no harm here, Mari called out. *Come out so we can talk.*

As she spoke, I moved in slow silence to the left, to confuse them about my position. *Leila, no one in our village would endorse this activity. Selling children is wrong.*

Sofi, you don't understand! Mari pleaded. *We are moving them to safer surroundings. Away from the Americans!*

Would you move our children this way? Slowly, I tiptoed to the side and lowered myself to the ground, raising my voice. *Provide false documents on their place of birth? It brings shame on us all. Mari, you can protect Leila and Jahangir. You've said it to me many times before—parents must protect children from themselves.*

As Mari dipped her head with shame, Leila reached out and shoved her.

Don't listen to her! Leila shouted. *You care more about her boys than my future?*

No noise! Jahangir scolded, before muffling his voice. *We cannot draw the Americans here.*

You promised you would take care of them, Leila scoffed.

What you're doing is wrong. I crawled, keeping my voice low and hypnotic, confusing them about my location. *What does Allah tell you to do?*

And what would you do to save your son? Jahangir called out. *What is he worth to you?*

Leila turned to Jahangir, pointed the gun that way, and shrieked. *We'll do nothing of the sort. The entire family will never stop watching us and judging us! It's why her first son is dead!*

Quiet, fool! Jahangir grasped her by the shoulders. *She doesn't have a gun, or she would have shot you by now.*

Shocked, I didn't know how to respond. My Ali. *Allah knows,* I said softly, crawling back and forth, slowly repeating this phrase over and over. *Allah knows.* Jahangir glared, and I could see the fear in his eyes. In his own way, the man was a believer.

But not Leila. There was no fear in her. Her head moved back and forth, her eyes scanning to find me in the darkness, aiming the weapon as if that might help her find me. *If you want your son, you must come out,* she demanded. Circling the fire, she moved toward the sound of my voice, trying to pinpoint my location. Jahangir followed, trying to wrest the gun away from her. But Leila pulled away.

Listen to your husband, Mari hissed.

I didn't trust Leila, yet rashly decided that it was better for my family if she shot me rather than Saddiq or Parsaa.

Emboldened, I stood and called out. *Allah knows! Let Allah decide.*

As I stepped down the slope, approaching the fire, Parsaa slowly lifted his hand toward the stars. *All matters are returned to Allah.*

Jahangir stared at us with terror, and that upset Leila. *You're so certain that Allah sides with you?* she screamed. Her headscarf had fallen to the ground, the hate in her eyes more terrifying than the scars.

I was ready to accept my fate, but couldn't keep my voice from shaking. *Yes.*

Slowly, she smiled and turned her back to me, raising the gun and pointing it at Parsaa. Jahangir lunged for the gun in her hand, but she was wild-eyed and twisted away. *No!* I screamed, despising my own arrogance.

Suddenly, huge lights encircled us, exposing the children clutching one another in terror near Parsaa on one side of the fire, the three adults on the other side of the fire, and me at the base of the hillside.

From a distance a shot fired, striking Leila in the right arm and swinging her around. *It's why their first son is dead*, she wailed, dropping to the ground. *He asked too many questions and wanted to go to school. He wanted to leave me!* Taking aim at me, she managed to pull the trigger. The weapon's retort was an empty click.

Weeping, Mari fell to her knees and clutched her daughter, tying her own headscarf around the girl's arm, pressing her fingers to the girl's mouth to quiet her. Parsaa aimed his rifle at Jahangir, as the driver took off running into the night and the cover of darkness. Saddiq dashed to my side, wrapping his arms around me and hiding his face. *I was so scared*, he said. *That father or you were helping Leila and Mari.* I had no words and gently folded my arms around him. No immediate explanation was needed. All that mattered was his safety.

Two American soldiers approached, weapons held high and ready to fire again. In the darkness, we heard someone tackling the driver and restraining him.

The man named Joey pointed an assault rifle on Jahangir, Mari, and Leila, and another soldier quickly applied handcuffs to the three. *The Americans have come for you. I warned you!* Jahangir shouted to the children. *You must fight them!*

Most of them didn't even look his way. Tears broke out, as Joey knelt in front of the scrawny children and spoke in Dari as he started in removing the restraints: *It's over now. You'll return to your villages and parents.*

Some children wept with joy, and the others who had known only hunger and abuse also cried, because they had counted on Jahangir's promises of a better life. One boy protested: *But I paid these men to take me to Pakistan. They promised us jobs!*

Joey and Parsaa exchanged sad glances, and my husband chided the boy. *The work is more difficult than you have ever known. You're better off with your families.*

You cannot trust the Americans! Jahangir screamed to the children. *Never! Help us destroy them . . .*

Leila sat up, cradling her arm. *We were helping these children. Everyone will know who colluded with the intruders! That you lie about us!*

Through the shouting, Joey explained to Jahangir and the women that they had violated both international law and the Afghan Law on Kidnapping and Human Trafficking.

Joey snapped orders that I didn't understand, and other men moved Leila and Mari away from the children. Parsaa and Joey kept their weapons ready as Saddiq and I helped distribute the remaining food and water among the children.

That was close, Joey said to Parsaa. *I was ready to move in without waiting for the signal.*

We had to wait until I knew who was involved, Parsaa explained.

The soldier turned to me. *Thank you. It helped that you drew Jahangir and the others away from the wagon and the children.*

Lowering my head, I stepped behind my husband, embarrassed for my village about meeting the American under such shameful circumstances, and I looked at Saddiq, terrified at how close we had come to losing another son. There was no need to thank me.

Parsaa admitted, *That wasn't part of the plan.*

Mari broke in with a plea. *Parsaa, we made a mistake listening to Jahangir—it's not too late to forgive us.*

You! Leila lashed out at her mother. *Begging his forgiveness! After his son ruined me!*

No, Leila . . . her mother protested.

Furious, Leila turned away from Mari. *You and everyone else saying that Ali was so alert and smart, how someday he'd lead our village. He didn't know what was best for him. He didn't see the rock aimed for his head!*

Leila! Mari wept. *He loved you. . . . Sofi, don't listen to her!*

No, mother, he chose school. Over me! She spat the words out with loathing for us and herself.

Parsaa joined Saddiq and me as we assisted the children. He did not look at or respond to Leila, other than to wrap his arms around us, as if to shield us and move us away to talk among ourselves. *It is over,* he whispered in my ear.

Tears came to my eyes. At last we understood our son's strange death, and my only worry was how this night of terror might weaken my other precious son. *Ali did no wrong,* I murmured. *Children are supposed to trust others.*

Parsaa laid his head on my shoulder and put his hand on the boy's head. *Our family is too strong not to trust,* Parsaa said. *We followed one another to protect one another.*

Saddiq nodded.

Then Parsaa teased me with a smile, asking why I had urged Leila to shoot the gun and then screamed no. *Isn't Allah with me as well?* Without words, I squeezed him tight.

A Humvee with bright lights pulled up, and Jahangir screamed to get Parsaa's attention, warning of wrath from neighboring tribes, Taliban leaders, the children's parents, Allah, and others. *You do not have to cooperate with the infidels! We can go on from here.*

Parsaa ignored him, and Joey shouted at his men. One soldier struggled to push Jahangir toward the rear of the truck as Jahangir fought, screaming and swinging his bound wrists like a club. Other soldiers joined them, and together they heaved the man into place, attaching his restraints to a metal bar lining the back of the truck.

Leila and the driver were compliant, but Mari panicked. The truck meant she wasn't returning to Laashekoh anytime soon. *Sofi, what about my daughters?* Mari cried out.

They'll be cared for, Parsaa promised shortly. *Until they do wrong.* Mari's moan was as dark as the night, but she had no choice. Everyone stared in silence as the soldier guided her into the truck and slammed the door.

Parsaa asked what would happen to the group, and Joey's mouth was set. *They'll go on trial and likely head to prison.* He lowered his voice. *How long they stay depends on whether they give us leads on the trafficking operations and how many children we find and return to their parents.*

I shuddered to think of encountering Mari or Leila again. But the men showed no signs of worry. Parsaa shrugged. The village had handled matters of justice before the Americans arrived and would do so again.

One of the soldiers pulled bright-colored boxes from a large pack, distributing them among the children. Opening their boxes with care, the children ate little cookies. The boy who had been so ready to cooperate with Jahangir ducked his head and tried to blend in with the others, and I could not help but pity him: He had miscalculated his future and would return to a small village where his cruelties would not be quickly forgotten.

Joey approached us and asked if we needed help getting the children settled for the night. Parsaa laughed and assured the man that his wife would have no trouble finding meals and beds for eighteen children.

The American thanked us. *In Laashekoh, the children are in good hands.*

The two men started to make arrangements for returning the children. Joey explained how he'd return with vehicles the following day for delivering the children to their villages and asked for Parsaa's help in collecting names and other details. *We'll need Afghans to accompany them for the return trip home.*

Parsaa nodded.

The American soldier embraced Parsaa and Saddiq, then thanked all of us for risking our lives. *These arrests will slow trafficking in this area for a while.*

We did what needed to be done, Parsaa replied. The two men said farewell and embraced again, more warmly than I could have ever imagined. But then, Mita and I had felt the same.

With the help of three of the oldest children, we linked our hands into a human chain that began climbing the hill, taking the easiest path back to Laashekoh.

Jahangir had been stopped. But I was troubled knowing how little control we had over those who intend to commit evil, cloaking it with the holy words—how we knew so little about the crimes practiced near our village.

As we trudged toward our village, a storm of thoughts went through my head. So many tasks for the hours ahead—knocking on doors and finding beds for children, giving them warm milk and hoping Saddiq and the rest of them would sleep without dreams of terror. Parsaa and I would craft explanations for Mari's children and other villagers.

But I was neither weary nor afraid. The pink light of dawn peered out over the distant mountains, spilling beauty and promises like the desert sand.

EPILOGUE

Take to forgiveness and enjoin good and turn aside from the ignorant.
—Koran 7:199

Our village is quiet. We don't talk about the events of the last year. The men work and travel to market. The women continue to cook, work in the fields, and care for children.

No one misses Jahangir at all.

The Americans have moved on.

I miss Mita terribly, and Parsaa misses Gul.

So much has changed, but if anything, Parsaa's and my love is stronger.

A year ago we despised the Americans, their decadence and depravity, and wanted no part of them as they searched for what they called the moderates in our midst. The men of our village took the term as an insult, a label for those not secure in their convictions.

After the clash between Jahangir and the Americans, we understood how to adjust our own feelings. Inside every person waits an extremist, ready to attack over political beliefs, humiliation, or the wrongful death of a beloved child.

Faith is beautiful, but it does not promise truth in matters beyond religion's reach. Believers can be wrong about some matters on this earth. The infidels can know some truths.

Arguing about religion is pointless, allowing extremism to take over the best parts of a mind. Shouting, bullying, forcing our opinions on others only weakens us over time. And the same is true for our opponents, whether they are Americans or Afghans. There are other, more powerful, ways to disagree.

As we gain more confidence and control, others can test and nudge our beliefs, yet the essence of who we are is not shaken.

Mita has arranged the delivery of small packages of books and articles—paid for by a company that includes more books about wheat than we could ever read or use—and I have followed her advice, setting up a library and encouraging others to borrow these books. The books teach on many topics, including what people of other lands think about us. And those strange opinions convinced the men that our village could benefit from its own school.

We have discovered that many people in the world would regard the people of our village as extremists. Some regard our efforts to fight off any who would interfere with our village life as dangerous to the world. People who understand our way of thinking, like Mita and Joey, are rare. We don't want to hurt others, but we want to control our own families and village.

The men of our village will go to great lengths to defend Laashekoh.

Mita has sent me articles that debate about whether moderate Taliban can even exist, and these arguments have forced me to reassess my own thoughts about Americans. Like us, the Americans have many differences and disagree on goals and methods, and the memories of myself are of a stranger I no longer understand.

Among the many books Mita sent, a favorite of mine is an old, heavy copy of a dictionary. I linger over that book, finding words used too often with so little thought. *Evil* is one. *Beauty* is another. Both require an observer, and both emerge as the result of another person's assessment. An individual can never be completely confident that she is beautiful or free of evil. The designation demands acknowledgment from another person.

A small village such as ours has few mechanisms for assessing and punishing evil. What is evil for some is justice for others. Standards we expect to last forever can change quickly. A person deft with words can make an argument for anything. Sadly, we must learn to live with some evil.

To guard against evil in ourselves, we can nurture the qualities that delight our senses and leave us thrilled for the future—a field green and ready for harvest, securing others against the crashing sounds of a stormy night with the warmth of a safe home, an image of a sleeping child, a book that presents ideas and hope. All these can catch our breath, changing how we think about the world or what we decide to do next with our lives, in ways big or small.

Beauty comes in many forms—work, faith, compassionate deeds and ideas—yet some fear when their senses are tested in strange, new ways. We cannot push others into enjoying what we experience and believe. I'd like to think that finding beauty brings pleasure and doing evil brings displeasure, but who can be sure? Like so much of human assessment, the two qualities intertwine, and one can feign the other. Any of us, with intention or not, is capable of creating beauty or evil, and we cannot judge or shame others for failing to appreciate what gives us purpose and helps us thrive.

Fearing beauty in itself is not evil. It's understandable to fear what's new or what we cannot control. The Koran warns against suspicion, and evil emerges when we prevent discovery of beauty by others. I'm sure more than ever before that it's best to live life intent on controlling ourselves more than on controlling others.

Early on, Mita's descriptions about so many new places and people and concepts saddened me. I felt so backward, and said as much as she handed over the dictionary and the other books.

Mita is never one for holding back a criticism, and she scolded me. *You explored before books. Some people have access to many more books, and they don't bother to explore what's available to them.* This surprised me, but I can only suppose they assume they have enough beauty in their lives and very little evil. Let me assure you, ownership of books or ideas does not guarantee complete understanding.

In my life, I have never met a person, if honest, who is satisfied with what he or she has already accomplished. For me, the search for truth and beauty—the assessing and reassessing, and mixing with others who do the same—will never end, and I no longer feel sad or left behind.

I have only one certainty in a world that never stops changing—that more must be learned and accomplished. This lack of certainty and the search are my freedom.

ACKNOWLEDGMENTS

M any have contributed to this book: Dan Mayer and the entire team at Seventh Street books, including Jade Zora Ballard, Grace M. Conti-Zilsberger, Meghan Quinn, Catherine Roberts-Abel, and Brian McMahon; Alison Picard, an understanding and patient agent; the encouraging Milton Kahn; Doug, the best husband a writer could ever have; Nick, for his advice on caves and much more; a wonderful family, including Joe Little and parents Joseph, Patricia, Roy, and Rory; Nayan Chanda, so generous with his insights on globalization; William Hixson; and the librarians and teachers who provided a lifetime of inspiration.

The author does not pretend to be an expert on the Koran and urges the curious to read such religious texts closely. This book relied on the online English version of the Koran, translated by M. H. Shakir, provided by the University of Michigan; the US Army *Ranger Handbook*, July 1992; Dari Dictionary (http://estragon.100megsfree5.com/dic .htm); and the unclassified confidential initial assessment on Afghanistan, from General Stanley A. McChrystal, then commander of the US forces in Afghanistan and the International Security Assistance Force–Afghanistan, to Secretary of Defense Robert Gates, August 30, 2009 (http://media.washingtonpost.com/wp-srv/politics/documents/ Assessment_Redacted_092109.pdf).

The lines of poetry recited by Joey Pearson, page 227, are from "Lines Composed a Few Miles above Tintern Abbey, on Revisiting the Banks of the Wye during a Tour. July 13, 1798," by William Wordsworth.

ABOUT THE AUTHOR

SUSAN FROETSCHEL is the author of three previous novels. In addition, she has written articles for the *New York Times*, the *Christian Science Monitor*, *Barron's*, and many other publications. She has taught at Yale University and Southern Connecticut State University, and she now writes and edits for *YaleGlobal Online* at the Yale Center for the Study of Globalization. She lives in Michigan.